HOW THE
WARRIOR
FELL

FALLING WARRIORS SERIES BOOK 1

NICOLE RENÉ

WARNING

This is a Dark Historical Romance taking place during a time way before there was such a thing as feminism, women's rights, and #equality.

If you're unable to put away your 21st century mindset whilst getting lost in these stories...then I strongly suggest you don't take a sip of this particular Kool-aid.

For those of you brave enough—bottoms up.

COPYRIGHT

GLOSSARY

Xavier: X-avier
Leawyn: Lee-uh-wen
Tyronian: Ty-row-knee-an
Namoriee: Nam-or-ree
Killix: Kill-ix
Deydrey: Dey-dré
Izayges: Iz-uh-gez
Rhoxolani: Rox-oh-lani
Siraces: Sir-aces
Asori: Uh-soar-ee
Cantos: Can-tos
Castic: Cas-tick
Asten: Ass-ten
Garnette: Gar-nett
Kisias: Kiss-ee-us
Yoro: Yo-ro
Boers: Bors
Dkésea: Duh-kay-sea

DEDICATION

To my family.
(Yes, you still have to skip over the sex scenes. Especially you, Grandma.)

1

"Leawyn?"

"Leawyn, where are you?"

Leawyn stood, turning her cerulean eyes in the direction the familiar voice was calling her from. Pushing a wayward strand of hair away from her face as she made her way down to her handmaiden, Brees.

"Leawyn, if you don't come here right now, I'll—"

"I'm here, Brees," she called out, her voice soft and melodic. She came around the corner of the small cove she was resting in. Brees whirled around to face her, a disapproving frown in place.

"Where have you been? I have been looking everywhere for you!" Brees snatched her by the wrist, her face twisted in a scowl.

"I was just—"

"I don't want to hear it!" Brees snapped, interrupting Leawyn mid-sentence. "I don't know how many times I've told you to not wander off when you have so much work to do."

Leawyn stayed silent, knowing that provoking Brees wouldn't do her any good as she was dragged up the sandy hill that separated the beach and their village.

Brees had been her handmaiden for as long as she could remember. Though, in Leawyn's eyes, Brees was more of a mother to her since her own mother died giving birth to her.

"What's the hurry, Brees?" Leawyn asked, amused by the woman's pace. She practically had to jog to keep alongside her fussy handmaiden.

Brees huffed, looking over her shoulder at Leawyn. "Have you forgotten?" Brees asked in her strange accent.

Brees wasn't born in the Rhoxolani like Leawyn was, and instead came to their humble village when Brees was just a young girl traveling with a band of sea merchants. It was here, in the Rhoxolani tribe, that Brees met and fell in love with a young Rhoxolani warrior whom she later married.

Gwan, unfortunately, was slain during one of the many tribe battles between the Izayges and Rhoxolani.

Leawyn's brows knitted together in confusion at her handmaiden's impatience. She couldn't think of anything particularly special about today. She woke up and did her chores just like any other day. Then, she took her mare, Deydrey, out for a ride on the beach. After she had put Deydrey back in the stables, she went out to the cliffs to sit and enjoy time to herself.

Was she supposed to do something else?

Leawyn smiled guiltily at Brees when she looked over her shoulder at her silence. "For Goddess's sakes, Leawyn! You were told earlier today!"

She opened her mouth, about to tell Brees that she had no idea what she was talking about. No one told Leawyn anything. But, judging by the annoyed scowl on Brees's face, she thought better of it and closed her mouth.

They reached the main hut, and a few moments later, Brees opened the partition to Leawyn's room and ushered her in. She watched as Brees went to her chest of gowns and searched through them.

"Wear this." Brees shoved a pale blue dress into her hands.

"What's wrong with what I'm wearing?" she asked, looking down to her modest brown gown.

At Brees's annoyed glare, Leawyn wisely didn't argue further and instead put on the garment. The color of the dress brought out Leawyn's eyes and made her golden hair that much brighter. It had a sweetheart neckline with long sleeves that tightly gripped Leawyn's arms before flaring out at her elbows. It was long, covering Leawyn's dainty feet and brushing the floor with each step she took.

Once she was done changing, Brees guided her to the stool in the middle of the room. Pushing down on Leawyn's shoulders, Brees reached around her, grabbed her brush and began combing her long hair.

It was silent between them for a few minutes, then, "Leawyn, you *do* know what tonight is, don't you?"

Leawyn hesitated, pulling a loose string from her dress before she answered. "I'm sorry, Brees, I truly have no idea what you're talking about."

She turned to look over her shoulder when Brees suddenly grew still. She grew worried by the way Brees looked at her.

It was as if she were about to tell Leawyn a terrible secret.

"No one told you?" Brees breathed out in shocked-horror.

"Tell me what?"

"Oh, Leawyn," Brees said tenderly. She ran the back of her hand down Leawyn's unblemished cheek. Her eyes misted over.

"Leawyn...your father received word this morning. The Izayges Chief grew tired of waiting and sent word that he would be arriving early." Brees hesitated. "That was six days ago."

Leawyn felt herself growing faint at the implications of what she was saying.

"No," Leawyn whispered, her eyes filling with panicked tears. She shook her head in denial. "I'm supposed to have until the winter. We weren't supposed to meet until the leaves fall!"

"Leawyn, he's arriving tonight," Brees informed her gently, as if her heart were breaking too.

Leawyn's world froze; icy fingers of dread gripped her heart. Tonight, her world would change forever.

Tonight, she would meet Xavier, the Chief of the Izayges.

The man who was the most dangerous warrior in Samaritan history.

Her betrothed.

Xavier stared out at the village before him as he sat atop his stallion, Killix. His face was emotionless, giving nothing away to the disgust he was feeling as he and his party traveled with him to meet with the Rhoxolani's chief and his daughter.

The daughter who was to become his wife.

He held in his sigh. He did not want to get married. He preferred the freedom he found in battle, and of taking common whores to satisfy his most primal desires. But, being the chief of the Izayges meant protecting his village, and the demand of breeding heirs was a priority. At thirty-two, he was the strongest and fiercest warrior in Izayges history.

What was he to do with a wife?

Xavier's eyes narrowed as his party grew closer to the little tribe that was the Rhoxolani. Their village was small—no more than a hundred people living there—and the smell of the ocean permeated the air, the aroma growing more prominent as they drew closer. The Rhoxolani were known to be light in every aspect. From their fair hair, sun-kissed skin, to their light-colored eyes.

They were nothing like his tribe, which was big and over four hundred strong. Unlike the Rhoxolani, the Izayges had an air of danger about them, and did not come across as friendly and rightfully so. They were a strong, fierce, and dangerous people.

It was no wonder the last marriage between his tribe and the Rhoxolani's didn't work out.

The long-fueled grudge between the two tribes started when the first marriage proposal between the Izayges and the Rhoxolani was offered. Chienef, who was the son of the Izayges chief, was set to marry Lyrical, daughter of the Rhoxolani chief. Chienef had caught his bride-to-be with another man on the night of their wedding. Furious over the betrayal, Chienef killed his betrothed and her lover. He accused the Rhoxolani people of being dishonorable, and a vicious battle took place between the two tribes, who never again attempted to form an allegiance through marriage.

Until now, that is.

He looked over to his second-in-command, Tristan.

"We make haste to the village. I want to arrive when there is yet sunlight," Xavier ordered, barely taking in Tristan's nod of understanding before he kicked his horse into a gallop.

It was time to meet his future wife.

avier and his small party, which included his fellow warriors and brother, arrived just as the sun was setting. Xavier's horse skidded to a stop in front of a big, blond man who lifted his arms high in welcome, a smile stretching across his chubby face.

"Welcome to Rhoxolani, Chief Xavier!" the man shouted merrily. "I am Boers, chief of this tribe." The chief hit himself in the chest and tilted his head down in greeting.

"Our horses need hay and water. I want to see your daughter before we marry. I don't plan on lingering here longer than I have to," Xavier said, skipping niceties and getting straight to the point. He stared Boers down through the fringe of his hair once he dismounted from Killix.

Boers seemed a bit put off by Xavier's dismissal, his jolly expression slipping before he caught himself, and his smile appeared on his face once again. "Of course, we will make sure all is taken care of," Boers promised. Turning to look behind him, he motioned his hand forward to the stable boys waiting.

"These boys will take your horses to our stables for you," Boers told Xavier as the boys ran up to them. Xavier snatched the wrist of the boy who went to take hold of Xavier's reins, stopping him.

The boy stared up at him in fear, while Boers looked shocked. Xavier stared back, impervious and unperturbed.

"We take care of our own horses," Xavier explained. "If they can just show us where we may board them."

Boers gave a nervous nod, signaling for the stable boys to do as he bid. Xavier released the wrist he was holding, and the boy quickly ran away from him to follow the others. Tristan walked past him leading both his and his brother's horse, and Xavier's eyes followed him for a moment before they cut back to Boers, who didn't look as jolly as he had before. Xavier held in his grin.

"Your daughter?"

Boers snapped to attention, meeting Xavier's gaze. His smile didn't quite reach his eyes when he said, "Yes, of course." He held his hand out toward the large hut stationed at the very top of the cliff that made up the Rhoxolani village.

"Come, I will take you to her."

Leawyn stared down at the sea-blue eyes that reflected at her with melancholy. Hit with sudden anger, she swiped the water in the basin roughly, erasing her reflection.

She turned away, heading toward her window that overlooked the ocean, when her head snapped up.

Footsteps; one set familiar, the other foreign.

Oh Gods, they're coming, she thought moments before the flap separating her room from the rest of the hut swung aside and in stepped her father and betrothed.

Cold brown eyes met hers, causing her to gasp at the utter emptiness that reflected inside of them.

Her betrothed stood to his full six-foot-six height, keeping his merciless eyes focused on her. His coal-colored hair brushed the tops of his broad shoulders, spread wide against his defined chest. His arms rested against his sides, and they were bunched with muscles.

He looked like a demi-god carved in stone.

The rumors she heard revolving around this man were all true, Leawyn realized, because looking at him now...all she could think of was danger.

She could still feel the heavy weight of his gaze when she looked to her father when he broke the tense silence by speaking.

"Daughter, this is your betrothed, Xavier," Boers said nervously as he glanced to Xavier before looking at her again. "Chief of the Izayges."

She looked to him again, the heat of his gaze making her uncomfortable. She lowered her dipped her head, bending her body slightly at the waist in greeting.

His response was to slowly rake his eyes up and down her body. She felt even smaller in front of him. As discreetly as possible, Leawyn peered up at him and studied him much like he did her.

He was massive.

His chest was bare, and he wore dark breeches that looked to be made of some type of tough animal skin, similar to leather. She could only spot four noticeable weapons on his person, but she doubted they were all he had on him. He had a long and wickedly curved sword strapped to his back, and another thick, straight blade that hung down from the side of his waist. On each side of his hip, Leawyn could see the hilt of a dagger peeking out of the waistband of his breeches. His abs were clearly defined and visible in divots. He had a beard, and a scar cut into his right eyebrow.

She looked down, heart rate spiking.

He was terrifying.

"Leave us," Xavier demanded gruffly. His deep voice caused the demand to come out more like a growl. Leawyn felt her eyes widen, looking to her father in fear.

Don't leave me, she thought.

Her father shifted uncomfortably but nodded his head. "Of course." He bowed to Xavier. Her father looked at her, and though he looked apologetic, he did nothing to save her. He just turned and lifted open the flap of the tent, leaving them alone.

She cast her eyes to the ground, chest tight with dread. She heard Xavier move closer to her, and she took a halting breath against the nervousness that seemed to choke her and keep her body paralyzed.

"Tell me your name, girl," Xavier demanded. She glanced up at him enough to show that he stared down at her. She was tiny compared to him. He easily towered over her.

"Leawyn," she answered softly, proud her voice didn't come out as shaky as she thought it would.

"Look at me."

When Leawyn's eyes failed to meet his fast enough, he reached down, gripped her chin, and lurched her face up to look at him.

"Your gaze will always meet my own," he told her sternly, staring down into her wide eyes. "You will only have eyes for me, do you understand?"

Her feelings of fear quickly morphed into annoyance. "Shall I call you master while I'm at it?" she asked sardonically, glaring at him defiantly. She wasn't prepared for his reaction.

"I don't appreciate the attitude, Leawyn. You will do well to remember exactly who you are talking to, and respect me," he growled down at her. He yanked her chin roughly, causing a whimper of pain to escape her.

"Do you understand?"

When she went to give him a nod, he tightened his grip before she could follow through with the motion. "The words, Leawyn. I want the words."

"Yes!" Leawyn gasped out against his painful hold, staring up at him with frightened eyes.

"Yes, I understand!"

She rubbed her aching jaw when he let go of her abruptly. She stepped away from him hastily, trying to blink back her tears.

"How old are you?" Xavier asked, watching her.

"E-eighteen summers," she stuttered. She knew he was much older than she, and the knowledge that she was expected to marry him made her stomach clench with sickness. But, Leawyn knew some girls' younger than herself were married to much older men. She told herself she should be somewhat grateful.

"We will be married in three days' time."

Leawyn tensed in shock, panic and dread washing over her.

"What?" She gaped at him. "We can't!"

She couldn't live with this man! This possessive, domineering man who didn't seem to care if he hurt her.

She didn't want to marry Xavier. Not after meeting him.

"I refuse to marry you," Leawyn said, her brows creasing as she stared up at him in determination.

Every muscle in Xavier's body stiffened. His eyes cut to hers, and Leawyn swallowed against the urge to run. She edged away from him, catching the dangerous glint that entered his eyes. The glint was that of a predator who caught sight of its prey right before attacking.

She had a feeling the prey was her.

"What did you just say?" Xavier asked. His voice was silky with promised danger.

She gulped but lifted her chin defiantly, staring at him with more bravery than she felt.

"I will not marry you," she repeated, backing away from him as he took slow, measured steps towards her.

He shook his head slowly, his icy eyes never leaving hers. "I'll ask you one more time, Leawyn. What did you say?"

"I refuse to marry—"

His eyes flashed furiously, then his hand shot out and wrapped around the back of her neck in a vice-like grip. Using his other hand, he gripped her jaw brutally.

"You will become my wife, Leawyn," he said in warning. He leaned in, rubbing his bearded cheek against her smooth one. "And if I find out you let another man between your legs come our wedding night..."

She could only emit a soft gasp of pain when Xavier's grip around her neck squeezed tighter.

"I'll kill you," he whispered softly into her ear.

Leawyn sucked in a sharp breath. He laughed humorlessly when he drew back and considered her frightened eyes.

How had her life come to this?

Three days later, Xavier sat at a table next to his wife, watching their wedding celebration. It seemed like half of the Izayges tribe came over to witness their union, making the six-day ride in record time. He scanned the crowd.

Distantly, he could hear the ocean waves as they crashed against the shore, the sound drowned out by all the laughter and talk that surrounded him. Huge bonfires provided light for the wedding party, and the air was rich with the aroma of smoked fish caught fresh for their wedding feast. Drums and flutes provided music for those who wished to dance. Long tables were arranged in a giant broken square, creating a perimeter for the festivities. Almost everywhere Xavier looked, there were smiling, happy faces.

Their wedding was a cause of celebration, for at last all the tribes in Samaria were connected. No longer was there a rift between the Izayges and the Rhoxolani.

It was funny to Xavier how two tribes fighting against each other for years came together by the same thing that drove them apart.

Chienef and Lyrical's wedding started the war; his and Leawyn's ended it.

He thought back to their wedding ceremony, and how Leawyn looked up at him in her white dress, eyes misted over with despair. Her dainty hands had trembled when he reached for them. He had held them still when the tribe elder said the marriage incantation that bound them together until death. She had flinched when he had slit his palm, and then hers, to press their hands together, joining their blood and sealing their marriage.

Xavier glanced over at his wife from the corner of his eyes and had to hold back the grin of male satisfaction.

Leawyn was beautiful, more so than the rumors portrayed her to be. For there *had* been rumors of the chief's daughter of the Rhoxolani. She was considered the most beautiful girl all of Samaria had ever seen. So lovely, it seemed the Gods blessed her, and the Goddess Ianna cursed her because she rivaled her own beauty.

Legend to have hair kissed by the sun, shining as bright as its rays in its loving light, and eyes made of teardrops from the clouds when the Gods wept from their loss of a daughter to mortals.

She was a child compared to him. Though, knowing that, all he felt was pleasure; pleasure for having a girl who would only belong to him. Someone who would be healthy to bear him enough heirs to keep his tribe protected. And she *would* be bearing him children—he would make sure of it come their wedding night.

Xavier felt a thrill go through him at the thought. Though he was no stranger to the opposite sex, none had made him experience this feeling of possessiveness he felt over Leawyn. The need to dominate her and make her his was so strong, it had his jaw clenching and blood rush straight to his cock.

Leawyn was beautiful, and she was going to be all his.

He glanced at Leawyn again. She was rumored to have a laugh so pure and heavenly, it was like the Gods laughed with her.

Xavier doubted that he would ever get to hear such laughter by the way she looked now.

Leawyn stared out at all the happy faces of her tribe as they ate and danced by the fire. She could hear the joyous laughter all around her —a sound that would usually make her heart melt with happiness— but tonight, she couldn't find it in herself to laugh with them.

Not when her heart clenched in such sadness.

After Xavier had left her room, he made arrangements for the wedding to take place exactly when he promised—three days' time.

Their tribes' people were probably in just as much shock as she was, but nonetheless, they had jumped into action to make it happen.

Three days was all it took for Leawyn to be forced to commit to a lifetime with someone she did not love.

Someone she was certain would treat her as nothing more than a broodmare to mate and give him little heartless warrior children.

Never again would she know the taste of freedom.

Leawyn tried to hold back tears against the feeling of absolute loneliness that invaded her. But she failed to conceal them, and soon felt the sudden pain of a hand gripping her thigh tightly and the scrape of a beard against her cheek.

"Weddings are a time of happiness. There's no room for tears—especially coming from you, my young wife," Xavier whispered in her ear, his voice hard under its honied exterior.

Leawyn tried to hide her tears by closing her eyes. To anyone looking at them, it would appear Xavier was nuzzling his new wife's neck and whispering loving words to her privately, eyes closed in contentment.

"Excuse me, brother, but I believe I haven't met your wife yet," an amused voice cut in smoothly.

Leawyn's eyes snapped open at the same time Xavier pulled his head away from her neck to look up and greet the person standing before them.

"Tristan."

Leawyn studied Tristan curiously. He was tall, but unlike his brother, who was broadly built, Tristan was sinewy. He had tattoos on each of his defined cheekbones, and his hair was shorter and straighter than Xavier's. He wore Izayges scouting armor, and he looked down at them with the same impassive face her husband wore.

It was his eyes that gave away his relation to Xavier.

Though they were lighter than his brother's, they held the same cold, almost wild look inside of them. Devoid of emotion, save but the tales of the souls they claimed with their swords.

Warrior eyes.

Leawyn startled when the eyes she studied met hers. Realizing she was staring, she tried to hide her blush by quickly looking down. When she was brave enough to look up again, she caught the slight twitch at the corner of Tristan's lips, as if he was forcing himself not to smile. Tristan looked to Xavier, who had silently studied the interaction between them.

"I was hoping I would get a dance with my new sister," Tristan drawled, shooting a quick glance at Leawyn, whose shoulders tensed at the question. "With your permission, of course."

Xavier studied Tristan for a bit then slowly bowing his head in consent.

"Of course," Xavier murmured. "I'm sure my wife would enjoy one dance before we retire."

Both brothers ignored the quick intake of breath from Leawyn in reaction to that comment.

"Thank you, brother." Tristan bowed his head to Xavier before offering his hand to her, palm up. She stared at it dumbly.

"I believe my brother just asked you to dance." She let out a hiss of pain when Xavier squeezed her thigh tightly.

"It would be rude not to accept," he growled, his grip growing more painful until she placed her hand in Tristan's.

Tristan's large hand closed around her much smaller one as he gently pulled her to her feet. He dragged her into the crowd of people dancing, whereas she glanced behind her to Xavier. He was glaring at her silently, his expression unreadable. The reflection of the fire glinted off his eyes and made him look more sinister. She suppressed a shiver and looked away.

Tristan swung her around in his arms, wrapping one arm around her waist and picked up her hand and held it above his shoulder. They swayed to the music as Leawyn moved stiffly against him. She focused on the shoulder design of the armor he wore.

He broke the silence first.

"It will get better."

His comment caught her off guard, and it took her a moment to figure out what he meant. She raised her head and met the eyes that were already looking down at her.

"Funny, you could say that, yet you are not forced to marry someone you've only just met, and I am," Leawyn said scathingly, glaring up at him for a moment more before looking away.

Tristan chuckled low—something that only further infuriated Leawyn— and spun her around with the rest of the dancers before they settled in a gentle sway again.

"It won't be as bad as it seems. Obey him, and you'll live."

Though the comment was said lightly, there was seriousness laced in his tone.

A warning.

She exhaled shakily, her throat clogged up with emotion.

"Tell me, Tristan...what would you do if you lost your freedom?"

She felt his shoulder tense beneath her hand. Her voice was hollow when she continued.

"To be forced to spend the rest of your life as nothing more than an object. Tied to a man who cares so little about you, he would feel no remorse for killing everything inside you." Leawyn looked up then, her eyes meeting his.

"Would you accept your fate?"

She saw a flash of something akin to anger in his eyes. Was he feeling protective of her? She couldn't tell, but she thought it was a possibility.

"No," Tristan answered her finally, his voice soft. He kept their eyes locked while he uttered the words that drove the spear through the little hope she had left within her.

"But you will, Leawyn."

The music around them ended, and they stopped dancing with their eyes still locked onto each other, holding a silent conversation with their souls.

It was when Leawyn felt the hand on her shoulder pulling her away from him that her first tear fell. She felt Tristan's gaze on her back as Xavier led her away to his horse and lifted her up onto the saddle. He climbed on behind her and kicked the horse into action.

The sound of the tribe cheering after them echoed loudly in Leawyn's ears as she rode away from the only life she had ever known.

~

They rode for what seemed like hours until, finally, Xavier pulled his horse to a stop. He landed on his feet lightly when he jumped down from his tall stallion's back and turned to her. He grasped Leawyn around her waist and pull her off until her feet touched the ground. She took in their surroundings.

There was a hut facing towards a small river, the water shimmering in the moonlight, reflecting the ripples of fish and other lake creatures as they swam. Beech-fir and foliage surrounded them, with trees towering high over their heads, creating a beautiful canopy.

"Where are we?" she asked, staring at the crudely made hut in interest.

"I had my men build this for us," Xavier answered without looking at her, too busy unsaddling his horse. "The ride to our village is too long. We'll stay here until the rest of my tribe reaches us. Together, we will all travel back to Izayges."

He lifted his saddle off his horse and threw it over a low-hanging branch.

"Why must we wait for the others? Why not just ride on?"

Xavier paused, leveling her with a look that made her heart pound. "You know why," he said quietly.

Leawyn looked away from him. Yes, she knew exactly why.

To consummate their marriage and claim her as his wife.

"Go inside and light the candles there. I will be in shortly."

Leawyn exhaled shakily, her legs trembling as she walked towards the hut to do as he bid. Her hand was on the rope that served as a door handle when his next words stopped her dead.

"There's nowhere to run, Leawyn. That door is the only way out. You can't escape me."

Leawyn closed her eyes; his meaning was clear. This was going to happen, and nothing she could do would stop him. Swallowing against the bile and fear choking her, Leawyn gathered her strength and wrenched open the door—sealing her fate.

~

Leawyn sat on the large bed staring down at her hands. She was still wearing her wedding gown, and her hair still had the small braids woven through it in the style of an Izayges.

She raised her head at the sound of the wooden door opening, standing when her husband's hulking frame came through. He stared at her as he closed the door behind him, the sound loud in the otherwise quiet room.

They squared off; the only sounds were the crackling of the fire Leawyn had lit and her shallow breathing. She trembled when he took slow, measured steps towards her, a predatory gleam in his eyes. He stopped within a breath away from her. She stared at the door behind his massive shoulders, avoiding his gaze.

It was when he reached up to untie the knot holding her dress together that she tried to run from him.

Leawyn screamed when Xavier wrapped his beefy arm around her waist and hoisted her up. Her legs kicked out wildly as she struggled in his grasp.

He threw her over his shoulder and onto the bed so that she landed on her back. He was on top of her in seconds, wedging himself in-between her legs. She lashed out at him, bucking her hips to try and dislodge him, aiming her dainty fists for his face.

Xavier reached up and grabbed her hands in his, holding them high above her head so it made her back arch. She shrieked again, struggling against his hold and sobbing.

"Enough!" Xavier barked, jolting her hard enough to make her head slam back onto the pillow. He glared down at her.

"You will accept this, Leawyn," he growled menacingly as he used his other hand to untie the knot and jerk her dress down her body, exposing her breasts.

She cried, shaking her head, fruitlessly struggling against him. She let out another loud sob when his hand trailed down her hip until it reached the underside of her thigh.

He grabbed a fistful of her dress and pushed it up so the material bunched around her waist.

"No!" she sobbed, trembling with her fear. Her eyes were wide as she looked at him pleadingly. "Please don't do this! *Please!* I'm not ready!"

Xavier snarled down at her, eyes furious. "You are my wife. You *will* accept this, and I will take you," he promised, his voice laced with steel. "You knew this would happen."

Leawyn cried. Fat tears rolled down her cheeks as she stared up at him fearfully. He traced one of her tears before dipping his head and catching it with his tongue. He turned, burying his face in her neck, inhaling the scent of her. He tilted his head, so his lips brushed her ear with every word he whispered.

"I can tie you down if you would prefer, or we can do this the easy way – willingly."

She choked around her sobs, her tiny form quivering. She felt his arousal through his breeches when it brushed against her thigh.

"Either way, I *will* claim you, Leawyn." He nipped her ear lightly, ignoring when she tried to jerk away from him. "And I'll enjoy every minute of it."

Leawyn let out a low moan; the sound resembled what a wounded animal would make. She jerked in his grasp, her one last attempt to try and escape.

To protect one of the only parts of herself she had left.

But it was futile.

"Do I need to grab my rope?" Xavier growled, his patience wearing thin. "Choice is yours."

"Willingly," Leawyn whispered numbly.

"Good girl," Xavier praised before his lips claimed her own in a possessive kiss. He reached up and ripped her dress completely off with one hand, while the other jerked down his pants.

Leawyn had just one moment to close her eyes before he gripped her thighs with both his hands and wrenched her legs apart, spreading her wide open so he could nestle between her.

"Mine," he hissed out. He slammed his hips forward with a brutal thrust that made her screech in pain as he tore through her virginal barrier with a swiftness that brought tears to her eyes and made her body seize in agony.

He groaned when she clawed at his shoulders, her nails leaving little crescent marks on his skin. He pulled out halfway, and Leawyn winced at the feeling before he slammed his pelvis forward and entered her once again, each thrust more powerful than the last.

"Please!" she blubbered in pain, the burn of him breaking her innocence only intensified with each movement of his hips.

Leawyn tried desperately to leave his grip, pushing against his shoulders and arching her back to try and crawl away from him, but it was no use. He simply reached up and grasped her hands, pinning them down onto the bed again with one hand while the other held her thigh closer to his body.

"The more you fight, the more painful I'll make it," Xavier snarled down at her, his eyes alight with his lust. He continued his merciless pace, pulling out and slamming back in with quick succession. The sounds of his flesh slapping against hers echoed around them.

"Please..." Leawyn sobbed her last attempt to reach out to whatever humanity Xavier had left.

He paused, and before she could hope for much, he pulled back and simply flipped her over, forcing her onto her stomach. He gripped her around her neck and forced her face down onto the pillow, holding her still while he wrapped his arm underneath her stomach and arched her hips up so she was on her knees. Taking her like the animal he was.

"I gave you a choice," Xavier hissed into her ear, then he thrust into her so hard and deep, she felt as if a hot dagger pierced her.

The pillow masked her screams and caught the tears that ran

down her cheeks as the flight left her completely. She lay beneath him, defeated.

Later that night, Leawyn lay stiffly in bed with Xavier's arm thrown possessively over her waist. Even in sleep, he controlled her.

Possessed her.

There was no going back after tonight, no escaping him.

She was his.

Forever.

Leawyn cried.

She cried for the freedom she lost, and the life she was forced to have.

She cried for her home, and she cried for the pain he made her feel.

But most of all, she cried because when she closed her eyes, she saw the hazel ones that belonged to the one she would miss the most.

The sun shone bright above, making the ocean's blue and green hues to sparkle from the reflective rays. The sound of seagulls squawking high overhead did nothing to diminish the tinkling sound of a child's joyous laughter as she chased after the waves.

Her blonde hair glowed bright when it caught the sun. The imprints of her feet marked the sand before the waves playfully drew them away, continuing the never-ending game of catch.

Leawyn giggled to herself and stared down at her feet as she squished her toes into the wet sand until they were buried. She watched in fascination as the water came and rinsed the sand away.

She should be back at her village with her caretaker, who was probably very upset with her for sneaking off, but Leawyn wanted to play, not do chores.

Growing tired of her game, she walked over to the dry part of sand and flopped down onto her back. She watched the seagulls overhead that grace-

fully glided with the wind and occasionally dropped down into the water to catch fish.

Before she even realized she was tired, she fell asleep right there on the sand.

~

It was quiet when she woke.

She could no longer hear the seagulls squawking overhead, and the beach wasn't as warm because the sun had long since set.

Leawyn shot up with a gasp, looking around in panic. She scrambled to her feet, wiping the sand off her hands by using her long skirt.

Brees was going to be so mad at her!

She gathered up her skirts and ran as quickly as her six-year-old legs could take her towards the hill that would lead back to her village. Leawyn's panic grew; everything was dark. Without a torch, it was hard to navigate.

It wasn't long that she was horribly lost.

Sliding down a rock slick with moss, she pulled her knees to her chest and began to cry.

"Why are you crying?"

She jerked violently sideways, her wide, blue eyes opening to see the pale face of a boy with a mop of curly brown hair standing a few steps in front of her.

He couldn't have been more than a few years older than her, standing at about four feet tall, he stared at her with curiosity and concern.

"I ran away from Brees, and now I don't know my way back." Leawyn sniffled, using the back of her hand to wipe away her tears. The boy's lips pursed as he took a step forward and knelt in front of her.

"Why did you run away?"

She sniffled again, her crystal eyes puddled as she answered. "I wanted to play, but she wouldn't let me."

"Why couldn't you play?"

"Papa doesn't like it when I play," Leawyn whispered sadly.

It got quiet between them, the boy lost in his thoughts, and Leawyn wishing she would have listened to her caretaker.

Her small shoulders shook as the beach carried a strong breeze. She jumped when a cloak was suddenly draped over her. Leawyn looked up at the boy as he stood, pulling her along with him.

"I will take you home."

"Wake up, Leawyn," the boy whispered in her ear.

She blinked open her eyes, looking up at him drowsily. "Your village is just up the hill." He nodded his head forward, gently setting Leawyn down onto her feet.

She smiled as she caught sight of her lit-up village, instantly feeling relieved. She was quick to run off, but just before she reached the top of the hill, she stopped to look over her shoulder when the boy did not follow.

"Are you not coming?" Leawyn asked, confused.

The boy silently shook his head. "This is not my home."

"But why—"

"You should go. I can hear them looking for you," the boy said calmly. Leawyn tilted her small head and listened. Her eyes widened when she heard he was right; they were looking for her.

"Go," the boy urged when the voices grew louder.

Leawyn nodded before she turned on her heel and once again started her way up to her village. She paused, whipping around with her mouth open, ready to ask him his name. She shut it abruptly.

No one was there.

The boy was gone.

Leawyn searched a moment more to see where he might have gone, but after not finding him, she shrugged and continued up the hill.

It never occurred to her to ask how the boy knew her name when she never told him.

The following morning, Leawyn lay frozen, staring at the ceiling of the hut. Xavier moved against her, the sounds of his groans of pleasure filling the silence. Her body moved with his movements, the thrusts quick, hard, and unrelenting as he held her legs captive, hooked around his forearms.

Leawyn tried desperately to hold in her winces of pain at his rough treatment. Her hands clenched around the bed furs beneath her, knuckles turning white with how tightly she held them. Her body, still unused to the act of pleasure, was ablaze with pain. Every time Xavier thrust inside of her, it felt as if a heated dagger was spearing her insides with brutal intensity. She squeezed her eyes shut. Tears of pain escaped from behind her closed eyelids, leaving a trail down her cheek.

Xavier's new wife cried out when he tightened his grip around her, pulling her forward sharply to meet his thrusts. He looked down at her, taking in her wide, frightened eyes. Her long hair was sprawled out on top of the pillow, and her back arched as he buried himself deep within her.

She was beautiful in his eyes, and he had no plans of ever letting her go.

Finally, he stilled, his body shuddering with his release. He collapsed on top of Leawyn, still completely astonished at the amount of pleasure her young, supple body provided. He groaned, still feeling his climax. The feeling of her untouched body clenching around him as it forced itself to accommodate him and his length. It drove him mad with lust.

She was so tight and warm around him, it was almost painful.

Xavier nuzzled his wife's neck, smirking when she shivered in reaction but otherwise did not pull away from him.

"You are learning," he commented smugly, kissing her neck.

She stiffened further when he moved his lips across her jaw. She jerked her head away with a glare when he went to capture her lips with his own. He stared down at her, his eyes boring into hers in warning. He dipped his head to capture her lips again.

He reached out and grabbed her jaw in one hand, a fistful of her hair in the other. He leveled his furious glare with her own as he tilted her head up.

"Why do you turn from me?" he asked in his deep, raspy voice. "Why do you deny me the touch of your lips, knowing they belong to me?"

Leawyn's eyes flashed. "They'll never belong to you," she hissed between clenched teeth as she struggled to release the pressure of his hand from her hair.

His expression became dangerous at her words. Did she not know that everything she was belonged to him now? She was his wife. His to own and possess.

His lips curled with his snarl as he shoved her down harder against the bed. He caught her wrists when she went to hit him, pinning them above her head.

"Everything you are belongs to me, Leawyn. You'll do well to remember that," he told her, brushing a strand of hair away from her face, ignoring her flinch when his hands touched her cheek, squeezing them together so that they puckered.

"Now be a good girl," he warned, dipping his head down to her lips.

This time, when he went to kiss her, she did not pull away.

Xavier pushed away from her quickly, uncaring of his nudity as he walked across the room to dress.

"Clean yourself up. We're leaving." And without a backward glance at her, he left.

∾

Leawyn lay on the bed for a moment longer before she slowly pushed herself into a sitting position. Taking a moment to collect herself, she stood up, whimpering at the pain between her thighs. Looking down, she saw her thighs were smeared with blood. She looked away, unable to bear the sight.

Gingerly, she made her way across the room until she stopped at the large basin of water there. Cupping her hands together, she plunged them into the cold liquid and splashed the glistening drops against her face. She dipped her hands into the water again and paused when she saw her reflection.

With a shaking hand, she fingered the bruises on her chin, the black and blue marks of fingerprints contrasting against her pale skin. Her hand trailed down, tracing her fingertips over the bruises on her neck.

Leawyn bit her lip, blinking away her tears so she could continue the survey of her body. She gave a muffled sob when her hands skimmed over her hips. Looking down, she noticed the cluster of bruises there, too. Bruises in the shape of fingerprints.

His fingerprints.

His mark.

His ownership.

Leawyn felt sore and stiff, as if she had been used. Well, she had, hadn't she?

Her face contorted in anger, and with a shout, she knocked the basin of water over. She watched as it crashed to the floor, the water soaked up by the animal skins littering the surface.

Her anger faded away, and all she was left with was the feeling of disgust for herself and the man she was forced to marry. Her shoulders shook, and, no longer able to hold herself up, she collapsed onto her knees and crumbled to the floor.

Her forehead met her hands as she wept.

"Our scouts have been reporting strange movements from these locations," Tristan said as he pointed to the areas on the map. "We don't know who they are or their reason for being on our land, but it's only a matter of time before they reach our borders."

Xavier sat silently as he processed the information Tristan provided. They were back in the Izayges village inside the war-hut, which housed maps of the land. It was where Xavier spent most of his time. The hut had three tables inside, two of which were pushed far against the wall that overflowed with various maps and rolled parchment. A long oak table was placed in the center of the room with several chairs neatly tucked in. The far wall held a flat timber Tristan had used to pin the map of their southern borders. Xavier leaned back in his chair, gripping the table corner. His face was impassive as he looked at the map in front of him, as if staring at it would give him the answers he sought. "Any chance of them being friendly travelers?"

Tristan shook his head. "I've never seen travelers equipped with that amount of armor and moving in such a large group."

"Send a message to all the patrols," Xavier finally said as he pushed himself away from the table. "Do not raise the alarm yet, but tell them to heed caution."

"What else will you have me do?" Tristan asked. He knew Xavier well enough to know he had more planned than just sending a warning.

He allowed a small smirk to tilt his lips up when he glanced at

Tristan. "We'll ride out ourselves. I need to know for myself and make judgment," he told him, looking to the map again. "I won't risk war on the assumption they're a threat."

"And if they are?" Tristan asked, raising a brow.

"Then we give them something to really fear before they die."

With a quick flick of his wrist, the knife Xavier held flew across the table and landed directly in the middle of the map they were both looking at.

"I'll ready the men, then." Tristan bowed his head in acknowledgment, quickly leaving to carry out his chief's orders.

Xavier stared at the dagger lodged into the wood. Knowing Tristan, the men would be ready to leave by nightfall. With no certainty of how long Xavier and his company would be gone, it meant he would be away from Leawyn for an indeterminate amount of time. For a reason unknown to him, that particular thought did not bode well. Xavier didn't want to be without her, and the thought of another man looking after her well-being while he was gone made his fists clench in anger and the bitter taste of jealousy fill his mouth.

His eyes narrowed. No doubt she would welcome the company and take advantage of his absence. Xavier growled as he marched to the map and ripped the knife from the wood savagely.

No, he thought as he left the tent and stalked past the many people in his village. They gave him a wide berth as he headed straight for the hut which contained his young wife. She would not be alone.

She'd never have the option to be with another man or take advantage of the chance to escape him. If he were to ever catch another man gazing at his wife with the same lust that ran through his veins whenever his eyes met hers, it would be that man's death.

Leawyn would go with him and his men.

The possessiveness of his thoughts startled him. Never had he felt this strongly about a woman.

What is she doing to me?

Even more aggravated than before, Xavier practically wrenched the door off his hut.

Leawyn jumped from the bed when the door banged open, watching as her husband ducked in. Xavier's presence seemed to fill the room. It was as if the air sensed the danger he possessed and crackled accordingly. He was dangerous, and powerful; she could only imagine what he was like on the battlefield. The thought made her shiver. She would never want to witness that, to see the true darkness in his eyes come to life.

They stood staring at one another across the room; the quiet intensity of his stare made her feel ill at ease. When Xavier took a step towards her, Leawyn couldn't help but take a step back.

"Don't," Xavier warned, his voice low. Leawyn stilled instantly, eyeing him warily as he slowly made his way to her. He took a couple more steps and stopped.

"Come here," he demanded.

Leawyn took a few timid steps forward. When she was within arm's reach, he caught her wrist and pulled her the rest of the way to him. With one hand, he pushed a lock of hair away from her face and hooked his thumb under her chin, tilting it to the side so that a freshly made bruise caught the light. He studied it, his dark eyes filled with intensity. Finally, Xavier did something Leawyn never would have expected.

His touch turned gentle as he tilted her chin up more and laid a gentle kiss on it. His kisses created a path down to her neck and collarbone, brushing the other bruises, both new and old, that marred her skin there.

"Pack a bag. You're accompanying me and my men," Xavier said against her skin. He kissed her neck one last time before turning and walking out the way he came.

Leawyn stared after him in bewilderment.

"Are you out of your mind?" Tristan demanded as soon as he reached Xavier.

Xavier said nothing in response, barely sparing Tristan a glance as he continued to load up his horse.

"I just saw Leawyn packing a bag. She said you demanded she go with us?" Tristan asked, pointing behind him in his wife's general direction. "Tell me my ears have mistaken me!"

Xavier tightened the girth of his saddle and continued to ignore his brother. Tristan gritted his teeth in frustration, stepping in front of Xavier and blocking his path.

"Xavier, she cannot go with us," Tristan said firmly.

"I don't believe I asked for your opinion, nor do you have a choice in the matter," Xavier said coolly. The fixed glare was the only warning Xavier gave his younger brother of the danger he invoked by questioning him.

"She cannot come with us, Xavier. It's no place for a woman," Tristan quietly reasoned with his brother.

When Xavier's eyes only narrowed in response, Tristan's anger grew.

"She could get killed!" Tristan yelled in frustration, drawing the attention of some of their tribesmen.

Xavier's temper got a hold of him, and he suddenly shoved Tristan against the tree behind him, forcing his back hard against the bark.

"Why the sudden concern for my wife, Brother?" Xavier asked as his grip tightened on Tristan's tunic. "What does it matter to you what I do with *my* wife?"

"She's a liability, Xavier," Tristan gritted out. "She'll get you killed. She'll get us *all* killed!"

"What I do with my wife is none of your concern!" Xavier hissed. "She's *mine*," he snarled possessively in Tristan's face.

They glared at each other, tense silence stretched between them. After several heated moments, Xavier released Tristan's tunic roughly as he backed away.

"Do not question me again, Brother," Xavier warned, his eyes telling of the promised danger if Tristan disobeyed.

Turning his back on Tristan, Xavier marched up the hill to go get his wife.

"You're making a mistake, Xavier!" Tristan yelled at his brother's back.

Xavier's steps paused, his fist clenching.

"She's going to be your downfall."

Xavier cocked his head and met Tristan's eyes. Moments passed before Xavier turned back around and continued walking away.

It took four days of hard riding to reach their destination. The only moments of respite Leawyn was granted was when they stopped to feed and water their horses. Leawyn and her horse, Deydrey, were unused to this type of traveling, and she worried the ride would be too much for her beloved mare. But Deydrey seemed to enjoy the run, which eased Leawyn's worry.

The only blessing of this whole adventure was the fact Leawyn did not have to be around her husband. In fact, she hardly saw him. Their company was about fifty men, and she was instructed to ride in the middle so that she was surrounded. Protected. Since the speed they were traveling hardly left room for conversation, Leawyn kept to herself. Even though she was happy to be away from her husband, she was sick of riding. Which was why when Xavier finally did call a stop, she sighed in relief.

With sore thighs and a numb bottom, she held back her groan as her feet touched solid ground. After taking a few minutes to stretch and try to bring feeling back into her limbs, she turned her attention to her horse and began the process of unsaddling her. She was in the middle of trying to lift the saddle with shaky arms when it was suddenly plucked out of her hands and set down on the ground.

Surprised, Leawyn whirled around, only to stare into the intricate design of breastplate armor. Tilting her head back, she stared into the dark eyes of her husband.

She glanced away from his stare and down to her saddle. Quickly coming out of her shock, she gave him a timid grateful smile.

"Thank you," she said, brushing a strand of her hair behind her ear in a nervous gesture.

"You're welcome," Xavier said gruffly.

He placed his hands on her slim hips, resting them there. Leawyn tensed, glancing over his shoulder to see his men were further up, busy setting up the camp.

Meaning that they were alone.

Xavier tightened his grip on her waist, his thumb brushing against her hip bone before he gently nudged her aside and stepped forward to finish what was left to unsaddle her horse.

She released the breath she didn't know she was holding and stared at his back for a moment in perplexity.

"I can do it," she protested, not wanting him to think her helpless. "You don't need to—"

"I want to," he interrupted her, staring into her eyes. Taking in her startled expression, he turned away from her and looked down at her horse's coat instead.

"I had a tent set up for you—us," he amended. "I know you must be tired. Go in and rest for a while." He glanced over his shoulder at her once more, meeting her blue eyes with his brown as she regarded him.

"Go." He turned his back on her again, his attention returned to his task. "I'll finish here."

Leawyn hesitated, watching him groom her mare. Not knowing what else to say, and not wanting to offend him because of his rare act of kindness, she turned on her heel in a daze and slowly made her way to the camp, all the while thinking, *what just happened?*

Once Leawyn made it to the encampment, she came to a stop, realizing she had no idea where she was supposed to go. She was in such a confused daze, she didn't think to ask Xavier *which* tent she was supposed to rest in. Since there was no way she was going to go back to her husband and *ask*, she was left standing there, looking like an idiot. Her shoulders slumped as she released a tired sigh.

"You look lost."

Leawyn whipped her head up and stared at Tristan as he made his way towards her, his lips tilted up in an amused smirk. She smiled, embarrassed. "Was I that obvious?"

"I'm afraid so." Tristan chuckled and she grimaced. "Then again, 'tis not often we see a woman in our camp," he added.

"I believe it." She sighed as she surveyed her surroundings. She watched Xavier's men as they built small fires, unloaded their horses, and settled in to relax after their long ride. She shook her head, turning her attention back to Tristan.

"What am I doing here, Tristan?" she asked him quietly, searching his eyes. "Why did he bring me here?"

"Come," he said instead of answering, grabbing her arm and leading her away. "I'll show you your tent."

Knowing he was not going to answer her, Leawyn sighed dejectedly and let him lead her away.

He stopped just outside a rather large green tent, pulled aside the front flap, and gestured for her to go in. Taking a step forward, Leawyn ducked her head down and looked around in wonder at the lavish tent.

In the middle was a large table filled with maps and knickknacks, no doubt marking out the land around them. Leawyn could see a small basin of water; the steam rising from it indicated it was still warm. There was a bed pallet in the far corner covered in thick animal skins with pillows littered all around it. Thick rugs covered the floor, and torch stands were spaced sporadically around the tent, creating a soft glow. It was a tent meant for the leader, and all in all it looked comfortable.

It made Leawyn feel a bit guilty to know she could sleep comfortably while the other men were left to sleep outside on the ground and in the cold.

She turned to thank Tristan, only to find he wasn't there.

She frowned. She was a bit put out he stuck around long enough to show her the way but didn't bother to tell her goodbye.

She didn't have long to think of that fact. Xavier stepped through the tent opening. He let the fabric used as the entrance of their tent slide from his fingers as he slowly straightened.

Leawyn felt a sudden sense of déjà vu when he took a step toward her, staring at her intently. She unconsciously took a step back and instantly regretted it when his eyes flashed irately. She braced herself when he marched towards her, knowing he was going to punish her for retreating from him.

But instead of grabbing her and forcing himself on her as she expected him to, he simply walked past her to the wash bin. She stared at him as he calmly grabbed the rag and started to run it over his face and down his arms.

"I'm going away for a few days," Xavier told her. "You are to stay here."

"Why did you bring me here, only for you to leave me? Why couldn't I stay behind in the village?"

His expression darkened. "So that you could find comfort in another man's arms?"

Leawyn recoiled, insulted. "I wouldn't—"

"I don't trust you," Xavier said bluntly, cutting her off. "And the only man I trust to ensure that doesn't happen is here. Tristan will be your keeper while I'm gone."

Leawyn bristled at the term "keeper." It was as if she were an insolent child. She wisely kept her mouth shut, knowing any remark she made would only rouse his anger.

"How long will you be away?" she asked instead. "We only just got here."

Xavier threw the rag back into the water with a small splash. He crossed his arms as he turned to face her.

"I am to scout ahead," he told her. He eyed her, watching her expression closely. "I don't know how long I'll be gone. It might be a few days to a week."

Leawyn tried not to show the small spark of hope that ignited inside her, even knowing he was gauging her reaction. If he were to leave for a few days, it would be the perfect time to try and escape.

She could finally be free of him and this trapped life.

"That is unfortunate," Leawyn murmured.

Xavier only smirked. "My dear, sweet wife," he said in a silky voice that instantly put her on alert. "Do you think me stupid?"

He raised his hand to cup her cheek. He stared into her eyes, and she tensed when he moved his hand to grip the nape of her neck.

"I know exactly what this opportunity presents," Xavier said, his other hand snaking up her throat.

His eyes turned icy, his grip on her neck tightened as he used his thumb to push down on her throat, forcibly titling her head back. "Know that if you try to escape, not only will you not get very far..."

Leawyn whimpered when his grip became unbearably painful. He slowly cut off her air supply by applying more pressure with his thumb. She closed her eyes at the feel of his beard scraping across her cheek, feeling his lips touch her ear.

"But you also won't like the consequences if I find out you tried to escape me," he whispered severely.

He pulled away from her, and before Leawyn could comprehend what was happening, he lifted her so she was flush against him. She let out a pained groan when her back met the large wooden beam holding up their tent.

"You're mine," Xavier growled. The sound of his belt unbuckling made Leawyn start to struggle against his hold, knowing what was coming. The slick head of his length brush her thigh as he yanked her skirts up. A moment later, he pushed himself inside her with a hard thrust. His grip bruised her thighs as he held them around his waist and thrust himself in and out of her with fast, jerky movements.

"You belong to me."

She cried out as her back and head painfully hit the beam behind her with each thrust of his hips.

"You'll never escape me, never!" he snarled manically. He pounded into her at a furious pace, punishing her with his body for a long while until, finally, he stiffened. He buried his face into her neck and Leawyn felt his seed spill into her. His thrusts slowed, and then stopped.

Xavier stepped back, and just as quickly he released his tight grip on her thighs so that she fell to the floor. He stared down at her seemingly without feeling as she crumbled around herself, her hair creating a barrier and hiding her tears as her shoulders shook.

He kneeled so his face was level with her head. She flinched when he calmly brushed her hair away from her cheek, turning her face toward him.

"You'll never escape me, Leawyn. Wherever you are, I'll find you," he promised, brushing a tear away. "You're mine. I'll kill anyone who tries to take you away from me," he said softly, his voice laced with steel and possessiveness.

With those parting words, he quickly rose to a standing position and left the tent, leaving Leawyn on the ground, shaking.

In that moment, any doubts that Xavier wasn't heartless were wiped away.

He was a monster, and he always would be.

She was going to escape him.

Even if it killed her.

"Asten!" a twelve-year old Leawyn shouted after the sixteen-year-old boy. He simply laughed at her and spurred his horse faster, holding the book he had taken away from her in the air teasingly.

Leawyn growled under her breath in annoyance.

"Deydrey, faster!" she urged her young mare, using her thighs to kick her into action. Deydrey snorted and pounded her hooves on the sand quicker, catching up to the quarter horse in front of her.

"Give it back!" Leawyn shouted at Asten when she and Deydrey pulled up beside his stallion.

Asten simply smirked at her, his hazel eyes sparkling in mischief and humor. "You want this, do you?" he shouted back.

His smirk grew at Leawyn's angry "Yes!"

"Go get it then!" he said before he chucked it forward toward the crashing waves.

Leawyn gasped in horror, watching the book sail high into the air. Asten's laughter sounded behind her when she and Deydrey flew ahead of him.

Without thinking, she stood up, threw herself off Deydrey's back and into the air, catching the book before she crashed into the ocean.

Deydrey instantly stopped when she felt her owner's weight leave her, sliding in the sand with her haste.

"Leawyn!" Asten yelled, pulling his horse to a hard stop and jumping off him. He rushed to the bank, ignoring the white of the water as it soaked his boots and pants. Leawyn gasped, her hair sticking to her face as she sputtered.

Asten stared at her drowned form before he burst out into heavy laughter. Leawyn scowled as she waddled to shore. "Oh yes, it's very funny!" she snapped, swatting at him as she passed.

Asten laughed harder, holding his sides as he bent forward. "You should have seen your face!" He managed to gasp out before his laughter continued.

Leawyn rolled her eyes heavenward.

. . .

"It's not funny; stop laughing!" she yelled at him, muttering curses under her breath when he fell on the beach in more laughter, not caring it got him wet.

She angrily wrung out her shoulder-length hair and her skirts, watching as the ocean water made a small puddle in the sand. Straightening, her lips curled in distaste as she plucked a string of seaweed off her shoulder blade.

"Gross," Leawyn muttered. She looked down at the book she held in her hands and knew that despite her efforts to save it, the drawings were now swirling together and wouldn't be readable.

She bit her lip hard to keep from crying in her anger, and instead she marched to her waiting horse so she could leave. She was just about to mount when a hand latched onto her wrist and spun her around.

"Hey!" Asten laughed. "Where are you going?"

Leawyn's eyes narrowed as she yanked herself out of his grip.

"I'm going away from you!" she yelled and shoved her finger into his chest. "You—you--" She struggled for an adequate word to call him. "Oaf!"

Asten's eyebrows shot up into his hairline. "Oaf?"

"You ruined my book!" She poked him again. "You ruined it, and now I'll never be able to finish!" she ranted, poking his chest, yet again, with each word.

Asten grinned, gently grabbing the offending finger and holding it in *his hands.*

"Come now, Lea, it's not the end of the world. I'll just buy you a new one!"

"Don't 'Lea' me, Asten!" she huffed, yanking her hand back from him. "That's not the point!"

"What is the point then, Lea?" Asten asked innocently, purposely using the nickname he knew she hated.

Leawyn's mouth dropped open. "What's the—? You— My—" Asten raised a brow in amusement as she struggled for words. It only infuriated her more.

"UGH!" Leawyn threw her hands up in the air and turned her back on him to mount Deydrey again. When strong arms wrapped around her waist and lifted her up and away from Deydrey, she started to kick her feet.

"Put me down!" she yelled, struggling even more when Asten continued to carry her. "Asten!" Leawyn said sharply in warning, trying to push away from him.

"Leawyn!" Asten mocked.

"I hate you," Leawyn pouted, folding her arms across her chest, giving up.

Asten just chuckled. "I know."

7

Xavier held in his sigh when he stepped out of the tent. He knew he was again too harsh with her, but he couldn't seem to rein in his anger at the thought of her trying to escape him. Not only did it cause a weird clenching sensation in his gut, but it was also extremely dangerous.

Stupid girl. Didn't she know they were far away from the tribes, and unfamiliar men were roaming our lands?

Xavier growled to himself in annoyance as he stalked to where he knew he would find his brother. His question was unnecessary since he knew the answer.

Of course, she didn't. How could she?

War was no place for a woman. Xavier knew that all too well. But he couldn't stand the thought of being away from her and, if anything, she would have a better chance at escaping him back in his village than she did here.

He couldn't allow her to escape him. She was his.

Whether she liked it or not, she was going to be with him forever.

"You're going to scout?" Tristan asked incredulously.

Xavier paused with his saddle in his hands, to give his brother an annoyed glare.

"Yes. Why is that such a hard thing to grasp?"

"Because you never scout, cousin." Tristan and Xavier turned their heads as the tall, heavily muscled blonde male made his way towards them.

"Tyronian!" Tristan exclaimed in surprise, a grin taking over his face. "When did you get back? And how did you find us? The Siraces get sick of you already?"

"Just now, I have my ways, and no one will ever get sick of me—I'm too handsome for that," Tyronian replied as he came to stand next to Tristan. He turned to Xavier. "Usually 'tis Tristan's expertise to scout, while yours is the maiming and stabbing," Tyronian grinned, showing his surprisingly white teeth around his blond beard.

Tristan smirked in humor while Xavier scowled at his cousin, who continued to grin.

"As much as we all enjoy your humor and input, Tyronian," Xavier said dryly, "I'm afraid that it is unwanted."

"Nonsense," Tyronian dismissed, waving his hand in front of his face as if he were swatting a fly. "My input is always wanted."

Tristan snorted.

Xavier tried to hold in his growl of annoyance at his cousin's teasing. Tyronian never was one to take things seriously, being the most laid-back among the three.

Besides Tristan, Tyronian was one of the few who did not cower from his glare or his moments of rage. Though part of him was thankful his cousin still treated him like kin instead of his commander, it was times like these he wished he had an effect over Tyronian.

"You're in charge of Leawyn," he told Tristan, turning to face him now that Killix was ready. "Do not let her out of your sight. She is not to go anywhere without you by her side, understood?" he commanded, giving Tristan a hard stare.

"Ah, yes! Your little wife." Tyronian clapped his hands together loudly, rubbing them together. "When do I get to meet my new cousin?" He asked excitedly, looking between Xavier and Tristan.

"You? Never," Xavier deadpanned.

"Ah, so she must be as lovely as the rumors portray her!"

"What does that have to do with anything?" Tristan asked Tyronian curiously, raising a brow.

"Why else wouldn't he let me meet her? He's afraid I'll sweep her right off her feet with my charm and good looks!"

Tristan chuckled, shaking his head at his cousin while Xavier scowled.

"How long do you suppose you'll be gone?" Tristan asked, getting back on topic, watching as Xavier lifted himself onto Killix's saddle.

"It depends on how quickly I find them, and if I decide they're a threat or not."

"And if they are?" Tyronian frowned.

"Then this will be the last land their feet touch."

Xavier turned his attention back to Tristan. "Remember what I said."

At Tristan's nod, Xavier gathered his reins tighter in his hands.

"Ride out!" Xavier called to his men loudly over his shoulder before he kicked Killix's side and took off in a gallop, twenty men following him on their own horses as they charged after the unknown.

It was dark. The once-roaring fires of the camp were now nothing but embers, and the men scattered all around the encampment were fast asleep.

Leawyn silently and stealthily made her way around the bodies, her booted feet making no sound as she quickly made her way to where the horses were. Spotting her mare, she rushed to her.

Deydrey nickered softly when she caught sight of her, and Leawyn hastily shushed her. "Quiet now, Deydrey," she whispered softly to her, petting her velvety nose. "We must be quiet."

When Deydrey made no more sounds, Leawyn made quick work of putting on the saddle and tying necessary items to hold her until she was farther away from her imprisonment. She was just about to grab the reins when a voice behind her caused her to freeze in her tracks.

"I wouldn't do that if I were you."

Leawyn whirled around and faced the person who spoke, feeling her heart drop when she met the boyish, dark brown eyes which belonged to Tristan. His face was void of any emotion as he stared at her; only his eyes glittered with unspoken words.

"You were just taking a quiet walk," Tristan said casually, taking measured steps towards her. "Because I know you weren't trying to escape...were you, Leawyn?" he asked her as he finally stopped in front of her, staring into her eyes intently.

"Please," she whispered. "I can't go back to him." She shook her head, her hands clutched into fists. "Please don't make me go back to him!" she pleaded, her eyes seem to shine in the moonlight reflecting off her unshed tears. Tristan didn't reply.

"I know you care; I can see it in your eyes." Leawyn's lip trembled as Tristan's brows furrowed, his eyes flashing with an unknown emotion.

By his expression, she could see she was right; he did care. He knew she was far too innocent and pure to deserve the treatment his older brother gave her.

"Please, let me go..." Leawyn begged desperately, searching Tristan's eyes for any indication he would let her leave. But he stood there, staring down at her much like he did at her wedding.

"Please."

Tristan's expression turned pained. For the second time, he drove the spear through what little hope she held.

"I can't," he whispered, his face scrunching up with mixed emotions.

Her heart broke as her tears slowly slid down her cheeks. She was so hurt that Tristan would betray her. But then again, why wouldn't he obey his brother and chief over helping her?

"He's my brother, and you are his wife," Tristan said as he gently but firmly grabbed her arm. Leawyn didn't fight him; she just let him take her away in defeat. When she felt she could no longer hold her own weight, he swung her up into his arms and carried her the rest of the way back to camp.

He placed her down on the bed, staring into her eyes as he gently took her wrists and tied them together, then secured them to the bedpost holding up the pallet. He pulled away, and Leawyn stared into his eyes. He looked sad and guilty. He leaned forward and kissed her cheek, wiping a salty tear from her face with his lips.

"I'm sorry, Leawyn," he whispered hoarsely, holding her head to his lips for a moment more before he rose to his feet and walked out, leaving her tied up to the bed like the prisoner she was.

I t had been almost five days since Tristan caught her trying to
sneak out, and Leawyn had never felt so much like a prisoner
than she did now.

Every day Tristan would come in and give her water and meals.
During the day, he would unbind her wrists. He knew she had no
chance of escape because he always had a guard posted outside
her tent.

The only time he let Leawyn outside was when she begged him to
because she was going stir crazy.

But even then, she was guarded with him by her side.

When nightfall came, Tristan would again tie her to the bed to
make sure she didn't try to escape.

The only good grace was that Tristan didn't tell anyone about her
trying to run away.

Sometimes, he would try to talk to her, but each time he did, she
ignored him. She knew she was being a bit irrational and childish to
be snubbing him like she was; it wasn't his fault she was stuck with a
man she didn't love. It wasn't his fault the man was his brother and
chief. Tristan would be held accountable for her actions, and the
repercussions of going against the chief of the tribe were dire.

It would be like Lyrical and Chienef all over again.

It was wrong of Leawyn to ask him to betray his brother for her.
But even with her rationalizing, she couldn't bring herself to forgive
him.

Eventually, Tristan stopped trying to talk to her and let her be.

Each night he would guard her tent, she would cry herself to sleep. She knew he could hear her.

~

Leawyn looked up at the sound of someone coming towards her tent. Figuring it was Tristan coming to bring her the evening meal, she turned her attention away, content on ignoring him.

However, the unfamiliar sound of another baritone voice caused her to whip her head back to look at the man in front of her in surprise.

"Who are you?" she asked, her tone a bit ruder than she intended.

She quickly cast her eyes down, worried she offended him. She didn't know much about the Izayges men, but if they were anything like her husband, they wouldn't appreciate her tone.

"Easy now, I only came to bring your meal." The man held up the small bowl in his hand as proof. "No need to kill the server," he chuckled, placing the bowl in her hands.

At Leawyn's look of surprise, the man chuckled again, his teeth showing as he gave her an attractive smile.

"Don't look so surprised, 'tis not like we want to starve you."

"I know that! It's just—" Leawyn flushed in embarrassment. "I was afraid I offended you."

She blinked when the man let out a booming laugh.

"I have no reason to be offended by a girl asking for a name of an unfamiliar man, now have I?" he asked with a raised eyebrow, his eyes twinkling with humor.

"Well, when you say it like that..." Leawyn mumbled. "Yet, you still fail to answer the question," she said when she got ahold of her embarrassment.

"Ah, you'd be correct! Tyronian, at your service!" He bowed down mockingly at her. At Leawyn's small giggle, he winked.

She took a moment to look at Tyronian. He was the only male besides her husband and Tristan with whom she'd had a real conversation.

Tyronian was tall, but not as tall as Xavier. He was built much like her husband, with broad shoulders and bulging muscles in both his arms and legs. Leawyn was certain that behind his armor he boasted a ripped, toned stomach.

He did not look at all like any of the other Izayges men she caught a glimpse of. In fact, he looked more like her people. Blond hair that stopped just above his shoulders and sparkling blue eyes. Tyronian was different; Leawyn could tell. He lacked the usual cold indifference most of the Izayges men had, and instead he was warm and welcoming. Already she had learned he had a good sense of humor.

She instantly liked him.

"Leawyn," she introduced before taking a small, hesitant sip of the soup in her bowl.

It was disgusting.

"I hope you like it. I made it myself."

Leawyn quickly stopped herself from spitting the soup back into her bowl.

"Hmm..." she forced herself to swallow it. "It's good," she coughed out, shooting a false reassuring smile at Tyronian. "Just hot."

He beamed at her. "That is because I put a special type of spice in it!"

"Are you Rhoxolani?" she asked to cover her grimace before she took another sip of the foul soup.

"No, but you are not the first one to ask." Tyronian chuckled, pulling up a seat in front of her. "My mother was Siraces, my father Izayges."

"Siraces?" Leawyn inquired, puzzled. "I thought the Siraces and the Izayges didn't get along. Since Lyrical slept with a Siraces man the night of her wedding," she pointed out unnecessarily.

"They don't really, but my father's brother thought it a good idea. So, he arranged for my father to marry the Siraces chief's daughter." He paused before he grinned impishly at Leawyn. "Y'know, for tribe unity and all."

She rolled her eyes. "I can see the Siraces relation now," Leawyn said dryly. "You said your 'father's brother.' Was your uncle the chief before?" she asked, readying herself to take another sip of the soup.

"He was," Tyronian nodded in agreement. "But when my father died, his son took over as chief."

He was quiet as he watched her take another spoonful of her soup.

"Xavier is my cousin."

This time Leawyn *did* spit out her soup.

Tyronian frowned when she went into a coughing fit. He thumped her on the back a couple of times—which almost knocked her off the bed.

"I'm fine!" Leawyn coughed out, waving his hand away. She took in a deep breath before she looked up at Tyronian with wide eyes.

"Xavier is your cousin?" she squeaked out in disbelief.

Tyronian frowned down at her again, his brows drawing together. "Well, yes. His father was my uncle and chief before Xavier took over. I am third in line, should anything happen to Tristan." He spoke slowly, as though he was explaining something complicated to a child.

"I know how it works!" Leawyn snapped, glaring at him. "I'm just surprised. You look nothing like him."

"'Tis a fact I'm very proud of!" Tyronian laughed, standing up from his chair. He bent down and placed his hand out to take the bowl back from Leawyn, which she gladly gave over to him. "I am better looking, after all."

In a daze, Leawyn watched him walk towards the flap of the tent.

"'Till next time, my Lady Chief!" Tyronian called over his shoulder. He flashed her one last mischievous grin before he ducked out of the tent.

She stared after him, waiting for him to come back and laugh at her for falling for his joke. But the longer she stared at the flap in stunned disbelief, the more she knew it wasn't a joke. Tyronian was Tristan's cousin, which meant he was Xavier, her *husband*'s, cousin. Third in line to be chief of the Izayges.

When she was fully able to process it, only two things remained on her mind.

If Tyronian was the chief, she imagined she would like the Izayges.

Why couldn't she marry *him?*

~

Over the next few days, Tyronian came and brought Leawyn her meals. It was something she was genuinely happy about, for she very much enjoyed his company, and even started to consider him a friend.

Tyronian made her forget her captivity. If only for a moment in time.

He was always able to make her laugh, especially when he would tell her stories of his childhood. It seemed Tristan and Tyronian were quite the troublemakers in their youth.

Leawyn found herself telling Tyronian things she hadn't told anyone else before. She told him about her village, and how she missed the sound of the waves crashing against the cliff rocks. He told her about his mother, and how she had died when he was just coming into manhood. Leawyn in turn told him how she never knew her mother, and how difficult it was for her father to be around her because of it.

It wasn't until Leawyn broached the subject of her husband one night during her evening meal that she saw the more serious side of her friend.

Leawyn told Tyronian about her wedding night, and how she always seemed to make Xavier angry. How mad she was at her father for making her marry a man who was always so cruel and uncaring. She told him how she felt like she was nothing but a prisoner, married to a man who was a monster. Tyronian's response surprised her.

"Do not be so quick to judge my cousin, Leawyn," he told her seriously, calling her by her name for the first time since she met him.

"There are many things you don't know about him. He's seen things that, if he were a lesser man, he would have gone mad over."

Tyronian's blue eyes met her own, staring into them deeply. His usual mischievous glint was absent.

"You're lucky that's all the monster he is, Leawyn."

After saying that, Tyronian didn't say any more, and went back to being his usual carefree, playful self.

But still, Leawyn couldn't get that conversation out of her head.

There was something in the way he said it, and how his eyes looked when he did.

She didn't know why, but it bothered her.

Later that night, when she finally succumbed to the heaviness of her eyes and fell into an uneasy sleep, she dreamed of her husband and the horrors of war.

Xavier and his men had been riding for days, following the trail of the unknown company of men who were swiftly making their way closer and closer to Samaria.

It was increasingly grating on Xavier's nerves that the mysterious men always seemed to be a step ahead of them. It was as if they were expecting someone to be looking for them and left different trails to throw them off.

They were playing a game Xavier did not understand, and it pissed him off.

"Xavier!"

Xavier snapped his head to the right when one of his most trusted scouts came rushing up to him. Xavier pushed himself to his feet as Crellio came to a skidding halt, bracing his hands on his knees as he panted, trying to catch his breath.

"What is it?" Xavier asked sharply, trying to hold in his growing ire as Crellio gasped for air, tilting his head to look up into his commander's eyes from his bent position.

"We found them."

"Where?" Xavier barked, already signaling the men around him to get ready to head out.

Crellio pushed himself up after finally getting a hold on his breathing.

"They're over by—"

Whatever Crellio was about to say was instantly cut off as an arrow lodged its way into his back and protruded out of his chest.

Crellio jerked, staring down at the arrow in shock. He slowly looked up at Xavier before he fell forward.

"Ambush!" Xavier yelled, stepping away from Crellio's fallen form and ripping his sword out of the sheath on his back as all hell broke loose.

All around him arrows flew as men burst out of the trees, surrounding them. They shouted war cries, their swords raised in the air.

Xavier raised his sword to block the one coming down at him. He snarled as he pushed it away and spun his body around, cutting his attacker's head clean from his shoulders.

Not pausing in his stride, Xavier ducked under another sword coming from the man beside him. He kicked him away while stabbing his own sword behind him, killing the coward who was just about to strike while his back was turned.

Xavier quickly lost himself in the battle as the cries of his men dying and steel clashing against steel echoed around him. He was already covered in blood from his own stack of bodies laid out on the ground around him when he looked around. They were clearly outnumbered.

For every man he struck down, two more seemed to take his place. Though he and his men were strong, they were quickly losing this battle.

Xavier gave an angry shout and swung his bloody sword in a high arc, cutting off the arm of another attacker. He quickly grabbed the dagger on his hip and speared the man through the eye.

His enemy gave a pained cry and was instantly silenced when Xavier slit his throat.

Disgusted, he kicked the body away from him. "Fall back!" he shouted at the few men he had left as he fought his way towards his horse. "Fall back!"

Xavier paused to swiftly dispatch two attackers before raising his bloody fingers to his mouth and letting out a piercing whistle. He ducked under yet another sword as Killix came barreling out of the trees, kicking and bucking at anyone who got in his way. He stopped in front of him, throwing his head and pawing the ground.

Xavier reached up, grabbed the saddle horn, and quickly flipped himself up as Killix started running off in the direction he came.

"Fall back! Go back!" He yelled as he passed his men, who were all fighting desperately to make it to their horses so they could escape, too.

He gritted his teeth as he ducked against an arrow that shot past his shoulder and landed in a tree in front of him. He reached down for his bow, quickly notching two arrows before he turned his body to release it. The arrow soared through the air and landed in its mark, killing two men. He turned back around in his seat and ducked low against Killix's neck as arrows continued to fall around him.

Killix's hooves flew over the ground as he tried to bring his master to safety. Xavier knew Killix's speed could not be matched by any horse, and in a few short moments, they outran their pursuers.

He only hoped some of his men got out.

The sound of loud shouts woke Leawyn up. She quickly threw the thick furs off her and marched to the opening of her tent to see what the commotion was.

She stopped in shock, taking in the men who'd rushed the front of the camp. Stepping out fully, she saw Tyronian run past her.

"Tyronian!" Leawyn called, grabbing onto his arm to stop him. "What's going on?"

Tyronian grabbed her and started to push her back towards her tent. "Get back inside, Leawyn!"

"What is it? What's wrong?" she asked, alarmed.

"Get inside, Leawyn!" he yelled at her, pushing her one last time towards her tent. She stopped her struggling at his raised voice.

"Tyronian!"

His head shot up to look over his shoulder before he turned back to Leawyn. "Go to the tent and don't come out until I get you!"

Leawyn could only nod before he ran off.

She burst into her tent, her heart beating wildly in her chest. She could still hear the men running all around the camp, seemingly in a panic. She took a deep breath, trying to calm herself down. She would be safe. Nothing would happen to her, she was surrounded by Izayges warriors.

Yes, but, what if something happens to them?

Leawyn blinked.

Her head whipped to the side at the sound of feet coming towards her. She backed up slightly, looking around for anything sharp she could use to protect herself. Before she could even grab something, the tent flap flipped open and Tristan burst in. Her breath rushed out, relieved. Smiling, she walked towards him, only to freeze in her tracks, her smile dropping.

Tyronian came in next, his arms around a slumped form.

"Oh Gods!" she gasped out, her hands flying to cover her mouth.

Leawyn stared in shock at the arrow sticking out of her husband's shoulder, dangerously close to his heart.

Tyronian and Tristan carried Xavier's slumped form over to the bed quickly and sat him down, sliding his arms off their shoulders. He slumped to the side, and only due to Tyronian's quick reflexes did he not fall sideways off the bed.

"We need to get the arrow out," Tristan told Tyronian grimly, who nodded in agreement.

She watched, still in shock, as Tristan took out a small knife and started to cut away Xavier's bloody clothes until his chest was bare. Her head snapped up to look at Tyronian when he said her name.

"We'll need someone to put pressure on the wound to stop the bleeding when we cut the arrow out," Tyronian said softly but sternly, looking her in the eyes. She could only nod, swallowing against the bile that rose in her throat. She walked over to the bed.

"We'll have to push the arrow forward. It looks like it went all the way through," Tristan said, looking at Xavier's back where the point of the arrow was visible. Tristan brought his knife up, and Leawyn had to look away when he started to cut the flesh around the arrow wound, trying to ensure it wasn't attached to bone.

"Get ready."

It was her only warning as Tristan snapped off the fletching before shoving the arrow forward, where Tyronian then grabbed onto it from the other side and yanked it out in one fluid motion. Xavier gave a coarse shout of pain before he slumped forward again.

She had to quickly swallow down the urge to vomit as blood gushed from Xavier's wound, and she caught him, pressing the cloth she held in her shaking hands against him firmly. The blue cloth quickly became red, soaked with Xavier's blood.

"Poison!" Tristan spat, throwing the arrow head to the floor in disgust.

"We have to get it out of him, before it spreads."

"How do we know it didn't already? Who knows how long he's had that arrow in."

"We don't have a choice!"

Leawyn looked up as a set of hands rested on her shoulders. Her eyes, full of helpless tears, met Tristan's as he looked down at her.

"Go outside, Leawyn," he told her softly, helping her rise to her feet and gently taking the soaked cloth away from her bloody hands.

"We'll get you when you can come back."

She nodded stiffly, still in shock as she ducked under his arm and out into the cold night air. She took a couple steps before she tensed and whipped around to look at the tent. She stared at it in wide-eyed horror as her husband's deep voice echoed out in a pained scream. A tear made its way down her cheek as she squeezed her eyes shut, and she flinched when another pained scream assaulted her ears.

A distressed whinny from a solid black stallion caught her attention as he paced from side to side, rearing up when some of the men tried to grab the reins to hold him. Before Leawyn could comprehend what she was doing, she rushed over to the horse.

"Stop!" she cried, grabbing a man's arm who was holding onto one of the reins. "Stop, let go!" she said desperately as the horse reared up in distress.

"My lady, he's too dangerous for you to—"

"Drop the reins!" Leawyn yelled, interrupting him. "Drop them now!"

The men slowly did as she asked, having no choice but to follow her orders as the Lady Chief. The stallion reared again, landing on his feet and pawing the ground while he paced sideways.

"Easy!" Leawyn soothed, putting her arms out in front of her as the stallion snorted angrily, throwing his head in agitation.

"Easy now! Easy!" Leawyn said again gently, keeping her hands out in front of her and bending her body inward in a nonthreatening manner. The horse began to calm down at her gentle ministrations. Gradually, his agitated pacing slowed until it came to a complete stop with one last throw of his head.

"There, see? All better," Leawyn whispered to the horse as she pets his huge nose. The horse snorted, nudging her in the shoulder. She laughed.

"He usually doesn't let anyone touch him."

Leawyn looked up at the sound of Tristan's voice, zeroing in on his bloody tunic. His shoulders were slumped, and she could see the distress in his brown eyes.

Leawyn swallowed as her throat suddenly became uncomfortably dry. She looked away from him and back down to the stallion's nose that was currently resting against her breast.

"How come?"

Tristan took a step towards her, eying her curiously.

"My brother is the only one Killix bestowed with that honor. Until now, at least."

"Killix," she smiled, running her hands down the horse's velvety nose. "I knew he was Xavier's horse, but I never knew his name." Killix let out another contented snort as she ran her fingers through his mane. "It suits him."

Leawyn patted Killix's muscled neck before stepping away and meeting Tristan's gaze once again.

"You can go see him now."

She hesitated. She was afraid of what she would find inside her tent. She stumbled forward when a nudge was given to her back.

Leawyn turned to see Killix's big form behind her.

"That wasn't very nice." She glared at Killix, who only snorted at her, before she made her way back to the tent.

The heavy hoof-falls assured her Killix was right behind her.

"Is he...?" Leawyn trailed off, staring at the still, sweating form of her husband.

Tyronian sighed as he pushed himself from his kneeling position by the bed to stand next to Leawyn.

"He's weak. The arrow was poisoned. We got out as much as we could, but only time will tell if we got it all," Tyronian said grimly, staring at the form of his cousin and leader sadly.

He sighed and rested his massive hand on Leawyn's shoulder, making her jump. "I'll take my leave now."

She could only nod, her eyes never leaving her husband's form.

"Leawyn?"

She looked to Tyronian, who was staring at her, one hand holding the flap of the tent.

"He needs you now," he told her softly. He looked at Xavier's form lying on the bed before looking back at Leawyn one last time and disappearing outside.

She stood staring at the space Tyronian occupied a moment ago before she slowly turned around so that she was facing her husband.

She took a slow, measured step towards the bed.

Then another.

Then another.

And another.

Before she knew it, she was looking down at her husband with a blank expression on her face.

His bare chest was covered in sweat. His breathing was shallow, his chest rising and falling in uneven pants. Dried blood covered him from his hair to his waist. His shoulder was already turning an angry red against the crude bandages covering the wound.

Her hands brushed his forehead, feeling that it was warm. Fever was already starting to set in. She pulled her hand away, and it was then she noticed the bloody dagger at her feet.

As if in a trance, Leawyn picked it up, holding it in front of her face. She glanced back down to her husband. Her eyes narrowed, brows creased together. Her lips thinned into a tight line. Her breast rose and fell with ragged pants as she held her shaking hand out, the dagger glistening off the firelight as she held it against his throat.

It would be so easy...

So easy to end his life and make her escape. Leawyn would be free from his terrible treatment. She could run away. She could save herself. Take Deydrey, and run.

She pressed the dagger into Xavier's skin, watching in fascination as beads of blood slowly swelled and dripped off the blade.

Do it, her mind whispered. *Save yourself. He deserves it.*

All she had to do was move her wrist, and she'd slit his throat.

Leawyn exhaled shakily and pulled her hand away, the dagger clattering to the floor. With a deep, mournful sigh, she sat down heavily beside Xavier on the bed, her shoulders sagging as the tension left her.

She picked up the wet rag from the basin of water beside the bed and lightly wiped the beads of blood away from her husband's throat, then started to dab it all over his head and body, trying to relieve his fever.

She was going to regret this.

The village was on fire.

All around him was chaos, the screams of the women in the village almost drowned out the clashing of metal as the warriors defended themselves against the men attacking them. It was a fierce battle, but the Izayges tribe was filled with the fiercest warriors of Samaria, and they would not go down easily.

Xavier's eyes flashed wildly, taking in the scene around him as he tried desperately to locate his father or mother. He was on the verge of panic when he finally spotted his father fighting with a massive man wielding a huge hammer.

His father's clothes were almost as bloody as the sword he wielded, his face locked in a look of concentration. Though the man his father was fighting was big, Xavier knew his father was going to slay him.

It only took a minute more before Xavier's father ducked under the swing of the hammer and sprung up, swinging his body around. With ease, he delivered the finishing blow by severing his head.

Xavier's relief was cut short when his eyes spotted the man behind his father. An arrow aimed straight at him.

"Father!" Xavier screamed loudly, running to him as fast as his seven-year-old legs could carry him.

Xavier's father whipped his head around, eyes darting through chaos around him before he spotted Xavier running towards him.

"Behind you!" Xavier screamed again, but his warning came too late.

Xavier watched in horror as the man holding the bow released the arrow and pierced his father's back.

Xavier's father raised his eyes to his son's, looking at him for what Xavier knew would be the last time.

Goroth, Xavier's father, looked up as a shadow fell over him, staring at the man in the eyes to bravely meet his fate. His attacker smiled, his rotten teeth showing as he readied another arrow to Goroth's head for the finishing blow.

"NO!"

Xavier let out a scream of pained anger as he swung a sword at the legs of his father's attacker, cutting them deeply.

The man bellowed as he fell forward, catching himself with one hand on the ground. He slowly turned his head to look at Xavier, his lips curling above his rotten teeth in a deadly snarl. Xavier swallowed thickly, raising the sword up in front of him and trying not to show his fear as the man stalked towards him.

He swatted Xavier's sword away easily and grabbed him by the throat, lifting him until their eyes met.

"Foolish boy," he snarled, tightening his grasp on Xavier's throat. "Now you die!"

The man raised his sword high over his head, ready to cut Xavier in half when he suddenly jerked. Pain flashed across his face as he dropped Xavier.

Xavier crumbled to the ground. He jerked back up, only to watch the man fall face forward as his uncle pulled out his sword from the barbarian's back.

Xavier scrambled to his feet and ran to his father, skidding on the grass to kneel in front of him.

"Father?" Xavier asked shakily, putting his hand on his father's shoulder.

His father looked up at him weakly; blood soaked his chest and spilled over his lip.

"Take care of your mother," his father gasped out, blood spitting out with each word he spoke.

"I will, Father," Xavier promised thickly. He held his father's eyes and watched as the life disappeared behind them, replaced with emptiness.

Xavier bowed his head. A firm hand pressed on his shoulder, and he looked up into his uncle's grave face.

"Find your mother, and get out of here as fast you can," Xavier's uncle told him sternly. "Hurry!" he shouted, throwing Xavier forward just before he managed to block another sword coming down at them.

Xavier raced forward, dodging fighting bodies in his search for mother.

By the time the battle was over, all the invading men were either dead or driven away.

Xavier blankly stared down at the corpse in front of him. The arrow protruding from the man's throat was a sure sign he was dead.

His mother's bow was still clenched in his tiny hand. The battle won wasn't without a price.

That day, both of Xavier's parents died.

He failed. He broke the last promise he'd made to his father.

That day, Xavier made his first kill at seven years old

That day was the day Xavier lost his innocence and became the youngest and fiercest warrior in Izayges history.

He had a fever.

Leawyn stared at her Xavier, lightly dabbing the cool cloth over his hot and sweaty forehead. His condition had grown progressively worse since he was brought in four days ago. The arrow wound was ghastly; the red and black edges of the burn inflicted by Tyronian and Tristan to stop the bleeding was now covered in green pus.

Signs of infection.

Though no one said anything, Leawyn could tell they did not think he would survive.

It was all over their faces.

She leaned back, wiped an arm across her forehead and sighed. Her eyes closed in exhaustion. She had been awake all-night caring for her abusive husband. Why?

She still had no idea.

Her eyes opened at the sound of a low moan. Her attention turned back to Xavier.

He was moaning in his sleep, his eyes flickering back and forth behind his closed lids. He was thrashing slightly, his hands clenched in tight fists.

She watched him for a moment, her brows creasing. He gave another moan, jerking forward in the bed as if he were struggling against something. She leaned forward, tilting her head to the side to listen to his quiet mumbling, trying to make sense of the words.

"Mother...!"

She jerked in surprise at his coarse shout.

"No...! Please..."

At that tortured whisper, she couldn't take it anymore. She leaned back and softly ran her hands through his sweaty and matted hair. When he continued to moan and thrash, without thinking, she started to sing softly under her breath.

Go home,
be free.
Like a swift breeze across the rolling green plains,
to the mighty mountain range.
Lay down the bloody blade of the dead,
lay ye weary head.

Her voice was very soft, whisper-like at first, but it seemed to be working. Xavier's struggles lessened. She sang louder.

Fight the wind and the rain,
fight against the pain in your heart. Be strong, be smart.
Fight, you'll see. You will come home to your mountains.
Stay here now, between the green trees, your home waits for thee.
Be free.
Go home.
Home to me.

Finally, he stopped struggling completely, and his moans quieted on the last note.

Leawyn sighed in relief and gently pulled the thick furs over Xavier's body again.

She stood, stretching her tired and sore limbs. She'd been cooped up in the tent for days, and she needed some air. She checked on her husband one more time, and seeing he was still resting quietly, she went outside.

She was only a little startled to see it was nighttime. Most of the men were lying on the ground next to the fires. She looked to her right, seeing that her guard tonight was Hassef, a young man not much older than she. She smiled a little and shook her head when she noticed he was sleeping, soft snores escaping him.

She hated to wake him, but someone needed to be with Xavier in case he woke up. Leawyn walked over to Hassef and shook his shoulder to rouse him.

She stepped back when he jerked awake, bringing his sword up with him. He had a moment of confusion in which he looked at his surroundings. She had to giggle when he blinked up at her.

"Lady Chief!" Hassef gasped, jumping to his feet. "I'm sorry. I didn't notice you there!"

"Yes, I imagine it's hard to notice anything when one is asleep," Leawyn teased.

Hassef's cheeks had a slight red color to them when he ducked his head in embarrassment and shame. "Sorry, Lady Chief. I-I failed in my duties."

She shook her head, resting her delicate hands on his shoulder. "I was merely teasing you, Hassef. I am not mad." She gave him a reassuring smile when he looked up at her hesitantly.

"I actually only woke you so that you may watch over Xavier while I get some fresh air," Leawyn explained.

Hassef looked up at her and frowned. "I should escort you then, Lady Chief. You shouldn't be walking in the dark alone."

She shook her head. "That will not be necessary, Hassef. I'll be perfectly fine on my own, and I'm not going to go far," she reassured.

When Hassef opened his mouth to disagree, Leawyn gave him a stern look. "You will allow me to walk by myself, and I will allow my memory to escape me and forget you were asleep on your watch post."

Hassef closed his mouth with a snap, glowering at her. "Not fair," he mumbled, shoulders slumping.

She smiled in triumph, patting his cheek lightly. "That's the spirit! Now, go on, I'll return shortly."

He sighed in resignation and started towards the tent. He turned around and gave her a strict look. "Be careful, and do not wander far, Lady Chief, I mean it."

Leawyn rolled her eyes and fluttered her hands over her shoulder. "Yes, yes, I know."

. . .

Leawyn slowly made her way to where the horses were. She made sure her footsteps were silent so she didn't wake the warriors scattered about the camp. Many would not be as kind as Hassef and would make her go back into the safety of her tent.

When she was a few steps away from the horses, both Killix and Deydrey lifted their heads. When they saw her, they gave her a soft nicker in hello, reaching their noses towards her. Leawyn smiled and quickened her steps towards them until she could rest her hands on their soft muzzles.

"Hello, you two, miss me?"

Deydrey nudged her with her nose, while Killix blew warm breath on top of her head, causing her to laugh.

"I'll take that as a yes then!" She smiled, taking turns in petting Deydrey and Killix, both of whom were fighting for her attention.

Since the night Xavier was attacked and returned to camp on Killix's back, Leawyn and Killix became fast friends. Killix seemed to take an interest in her, and she was the only one besides his master he willingly allowed to touch him.

The first couple of days *he* was the watch guard instead of one of Xavier's men, for he refused to leave his master alone. Leawyn was sure he would have stayed outside the tent the entire time Xavier was sick if she hadn't walked outside and made him stay with the other horses.

Even still, she would sometimes catch him sticking his head into the tent to say hello and watch over Leawyn and Xavier.

Leawyn shook her head in amusement at the memory, giving Killix a hard pat on his muscled neck before pulling her hand away. Killix turned his attention to Deydrey, nipping her side and causing her to kick her hind leg and whip her head around to nip him back, though she was a bit more aggressive with the "nip."

If Leawyn didn't know any better, she swore she saw Killix smirk.

Great. My husband's horse has a crush on my horse.

She rolled her eyes, stepping away from them in case things got more aggressive and not just playful.

Leawyn shivered, wrapping her arms around herself. She looked up at the sky. It had gotten increasingly colder, the ice surrounding the grass in the morning suggesting winter was fast approaching, and with it, snow.

She jumped when something smooth and warm was draped over her shoulders. Tristan moved out from behind her and stood by her side.

"Thank you," Leawyn said softly, pulling the wool cloak closer to her body. He nodded in response and turned his attention to watch the horses.

They stood together in silence, watching Killix and Deydrey interact before the silence was broken by Tristan's husky chuckle.

Leawyn titled her head to look over at Tristan. "What?" she asked, smiling.

He nodded at the two horses. "Looks like Killix has a crush."

Leawyn looked over at Killix and Deydrey again. She watched as Killix came behind Deydrey, grabbed her long tail, and pulled back. He jumped away, throwing his head when Deydrey responded by pinning her ears back and turning to bite him.

Leawyn laughed when Killix just trotted to Deydrey's side and blew on her ears.

"It seems you're right," she agreed, smiling at the stallion's antics. "Let's hope for Deydrey's sake, Killix isn't like his master in the ways of wooing women," she added dryly.

Tristan gave a short laugh. "Yes, I hope so too. But from the looks of things, he is very much like him."

"Poor Deydrey."

Tristan smirked again, turning his attention away from the two horses and over to Leawyn instead.

"You should go back to the tent. It's supposed to snow tonight."

Though he said it casually, Leawyn knew it was an order. She nodded, too tired to argue, and turned around, making her way back to the tent.

Leawyn was close to crying in frustration. It had been almost two and a half weeks, and Xavier's health showed almost no signs of improvement. It was a miracle he had survived this long.

And with reasons unknown to her, that scared her.

She scowled to herself, wiping Xavier's shoulder a bit harsher than needed. What did she care if he died? If he died, Tristan would take command over the tribe, and she would be free of her bonds tying her to Xavier. She would be free again. She should be happy, hopeful even, begging the Gods and Goddesses to take his life.

Yet, she was not.

It was extremely confusing, and it infuriated her.

Leawyn summed it up to her being a nice person. She'd always been too kind for her own good, according to Brees.

She pulled her hand away and dipped the now warm cloth back into the cool water that was mixed with healing herbs. She reached over and touched the cloth to his arrow wound, gently swiping it around the infected area, making sure to dip it back into the clean water to wash it away before repeating the process.

She was leaning over to soak the rag with the healing water again when her wrist was snatched up by a heated hand. The grip was tight, but not as tight as it used to be.

Leawyn gasped, her heart leaping to her throat as she stared down into the dark, glazed eyes of her husband.

"Xavier...?" she asked, her voice shaky.

Xavier remained silent, staring at her with feverish eyes. She wasn't sure if he even saw her, or if he was sucked up in the hallucinations of fever.

His eyes shifted to the rag Leawyn still held in her hand. Slowly, he looked back into her wide blue eyes.

The tent was dark, the only light coming from the burning fire in the room.

75

"Why are you doing this?" His voice was raspy and weak, so much different than his usual deep, commanding baritone.

Xavier didn't expect an answer, and instead was ready to accept the blackness that was slowly surrounding his vision, but then he heard her soft voice answering his loaded question in a whisper.

"Because it's the right thing to do."

Leawyn met his eyes bravely as he slowly released his grasp on her wrist. He watched her as she continued her task and carefully dabbed at his arrow wound with the medicine.

The only sounds were the cracking of the fire and the soft splash of a rag dipping in and out of water.

Over the next couple days, Xavier's health slowly returned under the care of Leawyn.

After that first night, he woke up only a handful of times. When he did, it wasn't for very long, and he didn't speak. Often times, Xavier would wake up when Leawyn was changing the bandages on his shoulder. He would also wake without her knowing, and would simply watch her as she went about her business.

But he almost always woke when she was singing.

Even though his health was improving enough to know he would survive, Leawyn never left his side. The only time she did was to relieve herself, or when Tristan and Tyronian would force her to.

The next time Xavier woke, it was his brother watching him instead of Leawyn.

"Tristan."

Tristan made his way quickly over to the bed, kneeling by his brother.

"Brother!" Tristan sighed in obvious relief, looking him over. "How are you faring?"

Xavier shifted, holding back his wince when he moved his still tender shoulder. "I've been better, but I'll live to see another day," he said, making his brother chuckle.

"No doubt thanks to Leawyn," Tristan told him, studying Xavier's face. "She never left your side."

Xavier swallowed, turning his eyes away from Tristan's and up at the tent ceiling. He was lost in thought for a few moments.

"She's different. She...confuses me," Xavier reluctantly told his brother, not meeting his eyes.

"She is a different creature, that is for certain," Tristan agreed with a chuckle.

Xavier didn't respond, and it grew quiet between the two of them for a while before Tristan spoke again. "She has taken Killix under her care while you were sick."

Xavier looked at Tristan sharply, and Tristan grinned at his expression. "Killix is quite taken with her, maybe even more so than he is with her mare."

Xavier grimaced, turning his head away. His stallion mating with Leawyn's mare was the last thing he needed.

"Don't worry; Deydrey isn't as welcoming to his attentions as Leawyn is."

Xavier allowed a small smirk to appear on his face. He had no doubt Killix wouldn't accept rejection for very long. He *was* his horse, after all.

Xavier sobered, looking to his brother. "What of my men?"

Tristan did not need to say anything; Xavier knew by his facial expression he was the only one who had survived. Xavier looked away, clenching his teeth together tightly in rage.

Many of them were good men, loyal to Xavier. They had trusted in his leadership, and he repaid them by leading them to their deaths.

That fact alone brought a burning desire to kill something. Xavier did not like to let his men down. He did not make a habit of being caught by surprise. He knew what to expect, and his battle strategies were legendary. It was the reason why the Izayges grew to be so powerful.

Xavier turned his burning gaze to Tristan. "Observing is over. They declared where they stand when they attacked me and my men," he growled out roughly, his glare heated by his rage and vengeance.

"What will you have me do?"

"Gather the men and tell them to get ready to ride back out to the village," he ordered, frowning in thought. "Leave some men behind here, the rest travel back."

Tristan stood. "I'll tell Tyronian to ready the men."

Xavier nodded, settling himself more comfortably as exhaustion set in. Just before Tristan exited the tent, he called out to him. "Tristan."

He paused, looking over his shoulder to meet his brother's eyes.

"We might have to tell the others."

Tristan raised his eyebrow, rotating his body so he was once again facing his brother. "You think it will come to that point?"

Xavier nodded, his eyes flashing to a memory only he could see.

Tristan sighed, turned back and exited the tent. The Izayges were the unofficial protectors of the tribes, since they were the most battle trained. Very rarely did they have to call upon other tribes.

But these men were dangerous. More than that, they were a threat.

eawyn made her way back towards the tent from her visit with the horses. She shivered, pulling her wool cloak closer to her slim body. The snow had begun to take over the land, creating a soft, cold blanket for everything it touched.

Snow had always been beautiful to Leawyn, however bitter the cold was. She wanted to make sure the weather didn't affect Xavier's health; his fever had only just broken, and he was finally beginning to regain some of his strength. She didn't want him to regress.

Leawyn hurried as best she could through the snow with that last thought. She stopped, letting out an irritated hiss when her feet slipped and she landed on her bottom on the cold ice. Grumbling to herself, she pushed herself up and tried to wipe the excess snow off her. Once she was satisfied, she let out a sharp whistle.

A moment passed before Leawyn heard a soft neigh and the sound of hooves crunching against the slush as they made their way to her.

She turned around and watched in amusement as Deydrey trudged through the snow to her, followed by her recent shadow, Killix. The mare blew on Leawyn's face when she finally reached her. Killix came trotting proudly next to her a second after, also greeting her. Deydrey pinned her ears back, turning her head sideways to nip at Killix before swiftly pulling her head back so the eager stallion couldn't return the favor.

Leawyn rolled her eyes and pet Deydrey. "Easy, girl."

Deydrey let out another snort, bending her neck so she could rest her nose on Leawyn's chest. Leawyn scratched her behind the ears a bit before she pulled her hand away.

"Mind giving me a ride? I'm afraid my legs aren't as strong against the snow as yours are," Leawyn told Deydrey lightly, giving her one last pat on the neck before she stepped away.

Deydrey shook out her mane before she bent her neck low and kneeled with her two front legs on the ground, bowing so Leawyn could climb on her back easily.

Leawyn hopped on, and only when she was settled comfortably did Deydrey spring up and start to make her way towards camp at Leawyn's gentle urging. Killix followed faithfully behind.

Leawyn held onto Deydrey's gray mane lightly, enjoying the gentle sway of the mare's relaxed walk. She looked up when the sounds of the camp reached her ears and stared in surprise to see some of the men packing up their things.

"Whoa," Leawyn said softly, hopping off Deydrey when she came to an immediate stop at her command.

"Go on now," Leawyn told Deydrey, waving both her hands in a "shoo" manner. Deydrey threw her head as she turned away and loped off the way she came, her white and gray coat easily disappearing within the snow.

Killix seemed to be debating whether to follow Deydrey or Leawyn. Turning his head, he looked in the direction Deydrey had cantered off to before swinging his muscled neck back to face Leawyn.

Killix was just like his master, and though Leawyn found it amusing, she also found herself worrying for Deydrey.

The poor mare didn't stand a chance.

"Oh, go on. I'll be fine, and I don't want to listen to your worrying," Leawyn told Killix in exasperated amusement.

Killix's ears flickered up towards her before they bent down as he listened, no doubt for the faraway sounds of the mare. He seemed to debate for a moment more before he swiftly turned and trotted his way proudly in Deydrey's direction.

Leawyn smiled after him for a moment, then turned her attention back to the encampment. She frowned. They were packing up, but where were they headed?

Her eyes searched for the familiar faces of her cousin and brother-in-law. Her eyebrows perked up when she caught a flash of blond hair that could only belong to one person besides herself.

"Tyronian!"

Tyronian stopped what he was doing and scanned the camp. He smiled when his eyes rested on Leawyn, and he uncaringly dropped the supplies he was holding, ignoring the grunt of irritation and glare Hassef gave him as he made his way over to her.

"Hello, beautiful! Finally decide to ditch your husband and come to me, have you?" Tyronian grinned shamelessly, wiggling his eyebrows. Leawyn laughed in amusement, used to his playful flirting.

"I'm afraid not, good sir. I came simply to ask a question."

He frowned in mock disappointment. "Well, that's no good."

Leawyn giggled, making Tyronian smile at the sound. He heaved a heavy sigh, his shoulders sagging. "I suppose since you have not come to accept my offer, I have no choice but to answer the question you have come to ask me."

Leawyn motioned her chin at the movement around the camp. "What's going on?"

Tyronian sighed yet again, taking off his own cloak and wrapping it around Leawyn's shoulders as he answered her. "We're packing up. Most of us are going back to the village while some men stay here to keep a lookout."

Leawyn frowned. "Who gave the order?" she asked, pulling Tyronian's big cloak closer to her body to snuggle into the warmth.

"Tristan did."

Her frown deepened as her eyes narrowed in thought. "Xavier isn't strong enough to travel. Why would he give such an order?"

Tyronian shrugged, not having the answer. "Perhaps you should ask him."

"Don't worry, I will," Leawyn snapped, her face scrunched in an adorable look of irritation only a woman could express. Tyronian wisely kept that thought to himself, though, and instead pointed to the direction he saw Tristan last.

"He went that way," Tyronian told her gleefully.

"Thank you, Tyronian," she nodded, patting his corded forearm before she held onto the cloak and trudged off in the direction he had pointed.

"Let me know if you get cold at night, I'll happily warm you up!" Tyronian called after her, chuckling at the way she waved at him over her shoulder. He sighed, resting his knuckles against both his hips.

"Poor Tristan," he chuckled to himself, shaking his head at the image of the little spitfire confronting his cousin. He turned back around, and frowned.

"Hassef, what is that doing there?" Tyronian pointed at the supplies he dropped. "It's suppose to be over there!"

"Did you give the order for the men to pack camp and move out?" Leawyn demanded, crossing her arms as she stopped behind Tristan.

Her brother-in-law sighed as he finished tying the dried meat into a straw sack before turning around to face her.

"Yes."

She narrowed her eyes. "Why would you do that?" she demanded, turning her body sideways as Tristan walked past her to the other side of the cluster of trees they were in and grabbed another straw sack.

"Because I can, and it's what we need to do." He threw the bag at his feet and kneeled to start putting more food into it.

"What about Xavier?"

"What about him?" Tristan replied, pulling the knot he created tighter.

Leawyn's mouth dropped open at his flippant tone. "Xavier is not strong enough to make this move, Tristan! He only just started to gain back his strength. If we move him, all the strength he regained and the recovery he made would diminish." She strode over to stand directly in his sight. "Tristan!" she said sharply when he did not respond.

She met his eyes dead on when he slowly turned his head to look up at her. "He cannot make this move," she repeated firmly, her expression unrelenting. She softened her tone to some degree as she stared at him in confusion. "How could you not care about that?"

Tristan shot to his feet. Leawyn reeled back when she suddenly found him in her face. "Why do you?" he hissed angrily.

"What do y—"

"You know exactly what I mean, Leawyn!" Tristan cut her off, his words sharp.

She recoiled more, her neck straining to put some space between Tristan's face and hers.

"He's my husband—"

Tristan scoffed, pushing himself away from her.

"What's wrong with you?" she asked, baffled.

Tristan whirled around, and Leawyn could not manage to hide her gasp when she suddenly found herself pressed against a tree, his furious face level with hers.

"I have watched what he has done to you!" Tristan bellowed, searing her with his heated gaze.

"It was my ears that burned with the sounds of your screams." Leawyn flinched, turning her face away from him. "It was I who heard your sobs as he left you like some common whore!" He raised his voice as he shook her a bit; causing her to straighten her shoulders and snap her gaze back to his.

"And yet you take care of him. Like a dutiful little wife, when, weeks before, it was *me* you begged to help you escape," he snarled bitterly, his expression transformed into a look of disgust as he let go of her shoulders and stepped away.

"Yet, here you stand, worried about his health." He laughed without humor, shaking his head. "You're pathetic," he spat.

Leawyn swallowed, her eyes clouding over with tears as she hugged herself. Never had Tristan raised his voice at her, or given any indication he felt this way. For the first time, she truly saw the resemblance between Tristan and Xavier.

"Xavier was nearly mortally wounded, Tristan. I couldn't just let him die," she said softly, wrapping her cloaks tighter around herself.

"It was the right thing to do, and if I was a lesser woman, I would have let him die. But I'm not." She raised her chin in proud defiance when he turned to look at her. "Out of everyone, I thought you understood that."

Tristan's jaw tightened as he looked away, not having a response. Leawyn looked down at the snow-covered ground and slowly turned around to head back to camp. She took a few steps before she paused and turned her body halfway to look back at him.

"I remember once, man told me to accept my fate," she said.

Tristan slowly looked up, his eyes meeting hers like they did what seemed now like so long ago.

"Those were the words that burned *my* ears."

Tristan flinched, the slight at him sharp and cutting. He looked away from her, and Leawyn didn't spare him a second more as she made her trek back to her tent.

Leawyn threw the flap over her shoulder with an angry jerk. She stopped, breathing in deeply to try and calm her raging emotions.

She looked down and grimaced in disgust at her wet clothing. She marched over to the place that held her other clothes and shrugged off both cloaks. She pulled the wet dress over her head quickly and threw it on the ground. Then she grabbed a thick, long-sleeved dress at random.

Leawyn sighed and closed her eyes, immediately feeling warmer now that she had on dry clothes. The angry words Tristan had thrown at her laid heavily on her mind. It brought back emotions she had tried to block away when she had first set eyes on Xavier.

She did not know what she was doing, and the feeling of being so hopelessly lost was weighing her down.

Leawyn bit her bottom lip hard to hold back the urge to cry.

Her eyes opened and landed at the fire that was growing dim. Deciding it was a task, and doing something would be better than doing nothing, Leawyn made her way over to the pit. It didn't take her very long to have the fire roaring once again.

She wrapped her arms around her legs and rested her head against her knees as she stared at the dancing flames.

Leawyn hadn't realized how tired she was until now. It was a struggle to keep her eyes open. She hadn't had much sleep; her time and energy was consumed with making sure Xavier survived the fever that tried many times to take his life. The few minutes of rest she did get was on top of the animal skins on the floor.

She didn't realize she had fallen asleep until she felt arms wrap under her head and under her knees. She startled awake, only to stare up into the dark eyes of her husband leaning over her, getting ready to pick her up.

"Xavier, what are you doing out of bed?" She felt groggy but, nevertheless, sat up. "You shouldn't be out of bed!" she admonished, frowning. She stood to try and usher him back to the pallets.

Xavier leaned back, allowing her to rise, but planted his feet, not permitting her to move him. "You should be in bed too."

Leawyn froze, caught by surprise. She glanced up to see he was looking down at her, his face the usual mask of indifference that made it difficult to know what he was thinking.

She shook her head. "I'm fine, but you need to lie down," she said as she tried once again to usher him back to bed.

Xavier didn't budge. Instead, he grabbed the hand she rested on his arm and held it with his own. Leawyn stilled at the contact, looking up slowly to meet his eyes.

"You need to sleep," he told her, pulling her body closer. "I know you haven't been sleeping much, and the floor is no place for you to try."

"But you need to—"

"And I will," Xavier interrupted her, tugging on her hand as he turned. "You're just going to go with me," he told her firmly.

Leawyn gazed past his shoulder to the bed pallets, looking at them wearily.

A warm hand cupped her jaw, urging her to look back up at him.

"Just sleep, Leawyn, nothing else," Xavier promised softly, keeping his gaze locked on her.

"Alright," she whispered, glancing up at him hesitantly. He said nothing. Instead, he turned back to the bed, keeping his hold on her hand until they reached it. He dropped her hand, and she settled down on the bed pallet obediently as he lay next to her, throwing the thick furs over them both.

Leawyn lay stiffly for a long while, trying to keep her erratic heartbeat from being made obvious through her breathing. She heard a sigh, and a moment later she was wrapped up by a muscled arm. Xavier tugged her closer until she settled with her head resting on his chest.

Satisfied, he kept his arm around Leawyn, holding her tight, and quickly fell asleep.

She didn't dare move, still in shock at the gesture. She peeked up at him and saw he really was asleep. She relaxed. She did not want to admit it, but being cuddled against him made her feel warmer, and she couldn't fight the shiver of delight that ran through her.

Surrounded by the warmth of her husband, Leawyn's body quickly relaxed, and soon she fell asleep with his arms wrapped around her protectively.

Leawyn wasn't sure what woke her up exactly, and it took her a minute to clear the grogginess out of her mind and tune into her surroundings.

The memory of Xavier waking her up before made her realize the feeling of his heavy arm draped over her possessively was absent. She sat up, holding the furs close to her body as she looked around.

Her blue eyes landed on the muscular back of her husband, who was standing a few paces away from the fire. Leawyn took a moment to truly look at her husband.

His muscles were much more defined than any other man's she'd seen, and they rippled whenever he moved. His shoulders were wide, and he had two bulging muscles that stood out on either side of his neck. His waist was slim, the V of his hips outlining the solid eight abdomen muscles. A small line of rough dark hair started from his navel and led the way down to a path he made sure she knew well.

She avoided those memories and instead returned her attention to his back again. She never noticed how many scars her husband had until now. The most recent one from the arrow was still an angry red color, the skin around the wound puckered.

One of the older scars was on his ribs, with a few smaller scars surrounding it. There was a long scar which started from his shoulder blade and traveled all the way down to his right hip. It must have been given to him by some unknown enemy who tried to kill him from behind.

Leawyn could see at least two other arrow wound scars. One was below his left shoulder, closer to his arm, and the other below the base of his neck. Had the arrow been shot a few inches higher, Xavier would be dead.

She knew if he were to turn around, there would be a different array of scars on his chest, arms, and legs.

His scars were the stories of the wars he had fought, and to acquire so many and still be able to draw breath was remarkable. Xavier was not only a warrior; he was also a survivor.

"You shouldn't be awake."

Her husband's voice snapped her out of the trance she was in, and she looked up, expecting to meet his gaze, but he hadn't turned around.

Leawyn's face flushed with the knowledge he had felt her staring.

"Yes, well..." she cleared her throat. "You shouldn't be out of bed," she countered smoothly, only to scowl when Xavier let out a throaty chuckle. Her scowl deepened when he didn't say anything more.

"We'll be leaving at dawn; I would get as much rest as possible.

We will be riding hard, and the only breaks we'll be taking are for the horses." Xavier looked over his shoulder, studying her before he turned back around and walked to the far end of the tent.

Leawyn watched him with growing curiosity as he rummaged through a few things and then made his way over to her.

"Do you know how to use this?" he asked. In his hands, he held a small bow and a few arrows that were most likely used for hunting.

Leawyn's brow creased in confusion. "Yes, well enough. I was trained a bit when I was a child."

Xavier nodded in approval. "Most Samaritans are trained in battle, as they should be. It pleases me to hear the Rhoxolani have upheld the tradition."

Leawyn bristled, narrowing her eyes and giving him a nasty glare. "Are you accusing my people of having no respect for our traditions and heritage?"

Xavier met her gaze calmly, not at all fazed by her outburst. "Rhoxolani people haven't gone to battle in years, and very rarely venture out of their village. It wouldn't surprise me if they didn't feel the need to prepare themselves for an attack, nor train their women to protect themselves should the need arise."

Leawyn's mouth dropped open and closed for a moment in disbelief. Her disbelief turned into anger, and she snatched the bow and arrow out of his hands. Huffing, she turned on her heel and marched outside.

Xavier blinked at the space Leawyn had been in a moment before, and then he quickly walked after her.

"Leawyn!" he barked, throwing the tent flap over his shoulder in annoyance. His irritation grew when she simply ignored him and stopped towards the end of the camp.

"What do you think you're doing?" Xavier seethed, trudging through the snow quickly. His shout roused the attention of some of his men who were awake, including Tristan and Tyronian, who both watched curiously.

Leawyn looked up at the sky, her head turning as her eyes searched for something. He was just about to yank her backwards to him when she suddenly notched an arrow and aimed the bow high. She released it before Xavier could stop her.

A moment later, a bird fell out of the sky and dropped to the ground with an arrow lodged in its chest.

He stared at it in shock. When he lifted his eyes to meet Leawyn's smug look, she roughly pushed the bow to his chest. On reflex, he clutched it to him so it wouldn't fall to the ground.

"Just so you know, the women of my tribe are usually the ones to hunt," Leawyn said haughtily and walked past him into the tent without another word.

Xavier followed her with his eyes before turning back to the bird on the ground.

Tyronian strutted up to it and let out a low whistle, holding the arrow to his face. "Shot it right in the chest!" he said admiringly, walking a few paces to stand in front of his cousin.

"Guess she showed you," he said cheekily.

Xavier scowled at him before he swiftly turned on his heel and marched back into the tent after his wife. His cousin's laughter followed him in.

avier chuckled quietly as he watched his wife arguing with his horse. She didn't know he was there, which made it even more entertaining.

"Killix! I swear, if you don't get out of my way, I'm going to use you for horse meat!" Leawyn huffed when all Killix did was pull his lips up over his teeth and continue to stand in the way of her mare and the saddle she held in her hands.

Deydrey snorted, pinning her ears back at Killix. It was like she huffed and glared at the stubborn stallion the same way Leawyn did.

When his tiny wife attempted to push the giant stallion out of the way again, the horse turned his neck and nipped her fingers.

"Ow!" Leawyn exclaimed, dropping the saddle as she clutched her fingers. "You bit me!"

Killix let out a long whinny, his sides shaking with the sound.

"Are you *laughing* at me?"

Leawyn scowled at Killix, who threw his head upwards before snapping it back down several times. Xavier let out a whistle then, and Killix instantly stopped, ears flicking up as he turned his head to look behind Leawyn. She rotated her body to watch Killix trot off.

Xavier lifted his hand and patted Killix's neck, leaning over to stare at Leawyn. He couldn't help himself, and grinned ever so slightly.

"Have you been there the whole time?" She exclaimed in annoyance.

Her ire seemed to grow when Xavier felt his smirk widen.

Leawyn glared at them both (especially Killix), picked the saddle up off the ground, and threw it over Deydrey, who was now free to stand in front of Leawyn.

"Unbelievable," she muttered angrily under her breath. Deydrey snorted, agreeing with her.

"I heard that Killix had a crush on your mare, but I didn't believe it until now."

"Yes, well," Leawyn threw the reins around Deydrey's neck, "he's been unbelievingly annoying with the whole thing. It's unattractive, quite frankly." She climbed up onto Deydrey's back.

"So, you can just forget it!" She gave them both another dirty glare before she kicked her heels and Deydrey took off.

Xavier and Killix watched both their respective females trot off.

"I think you made her angry," he said wryly, glancing over at Killix when he turned his head to look at him. "If she's anything like Leawyn, I'm afraid you have your work cut out for you."

Killix stared at Xavier a bit longer before he again turned his attention to Deydrey, snorting dismissively.

"If you say so," Xavier chuckled, shaking his head.

He pushed himself away from where he learned on his horse and lifted himself onto the saddle. He didn't even need to urge Killix to go before he was making his way all too eagerly to the company of men waiting to move out.

Or more likely, making his way to Deydrey.

They rode just as hard as they had before.

Once again Leawyn was determined to prove her worth and show that she and Deydrey could handle such a hard ride. But it was difficult.

Well, for Leawyn it was.

There was a sense of urgency in the way Xavier had the men riding, almost as if he was eager to return home. Leawyn looked over in front of her, watching him closely. She still didn't agree in leaving so early with Xavier still recovering, but she had to admit he seemed to be doing fine.

Still...

Leawyn might not be battle trained, in fact, she knew next to nothing about war, but she couldn't help feel something bad was coming. Like everything was about to change—and not in a good way.

She shivered, shaking off her ominous thoughts and instead focused on riding Deydrey safely through the snow. Good thing too, because she almost ran right into the back of Tyronian's horse as they came to a sudden stop.

Tyronian turned in his saddle, raising his brow at her. Leawyn shot him a sheepish look.

"Sorry," she mouthed.

Tyronian grinned, shook his head, and turned his attention back to the front where Xavier and Tristan were stopped.

Leawyn nudged Deydrey so she was positioned beside him and his horse.

"What's going on?" she asked, straining her neck to see over the men in front of her.

"The lake is frozen," Tyronian frowned.

She snapped her head to look over at Tyronian.

"Lake? I don't remember a lake on our way here."

"Aye," Tyronian nodded, still staring in front of him. He watched Tristan and Xavier, who looked to be in a heated discussion.

"We went around it before."

"I don't get it," Leawyn said in confusion. "If we went it around it before, why can't we now?"

Tyronian shrugged. "Guess we'll have to wait and find out," he told her. She could tell there was something he was keeping from her, but she didn't press him further.

So, they waited.

"Do you have a plan?"

Xavier held in his sigh and gave the frozen water in front of him a brooding glare from his kneeled position.

"We cross," Xavier said, standing to his full height.

"You cannot be serious?" Tristan asked incredulously, staring at him like he was mad.

Xavier gave a slight nod, and Tristan looked to the lake. He heard his brother's jaw ticking.

"The lake is not frozen all the way," Tristan said. "There is no chance it will hold all our weight without cracking."

"It's the only way. We'll spread out; have the men dismount when they cross."

"Xavier," Tristan said quietly. "We cannot cross; we will fall to our doom if we do. We should go back the way we came."

"That road is too dangerous now." Xavier shook his head adamantly. "They'll expect us to go the safer route. We would be walking right into an ambush," he told Tristan, his voice also low.

"The ice will crack under our weight, and we'll all be killed. I know it, and so do you."

"We will all die if we go back the way we came!" Xavier stepped up to his brother, his glare heavy with authority. "We cross the lake. Now ready the men," he hissed before he brushed by Tristan and stalked away to find his wife.

As more time passed, Tyronian seemed to grow more and more restless, which in turn made Leawyn nervous.

Finally, after what seemed like days, Tyronian stood straighter when Xavier approached him with a solemn look on his face.

"We cross the lake."

Noticing the tension, Leawyn looked between Tyronian and her husband.

Tyronian quickly rushed to Xavier, ducking his head as he whispered hurried words with him.

She watched with growing anxiety as Xavier and Tyronian argued, Xavier shaking his head every so often and saying clipped words in response. Her husband said something to Tyronian with finality, which caused Tyronian to shake his head and stalk off.

Leawyn gave Xavier a questioning look when he stopped in front of her.

"You will have to lead Deydrey across the lake on foot; the less weight, the better," Xavier ordered her in a clipped tone.

"Xavier, what's going on?" Leawyn questioned softly, her brows drawing together in worry. "Why not just go the way we came?"

His lips firmed, staring down at her solemnly. "Those roads are out of the question."

"Why?"

Scowling down at her, he snapped, "We cross the lake. End of discussion. Now get ready to move out and meet me at the front." He turned his back on her then and returned to where Tristan and Tyronian were waiting for him, barking out orders as he walked by the rest of his men.

Well. Alright, then.

Leawyn sighed. Grabbing hold of Deydrey's reins, she silently led her horse to the front.

~

This was a very, very bad idea, Leawyn thought to herself, staring down at the frozen water in apprehension.

She had to stop and hold her breath frequently whenever the ice groaned under her weight.

The men were all scattered about, each one of them doing the exact same thing Leawyn was. This lake was not nearly frozen enough for them to be walking on, and she couldn't understand why Xavier would order them to attempt to cross it. Though, she knew by now there was no use trying to ask questions or change his mind.

He was stubborn as a mule and didn't listen to anyone.

The ice gave another loud groan. Leawyn immediately stopped.

"We should go back!"

She couldn't help but agree with whoever had called that out.

"Keep moving and spread out more," Xavier ordered. No one said anything more, and instead followed their chief's orders.

"Nice and steady, Deydrey. Atta girl," Leawyn murmured soothingly to her restless mare.

They all went at a slow pace, avoiding the areas that seemed weaker than the others. Some men were already across on stronger ice and waiting for them.

Leawyn took a step forward slowly, keeping her eyes on the ground at all times. She stopped, her heart going to her throat as the ice groaned disapprovingly and a small break appeared.

She stared down at the crack in mounting horror as it spread, the sound of the ice splitting loud in her ears.

Oh, Goddess, no.

She only had a second to scream out Xavier's name before the ice under her feet collapsed and she plummeted into the deathly cold ice water.

14

Xavier knew his men, brother, and cousin did not agree with his choice of crossing the ice, but it was the only way.

He couldn't risk the chance of the only safe road being ambushed. If it were just his men with him, he might have considered it, having faith in their fighting capabilities. But it wasn't just him and his men. He had Leawyn to consider, and he refused to take the chance she would be caught in the crossfire and get hurt.

He would not risk her life.

Though, even he had to admit the bird she shot out of the sky was impressive.

But he'd never tell that to her face.

Ever.

They were almost across the frozen lake, most of his men already standing on the bank, waiting for the rest of them to cross safely. He was just about to exhale a sigh of relief when he heard it.

A low groan followed by the sound of cracking ice and a sharp, shrill scream.

Her scream.

"Xavier!"

He whipped around just in time to see the ice collapse under his wife's feet, plunging her into the icy depths below.

Xavier didn't even think as he ran towards her, watching as the ice cracked more. Deydrey fell into the water too; the mare gave a shrill cry of distress as she struggled to swim and jump back on the ice.

Xavier skidded to a stop a few inches away from the gaping hole and searched frantically for Leawyn, barely noticing Tyronian did the same.

"Leawyn!" Xavier shouted, plunging his arm into the icy water and searching for her, trying desperately to grab anything. He lifted his arm out of the water; the freezing temperature caused pain to shoot through his arm, which quickly became numb. He ignored it and plunged back into the water again.

"I don't see her!" Tyronian shouted, his eyes scanning the murky water, his expression grim. Tristan struggled to pull Deydrey up, but the panicked mare was so frantic on surviving she only dug herself deeper into the icy water.

"Keep looking!" Xavier ordered, frantically continuing his search. He couldn't lose her. He had to find her.

He needed to save her.

He could feel his heart constrict in horrible pain with the knowledge that the chance of Leawyn surviving was next to none. A burning sensation was building behind his eyes as he pulled his arm back from the water; his limb was so numb, he no longer had the strength to move it. It seemed like time had slowed and hours passed until Xavier slowly stood.

He looked up, his face pinched in despair as he gazed around. Tristan's mouth moved in slow motion as he yelled and dragged Deydrey up. Killix's shrill whinny was loud and drawn out, echoing in his ears. His men held him back from charging onto the ice. Tyronian was still searching the ice around him, his face frozen in a look of desperation.

Xavier was about to numbly tell them to stop looking, that it was no use. Leawyn was gone.

That he had killed his wife with his decision to bring her with him, and to cross the frozen lake.

That he failed her. Just like his mother.

But that's when he saw it.

A palm pressed against the ice, and floating blonde hair.

Xavier didn't realize he shouted out to Tyronian and Tristan as he rushed to the spot, pulling out his sword as he did so. He fell to his knees and looked down, just in time for the hand to hit against the ice one more time and disappear.

Xavier lifted his sword high in the air above him and plunged it down straight into the ice, hilt first. It barely cracked, but Xavier refused to give up and continued to ram his sword onto the lake. When Xavier's sword was raised, Tyronian's blade took its place and slammed down onto the ice.

Together, they hacked frantically at the frozen surface, and with one last hard thrust, it cracked and split open. Xavier threw his sword to the side and reached down into the dark depths. Tyronian quickly followed suit, and together they blindly tried to grasp Leawyn's hand.

Xavier moved his arm to the left and brushed against something soft. He instantly turned and grabbed it.

"Tyronian!" Xavier yelled as he put both hands into the water and started pulling. Tyronian reached down and grabbed on, pulling with Xavier until Leawyn's head popped out above the water. They each took a shoulder and pulled upwards until she was sprawled on top of the ice. Then they dragged her lifeless form away from the weakened ice and onto solid ground.

Xavier and Tyronian took in Leawyn's unconscious form, quickly shedding their cloaks and wrapping them around her. Her lips were dark blue, her skin was deathly pale, and some of her long locks of hair had ice clinging to them.

"She's not breathing!" Xavier yelled, taking in her still chest.

"Blankets! We need blankets!" Tyronian yelled loudly, turning his head towards the rest of the men. "Quickly!"

Xavier bent over and started to pound on her chest, trying to shock her heart into beating again.

"C'mon, c'mon!" he mumbled, pushing onto her chest harder.

Xavier lifted Leawyn up and shook her. "Breathe, Leawyn! Breathe!" He took several of the blankets offered to him and wrapped them around her. "Leawyn!" he shouted down to her, shaking her more roughly.

Tyronian and Tristan crowded around Xavier, Tyronian's eyes openly spilling over with his tears.

"Xavier..." Tristan said quietly, his voice thick as he rested a hand on Xavier's broad shoulder.

"No!" Xavier shouted at him, shrugging his hand off and pushing down on her chest again. "She's not dead!"

"Xavier, she's gone," Tyronian choked out, staring down at Leawyn's frozen body. "She's gone."

"She's not dead!" Xavier hissed out, his eyes on her pale face. "I refuse to believe she's dead!"

Tyronian and Tristan were silent, each of their faces drawn up tightly with their pain.

"Wake up!" Xavier yelled down at Leawyn, scooping her still form into his arms. Leawyn's head rolled to the side limply, her arms sprawled over Xavier's bent arms. He stared down at her as he continued to desperately will her to breathe.

She didn't.

He threw his head back. The anguished scream ripped out of his throat and echoed throughout the mountain as he clutched her limp body tighter to his chest. Tyronian and Tristan bowed their heads, sitting back on their heels as Xavier continued to shout his pain to the heavens.

Then Xavier grew silent, staring down at the once lively face of his wife. He traced a calloused finger down her cheek, brushing a wet strand of hair away from her face. He tightened his grip around her, cradling her as he stood up and made his way to the bank where all his men were standing, silent. He tried to ignore the fact that Leawyn's head lay over his elbow limply, and instead forced himself to think she was sleeping.

He said nothing as he passed his men, who made a path for Xavier to walk through, each staring sadly at their lady chief in his arms. He made his way towards his horse, who was leaning over Deydrey's form on the ground. When Xavier stopped in front of him, Killix lifted his head and put his muzzle on Leawyn's cheek, blowing air on it as he nudged her gently a few times. Xavier was just about to pull her away from Killix, when a soft moan escaped her blue lips.

Xavier looked down, holding his breath, hope making him immobile. Her blue eyes fluttered open, and she squinted up at him. "X-Xa-Xavier?" she stuttered in a hoarse whisper.

He nodded quickly, pulling her up closer to him. "Yes, Leawyn." He breathed in relief. "You're safe."

Leawyn moaned again, shivering. "Deydrey?" Leawyn asked weakly.

Xavier over at Deydrey, who was still on the ground. He completely forgot about her horse.

Xavier shook his head, his lips thinning. "I don't know."

Leawyn's eyes closed tightly, her face scrunching up in pain. "S-save her. Pl-ease," she whispered through chattering teeth before her eyes closed again. Xavier had a moment of panic, thinking she was once again lost to him, but then he saw her shallow breathing.

"She's alive!" Xavier called out to his men in joy. Tyronian and Tristan pushed their way through and stopped beside him.

"I can't believe it," Tyronian cried in awe.

"Tristan, build a tent and a fire. We need to get her as warm as possible before we attempt to travel home again," Xavier ordered. Tristan wasted no time and quickly rushed away from him, shouting out orders to the men as they all rushed to do as Xavier said.

"Tyronian—"

"Don't worry, I know," Tyronian interrupted. He looked down at Leawyn one last time before he hurried over to Deydrey.

It felt like forever to Xavier as he waited for Tristan to set up the tent. Each moment that passed, his anxiety grew. Finally, Tristan called him over and Xavier rearranged his grip on Leawyn as he walked to the tent his brother and men hastily set up. He set her down gently on the animal fur on the ground by the fire. After unraveling the damp blankets from around her, he noticed she was only in a slip. Realizing she must have taken it off underwater to get rid of the extra weight, Xavier couldn't help but quirk his lips.

"Smart girl," he murmured as he reached out with his small dagger and cut the slip in half. He pulled it from her body so she was completely naked. Not giving her nudity much attention, he stood up and quickly shrugged out of his own clothes until he too was bare.

Lying down behind his wife, he pulled her tightly into his arms so she was flush against him and piled the stack of blankets the men left over them both.

He needed to get her warm, and he needed to take her home where she belonged.

The first thing Leawyn realized as she slowly gained consciousness was the warmth surrounding her. The second thing was she felt very ill. Thirdly, there was someone rubbing something cool over her forehead.

Blue eyes met green as she stared at the young face of a girl she had never seen before.

"Who are you?" Leawyn winced at how scratchy her voice sounded.

The girl gave her a kind smile, though she noted it was a bit hesitant. She instantly felt bad for the way she addressed the obviously young girl.

"I'm sorry," Leawyn said softly. "That was very rude of me."

The girl's green eyes widened before she quickly shook her head. "'Tis not r-r-rude, Lady Chief. It was m-m-my fault. I shouldn't have—"

She raised a brow at the girl and smiled kindly when she instantly stopped talking.

"I don't see how taking care of an unconscious sick person, who suddenly wakes up and demands answers in the rudest way, is your fault," Leawyn said, giving the girl a look of amusement. "Now, I will ask again—though much kindlier." She smiled when the girl giggled. "Who are you?"

"Namoriee," the girl said quietly, looking away from Leawyn's eyes shyly. She was a skittish little thing.

"Namoriee, what a pretty name!" Leawyn praised. "How old are you, Namoriee?" Her grin grew when Namoriee ducked her head again, blushing. "S-sixteen s-s-summers," Namoriee mumbled quietly.

"Why haven't I seen you around the village?"

"I was at the Asori tribe with the healer I serve."

Leawyn nodded in understanding. It was not unheard of for healers from other tribes to go to the Asori. They were the best, after all.

"Have you been taking care of me this whole time?"

Namoriee shook her head once. "No, I only recently—"

The door opened, cutting her off mid-sentence. Both girls looked over to see Xavier's massive form entering the hut, his eyes instantly landing on Leawyn.

Namoriee immediately shot to her feet. "Chief X-Xavier. I was j-just going to g-g-get you," she stuttered fearfully, avoiding Xavier's eyes by staring down at her feet.

"I just woke up," Leawyn agreed, taking pity on Namoriee, who was obviously fearful of her husband. Not that she could blame the girl.

"Leave us." Xavier's eyes never left Leawyn's.

Leawyn's brows drew together, giving Namoriee one last kind smile as she quickly made her way out of the hut. She eased her way past Xavier and practically ran out of the door once she did.

"You could have said that a bit kindlier. She's obviously skittish." Leawyn glared disapprovingly.

Xavier said nothing, and Leawyn's apprehension grew when he made his way over to her, his massive form giving off an aura she couldn't distinguish.

"Xavier?" She questioned wearily, eyeing him.

Without warning, he hauled her into his arms and crushed her to his chest. Leawyn gasped. He grabbed a fistful of her golden locks and angled her head before he gave her a hungry kiss that knocked her breath away. She stiffened, eyes wide in surprise. He pulled back and stared into her eyes intently. She felt her heart skip when they flashed with an emotion she'd never seen before.

He stared at her a moment longer before he dipped his head and captured her lips with his own again. This time, his kiss was gentle, even though his grip was fierce. His lips were soft against her own as his tongue swept into her mouth and caressed hers. He lowered Leawyn down until her back was pressed against the soft bed pallets, and hovered over her.

They stayed like that for a while, lips meshed together. Xavier's kiss was bold and strong and consuming. He pulled away so his head rested against hers, their faces so close Leawyn could feel his lips and his warm breath.

Keeping her gaze captive, his hand traveled down the side of her body until he gripped the edges of the slip she was wearing and slowly inched it up over her hips. Leawyn's breath shuddered as she felt his calloused hands travel over her right hipbone, the touch butterfly-soft, and move down to the inside of her thigh. He stopped his hand when it rested over the place that had been touched only by him.

He pulled back a bit to watch her face as he gently petted her. Leawyn bit her bottom lip, her breath hitching at the slow build of pleasure from the tiny, swollen bundle of nerves he was touching. His thumb flicked against the sensitive spot, while his fingers dipped into the wetness gathering there. She moaned softly when he eased his thick finger inside her, her hips bucking involuntarily at the sensation.

"Xavier..." Leawyn whimpered, the sound both scared and confused.

"Shh," he soothed, stopping to add another finger inside her before he continued pumping them slowly in and out of her. "Just let it come."

She moaned, a tremble starting within her. Her body felt hot and tense. The pleasure shooting from her core at Xavier's ministrations made her breathless. Soon the sensation became too much, and she gripped his shoulders in fear at the overwhelming feeling.

"Xavier!"

"It's okay," Xavier whispered, nuzzling her cheek. "You're okay. Don't fight it."

He moved faster, and she gasped at the feeling.

"That's it. You're such a good girl," he said as he watched her with heated eyes

With those whispered words, Leawyn's body grew rigid, her back arching off the bed as her world shattered apart.

She barely noticed when Xavier's hand left her hair or heard his belt unbuckling. She was too lost in the moment. He dipped his head and sealed his mouth to hers to muffle her cry as he pushed into her warm depth without warning.

Leawyn didn't know what was happening, nor what to think. She knew better than to fight him when he wanted something—not that he would care anyway—but in this case, something was different. She didn't feel the usual pain when he entered her against her will, and she didn't feel the sharp burn his rough treatment caused her insides.

He did enter her without asking, yes, but he was almost being...gentle.

Instead of pain, she felt a different burning sensation than she had never experienced before now. Leawyn couldn't hold in her gasp when Xavier's slow, gentle rocking started to gain more momentum. She tilted her neck to the side when his mouth latched onto her pulse point, giving it a sharp nip with his teeth. She cried out at the pain of the action, but it quickly turned into a whimper of need as his tongue soothed the hurt away.

"Look at me," Xavier ordered huskily. He exhaled roughly when her eyes flew open and did what he asked. He cupped her throat, his thumb brushing over her bottom lip. "Don't take your eyes off me."

He continued to thrust into her for a long while, the sound of their bodies joining loud in the otherwise quiet room. Her responding whimpers of pleasure urged him on until he stilled, shuddering as he spilled his seed inside her.

It was silent as they each took a moment to catch their breaths. Xavier gently rolled off her and the bed. He avoided looking at her as he gathered his clothes up, pulled them on, and exited the hut as quickly as he came in.

Leawyn stared at the closed door with a mixture of confusion, anger and...hurt.

Closing her eyes in embarrassment, she pulled the furs over herself and righted her slip. Leawyn pointedly ignored the tear that slipped behind her closed eyes and made its way silently down her cheek.

~

Xavier stared out into the rolling hills that surrounded his village, deep in thought. He stayed passive even as Tristan settled himself beside him. They sat together in silence for a long while and watched the hustle and bustle of their village.

"She's awake?"

Xavier nodded silently. He could see Tristan nod from the corner of his eye.

"Are you going to tell her?" Tristan asked morosely. Xavier avoided his brother's questioning gaze and kept his eyes glued to the village below.

Xavier stayed silent, a muscle ticking in his jaw. He thought about the day he brought Leawyn back to the village after she fell into the ice...only for the healer to tell him the baby he never knew she was carrying was lost.

"No."

The silence between them was tense. He knew Tristan wanted to bring him solace, but he just wanted to be alone. Finally, Tristan stood and turned to make his way back home. He paused, hesitated, then put his hand on Xavier's shoulder in comfort and sympathy before he continued his way and left Xavier alone with his thoughts.

Xavier waited until he was certain he was once again alone. Only then did he let his emotions show. He covered his head with his hands and wept for the first time since he was seven years old, when he watched his mother get raped and killed in front of his eyes.

Leawyn was forced to stay in bed, her body still weak and recovering. She hardly saw Xavier since the night she woke up. Her treacherous thoughts would travel to that night often. She thought of the way his hands felt on her body as he touched her, and of the new pleasure it 7uuyhbrought her when he was moving inside of her. It shamed her to long for that connection again. It was why she welcomed the distraction Namoriee presented when she stopped by her hut.

Their friendship came easily, and Leawyn was ecstatic when Namoriee informed her she was to be her new handmaiden. She refused to consider her the slave Namoriee claimed herself to be.

The girls were still giggling wildly about the newest antics of Killix and his quest to win Deydrey's affections when Tyronian strolled in. He propped his hip on the door as he took in the laughing girls with a smile.

"And what is so funny?" he asked, causing the laughter to stop abruptly when they finally noticed his presence.

"Tyronian!" Leawyn exclaimed, shooting him a smile. "I did not hear you come in. What a pleasant surprise!"

He chuckled, pushing himself off the doorjamb and making his way over to the girls. "Not surprising, the whole village could hear you laughing." He grinned, bending his tall form to kiss Leawyn on the cheek before he settled himself on the vacant chair next to her bed. Namoriee ducked her head when his stormy blue eyes pierced hers. "Namoriee, how do you fare?" he asked, keeping his gaze on the dark brown locks hiding the girl's face.

Namoriee gave a quick, jerky nod in answer before she rose to her feet. She peeked at Leawyn through her brown fringe. "I'll take my leave now, Lady Chief."

Leawyn frowned, her brows drawing together. Before she could even utter her protest, Namoriee was out of the hut, the door shutting soundly behind her. She shook her head at Namoriee's sudden departure. She turned her attention back to Tyronian to see his eyes locked on the closed door. A sly smile quirked her lips.

"It seems you find my door very appealing," Leawyn commented lightly, causing Tyronian to jerk to attention, blinking out of his daze.

"Yes, well." He cleared his throat and shifted in his seat uncomfortably. "It's a very nice door," he defended.

Leawyn snorted. When he glowered at her, she laughed.

Tyronian huffed and rolled his eyes. "Right. Well," he said, standing up to his full six-foot-five height quickly, "I best be off. I only came in here to tell you Deydrey is recovering well."

"So, I've heard." Leawyn smiled, staring up at Tyronian. "Thank you for telling me."

He narrowed his eyes at her, trying to distinguish the look she was giving him. He gave up when all she did was continue to stare up at him innocently, and he strode to the door.

"Where are you going?" she asked, amused.

"Away from you!" Tyronian snapped, suddenly grumpy.

Leawyn laughed. "Tell Namoriee she must come visit me again when she has time!" she called out as he opened the door.

He paused, his hand resting on the wooden knob before he huffed and slammed the door closed behind him.

Leawyn was still laughing under her breath as she lay back down onto her bed pallet and snuggled into the soft animal furs. She sighed in comfort.

"Poor Namoriee. She won't stand a chance," she mumbled before she closed her eyes and slept.

~

Later that night, Xavier, Tyronian, and Tristan stared down at a map of the land on the large oak table in the middle of the war room.

Xavier had called in his counsel almost immediately when they had first arrived back in the village. After a heavy discussion, it was agreed to send out another scouting party to track the whereabouts of the mysterious army and to learn anything they could about them. But when they didn't report back, they sent a few more men to meet up with the previous party.

That was almost six nights ago.

"Still no word from the Siraces?" Xavier asked. Tyronian's frown was deep when he shook his head.

"Tristan?"

Xavier gave a low growl of annoyance and frustration when Tristan shook his head as well.

"Who are these bastards?" Tyronian muttered.

"One army does not simply appear and disappear," Tristan reasoned. "They have to be hiding somewhere."

"Yes, but the question is *where*?" Tyronian sighed, rubbing his beard thoughtfully.

Xavier narrowed his eyes at the map in front of him, his annoyance quickly turning into ire. This army was toying with him, goading him to find them and attack. They were biding their time and making a fool out of him all at the same time. Not many men were able to catch him off guard. But they did, and that fact alone enraged Xavier.

They were all brooding down at the map, getting more and more frustrated, when a series of shouts met their ears.

Without another glance at each other, they each made their way outside and watched as two horses came barreling toward them.

The stallion slid to a stop in front of them, rearing a moment before his front legs landed on the ground with a thud. The rider hopped off, throwing a crossbow down at Xavier's feet.

Xavier glanced down at it before raising his brown eyes to meet Tidas's grim face, waiting for him to reveal what Xavier already knew.

"Armor piercing."

Tristan frowned, snatching up the crossbow and raising it to eye-level, scrutinizing it.

"That's obvious," Tyronian commented, his voice laced heavily in derision.

Tidas shot Tyronian a look before focusing on his chief, his eyes piercing Xavier's.

"There's more," Tidas said gravely. Xavier watched as Tidas made his way to the other horse and snatched up what looked like a ruck-sack. He brought it back to Xavier, placing it in his hands.

"A message."

Xavier glanced at Tidas briefly, then turned his attention to the bundle. He held onto it with one hand while his other unraveled the tightly wrapped string holding the bag together.

Once he could unknot it, he flipped the lappet over and looked into the bag.

He stilled, his face twisting in fury as he stared down at what he held in his hand. He looked up slowly, and everyone took a step back at the savage look clouding his eyes.

Xavier glanced down at the rucksack again, his back molars grinding together in anger as his fists clenched. He let out a roar of rage, his voice echoing through the dense forest surrounding them as he turned around and threw the rucksack. It landed against the earth with a thud that resounded loudly against the silence before tumbling forward.

Without another word, Xavier stomped away.

The silence was deafening. The men all watched quietly with antici-pation as Tristan slowly walked to the bag. He bent down, picked up it up, and considered it.

"What is it?" Tyronian asked, his voice tense.

Tristan lifted his gaze to meet his cousin's at the same time he turned and pulled out what was hidden inside, revealing the head of one of the scouts sent to follow the army.

Tyronian clenched his fist, his throat constricting as he swallowed. He looked over to his right when one of the soldiers asked the question they were all wondering.

"What does it mean?"

Tyronian's and Tristan's eyes met, each reflecting the knowledge of what was to come.

"War," Tristan growled, his voice filled with death. He looked down at the head in his hands one last time and released the grip he had on it.

The head landed against the earth with sickening sound, tilting so the warrior's last expression of shock was facing everyone.

"This means war."

17

Leawyn was startled awake by the sound of the door slamming open as her husband stormed in. She instantly went on guard when she saw the murderous glint in his eye. He said nothing to her as he marched straight to where his armor was and started to strap it on, his movements fluid.

When the tense silence became too much for her, she took in a breath to prepare herself.

"Xavier?" she asked timorously.

He stiffened, his fingers pausing in strapping his sword to his hip. His back and shoulder muscles bulged as his entire posture coiled at her tone. Slowly, he turned and met her eyes.

Leawyn felt her heart skip a beat with her quick intake of breath. He looked ready to kill.

Xavier kept his eyes locked on hers as he made his way to her. With each step that drew him closer, her apprehension grew. He stared down at her, his eyes boring deep within her soul.

When she was within arm's reach, his hands struck out lightning fast, giving Leawyn a second to let out a surprised gasp before she found herself hauled into her husband's muscled arms. He continued to stare at her, as if committing every single one of her features to memory.

Besides the fire crackling in their room, the only other sound Leawyn could hear was her beating heart. She stayed in his arms rigidly, her guard up for any action he might take.

One thing she had learned about her husband was he was

anything but predictable. He was like a wild stallion, big and power-ful, but with an elegant grace that could leave her awestruck.

Slowly—ever so slowly—she felt herself relax in his arms. He shifted her so he could bring one hand up to slide a callused finger down her cheek. Her lips parted, her breath hitching at the gentle touch.

"Do you hate me, Leawyn?" Xavier asked, his voice a low timbre.

"Yes."

Xavier said nothing in response and instead bent down until Leawyn's back was against the animal furs on their bed again. He rested his weight on his elbows as he hovered above her. He then dipped his head and put his mouth against hers, thrusting his tongue past her lips when she didn't respond.

Leawyn went rigid, not knowing how respond to his advances. As if sensing her hesitation, her husband grabbed a fistful of her blonde hair and tugged until her head was arched back, using her gasp of pain to further his exploration of her hot mouth.

She didn't know what caused this sudden attention, but she did know it wouldn't be like last time. He was not going to be gentle. Something set him off, and she knew from experience it wasn't going to be a pleasurable interaction.

He tore his mouth away from hers, staring down at her with lust-filled eyes.

"Kiss me," he demanded roughly, and his lips resumed their attack. Tightening the grip he had on her hair, he gave it a slight jerk to further motivate her when she didn't follow his order right away.

Leawyn squeezed her eyes shut, feeling her neck strain from the way he arched her. The pain of her hair being pulled into a tight grip made her eyes water. When Xavier bit her lip sharply, getting impa-tient, she brushed her tongue against his to save herself further pain.

She felt his erection against her thigh then, and she let out a whimper when he yanked his mouth away from her lips and buried it in the juncture of her neck, biting down on the skin harshly. She gave a short yelp of pain.

He released her hair and ran his rough hands down her chest

until he held the fabric of her flimsy dress. Leawyn's body jerked, the sound of fabric ripping split through the otherwise silent room as Xavier tore it completely off her. Another pain-filled yelp escaped her mouth when she felt his teeth clasp onto her right breast, hard.

Not giving her time to recover, he quickly picked her body up and flipped her around so her face was pushed down into the plush pillow. His rough hand pushed her shoulders down and his thighs splayed her legs open when he wedged them between her. He gripped her hips, fingers digging into her flesh, and entered her with one deep thrust. Her scream was shrill from the swift intrusion.

A loud groan escaped his throat. Resuming his fistful of her hair, he yanked her head up until her neck was straining toward him. He relentlessly thrust into her, her body sliding away from each time their hips connected from the force of their joining. Leawyn's pain-induced tears spilled over her eyelashes and made a trail down her smooth cheeks from Xavier's rough assault.

Her hands scrambled to get purchase, trying to pull her body away and escape him, but his hard thrusts kept her body off the bed for no more than a second. He gripped her hips harder to keep her still and buried his face deep into her neck. The sound of his growls and grunts were loud in her ear.

"Xavier, please!" she whimpered weakly in protest.

Ignoring her pleas of respite, Xavier picked up the pace of the teeth-clattering thrusts as he plunged into her body time and time again, driving as deep into her as he was able.

"Mine," he growled into her ear. "You're mine, Leawyn." He groaned, sweat dripping down his brow as he pushed into her harder still. "MINE!"

With one last sharp twist of his hips, Xavier's breath escaped as his release came, his seed pulsing into her and solidifying his ownership.

It was silent as he threw himself off her body. She was motionless as he tucked her stiff and shaking body against his side. He kept a tight hold of her, his arm thrown possessively across her hip.

The sob Leawyn was trying to hold in broke free when she felt the sticky substance of Xavier's climax running down her thighs.

"I hate you," she cried coarsely, squeezing her eyes shut tightly against the pain of her abused body and emotions. "I hate you!"

Xavier ignored her, staring up at the ceiling.

"I hate you," Leawyn chanted repeatedly, until she had no more energy to cry or speak.

"I hate you..." she whispered one last time before she gave in to the blackness and slipped into a restless sleep.

The next morning, Xavier woke to the quiet of his hut and faint sounds of his village waking up.

Blinking against the stream of sunlight, he slowly sat up and turned his head to look down at his wife.

His eyes took in her bruised lip, the bruises in the shape of his fingers on her hips, and the various bite marks covering her body. His gaze shifted to her breast, the skin around the area raised and red from his bite. His semen was still visible on her thighs.

Xavier looked away with a grimace. He knew she wouldn't be forgiving, and a part of him was angry at himself for losing control, but the other—the more savage part of him—was filled with pride and satisfaction of his doing.

He marked her like no one had; his ownership was there for everyone to see. Everyone would know she was his. He'd kill any man who tried to touch her the way he had.

He thought of the way it felt to take her so mercilessly—the feel of her body clasped tight around him and the knowledge she was his —no one else had ever been given the privilege he had with his young wife, and it constantly drove him insane with lust. He wanted to dominate her. Possess her.

It didn't matter that she hated him, or that an unknown army was swiftly coming to try and destroy his village. All that had mattered in that moment was the feel of Leawyn against him.

Xavier smirked, his eyes glittering with dark possession at the knowledge. He gave himself a moment more to admire his wife before he rose from the bed and strode shamelessly to the chest holding his clothes and armor.

Leawyn regretted coming aware of her surroundings the moment she tried to shift herself to a sitting position. The sharp sting of pain had her body protesting at each small movement. Every part of her felt like it had been run over by a horse. The pain in her thighs and inner muscles made her eyes water.

"You will stay in the hut today."

Leawyn shivered at the sound of her husband's cold voice. She turned her head, bringing her narrowed gaze to match his.

"And if I don't?"

Xavier's eyes flashed. Growling, he strode over to her in two quick strides until his nose was pushed against hers.

"If you disobey me, you will be punished." His hands struck fast and grabbed her chin.

"You will stay here," Xavier repeated lowly, staring her in the eyes. "You will be waiting for my return." He leaned in closer, firming his grip on her chin when she tried to jerk away from him. "And you will be prepared to please me, Leawyn."

She tensed. He let her go abruptly and stood, turning away from her.

She held her breath until the slamming of her hut's door. She lay back down on the bed and buried her face into the pillow, letting it catch her tears. Her small hands tightened into a fist, hitting the pillow as she screamed. She screamed, and screamed, and screamed. Each scream became more gut-wrenching than the rest.

She didn't stop screaming, even as Namoriee's warm arms embraced her. In silent comfort, Namoriee stayed like that as Leawyn broke apart.

Slowly, Leawyn's body began to heal. Each day Namoriee came to help her recover, and it was with her encouragement Leawyn finally left the shelter of her hut.

"The village knows who their chief is," Namoriee said. "They know nothing of the woman who now runs the Izayges."

"They know who I am! I've been here for a while," Leawyn defended, a bit insulted.

"No, they don't," Namoriee flatly disagreed. "They might have seen you, but they don't know *who* you are. Do you even know how long it's been since the Izayges have had a lady chief?" Namoriee skewed her with a pointed look.

Leawyn slowly shook her head. She had a feeling it had been a long time.

"They are desperate for you, my lady. There was great excitement when the chief announced his intent to marry. You need to stop hiding."

Leawyn knew Namoriee was right, and it was with that sole reason she went out to meet the people of her new home.

Just because her husband was a cruel and heartless man, didn't mean all the Izayges were the same.

Weary at first, the village people stayed clear of her the first few days she walked around the tribe with Namoriee by her side explaining their way of life and pointing things out. It made Leawyn's guilt mount because she knew it was her fault.

Namoriee was right; Leawyn was hiding.

But, she didn't give up. Every day she went out, with or without Namoriee, and tried to be involved in the day-to-day activities of the village whenever she could. The villagers noticed, and bit by bit they became more willing to interact with her.

One thing Leawyn noticed right away was there weren't many children in the tribe, even though there were quite a few women with child. When she asked Namoriee about it, the girl's face grew pained.

"Without a proper midwife, it is hard to give birth to a child and have them live," Namoriee told her sadly.

Leawyn did not ask again. A week later, she arranged for a healer from the Asori tribe to come and teach her the ways of being a midwife. She couldn't stand the thought of the mothers' pain in losing their children, and she was determined it would not happen again.

The villagers didn't say anything publicly, but the next day the women of the tribe showed their appreciation the only way they knew how: making her a beautiful sword and bow and secretly training her in the ways of being an Izayges shield maiden of old.

"Lady Chief! Lady Chief!"

Leawyn turned her attention to the voice shouting her name, rising quickly when the young boy, Castic, came running to her.

"Castic? What's the matter?" Leawyn asked in alarm, meeting him halfway.

Castic heaved lungs full of air, winded from his sprint. In between panted breaths, he tried to calm himself enough to speak.

"Come...help...Garnette..."

Leawyn's brow furrowed, not at all making sense of what the eight-year-old was trying to say.

"Calm down, Castic," Leawyn soothed as she brushed his dark hair away from his sweaty forehead. "Tell me what happened."

"Garnette is missing!" Castic finally burst out, panicked.

Leawyn sucked in a sharp breath as her heart sped up in fear.

Keeping her face neutral so that she did not frighten the boy more, her voice came out calm when she asked her next question.

"What happened?"

"We were playing hide and seek, and it was her turn to hide," Castic explained hurriedly. "I was done counting and went to find her. Garnette always hides in the same spot, *always*," he stressed, causing her lips to twitch in amusement. "But when I went to find her, she wasn't there!"

Leawyn sighed in relief at that explanation. It wasn't as serious as she feared.

"Maybe she simply hid in a different spot. Did you look for her?" she suggested, but even as she was speaking, he shook his head.

"You don't understand!" Castic cried. "I went over there and there were markings—*foot* markings!"

Leawyn's blood ran cold. She thought about the mysterious army that had attacked and almost killed Xavier. She crouched down so she was eye level with the boy.

"Castic, are you certain?" she asked, her usual carefree tone gone.

Castic didn't hesitate in his answer. "Yes."

Leawyn needed no further confirmation and quickly sprang into action.

"Where is her hiding place?" she asked as she walked with hurried steps to the horse pasture.

"Between the three trees and the rock that looks like a sword," Castic explained, trying to keep up with her long strides. "She always climbs the lowest branch of the third tree and hides there."

"I want you to go to your mother and stay with her," Leawyn ordered. She whistled loudly. Deydrey's head snapped up, and when she saw her mistress, the mare trotted her way obediently.

"Tell the first warrior you see that I ordered you to tell everyone to go inside their huts and stay there until I return. Have them set up perimeters around the tribe." Castic nodded and started to rush off to follow his lady chief's orders. He was quickly yanked backwards by his shirt.

"If I do not return by the time my husband and his company arrive, tell them the same thing you told me. Understand?"

She could see that Castic grew worried, as if he had gotten the feeling that something more serious had happened than his friend going missing.

"Yes, Lady Chief. I swear I will."

"Good," Leawyn said, running her hand down his cheek. "Now go." She nudged him towards the village.

Castic hesitated, his face contorting in worry. "What are you going to do?"

"Don't worry, I'll be fine." Leawyn smiled to help ease his worries. "Now go." She pushed him again, finally getting him to run back to the village. When he was far enough away, she dropped her smile.

Without wasting any more time, Leawyn climbed onto Deydrey's back and rode fast to where Castic told her to go, grass and dust flying behind her from the mare's speed, all the while hoping her feeling that something horrible was about to happen was nothing more than nerves.

Xavier held in his urge to growl at the Asori tribe leader.

After Xavier left Leawyn that night, he, Tyronian, and Tristan traveled to all the other tribes to warn them of the oncoming threat and potential war. It seemed the other tribes were not as willing to risk their lives when it came to protecting their land.

"How do you know this army is a threat?" Yoro, the Chief of the Asori, asked.

"Besides the attack on me and my men and the message of a severed head, you mean?" Xavier bit out angrily. He was quickly losing his patience with this useless talk and the dim-witted Asori.

Yoro looked at Xavier, his eyes masking how uncomfortable he was to have Xavier in such proximity. "As it sounds, it seems they only threaten *you*."

Xavier shot out of his chair so fast it toppled over. Tristan quickly held out his arm to keep his brother from attacking.

"Just what do you think will happen if we're not able to hold them back?" Tyronian asked Yoro calmly, glancing between the Asori chief and his own.

"They will not simply walk away. They *will* come after you."

Xavier shrugged Tristan's arms off him with an angry jerk of his shoulders.

"The Asori have no reason to go into battle and attack an army that might not even be a threat," Yoro said firmly. "We haven't been to war in years, and I will not blindly lead my men into battle without the right cause."

Xavier scoffed, his fists clenched with his anger at the naiveté of Yoro.

"Yoro," Tyronian began, barely able to keep the steel out of his voice. "You are placing your men, women and children in danger by not acknowledging this threat."

Yoro turned his attention from Xavier to give Tyronian a cold look. "It is your job to ensure that doesn't happen."

"You fool!" Xavier yelled. He got some satisfaction when Yoro jerked at his raised voice.

"We have been protecting your tribe and the others for years, and now that we call upon you, you cower away? You are a coward!" Xavier hissed out between clenched teeth. Yoro's expression grew stormy, but before he could utter a word, Xavier turned his back and stomped out.

He had tunnel vision as he marched to Killix. Tyronian and Tristan caught up with him.

"If that fool won't help us, then we shall not help him!"

Tristan and Tyronian shared a look over his shoulder. Tyronian cleared his throat.

"Xavier, he's blind, but soon the fog will lift from his eyes. We cannot leave the women and children to fend for themselves."

"Then they can go to a different tribe!" Xavier growled before he lifted himself up on Killix.

"Xavier, you're angry, don't make any rash decisions."

"No! If they were to fall, it would be because of their coward of a leader! Izayges shall not help the Asori until they help us!" Xavier glared down at Tyronian and Tristan one last time before he spurred Killix roughly, causing Killix to rear before galloping away.

"Well, that went well," Tyronian sighed, rubbing his temples, which were starting to ache.

"I will follow him, you work on Yoro," Tristan ordered Tyronian, climbing up onto his own horse.

When Tristan was settled in his saddle, he said to Tyronian, "If he does not come around, make him."

"I will see it done." Tyronian's grin was all teeth.

Tristan jerked his head in response before he galloped after his brother.

Leawyn jerked Deydrey to a sliding stop when she finally spotted the place Castic described.

Right away she knew something wasn't right. Castic luckily hadn't noticed what Leawyn did. There were footprints all right, but the lower branch where Garnette had been hiding was an even more alarming sight. It was snapped, and there was a weird line that ran below it.

They must have dragged her down, then picked her up to stop her struggling, she thought.

Leawyn's heart sank, imagining what the young girl must have gone through. Knowing she couldn't wait for her husband to come and save the young girl, she urged Deydrey into a gallop again.

She would not make Garnette suffer more than she had too.

Leawyn pushed the thick branch away from her face and looked down on the camp below her.

She didn't like what she saw.

It seemed there were at least forty or so men, and every one of them were armed.

"Garnette, what have you gotten me into?" she mumbled to herself. Her blue eyes took in everything around her, trying to find said girl. It didn't take long for Leawyn to spot her.

Garnette was "settled" against a tree a few feet away from the men, their backs turned to her. They were huddled against the fire, trying to keep warm against the snow. The irritated glare the child was shooting at them would have been comical under different circumstances. Knowing time was of the essence, Leawyn began her slow descent down the incline and to her charge.

When she thought she was within hearing distance, she crouched down low behind a bush and called the girl's name, trying to whisper, but at the same time get the girl's attention. "Garnette!"

The poor girl looked upset, but at the sound of Leawyn's voice, she narrowed her eyes and sat up straighter, searching for whomever had called her name.

"Garnette!" Leawyn dared to call again.

"Lady Chief?" Garnette asked, looking confused. She looked around again and perked up when she spotted Leawyn peeking out of the bush.

"Lady Chief!" Garnette exclaimed happily. "What are you—"

"Shh! Not too loud," Leawyn whispered frantically. She shot a look towards the men to see if they heard.

Garnette also looked at them, then looked back at her lady chief.

"What are you doing here?" Garnette finished, her voice much quieter.

"I'm here to get you out of trouble. Are you okay?" Leawyn crawled over to her on her stomach. "They did not harm you, did they?"

Garnette shook her head. "No, I am not harmed." She pouted. "They broke my hiding branch, though."

Leawyn paused in untying Garnette's hands and gave her a stern look. "That's the least you should be worried about."

Once the knots were undone, she quickly put a hand on Garnette's shoulder so the young girl couldn't spring up and alert the entire encampment of her freedom.

"Garnette, you must listen very carefully. Do you see those bushes over there?" Leawyn whispered, pointing to the brush that was just to the side of the girl a few paces away.

Garnette followed her pointed finger and nodded. "Yes, I see them."

"Good. I want you to slowly crawl your way over there. Once you do, climb up the tree until you reach the top of the hill," Leawyn urged quietly. "You must stay on your belly and stay low to the ground. Understand?"

"Yes, Lady Chief."

"Good. Now go. I'll be right behind you."

No comment passed as Garnette followed her Lady's instructions. Leawyn waited until the child's tiny feet disappeared into the bush before she followed.

When Leawyn pulled herself up the ledge, Garnette was waiting for her.

"Come now, Garnette. Deydrey is waiting for us," Leawyn said hurriedly. She grabbed the girl's hand and pulled her along. It wasn't very long until shouts rang out nearby. The men had noticed Garnette's disappearance. Not wasting any more time, Leawyn swung

Garnette up into her arms and ran as fast as she could. She skidded to a stop when one of the men hopped out of the trees and blocked their path.

"Now, looky wha' I found," the man grinned, showing off his foul teeth. "Where you think you're goin'?"

Leawyn placed Garnette on the ground and pushed her behind her back. She'd known there was a chance of her being caught, but she never got as far as planning what she would do if that happened.

"Garnette, whatever happens, you have to run. Even if it's without me," Leawyn told Garnette quietly.

"I dun think that will be happenin', sweets," the burly man chuckled, brandishing his sword. She heard multiple feet coming toward them. Soon Leawyn and Garnette would be surrounded with no chance for either of them to escape.

To Leawyn's surprise, a rock flew and landed squarely in the man's crotch. The man crumpled to his knees with a squeal rivaling a girl's, and Leawyn took the opportunity to quickly pull her bow over her shoulder and let an arrow fly. It killed him instantly.

Leawyn looked down.

"Castic taught me how to throw. He's the best at skipping rocks." The innocent proclamation was so nonchalant, Leawyn couldn't help but roll her eyes.

The sound of men yelling behind them alerted Leawyn. She quickly picked up Garnette again and ran for all she was worth. Turning to glance over her shoulder, she wasn't at all surprised to see the men right on her heels. She saw Deydrey in the distance but was afraid she wouldn't make it in time.

Leawyn whistled for her mare. "Deydrey!" she called desperately, relieved when her horse galloped toward her.

They met halfway, and Leawyn quickly swung Garnette on Deydrey's back and handed her the reins. She looked behind her again. She was out of time. Leawyn felt the heat of the oncoming men behind her, and knew what she had to do.

"Run!" she shouted. And with a slap on the rump, Deydrey took off, with Garnette screaming for Leawyn as she did.

Leawyn watched their escape until only seconds later, when several men grabbed her, hauling her away as she kicked and screamed in protest.

~

Xavier knew something was wrong the moment he rode into his village. He scanned the faces of his villagers and noticed how none of them would quite meet his eyes.

"Something's not right." Tristan stated what Xavier himself was thinking when he brought his stallion up to walk beside Killix. They both pulled their horses to a stop and fluidly dismounted when they reached the massive stables. Xavier paused in taking off the saddle when Killix looked around, stomping his feet anxiously and snorting in distress.

He knew only one reason that could cause a reaction like that from his horse. A terrible feeling pooled in his stomach. Xavier rushed around Killix and to the pasture Deydrey would be resting in.

The mare wasn't there. Leawyn was gone. Xavier whipped around, fury reflecting in his eyes. She disobeyed him! She ran as soon as Xavier left. He was a fool to trust her.

"What is it?" Tristan asked in alarm.

A piercing whinny sounded out seconds before Deydrey burst through the trees at a neck-breaking speed, stalling Xavier's answer.

Absent was the body of her owner on her back. Instead, it was a child.

Xavier stepped in front of Deydrey, intercepting her. He grabbed the mare's reins when she threw her dapple grey head in distress. Deydrey stomped in place, letting out earsplitting cries of suffering. Xavier looked up into the watery eyes of Garnette.

"Chief!" Garnette cried in sorrow and desperation. She practically threw herself off Deydrey's tall back and into Tristan's arms, who was quick to catch her and save her from hurting herself.

The little girl impatiently shrugged out of Tristan's hold and ran to Xavier's feet, grabbing hold of his shirt at the wrist and pulling him back toward Deydrey, all the while brokenly trying to explain through her sobs.

"You have to hurry... Lady Chief... You have to help!"

Xavier planted his feet and placed his hands on the small girl's shoulders to still her.

"Garnette, what has happened?"

"It's all my fault!" Garnette wailed, her tears sliding down her cheeks like a waterfall. "Save her, Chief, save her, please!"

"What happened?" He yelled, shaking Garnette's shoulders with impatience. "Where is she?"

"They took her!" Garnette burst out. "The men took her! She tried to save me, and they took her!"

Garnette sobbed as Xavier quickly released her and climbed onto Deydrey's back.

He wasn't even properly seated in the saddle when Deydrey shot off in a furious gallop, leaving grass and dust in her wake. Only one thing ran through Xavier's mind.

Save her.

Save his wife.

Leawyn's head snapped to the side at the sharp slap against her cheek. She licked her already cracked lip before she slowly turned her head back to glare at the man who laid a hand on her.

"Tell us!"

Leawyn stubbornly kept her mouth shut, which earned her another slap. The men who had captured her were holding her hostage inside a large tent that was completely bare of furniture. Her hands were bound in front of her, held tightly together by a coarse rope that chafed her skin. The semi-dried blood trailing down from her cut eyebrow plastered her blonde hair to the side of her face.

Her five captors had tried to get information from her for quite some time. *What tribe is she from? Where is it? Who is she? Does she know where Xavier is?* Leawyn refused to answer any of their questions. She didn't give them the satisfaction of even making a sound as they continued to beat her to try and force the information from her. They didn't know she was Samaritan, Lady Chief of the Izayges, and married to the most fearsome warrior in history.

This was child's play.

They only thing that kept her from breaking was the satisfaction she would get when Xavier came to save her. Because he *would* come for her, and when he did, all the men holding her captive would die.

That thought alone caused a smirk to cover her face. It infuriated the man and earned her another hit, this time with his beefy fists.

That hurt.

Leawyn closed her eyes against the black dots that controlled her vision, shaking her head to try and clear them away.

She grunted in pain when the man grabbed her hair and yanked her head back. Her blue eyes stared down at the blade he trailed across her cheek, barely flinching when it dipped into her skin to make a shallow cut.

"Yer awful pretty," the man leered in his strange accent, his rotten breath making Leawyn gag. "It would be a shame ta cut ya an' mark that smile."

Her captor chuckled and looked over his shoulder to the other men, who were also laughing. All the men looked unfamiliar, which made Leawyn confused. Were they the men who had ambushed Xavier? Their chests were bare, and they wore dark breeches made of a material Leawyn wasn't familiar with. They had incredibly poor hygiene, as if they never soaked in oils, and their facial hair was ragged and untamed.

The laughter instantly ceased when bloody spittle landed on his face and slowly trailed down his cheek and chin. He turned murderous eyes to Leawyn as he wiped the spit away with the back of his hand. "You'll pay for that, ya bitch."

Before Leawyn could prepare herself, she was thrown roughly on the ground. She screamed in pain when she landed hard on her shoulder. It made a horrible popping sound as it disconnected.

She had no time to recuperate; she was roughly turned over onto her back and straddled by the man who was abusing her. Struggling violently, kicking and clawing at the man's face, she tried to throw him off her by bucking her hips and kicking out with her feet.

The powerful punch he landed to her face disoriented her enough that he was able to gain an advantage and grab both her wrists to hold them above her head. Leawyn shrieked at the agony the action caused her dislocated shoulder.

"Grab 'er!"

Another pair of hands held Leawyn's wrists down so the man on top of her could shimmy down her body. He grabbed her thighs and spread them open, resting his body between them.

"Now you fight and I'll actually enjoy it!" the man leered, reaching down with one hand to unbuckle his belt and pull down his pants.

"No!" Leawyn's heart seized in horror at the realization of what he intended to do to her. She renewed her struggle.

"I want a turn afta' ya!" The man holding her wrists down said. Her soon-to-be rapist laughed his agreement as he positioned himself. Leawyn felt sick when his arousal brushed her inner thigh.

She squeezed her eyes shut—refusing to look into his eyes and give him any kind of enjoyment of his deed. She felt the stiffness of him brush against her opening. Leawyn bit her lip hard enough to draw blood, determined not to make a sound. The tip started to push inside her.

Shouts of alarm rang out. Suddenly, the man on top of her was roughly yanked off her and thrown across the room.

Leawyn's eyes flew open, and she stared in shock at the man before her.

"Asten!" Leawyn yelled, sprinting through the trees as tears clouded her eyes.

"Asten!" she called again, her voice cloaked with fear and desperation.

"Lea? What is it? What's wrong?" Asten asked in concern. He stumbled back a step when she flung herself into his arms, clinging to him desperately and soaking his tunic quickly with her sobs.

"Lea?" Asten asked in alarm, though his voice was as gentle as his arms when he wrapped them around her and rubbed her back.

"What's wrong?" Asten whispered in her ear. His only answer was for her to clench her hands tighter around his tunic, making her knuckles turn white.

"I-I—" Leawyn tried, but couldn't seem to speak around her gut-wrenching sobs.

"Shh, calm down," Asten whispered soothingly. He continued to rub her back. "It's okay, you're okay."

"No!" Leawyn croaked, tilting her face up so she could meet his eyes.

"I-I'm not okay! Everything isn't okay!" she sobbed brokenly, her eyes shining as they overflowed with tears that made her eyelashes clump together.

"What happened?"

Leawyn's lip trembled, and Asten caught a tear with his thumb, only for it to miss another. "My father, he—" she sobbed, bowing her head.

Asten moved his hands so they were holding each of her cheeks, forcing her head up so he could stare down at her.

"He what?" he prompted.

"He's making me marry him," Leawyn whispered.

Asten froze, his grip on her cheeks tightening in his shock.

"He's making me marry the Chief of the Izayges!" Leawyn crumbled around him, and he stiffly but gently tugged her back into his chest and held her as she cried.

They both stood there, Leawyn sobbing into the arms of her childhood friend, knowing this might be the last time they would ever be together.

The man in front of her was tall and fit. His thick arms were curled around the man who was just moments before on top of her, holding him by his neck so high her attacker's feet skimmed the ground.

Her rescuer's hair was cut short, except for the mop of curly hair on top.

"Asten?" Leawyn breathed when the man in question glanced at her, and she looked into the hazel eyes that haunted her dreams.

Asten tilted his head in slight acknowledgment before his furious eyes turned to her attacker. His gaze narrowed, and he snarled as he dug his fingers into the man's throat, causing him to choke.

"The lady said no," Asten told him calmly, but his voice was thick with malice. Her attacker's eyes widened, his face flushed from the lack of oxygen. "I-I-I'm s-so—"

"I'm not interested in excuses," he snarled, and without a second thought, he quickly crushed the man's windpipe with a sickening crunch.

Leawyn let out a strangled scream when Asten dropped the dead body to the ground, his eyes forever frozen wide with shock and fear.

She looked away from the corpse and back up to her childhood friend as he positioned himself in front of her. He pulled out his wickedly curved sword, pointing it to the men still gathered around.

Asten looked over his shoulder down at her, his eyes flashing.

"Run," he ordered before he swung his blade up and cut off the arm of the closest man standing next to him.

She screamed again as the men all around her charged at Asten, who quickly matched their attacks with a viciousness she'd never seen from him before.

Leawyn quickly stood to follow his advice when she saw one come at him from behind.

"Asten!" she yelled out in warning and, without thinking, swiped a dagger from a recent corpse and threw it forward.

Asten swung around with his sword poised above him, but faltered when a knife suddenly protruded through the throat of his potential attacker, who then fell at his feet.

He looked at Leawyn, bewildered. She felt just as shocked as he looked. "I thought I told you to run?" Asten quipped.

"I..." Leawyn trailed off when more shouts sounded out behind her—shouts of pain and fear.

Since Asten was here with her, she knew only one other man who could cause a reaction like that.

"Xavier," she sighed in relief. Turning her head, she addressed her first savior. "Asten, my husband is—"

Leawyn choked on her words, eyes taking in the space where Asten had been standing.

He was gone.

Xavier snarled when he saw the blurs of men in front of him. His vision turned red in his rage. He didn't feel when he threw himself off his wife's mare and tackled the first man he saw. He pulled his arm back and sent his fist sailing into the man's face. The blow instantly killed the man by breaking his nose and pushing the fractured bone into his brain. It was less than a second before he was on to the next man, swiftly cutting the head off his body.

Xavier was a flurry of motion, his sword stained red with blood as he ruthlessly cut down every man who came between him and his wife. He didn't flinch or feel the blood that splattered on his face and armor. His rage was all-consuming, and it was no time at all until he stood outside of a crudely made tent.

He felt his gut clench. His instinct told him his prize was inside that tent.

Six pairs of eyes met Xavier when he walked inside. They all had their swords and daggers pointed at him, but he paid them no mind. His sole focus was on his wife and the man holding a sword to her throat.

"Put yer sword down or I'll cut 'er!" the man holding Leawyn hostage ordered crudely, tightening his grip on his wife.

Xavier glanced over at Leawyn. He took in her split lip, every cut and bruise on her beautiful body and face, and the fact that her hair was matted to her cheek by her blood. Her shoulder was hanging at an odd angle, and he knew it was dislocated. He was instantly filled with more rage.

"Release her." His growl was almost inhuman.

The man holding his wife trembled with fear. Rightfully so. Xavier knew he was a sight to see covered in blood from head to toe. His shiny gold and black armor was now completely red, and his long hair stuck together with both sweat and blood. One strand was literally dripping with it. His face was specked with blood, but none of it his. He felt every bit the fearsome warrior the stories made him out to be.

"I said drop it!" her captor yelled again. He jerked Leawyn by her hair and arched her throat so that it was right on top of the blade; a thin trail of blood pooled and slid off the gleaming steel.

Xavier stiffened, his eyes zeroing in on his wife's dripping blood. He looked back up.

"Wrong move," he growled, and in the blink of an eye, Leawyn found Xavier's sword through her attacker's head, pinning him to the post behind him so he was still standing.

She screamed when brain matter and blood coated her locks and splashed in her face.

It was her reaction that spurred all the men to attack Xavier at once, thinking they had the advantage since he was without a weapon.

They could not have been more wrong.

It seemed like only moments before Leawyn found herself wrapped in her husband's arms after he disposed of the men who had snuck up on her from behind after Asten disappeared. Did Asten already know Xavier was outside taking care of the other men, and that was why he left her alone? When she thought about Asten and Xavier meeting and having to explain to her husband how she knew him...it caused a shiver to go down her spine. Xavier was over-the-top possessive of her. He would kill Asten.

Xavier crushed her to his chest, effectively snapping her out of her thoughts.

"Leawyn," Xavier breathed out in relief. His muscles instantly relaxed as soon as she was safe in his arms.

"Are you badly hurt?" he asked gruffly, but even Leawyn could hear the concern in his voice.

Silently, she shook her head but didn't resist when his hands traveled over her to check and reassure himself.

"I knew you'd come for me."

Xavier froze, slowly raising his eyes to look into hers. She met his stare evenly, and despite her black eye, her eyes shone beautifully.

"I knew you would save me," Leawyn whispered.

She kept eye contact when his calloused hand rested on her cheek, gently moving his thumb to wipe away blood.

"Always," Xavier promised, his voice low and rough. "I'll always come and save you, Leawyn."

Her smile immediately turned into a wince when the action caused her split lip to stretch and reopen.

Xavier scowled at the sight. He dipped down and swung her into his arms with ease and carried her out of the tent and over to her horse. She let out a tired sigh and rested her head against his chest as he walked. They were almost to her horse, who whinnied loudly when she saw him carrying her mistress. She stared over Xavier's massive shoulders, thinking about the man who had saved her first.

Asten...

~

Xavier and Deydrey burst into the village. He held a motionless Leawyn close to his chest.

"Get the healer immediately," Xavier ordered.

"She's already waiting inside," Tristan assured his brother, glancing down at the beaten body of his sister.

"Lady Chief!" a small voice cried out, running up to Xavier. Garnette slipped out of Tyronian's grasp when he tried to grab her to stop her.

"Lady Chief! I'm so sorry!" Garnette cried when she looked up to see how hurt Leawyn was.

Xavier stopped and looked down at the child, a bit surprised at her reaction, but more annoyed she was slowing him down to take his wife to the healer.

"Garnette, let go," Castic said, his voice calm, even though it was clear he was trying his best not to cry at the sight of his lady chief, too. The young boy gently pulled Garnette way from Leawyn before picking the small girl up as she cried into his chest.

Xavier gave the boy a nod as he quickly resumed his pace to his hut.

~

"Lay her down here," the old healer ordered when Xavier, Tristan, and Tyronian walked in. She pushed them aside impatiently, bending down to examine Leawyn, frowning in concentration.

"Her head is badly cut," the healer murmured. "Namoriee, bring me my mixing bowl."

Namoriee quickly did as the healer bid, handing the bowl and herbs to her. She gasped when she saw Leawyn's face, her eyes pooling with tears. Her face was much more swollen than when Xavier first found her. Her left eye was a dark blue and purple, looking close to swelling shut, and her split lip was puffy.

The healer ordered Namoriee to take care of her lip and eye, and Xavier noticed the slight tremble in Namoriee's small hand as she spread different kind of pastes on his wife's face. It killed Xavier to simply watch as both the tribe healer and Namoriee worked on his wife. He had trouble keeping his face stoic and keeping a grip on his emotions. He didn't know how to deal with this feeling of helplessness and rage.

The rustling of herbs and the quiet directions the healer gave Namoriee were the only sounds inside the hut. Tristan, Tyronian and Xavier stayed out of the healer's way, all three of them staring down at Leawyn's prone form with the need to seek vengeance.

Finally, the healer stood with a sigh. She looked to Xavier. "The bruises will heal. Her head had a deep cut in the back of it, which I had to sew shut. You will have to administer her medicine to try and fight infection. But she should be fine."

"Thank you," Xavier said gruffly, and the healer nodded before taking her leave.

Xavier noticed Namoriee standing off to the side, shifting nervously. She seemed to want to say something but was hesitant to do so. Finally, her spine straightened, a look of determination on her face. The girl finally walked up to him.

"I gave her a s-s-sleeping draught. She will need rest in order to heal." Namoriee paused, faltering slightly, before she continued. "Sh-she does not need more done to her than what she has a-a-already endured. She needs gentle caring for, and it would be wise to r-r-remember that."

Xavier raised his brow at the slight girl. It was a politely spoken threat.

Namoriee bowed to her chief and scurried out of the room. The three men followed her with their eyes, in shock and grudging respect. It didn't slip Xavier's notice how Tyronian's eyes lingered on her and the door she slipped out of with a different kind of emotion altogether.

"**T**ell me again, Asten..." Leawyn whispered, turning her head slightly to look up at her best friend lying beside her whose arm she was using as a pillow. "Tell me again about the fallen warriors and their horses."

Asten chuckled, shaking his head a little, turning his attention away from the stars and down into Leawyn's blue eyes. "You've heard this legend many times; I imagine you know it by heart. You tell me!"

Leawyn smiled sweetly up at him. "But I like the way you tell it; I could never tell the tale like you can."

Asten smirked, raising his other arm to push a lock of gold hair away from her eyes. "Well, that's because these aren't tales, Lea; it's our history." Asten heaved a big sigh, pretending to be annoyed. "But very well, I will tell you since you seem to need another history lesson."

Leawyn smiled and rested her head back on his arm. Her attention turned to the stars. They were both lying in their spot, using the horses' blankets to lie on the sand as they star-gazed.

Once Asten knew Lea was comfortable he began, "There was once a great warrior who protected all the land, before it was divided into tribes. His name was—"

"Saviero," Leawyn whispered.

"Yes, Saviero. Now Saviero was a quiet, intimidating man. He was over seven feet tall, with hands as big as an axe, equipped with the skill to crush any enemies' brains out!"

He laughed at Leawyn's disgusted look.

"Saviero was legendary for his skills in battle, second only to the God of War, whom he himself was a part of. The God had used his skin to shape Saviero and passed on some of his knowledge of warfare. Being the successor, Saviero was considered unstoppable."

Asten paused, staring at the stars for a bit until he turned his attention down to Leawyn. "But though Saviero was made from a God, he was still a man, mortal, and with mortality, there is death," Asten said in a grave voice.

"It was on a day the sun was not shining that Saviero met his fate when an army came and invaded his beloved land. The townspeople, not accustomed to protecting themselves and not prepared to fight, were being slaughtered.

"Saviero tried his best to fight the army off, to save his townspeople, but he was one man, and there were many. Terrified for his people, Saviero ran to the forest looking for the mage hidden there. He ran deep into the forest, but instead of the mage he was searching for, he came across the great Goddess, Ianna, who was known for warfare and her...sexual love." Asten grinned, wiggling his eyebrows. Leawyn rolled her eyes.

"Upon seeing the Goddess, Saviero sighed with relief and hope. 'Please, Goddess, help me save my people!' Saviero pled. The beautiful Goddess just smiled at Saviero.

"'What will it do for me to save your people,' she asked, 'when there is nothing for me, and I have no attachment to the lives of your kin?'

"Saviero's heart was heavy with dread; he could hear the screams of his people dying in the background, and he was desperate to save them. 'My goddess, I will do anything if you but save them!' Saviero cried.

"But Ianna just smiled again; her eyes cold as she stared at the warrior her kin made. 'I will answer your prayer,' she said, 'but it will be at the price of you.'

"Without hesitating, Saviero replied, 'Anything. I will give you anything.'

"Saviero then named off all the riches he could think of, promising the Goddess animals, jewels and clothes that he would give her in return—"

"I always hate this part," Leawyn whispered, shivering from the cold. Asten paused to reach over and wrap his cloak around her.

"Aye, but it is part of the history I cannot skip," Asten sighed and continued his tale. "'I do not want any of those things,' Ianna interrupted, and Saviero's heart broke. 'I will give you three of my war horses, whose strength will be able to conquer any who threaten you now. You will keep them for three years.'

"Saviero's heart swelled with happiness, and his relief over the knowledge that his people would be saved made him weak. Saviero crumpled to his knees in front of the Goddess, bowing to her in his gratitude.

"But the cunning Goddess was not done. 'In return, you will give yourself to me, Saviero, fully. I will take you, and you will be mine for all eternity. You will love no one else but me, and after the three years are up, no one will remember your name. That is the price you will pay for me to save your people.'

"Saviero was crushed, for he was a man who enjoyed his freedom and longed to be legendary, but he knew if he didn't take her offer, the people he'd cared for and grown to love would perish, so he agreed, and she took him then and there.

"She used her magic to overcome his grief and instead gave him unimaginable pleasure in their joining. Once finished, she took her dagger and slit her wrist so that only three drops of blood fell, which shaped into four massive black horses.

"'Go now with Rhoxolani, Asori, and Siraces to defeat this threat,' Ianna said, watching as Saviero quickly dressed, mounted one of the war horses and galloped away. But Ianna, who was also known for her trickery, did not tell Saviero what would become of him if he were to disobey and give himself to another, for he did not ask. If he did that, Saviero would be damned."

"I don't want to hear the rest; just skip to the good part." Leawyn yawned, rolling so she was completely on her side, snuggled into Asten's chest.

Asten grinned, putting his arm around her. "You don't want to hear about the battle?"

Leawyn shook her head. "Too gruesome."

Asten chuckled again but shrugged. "Very well. I'll skip the battle."

"And so, with Ianna's gift, Saviero was able to defeat the army attacking his village. For two years he kept his promise to Ianna; he did not love or give himself to any other, but one day during one of the raids, he saved a girl.

"Though the girl was not beautiful, Saviero was drawn to her. She was the lightness in his dark world, and it was fairly quickly that she fell in love with him. No matter how much Saviero tried, he could not keep his mind off her. One night his strong hold of self-control snapped, and they made love on the beach. As she whispered that she loved him, Saviero could not hold the words in his heart, and returned the sentiment. And together they fell asleep, with his arms wrapped around his love.

"Later that night, a sharp pain woke Saviero, and not wanting to wake his love, he stumbled to his feet and walked further down the beach. Soon the pain became too much, and he crumbled onto all fours, howling at the moon.

"'You disobeyed me, Saviero. You have given yourself and your heart to another,' the Goddess Ianna said, appearing in front of him, staring down at him with cold eyes.

"'Ianna! My Goddess, please! I am only yours!'

"Ianna, furious over his lie, snarled, 'You are not, and because of that, you will learn what happens when you break a promise to me!'

"Saviero screamed in agony as the pain became unbearable, and before his eyes his hands turned into hoofs, and his hair grew into a mane. And before long he was changed completely into one of the black war horses Ianna gifted him with.

"'Now you will roam these lands as a war horse that I promised you, knowing your love will never know who you are, and your people will forget you. For you are no longer Saviero, hero of Samira. You are now Izayges, my servant and war horse forever.'

"With those parting words, Ianna disappeared, leaving her new beast on the beach. He stayed there and cried, but instead of a man's cry, it was a whinny of a stallion.

"The end!" Asten proclaimed, grinning.

Leawyn sat up fully, glaring down at him. "That's not the end, and you know it! Finish the story!"

Asten shook his head, smirking. "But Lea, you already know the rest; why do I need to tell you?"

Leawyn frowned and slapped his chest, causing Asten to laugh.

"Asten!" Leawyn whined, her lips forming in a pout.

With that look, Asten stopped his teasing, rolling his eyes. "Alright, alright, I'll finish."

Leawyn settled back down against him.

"Brat," Asten said affectionately, but nevertheless continued with his tale.

"And so, the great war horse Izayges, who was once a man, did his duty to the Goddess whom he crossed roaming the rolling hills and beach. Days passed and turned into months, then into years, and soon the hero Saviero had been became a distant memory.

"There was one, however, who never forgot the man she gave herself to, who loved, nurtured and eventually gave birth to his seed.

"Times were peaceful, until the terrible army that threatened the people years ago came back with their own great warrior that only held vengeance for one man: Saviero. Thinking the people were hiding the great warrior from him, the warrior held the townspeople hostage, and each day Saviero did not come, a life was taken in his place. From afar, the black war horse watched the execution of the people he loved, unable to save them.

"It was on the second week that he could no longer stand idle, because there before him was the woman he loved.

"Izayges charged down the hill, letting out a piercing whinny that had the man whipping around. Izayges raised up on his legs and kicked the sword out of his hand, knocking him down.

"'Kill it!' the man roared at his men, who quickly snapped out of their stupor and charged at the raging war horse, letting out arrows and stabbing with their swords.

"Izayges fought the best he could in his horse form, kicking out with his legs and ramming them with his body.

"Though the townspeople, who were inspired by the war horse's courage, fought back, Izayges was just a horse, and, in turn, no match for a man. He was stabbed by the leader, his sword going straight into Izayges' chest.

"'No!' his love cried, and in her anger and despair, she picked up a fallen sword and stabbed the leader in the back, her aim strong and true as it pierced his heart.

"She ran to the horse's side, crying at the sight of the blood covering his black coat and its short, painful breaths.

The horse was dying.

"'Thank you,' she whispered through her tears, running her hand through its soft mane.

"With great effort, the horse lifted its head so that its nose could brush against her lips, black eyes meeting hers. The woman gasped at the emotion she saw reflecting from them. There was only one other person, besides her child, who had looked at her like that.

"'Saviero?' she gasped around a sob, as ever so slightly the horse bowed its head.

"'Oh Saviero!' she sobbed, staring down as the great war horse's breaths grew more ragged as it fought to stay alive.

"'I'm sorry; I'm so sorry...' she whispered, brushing his mane away from his eyes. 'Thank you for saving me; I love you.' The war horse blinked its dark eyes as they grew heavier, but as his love uttered those three words, the dark penetrating eyes of the war horse kept hers until his last breath.

"So—"

Leawyn's sniffle caused Asten to tilt his chin down to look at her. "Are you crying?" he asked incredulously.

"No," Leawyn said stubbornly, followed by another sniffle.

Asten blinked at her, before he chuckled and shook his head in disbelief. "You've heard this story before."

"So?! Doesn't mean it's not still sad," Leawyn pouted, wiping her eyes.

"Oh, Lea," Asten sighed with a grin, pulling her closer to him. "I'll just speed this along then."

"The woman he loved continued to cry over the body of her man-turned-horse, until something...peculiar happened. Ianna, the jealous Goddess appeared, looking down at the woman.

"'You have broken the spell,' Ianna said, 'and for that, I applaud you, for not many have conquered my riddles.'

"*Izayges' love stared up at Ianna, both amazed and furious. 'You are the Goddess Ianna, the one who turned Saviero into what he is now,' she stated with narrowed eyes, even as tears continued to spill down her cheeks.*

"*Ianna nodded her head, a slight smile quirking her lips. 'I am,' she agreed. 'I am also the Goddess who will bless you with a gift. I gave Saviero my own horses to save your village, and then I cursed him to become one cause he made a promise he could not keep.'*

"*Ianna looked down at the massive black horse Izayges. 'Saviero signed his future away for the love of this village, and he has laid his life down for the same reason, as Izayges.'*

"*Ianna lifted her gaze to the woman whom Izayges loved. 'He died because your life was more important than his own. He has a strong heart, and that is something I cannot ignore.'*

"*'I don't understand,' the woman replied.*

"*'I do not expect you to understand, but understand this: from this day forth any who possess the heart, courage, and strength that Saviero showed me, will be reborn as a great war horse to protect the land, and any who deserve it. That is my gift to you.'*

"*With nothing else to say, Ianna leaned down over Izayges and kissed both his closed eyes, then disappeared as quickly as she came, leaving the body of not only Izayges, but of Saviero, whose village gave him a burial fit for a king.*

"*And thus began the Samaritan people, who divided and took the names of the war horses that saved them, and whose warriors were protected by their fallen kin....as war horses,*" Asten finished, glancing down to Leawyn, whose eyes were closed.

"*Thank you for telling me,*" she whispered sleepily.

Asten brushed a lock of hair away from her face. "*You're welcome, Lea. Go to sleep now,*" he whispered before he moved his hands so that one was under her knees and the other under her head. He stood cradling her against his chest and started to walk.

"*Asten?*" Leawyn asked, her voice muffled by both his chest and sleep.

"*Yes, Lea?*"

She tilted her head up to meet Asten's hazel gaze. *She was always so*

145

fascinated with them and how they did not hold just one color in the iris. Sometimes they were a bluish-green, and other times they were a dewy green, with specks of amber. She took in his face, and the slight beard that started to grow there. He was turning into a man. His eyes bore into hers, and she felt her heartbeat pick up. Asten was her best friend, her closest confident, but lately, Leawyn found that her heart did weird things in her chest when he smiled at her. Or when she heard his laugh. It scared her a bit because she knew those reactions were not just in a friendly manner.

She was afraid feelings of friendship were turning into feelings of her very first crush. Asten raised an eyebrow at her silence, which prompted her to finish her sentence.

"I think you'll be a great war horse."

Leawyn's heart skipped again when he smiled down at her gently. His eyes grew serious, and he dipped his head down towards her.

"You know I'll do anything for you, Lea, don't you?"

She furrowed her brow, puzzled. "Yes...?" She wasn't sure where he was going with this.

"I'll always protect you. I'd give my life for yours," Asten said, his voice solemn. "There's nothing I won't do for you, because you're mine, and I'm yours. Right?"

Leawyn nodded slowly. Was this his way of saying he was starting to feel the same way she did? Her breath hitched when he pulled her closer, their lips mere inches apart. Was he going to kiss her?

"You're the most important person in my life, Lea. You're all I have left," he whispered, a strange expression on his face. "Nothing can take you away from me. You're mine, always mine."

He wasn't making any sense.

"What do you mean?" Leawyn whispered back. She watched as the weird expression disappear as his face smoothed out, the mischievous sparkle back in his eyes as he smiled down at her.

"Go to sleep, Lea," he dismissed. His hand urged her head to rest against his chest again. "I'll wake you when we're back at your village."

Having no choice but to comply, Leawyn closed her eyes and tried her best to let the gentle sway of his arms as he carried her back to her village lull her to sleep.

If only her heartbeat would slow down.

Leawyn woke inside her own hut. She blinked her eyes furiously to try and clear the haze of her deep sleep. She winced when she was greeted with a splitting headache and pain all throughout her body.

"Here, drink this."

Xavier appeared, holding out a cup of bitter-smelling liquid. He held the back of her head gently to support her as he helped her sip the medicine. Leawyn gagged at the horrible taste. When she was done, she lay back down against the pillows with a sigh.

He reached behind him and placed the now empty cup on the ground before turning back around to face her. It was silent as they stared at each other. The quiet was broken when she cupped her face with her hands and cried. She turned her face into the strong chest of her husband as he silently slipped into bed with her, and wrapped his arms around her. He held her until her sobs turned into silent tears.

"They hurt me," Leawyn whispered, her voice thick with emotion. "They hurt me because I wouldn't tell them where I came from." She lifted her head, looking up at the stony-faced Xavier, who was staring down at her. "They hurt me because I wouldn't tell them about you."

He stiffened.

"Each question they asked that I did not answer, they would beat me. It wasn't until he was about to rape me that I realized something."

Xavier whipped his head down, fury reflecting in his dark orbs. "What was it?"

Leawyn stared into his eyes, not answering right away. "I should be used to my body being taken," she finally whispered, tilting her head away from his to stare blankly at the fire that was lit inside their tent to keep them warm from the winter. "You do it all the time."

He flinched.

"I realized today—" Her voice hitched. "I realized I didn't want anyone else inside me...I only wanted you." Leawyn turned her head to look at him. She sat up so she was level with his eyes. "Why?" she asked, a frenzied look on her face. "Why do I want you to be the only one inside me? To hurt me?"

She choked around a sob, even as she brought her face closer to his. Her lips brushed across his. Once, twice, three times, before Xavier grabbed her shoulders and pushed her away from him, breathing heavily.

"Leawyn—" he started, his tone harsh as he scrambled for control.

"Please!" Leawyn cried, moving forward again to catch his lips again. "Please, Xavier, make me forget," she said against his lips, continuing with her attack. "I can feel him. I feel his body on top of mine," she groaned in despair. "I want you. Please, just make me feel something other than this. Make me forget."

Xavier's eyes clenched shut. His fingers dug into her shoulders as his arms shook with his restraint.

"You don't know what you're asking," he warned her harshly.

"Yes, I do," she whimpered. "I need you."

His control snapped.

He pulled her in for a rough kiss, his tongue pushing into her mouth forcefully as he yanked her up his body and pushed her dress up with one hand. Leawyn met his kiss just as hungrily as she bit his bottom lip with enough force to draw blood. He groaned low in his throat at the pain.

He sat up, his hands under her bottom as he tugged her to him. Her nails bit into the skin on his shoulders when he surged upwards, and with a quick thrust he was inside her, filling her to the brim.

Leawyn cried out against his lips at the sudden fullness, but she met his thrusts with her own.

Her body jerked as Xavier continued to slam into her. The sounds of their skin slapping together rapidly echoed throughout the room, making her shiver in pleasure. Leawyn moaned, gripping a fist full of his long hair and holding it tightly. He leaned forward and took her breast into his mouth, suckling softly. She groaned low in her throat when his teeth clamped down on the soft flesh. The painful pleasure of the action was shocking.

She used her grip on his hair to yank his mouth up to hers. She then pushed him onto his back, braced her hands on his chest, and started to lift herself above him. She knew her movements were inexperienced, fast, and clumsy with her need to fill the hole inside of her soul he created.

Xavier sat up and spun them around so he was on top of her. He used his grip on one of her thighs to pull her leg up and over his shoulder.

"Xavier!" Leawyn yelped and clawed his back, trying to bring him closer to her.

He faltered slightly with a grunt when she squeezed herself around him and bit sharply into the juncture of his neck and shoulder.

"Mine," Xavier growled roughly, nipping her ear. "You're mine, Leawyn."

She couldn't breathe. She was dying. There was a volcano inside of her that was ready to erupt, but unable to do so. He was thrusting into her at a teeth-clattering pace; the pleasure/pain of his lovemaking brought on a burning need within her that had her writhing beneath him in desperation.

It wasn't enough. She needed more.

"Xavier!" Leawyn sobbed, holding onto him tightly. "Please!"

"Say you're mine, Leawyn," Xavier growled huskily into her ear, his tone thick with pleasure and need. "Tell me you're mine. Admit it!"

"I'm yours!" she gasped, tears pooled in her eyes and slid down her cheeks. "I've always been yours."

Hearing the words come out of her mouth made something inside him snap, and with wild abandon he lost himself. Her sharp cries spurred on something primal within him. The groans that slipped out of his mouth were almost an inhuman growl. Xavier let out a hoarse shout when his release rippled through him. He held onto her just as tightly as she was clinging to him as she shattered around him.

He shuddered, unable to control the spasms of his body as he rested his head in the crook of her slender shoulders. Leawyn lay shaking in his arms, her nails still holding him to her tightly.

Their breathing was still ragged when Xavier lifted his head and looked down into her crystal-blue eyes. With a shaking hand, Leawyn pushed his sweaty mane away from his face, her fingers light against his cheek as she leaned up and caught his lips with hers in a soft kiss.

"Thank you," she whispered.

Xavier swallowed against the lump that suddenly found itself in his throat. He managed to nod as he caught a tear with his thumb and wiped it away.

He braced his hands above her head to slide off her, but glanced down in surprise when Leawyn clamped her thighs around him and tightened the hold she had on his shoulders.

"Stay," she commanded sleepily. "Don't run. Please, just stay with me." She peeked open an eye and looked at him, telling him everything he needed to know.

He nodded, his voice escaping him. He relaxed his shoulders and moved his body so his full weight wasn't resting on her. His wife snuggled into his chest, throwing a leg over him and intertwining it with his own.

She drifted off to sleep quickly, but not before she whispered one last order.

"No more running."

He didn't know if the command was for herself, or for him.

Either way, she was his, and he had no plans on ever letting her leave him.

The loud crack of lightning followed by the boom of thunder startled Leawyn awake.

She shivered, pulling the thick furs closer against her naked chest as she sat up. Her gold curls tumbled over her shoulders and down her back as she pushed the tousled strands away from her face.

She looked around her hut for her husband, frowning when she found he wasn't there. Wincing slightly at the soreness in her thighs as she stood, Leawyn reached over and grabbed the soft material of her robe and wrapped it around herself quickly.

Crossing the room, she pooled her hands before dipping them into the now cold water and splashed it against her face, gasping slightly at the temperature—it was colder than she expected.

Another boom of thunder made her jump.

"The storm must be getting worse," Leawyn murmured.

As if to prove her point, the small window across from her decided to burst open, letting in huge gusts of wind and rain. She shrieked and raced across the room to try to slam it shut.

"Damn!" she cursed when it wouldn't budge. No matter how hard she forced it closed, the wind kept blowing it back.

Suddenly a tan, muscled arm shot out over her shoulder, and with Xavier's help she managed to close it. Leawyn quickly latched it shut again, sighing in relief when it did so easily.

She wiped the water off her face, shaking her hands out as she looked down at herself. She was soaking wet, her robe clinging to her figure, the wet strands of her hair stuck to her lips and cheek. She glanced up at her husband, noticing he too was wet, and though he still looked formidable, she had never seen him look so...normal.

A soft giggle escaped her lips.

Xavier glanced down at Leawyn.

"Sorry," she mumbled, biting her lip to stifle her laughter.

When he merely raised a scarred eyebrow at her, Leawyn let another giggle slip. Soon it was full-blown peals of laughter.

"I'm sorry!" she gasped around her laughter. "It's just...you look so," she waved her dainty hand, vaguely encompassing his person, "so drowned!"

Xavier's lip twitched, fighting a smirk. "You don't look much better."

She looked down at herself, laughing as she shook her head. "No, I suppose not."

Leawyn was still giggling quietly, but sobered when Xavier's fingers gently took one of her wet strands and pushed it over her shoulder.

She caught his hand, pausing at its soft stroke of her cheek. Bravely, she stepped away from him. Keeping her hold on his hand, she slowly moved them backwards, stopping when she reached their bed.

With a slightly shaking hand, she caressed his hard abdominals for a moment before putting more pressure on them until he sat down. Xavier stared up at her warily, unused to this new Leawyn. His eyes darkened when she took a deep breath and untied the knot to her robe, lowering her arms so the fabric pooled to the floor at her feet, leaving her bare to him. Keeping eye contact, she straddled his lap, resting her hands on his shoulders and dipping her head so her lips were level with his.

Xavier's hand shot up, grasping her jaw, effectively stopping her lips from touching his.

"Why are you doing this?" he growled, his eyes narrowing in suspicion. "Never have you asked for my touch, yet now you are, two days in a row." When his question was not met right away, he squeezed her jaw harder.

Leawyn closed her eyes against the pain, gripping his hand with hers.

"Xavier..." she pleaded softly.

"Why?" he growled, making her wince. "Tell me!"

"Because I'm tired of feeling empty!" she cried out, glaring at him defiantly as her eyes glistened with unshed tears of sorrow and pain.

Xavier stilled, his grip going slack. She jerked her head away from him, and he quickly grabbed a fistful of her hair at the nape of her neck to still her.

"Do you want me?" he asked, voice low.

Leawyn closed her eyes and took a shuddering breath. On her exhale, she opened her eyes. "I shouldn't, but...yes," she whispered. "I want you."

Xavier used the grip he had on her hair and tugged downward, making her head tilt back and exposing her neck. He brushed his lips against her silky skin, his tongue tasting her. Her breath hiccupped, shuddering when his breath cooled her heated skin.

"How?" His tongue flicked against her throat again. "Slowly? You want me to—" Xavier's lip trailed up to the underside of her ear. "Make *love* to you?" His eyes matched his mocking tone when he pulled away to meet hers.

"No," Leawyn whispered, reaching up and watching her fingers as she traced one of the scars on his face. "No," she said again, her head giving a small shake as she brushed her thumb against his lips, pausing to meet his eyes once again. "I imagine you're not capable of love." She pushed his face away roughly. Xavier narrowed his eyes as they flashed darkly. He smirked for the briefest second before his lips grew still.

Using his knee, he quickly thrust it upwards, throwing her off balance. She let out a quick gasp of surprise before her chest collided with his. Using his grip on her hair, which tightened to bruising force as he pulled her even closer against him, he stilled her meager struggles to put space between them. Xavier grasped her jaw with his fingers, looking her straight in her eyes.

"Do you still hate me?" His voice was a deep timbre as he asked the heavy question.

The tension thickened as they stared at each other, engaged in a deadly game of cat and mouse. Every unsaid word was spoken through their eyes.

"Yes," Leawyn hissed in his face, her eyes burning. "I still hate you."

Xavier closed his eyes at her confession. Leaning forward, he buried his nose into her hair and inhaled her sweet scent.

"I don't care," he said bluntly. "You will never escape me, Leawyn. You're mine, forever." He breathed the words into her ear, nuzzling her cheek before pulling back.

Leawyn's breath blew harshly out of her nose. It was the calm before the storm.

Quick as a snake, she lashed out, grabbing hold of his lip with her teeth and pulling as her nails dug into his scalp. Xavier grunted in pain and quickly flipped her over onto her stomach, jerking her hips up. He grabbed hold of both of her hands with one of his and placed them high above her head.

Leawyn struggled with all her might before gasping when Xavier attacked her neck with his lips. His other hand bunched the material of her dress and dragged it upwards. As he tilted her neck to give himself better access, he gave a sharp, quick thrust of his pelvis, and she groaned when the feel of him filled her from behind.

The storm masked the sounds of their pleasure.

24

"Once the Rhoxolani join, we'll have all the tribes at our side so we can officially plan our attack and get rid of this nuisance of an army once and for all."

"Hear, hear!" Tyronian approved, slamming his fist down on the wooden table, causing the candles to rattle.

Tristan shot an amused look at Tyronian.

"When will we leave?" Tristan asked.

"You will stay, brother. Tyronian will go with me."

Tyronian's eyebrows shot up in surprise. He used the sudden tension that filled the room as his cue to leave.

"I shall prepare, then." Tyronian pushed himself from the table. The door shut behind him, leaving Xavier and Tristan alone.

Xavier leaned back in his chair, his arm extended out on the table in a relaxed manner while he studied Tristan. There was a war behind his brother's eyes when they met his own.

"You will have our cousin go with you, but not me? Why?"

"You are needed here."

Tristan slammed his hand flat on the table in a quick moment of anger at that. Tristan braced his hands on the table and leaned forward into Xavier's space.

"You're lying," Tristan accused through clenched teeth.

Xavier's eyes flashed with ire before he flew out of his seat, grabbing hold of Tristan's neck and shoving him down so that his cheek pressed against the wood.

"You disobey me!" Xavier bellowed. "You want what is mine, always!"

Tristan struggled against his hand, but Xavier held firm, digging his elbow between Tristan's shoulder-blades.

"You don't think I see the way you look at her?" he seethed, jerking Tristan up and throwing him away from him. "You will never have what I have, Tristan. Ever."

"What exactly do you think you have?" Tristan yelled back furiously, stalking back to Xavier until they were nose to nose. "You have nothing! She feels *nothing* for you!"

Xavier shoved Tristan out of his face. "And she feels for you?"

"She feels more for me than she ever will you! I don't treat her like my slave! I do not force myself on her as you do." Tristan glared down at him in disgust. "If it weren't for me, she would have escaped you the night you left to scout. She wouldn't have been able to save you, and she wouldn't have lost the baby because you were too weak to protect her in the first place."

Xavier eyes turned glacier. Before Tristan could protect himself, he pulled back his arm and punched Tristan in the jaw, drawing blood and brought him to his knees.

Xavier stood staring down at his groaning brother, his breaths heavy. He fists clenched with the effort it took to hold himself back from attacking his brother again.

Tristan pushed himself up with one hand, his other coming to his lip. When it came back bloody, he chuckled humorlessly.

"She's going to destroy you," Tristan panted, looking up at Xavier with a look he couldn't decipher.

"And you will fall, in every way. But she will never want you the way you want her."

He stood unsteadily to his feet, and Xavier watched him walk passed him, only stopping when he was halfway out of the tent.

"She will never love you, Xavier," he promised quietly.

The moment he was gone, Xavier flipped over the table and screamed with his rage.

⁓

Deydrey was going into season. It was the only way to explain her attitude.

"We have to make sure she stays away from the males. Especially Killix."

Namoriee grinned at that, which caused Leawyn to glower at her.

"I don't know why you're smiling. I'm serious," Leawyn grumbled, pulling her hand away from Deydrey's stomach and quickly stepping back when the mare raised her hind leg as if to kick her.

"Oh, I think it would be quite exciting if Killix was the sire," Namoriee said as she led Deydrey behind her while they walked. Her enthusiasm was as contagious as the big smile that lit her face.

Leawyn could clearly see why Tyronian was so smitten with the sixteen-year-old. She was beautiful, and good, but with just enough defiance to keep Tyronian from completely controlling her. Leawyn smirked at the thought. It was mean, but she couldn't wait until Tyronian tried to claim Namoriee. She almost felt bad for him.

Almost.

"Right. Just what we need, another Killix," Leawyn scoffed, dodging Garnette's small body as she ran past them, Castic quick on her heels, yelling after her as Garnette laughed.

Namoriee grinned at her lady chief. "Maybe it will take after Deydrey."

They both stopped, watching as Killix pranced around with his rope halter in his mouth, taunting the stable boy as he rushed to try and get it back.

They both turned and looked at each other simultaneously.

"It better," Leawyn deadpanned. "We'll have to separate them, I think."

Namoriee nodded in agreement. "I'll put her in the front pasture, the one behind your hut, so it will be easier to keep an eye on her, if that pleases you?"

Leawyn smiled. "Namoriee, how many times have I told you? Yes,

I am your lady chief, but I am also your friend. No need to sound so formal." She smiled wider at the blush that quickly covered Namoriee's cheeks. "You go ahead and put Deydrey in while I go and try to find Xavier so he knows where Killix is."

"Yes, Lady Chief," Namoriee mumbled, still embarrassed as she quickly led Deydrey away.

Leawyn laughed quietly under her breath as she walked in the opposite direction to find Xavier.

"Your stupid horse is going to get my mare pregnant."

Xavier paused in tying his sword strap to his waist and raised his scarred eyebrow, the only sign he allowed to show his amusement at Leawyn's aggravated proclamation as she threw herself down on their bed.

He continued getting dressed. "How do you know it will be my stupid horse?"

Leawyn slapped her hands down on the pallets and lifted herself up, giving him an unimpressed look before flopping back down. Xavier chuckled.

Giving his scabbard one final jerk, he made his way to his wife, leaning his massive body against the table by their bed and crossing his arms over his chest.

"Are you certain she's in season?" Even before he finished asking, Leawyn was nodding.

"She's moody, she's winking, and Killix won't leave her alone." She paused, grinning. "Well, more than usual, at least," she added.

Xavier smirked, but his face quickly sobered as he studied her. She was still as beautiful as the moment he laid eyes on her, but everyday it was as if her beauty enhanced. No longer did she wear her tribe's clothing, and instead covered herself in the usual Izayges female garb. Her long hair was pulled high away from her face, tied by a small leather strip.

Xavier found he didn't like it.

Without fully realizing his body was in motion, he strode over to her, snagged her wrists, and pulled her to her feet until she was flush against his chest—all in one swift move.

He ignored the flinch she gave when he raised his hand to her cheek. He stroked the soft skin there before his hands tangled in her hair and pulled, releasing the leather strip. Her sun-kissed curls tumbled down her back and over her shoulders, creating a halo around her face.

His wife closed her eyes, taking a breath as he ran his fingers through the strands. She moved so their stance was reversed. He shifted when she leaned her weight forward until his lips brushed hers. She kept pressing forward, following his body as his back met their bed.

With a sharp nip from him on her bottom lip, Leawyn opened her mouth for him. She let out a soft moan when his tongue brushed against hers. Pulling away from her, Xavier leaned up and pulled the strap of the scabbard he had just put on, throwing it away from him carelessly. The swords made a clang when they landed on the floor. He tugged her to him again.

Leawyn met him halfway and started a trail of kisses from his ear to his neck. Xavier felt his body shudder in response, which seemed to encourage her as she brushed her fingers over the buttons of his tunic, popping them open one by one. She pushed it completely off his shoulders until it came free, her fingers moving to his breeches.

"You're getting bold, little girl." There was a slight growl in his voice, but his body was responding to her hesitant touches.

"You seem to enjoy it," Leawyn whispered against his lips before pressing hers against his again, taking them.

He traced his calloused fingers up her back, his nails scratching against her soft skin until he stopped at her neck.

Suddenly, he dug his hand into her hair and pulled back sharply. She let out a whimper and looked up at him. His eyes bore into hers seriously, but he felt a smirk tugging on his lips.

"You forget who's in charge, Leawyn."

"I didn't—"

"You have. But I'm going to make damn sure that you don't again."

So, he did.

Leawyn was silent, but Xavier found he didn't mind. He ran his fingers through her hair and down her back, stopping, and then repeating the process.

Leawyn was lax and sweet against him, and it caused a tug against his rib cage that he ignored. He could feel her about to slip into a relaxed sleep when he broke the silence.

"I am leaving again, to visit another tribe. I should be back in a week's time."

"A week?" she replied, brow furrowing. "But the only tribe that far away is—"

He felt her tense, and he tightened the grip he had on her hair to still her when she tried to raise herself up to look at him.

"You're staying here."

It was a command.

He felt her tears against his skin. It caused that uncomfortable feeling to tug at his chest again.

"Xavier, please," she begged softly, her tears causing her voice to crack. "Let me go with you."

"No." He untangled his hand and pushed himself off the bed to get dressed again. He stiffened when he felt her small hand grab his wrist, clutching it tightly. Slowly, he turned his head to glare down at her. She was on her knees, her hair over her right shoulder, leaving her naked left breast exposed to his eyes.

"It's my home. I haven't seen anyone—" She stopped, swallowing and collecting herself. "Please, Xavier. I'm begging you."

He tugged himself from her weak grasp. He bent and grabbed her neck, lifting her off the bed and towering over her. He squeezed his fingers around her neck slowly, giving just enough pressure to make it uncomfortable, but not enough to make it painful. Yet.

"This," Xavier furiously hissed down at her, "is your home." He squeezed harder, and her hand flew up to grab his wrist, tugging it weakly. "*I'm* your home." With a sneer, he shoved her away from him.

"Rhoxolani is not your home. Not anymore."

Xavier turned away from her and resumed dressing. He was buckling his sword to his hip again, when she spoke softly.

"I'll do anything."

He slowly turned his head to look at her. She met his eyes bravely, resolutely, despite the tears coursing down both her cheeks and chin.

"What?" Xavier asked, his voice low. He turned around to give her his full attention.

"I'll do anything," she said again, flinching when he stalked back to her slowly, like a predator.

"Say it again," he ordered, looking down at her.

"I'll do anything," she repeated, her voice firmer. "I'll do anything you ask of me. Just let me go with you. Let me go ho—" She cut herself off, and he narrowed his eyes at her. Swallowing nervously, she tried again. "Let me go with you, to my old tribe. Take me with you, please, Husband."

Xavier was silent as he studied her. He tilted her chin up with his thumb. "Why? You have nothing left there."

Leawyn's lip trembled, but she didn't try and correct him. "I would like to see the sea again," she whispered. "I miss the smell of the ocean, of the seagulls squawking, and the sound of waves crashing against the cliffs."

Xavier kept his narrowed eyes on her own, trying to find untruth in her words.

"Is that all?" he asked, his voice a suspicious growl. Leawyn nodded as much as she could against his grip. "Yes! That's all. I swear."

Trying a different tactic to convince him, she leaned forward and kissed his chin. She placed her hand on his chest, stroking it sooth-ingly. "I promise I won't try to leave you. I only want to see the ocean. Maybe my old handmaiden, she was like a mother to me. See my father again..." she trailed off.

Xavier continued his silence, knowing what she was trying to do. But her desperation and willingness pleased him, and he could use it to his advantage. Decided, he grabbed her hair again and tugged it downward until her neck was arched and she was looking up into his dark eyes once more.

"You will stop fighting me," he told her. "You will do whatever I say, whenever I say it. You will stay by my side, *always*." Her eyes widened, both in shock and excitement, and she quickly agreed.

Xavier smirked, trailing his finger down her cheek. "I'm not done."

Leawyn paused uncertainly. "When we get back, you will give me a baby."

She sucked in a sharp breath, and her body started to tremble.

"You will get my mark," he trailed his hand down her body, watching its descent until it stopped on her hip, "right here." Xavier stared at his fingers splayed over her naked hip. "And it will be the old, traditional way."

He felt Leawyn shudder, and she closed her eyes, presumably to hide her dread from him. The marking ceremony was very uncommon to most of the tribes and rarely used. It took place in front of all the men of the tribe to witness the mark being placed, to make it known the woman was forever owned.

The mark itself was a tattoo of the husband's family symbol. Taking pleasure in a marked woman's body, without the husband's permission, was punishable by death. Death to both the offending lover...and the wife.

Using ink to tattoo the symbol on the skin was the new way; the old way was much more barbaric, and much more painful. It resem-bled the way a horse would be marked. A heated iron wrought with the desired symbol was burned onto the skin, etching the brand and leaving a permanent scar of the symbol.

It had stopped being the common practice more than a hundred moons ago.

Either way, the fire branding was stronger than marriage and the tattoo. For even if a branded woman's husband were to die in battle, she could never marry or lay with another man again.

No man would take her.

It was the most absolute way of ownership and possession.

Leawyn closed her eyes tightly, a lone tear slowly trailing down her smooth cheek as her lip quivered. Xavier watched her, giving her a moment. "Are we understood?"

He waited, until finally, her body deflated and she gave a slight jerk of her head, nodding her consent while staring at the floor.

Xavier cupped her cheeks and made her look at him, and kissed her lips softly.

"Good girl," he breathed out before claiming her lips completely in a hungry, primal kiss that oozed satisfaction. He pulled back and turned her so his chest pressed against her back. Wrapping his arms around her, he bent down to her ear. "Now, get dressed, and pack a bag. We're leaving as soon as you're done." He gave her an encouraging nudge toward her chest containing her clothes.

When she took two steps away from him, he reached for his dagger on the floor and quickly unsheathed it. His arm shot out swiftly and silently, pulling her back against him roughly.

"If you break your word to me, Leawyn..." Xavier raised the small dagger and held it in front of her to see before he lowered it slowly to rest against her neck. She hissed when he pressed the steel just hard enough to make a small cut below her throat.

"I will kill you, and send your body back to the Rhoxolani you miss so much, and into your father's hands. And any alliance we have set up will be broken. All because the chief's daughter didn't know how to behave."

Leawyn trembled in his arms, but he tilted his head to bite her earlobe. Her breath hitched.

"Then, I will kill them all."

Xavier turned and exited their hut, leaving Leawyn to stand there trembling in shock and horror.

∽

The travel to Rhoxolani was long, but it was worth it the minute Leawyn smelled the ocean air. When she heard the call of seagulls, her body tightened with excitement, causing Killix to flick his ears forward.

When she heard waves crashing against the rocks, she smiled.

When her village first came into view on the crest of the cliffs, she could do nothing to try to hold back the tears.

When they got closer, Leawyn couldn't hold in her cry.

There were bodies everywhere, dead.

Nothing was left of her village except the charred remains of some of the huts.

The Rhoxolani had been destroyed.

"NOOO!"

She didn't give Xavier any time to stop her from throwing herself off Killix's back. She faltered but scrambled forward, stumbling in her haste. She threw herself down, grabbing her hair against her face as she stared out in horror.

"No!" she moaned pitifully, shaking her head against her tears. "No, no, no!" she wailed, choking against her sobs.

"Leawyn..." Her husband's hand touched her shoulder gently. "We need to go."

She shook her head, shrugging his hand off her.

"Leawyn—" he tried again, pulling her towards him. "We need to go, Leawyn."

"No! Let me go!" she screamed, struggling against his hold, turning into his chest and raising her small fists, beating them against him.

"Leawyn!" Xavier shouted, narrowly avoiding her nails as she went to scratch his eyes. "Leawyn!" he screamed into her face, shaking her roughly until she stopped.

"We need to go," he said sternly. She could barely see from the tears spilling over her eyes, but she could tell his expression softened, and he brushed her hair away from her face with gentle fingers.

"It's not safe here. We need to go," he said more gently as he slowly lifted her up with him.

She could barely walk, and her legs gave out halfway to his horse. Xavier swooped her up and placed her on top of Killix before swinging himself up.

"Ten of you stay, look for any survivors," he ordered quickly before yanking Killix's head around by the reins and taking off at a full gallop, leaving her tribe's grave behind them.

They rode past a lone pike with a human head on top of it.

Leawyn's father.

26

They were in their spot.

It was the spot Leawyn would always run to when she wanted to play, when she was sad, or when she needed to escape from the duties that were expected of her as the chief's daughter.

Leawyn knew Asten would always be there, waiting for her. He was her best friend, her savior.

If only he could save her from him.

"Lea..."

Leawyn closed her eyes briefly; his gravelly voice washed over her, and she wanted to savor the sound. She knew their time was coming to an end.

"Look at me, Leawyn."

Asten used her full name. Leawyn could do nothing but fight the sting of tears. He only used her full name when he was serious. He was many things, but serious was not one of them. She didn't want to look at him. She didn't want to hear what she knew he was going to say.

She didn't want to say goodbye. His hand cupped her chin gently and urged her to look up at him. He knew, and he wasn't giving her a choice. Leawyn stopped fighting him and opened her eyes.

Don't cry. Don't cry, she thought.

Asten smiled. It was a sad, gentle smile. He brushed his thumb underneath her eyes. "You're going to be okay, Lea."

The tears she fought so hard to keep back slid down her cheeks.

"You're strong, and smart. You'll be fine," he continued.

Leawyn bit her lip against the sob that wanted to escape.

"Let's just run away," she whispered. She grew desperate when Asten's

frown deepened and he sighed sadly. "We can take a boat, sail east and make our own way. No one can find us, we—"

Asten placed his finger on Leawyn's lips, silencing her.

"You know we can't." He shook his head, pushing a lock of golden hair away from her damp cheek.

"Why?" her voice cracked with tears. "Why can't we?" He tugged her into his arms. She pressed her face against his tunic, soaking it with her sobs.

"Because you don't deserve that life, Leawyn. You deserve better." She sobbed harder when his voice wavered, unsteady with his emotion. She was about to lose her best friend as well as her freedom.

"Don't say it. Please don't say it," she begged, barely able to speak through her ragged breaths. "I don't want to say goodbye. Please!"

Asten didn't say anything back, just pulled her tighter against him and let her cry until she exhausted herself to the point of sleep. No matter how hard Leawyn blinked, she couldn't fight the darkness trying to take her.

She was on the verge of sleep when his soft voice broke through the fog enough for her to hear him.

"I love you, Leawyn."

She relaxed against him and let sleep claim her, his lone tear mixed with her own.

The next morning, he was gone. Even when Leawyn returned to their spot days later, he wasn't there. He didn't come.

After a week, she stopped waiting for him and accepted what she already knew—that night he said goodbye and let her go.

27

Leawyn continued to cry into Xavier's arms as he sprinted Killix away from her decimated village.

All her once-vibrant and beautiful people, who were loving and strong, laid waste behind them in a giant charred mess.

They didn't deserve that.

Her father...

Brees...

Leawyn let out another sob, nearly crumbling with her grief.

They were gone.

All gone.

She was the last there was of her tribe.

She truly was an Izayges now.

"How could we have missed this?" Xavier thundered as he paced furiously in front of Tyronian, throwing him a murderous glare as he did.

"This shouldn't have been able to happen, Tyronian. We're the first in line, damn it!"

Tyronian eyed him as he paced. Xavier could barely restrain his anger as he stepped with quick, jerky movements.

"Perhaps Leawyn might know of a route that could explain how they were able to slip by the Rhoxolani guards. She's from the land, after all; she would know the schedule and routes."

"That's to say if they even had guards!" Xavier snapped, jerking his head to Tyronian as he passed by. "I always said the Rhoxolani were getting lax," he seethed before Tyronian could comment. "They didn't believe anything could encroach with their precious sea and the Izayges protecting their back."

He jerked to a standstill, his back to Tyronian, knuckles cracking when he clenched them in a tight fist. "We lost a tribe today. My wife —*Leawyn's* tribe."

Tyronian nodded solemnly. "What will you have us do?"

Xavier stared outward to the darkened tent where he had left his wife once she'd finally exhausted herself to sleep from sobbing. "They need to be destroyed." He whirled around to Tyronian. "Send the message. The tribes must gather. This isn't a potential threat anymore—it's a full-fledged one."

Tyronian nodded, clasping his hand hard on Xavier's shoulder. "I think—"

"Chief Xavier!" Both their heads snapped to the side at the panicked yell.

Hassef ran in, looking frantic. Tyronian and Xavier were instantly alert, their dominant hands reaching for their swords.

"It's Lady Chief!"

Xavier's muscles tensed, a feeling of dread filling him.

"What about her?" Xavier gritted out.

"She's gone!"

The sight of her desecrated village wasn't any easier to view in the cover of darkness than it had been in the light of the sun.

Though it was harder to see all the bodies littered across the fields, she could still smell the stench of death. The aroma of burnt, rotting flesh with the added stink of old blood drying mixed together was so pungent it made her gag.

But still, she continued. She silently made her way through the remains of her little village, stepping around the bodies of her people, animals, and the few charred remains left of their homes.

Killix was her ever faithful companion, trotting steadily behind her. Ever watchful, his ears constantly flickered with the sounds only he could hear, craning his neck this way and that, alert to the possibility of protecting her. Leawyn had no doubt Killix was once a great warrior before he was reborn again into his mighty stallion form.

She walked until she reached the path that would take her to the destination that had been her plan all along.

The reason she had agreed to Xavier's mark.

It was the way to their spot.

Leawyn turned, reaching up and catching Killix's muzzle until he bent his head into her arm. "Wait here. Please."

Killix stared into her eyes, and she could almost hear him speak with that look.

Not a chance.

She simply sighed and continued on her way.

~

"I knew you would come."

Leawyn's shoulders relaxed, her breath leaving her as Asten turned from looking out at the ocean, to her.

He was so different now. His curly hair was styled differently, and his physique almost rivaled that of her husband's.

He was broad, silent, and powerful. While she was away, her friend had turned into a warrior.

"Why are you here?" Leawyn asked softly as she took a timid step forward.

Asten smiled at her, just a quick uplift of his lips as he caressed her face with his eyes. "The same reason why I expect you are, Lea," he said just as softly. "I knew it would be only a matter of time after I saved you that you would come looking for me." His lips curved upwards with a wry grin as he took slow, measured steps to her. "You always were too curious for your own good."

Leawyn had to tilt her head back when Asten stopped walking so she could meet his eyes.

"Lea..." he whispered, reaching up to stroke her cheek.

Her eyes closed, fighting the different array of emotions coursing through her.

Happiness.

Confusion.

Hurt.

"I've missed you."

Anger.

She flinched away from his hand with that proclamation, turning her back on him as she moved away to put some space between them. She crossed her arms protectively over her chest. "Why are you here, Asten?"

"Why are *you* here, Leawyn?" he asked in return, taking a step towards her again. "You came here. Some part of you knew I would be here waiting for you." He didn't stop his advance until she could feel his heat behind her, his solid muscular chest flush against her back.

She suppressed her shiver as his hands heated a path down her shoulders and trailed down softly to her wrists. The brush of his beard scraping against the side of her neck as he nuzzled her made her head tilt away from him.

"Why do you flinch from me so?" he breathed into her ear, following her movement.

"You left me!" Leawyn cried, spinning around and, bracing both her hands on his chest, shoved him away from her.

"I asked you to save me—to run away with me." She pushed at his chest again. He stumbled back with a shocked look on his face.

"You left me to *him*!" She shoved him again, harder. "To marry a man, I *hate*!" she cried angrily. "To a man who only knows how to hurt me."

"Leawyn—" Asten started, his arms reaching for her.

"No!" she shouted, shoving him away. "You bastard! How could you do that to me!" she sobbed. Completely worked up, she slapped his face, the force of it causing his head to turn. He winced, but he took it without complaint.

"I asked you to save me, and you left!" Leawyn shouted hoarsely against the emotion clogging her throat. "I hate you," she choked out, staring up at him through bleary eyes.

Asten's face hardened, and before she could react, he rushed her. Grabbing ahold of her wrists, he brought them behind her back and held them there, jerking her chest into his.

"You want to know why I left?" he growled out behind bared teeth, tightening his grip around her wrists when she struggled to break his hold.

"Do you?" Asten demanded, jerking her against him again.

"Let me go!" she screamed in his face, struggling.

"Because I know the kind of woman you are!" he bellowed back at her, shaking her hard enough her teeth rattled.

"The truth is, I wanted to take you away," he yelled down into her bewildered face, his eyes flashing with his frustration and anger. "I wanted to run away and never look back." She sucked in a sharp breath. "But I couldn't live with myself knowing I shamed you," he choked out before he slammed his lips onto hers.

Leawyn whimpered weakly as Asten dropped her arms and bent down, grabbed the backs of her thighs and lifted her up against him, slamming her back against the tree nearest to them in one fluid motion. She gasped in surprise at the contact, but it was swallowed by his mouth, his greedy lips taking every sound she made.

"I've loved you since I was sixteen years old," Asten growled against her mouth, moving down her neck with little nips and kisses. "I still do. I never stopped loving you." He pulled back, reaching up to grasp her chin and tilt her head back until her eyes met his.

"I'll always love you, Lea."

Leawyn didn't know what to do. She was conflicted. Part of her rejoiced in hearing those words coming from his mouth. They were the words she longed to hear in her childhood.

So why wasn't she happy now? She refused to believe it was because of Xavier.

So, this time, Leawyn was the one to kiss him, and she tried desperately to ignore the regret that wracked her as soon as she did.

～

They were lying in the sand, staring up at the stars. Leawyn was wrapped up in Asten's strong arms. He blanketed her in his warmth as he lightly brushed his hand through her long locks.

It was as if she'd never left.

After Leawyn kissed him earlier, she could tell Asten wanted to do more. She felt his want through his breeches as he held her up and pressed her back against the tree. When he started to guide his hand between her thighs, Leawyn had tried to convince herself to just let him touch her *there*. She thought about letting Asten claim her body.

But...she couldn't do it.

When she thought about joining with Asten, her body felt cold, and her heart raced in such a way she knew wasn't from anticipation or pleasure. She stopped his advances, and, though disappointed, he understood. He made no further attempts after that.

It was Killix who warned them. He lifted his head and looked into the distance, his ears flicking forward. That's when they heard it— her name being called.

They both shot up, Leawyn staring in horror at the sound of Xavier's voice growing closer.

"You have to go," she said quickly, fear laced heavily in her voice. She turned and started to push Asten back, towards the cover of the trees surrounding them.

Asten shook his head, grabbing her wrist. "I'm not letting you go."

Leawyn shook her head, her eyes filling with tears again. "He'll kill you!" she cried, pushing him back again. He didn't budge. "Please, go," she begged.

Asten's eyes narrowed in determination. "I'm not leaving you again," he growled.

"You have to!" Leawyn cried desperately, looking over her shoulder and growing more frantic when she heard the sound of hooves getting closer. She turned back to Asten, her fear and desperation evident on her face.

"Please, Asten, leave. Go! He'll kill you if he sees me with you, and then he'll kill me. Please," she begged, shoving him back hard. "Just go."

Asten groaned deep in his throat, bending down and kissing her roughly. It was hard and desperate.

"Listen—" Asten said quickly, turning Leawyn's face back to his when she looked over her shoulder. "I'll find you, and I'll save you. I promise."

"Go!" she whispered brokenly. With one last longing look, Asten turned and disappeared out of sight just as Leawyn whipped around and Xavier crested the corner.

The icy look in his eyes caused fear to strike straight into her heart.

"Xavier, I can ex—"

Leawyn never got to finish. Quicker than a flash of lighting, the back of Xavier's hand connected to her cheek.

The force of the blow would have caused her to fall back if it wasn't for the fact Xavier's hand buried in her hair and tugged her upright.

"Do you have any idea what could have happened to you?" He yanked her roughly around, his hand flying out and tightening around her throat. "You could have been killed!"

Leawyn whimpered in pain, her chest heaving with fear. She'd never seen him this angry before.

"How dare you try and leave me," Xavier hissed, the red gaze of his anger clouding his eyes. His hand was squeezing her throat dangerously tight. All it would take was a little more pressure, and he could snap her windpipe.

"Xavier..." Leawyn choked out, her weak attempts to pry his hand away growing even weaker. Her vision was clouding with little black spots, and she knew she was going to pass out if he didn't let go.

He watched as her struggles lessened, keeping his eyes on hers as they started to flutter closed. He lifted his arms, bringing her close enough so he could whisper in her ear. "When we get home, you'll wish you never ran away."

It was the last thing Leawyn heard before she slipped into unconsciousness.

~

Xavier charged into the camp his men had set up, sliding Killix into a quick stop, the horse he took to find Leawyn doing the same. Tyronian slowly sat up from where he was lying by one of the campfires, his eyes going to Leawyn's unconscious form shrugged over the front of Killix's saddle, then back to Xavier's.

"What happened?"

Xavier said nothing, hopping off Killix and slinging Leawyn over his shoulder when he turned back to her.

"Send a message for the rest of our men to be prepared to meet at Cortagaver when we return."

Tyronian followed closely behind Xavier. "Cortagaver? But that's only used for—"

"The marking ceremony," he cut him off briskly. "Send the message."

Tyronian stopped, grabbing Xavier's elbow and swinging him around.

"Xavier..." he trailed off apprehensively, shaking his head. "You don't mean to actually brand her, do you?"

Xavier curled his lip, looking pointedly down at the hand holding his elbow prisoner. "What I do with my wife is none of your concern." He shook off Tyronian's hand and continued to his tent.

"Xavier!" Tyronian shouted, jerking him to a stop yet again. "You can't do that! That practice has not been used in a hundred winters. You can't—"

"I'm getting very tired of people telling me what I can and cannot do," Xavier practically snarled, spinning around to throw Tyronian a furious glare.

"She's my wife! *Mine*! What I do to her is *my* business."

Tyronian reeled back in shock, and Xavier came right up to his face. "Now, your chief gave you an order. I expect you to follow it," he said dangerously.

Tyronian looked down at Leawyn, who was still draped carelessly over Xavier's shoulders. "You're making a mistake," he said quietly. He gave Leawyn one last sad look before turning and doing what his chief asked.

Xavier stared after him, his jaw ticking in anger. Growling in annoyance, he turned on his heel and continued to his tent.

It was time to take care of his wife.

Leawyn blinked her eyes open, taking in the dark room around her in confusion.

Then she remembered.

Asten.

Xavier.

She gasped, hands flying up to her throat and wincing.

"Leawyn."

She stiffened, her eyes shooting to the corner of the room. The shadowed form of Xavier made her heart race.

"Xavier, please I was just—" Leawyn winced again. Her throat felt scratchy, and it hurt to talk.

"I'm not interested in your excuses, Wife." Xavier slowly stood up, his face outlined by the fire as he took a step forward.

"You disobeyed me." He took another step, and Leawyn clenched the sheets beneath her, shrinking back as he grew closer.

Swallowing around her fear, she spoke. "I didn't."

"Don't lie to me," he growled.

"Xavier, please, I—"

Leawyn gasped in pain when Xavier reached down, quickly gathering her up into his arms.

"You ran away!" he roared, shaking her and tightening his grip around her arms until they bruised. "I took a chance, and you ran away from me."

"I was going to come back!" Leawyn cried out.

Xavier snarled, throwing her down on the bed roughly. She yelped when his weight settled on her, grasping her wrists and slamming them above her head. He grabbed her chin, jerking her face up until they were nose to nose, his dark eyes boring into hers.

"I trusted you," he said, his voice dark.

Leawyn squeezed her eyes shut against the betrayal she heard in his voice. "I know. I'm sorry," she whispered, lips trembling.

Xavier leaned forward, taking her lips in a brutal kiss, expressing everything he couldn't say. He pulled back, grabbing the front of her dress. With one sharp tug sideways, it ripped in half.

"You will be," he hissed in her ear right before he flipped her over. With a fistful of her hair to hold her steady, a quick thrust of his hips was all it took for him to fill her.

It was relentless and painful, just like their wedding night.

And Leawyn took it, because somewhere in her heart, she knew she had hurt him.

28

"I'll let you do it."

Leawyn jumped, whirling around. Her eyes landed on Tristan, who looked at her with an odd expression. She frowned. "What?"

"Leave," Tristan said, nodding behind her to her horse. "I won't stop you this time."

Leawyn's eyes followed him, tilting her head back when he came to stand in front of her.

"Leave. Before it's too late."

"He'd find me," she whispered.

"He won't," he promised. "I'll make sure of it."

She studied Tristan, gauging to see if he was serious or not. He met her eyes calmly.

"This isn't a trick, Leawyn. I should have helped you that night at the camp. Your mare is saddled and ready." Tristan lifted his hand, and she was startled to see he held up a thick bag.

"This has everything you need for you to reach the sea. From there, you can catch a merchant ship and sail far from this land, to wherever you wish." Tristan held the bag out to her, and, on instinct, Leawyn took it.

"You'd be betraying your brother..."

"I don't care," Tristan replied bluntly. "He's going to mark you, Leawyn. It will be painful, humiliating, and binding. You need to leave. If you don't go now...you'll be his forever." He cupped her cheeks with both palms, bending to ensnare her eyes with his.

"Go, Leawyn. *Run*."

She turned away, looking down at the lights of her village. The setting sun created a brilliant collage of colors, making the Izayges village shimmer. They had arrived earlier that morning, the marking ceremony set to take place as soon as the moon was up. Leawyn felt anxiety just thinking about it. Every male—young and old—would bear witness to Xavier branding her with his mark. It was to ensure all the males saw she was irrevocably his.

She looked down at the pack in her hand. She was silent for a long while, until, finally, she sighed. It was a heavy sigh, filled with conflicting emotions and desires.

"He told me what would happen." Leawyn turned back around to face Tristan. "He gave me a chance to refuse."

"Leawyn..."

"It's *my* choice, Tristan. I accept responsibility for my actions." She offered the bag back to him, who took it reluctantly. She smiled —a swift upturn of her lips that quickly smoothed back into a grim line.

As she walked away, Tristan called out to her. "You'll regret this."

She paused, looking at him over her shoulder. "I know."

And after giving him another half-hearted smile, she walked out of sight.

"Please, Xavier, don't make me go through this," Leawyn trembled softly, her whispered plea too quiet for the men around them to hear.

"I'm sorry," Xavier said, caressing her bruised cheek with the back of his hand. "But you already tried to run twice."

He didn't say anything more, just wrapped his right arm across her chest while the other cut a slit up her ceremonial dress, exposing her leg and hip bone in response.

"I'm yours; you know I am!" she begged desperately.

"It will be quick. The more you struggle, the more painful it will be," Xavier said, his voice low in her ear. Kissing the side of her head softly, he tightened his grip around her when she tensed in fearful anticipation. Reaching to the side of him, he gripped the heated prod and brought it over so it hovered between them.

Leawyn turned her head away, the heat from the iron spreading across her skin. Her eyes met the stony faces of Tyronian and Tristan. Tyronian openly showed his anger, his jaw locked.

She whimpered pitifully when Xavier said the joining incantation.

"I can't watch this," Tyronian ground out, clenching his eyes shut and turning his head away.

"You have to watch it. It's the tradition," Tristan murmured. "If you leave now, she will have to endure it again. Every man must bear witness."

Tyronian exhaled shakily and returned his gaze to Leawyn.

She held Tristan's and Tyronian's gazes until the searing, wrought iron symbol sizzled into her skin, making her screech and buck wildly against the pain.

Her scream was so filled with deep, horrified, anguish, it echoed throughout the village. It was a sound Tyronian knew would haunt him for the rest of his life. She continued to scream until her voice became hoarse and her body couldn't take it anymore. They watched as she slumped against Xavier's form, unconscious.

One by one the village men left until only Tristan remained. Tyronian was the first to leave, unable to bear the sight of his cousin's slumped form and the lingering scent of her burnt flesh.

"I hope you're happy now, Brother," Tristan said, staring down at Leawyn, her blonde hair bright against her pale, sweat-soaked skin.

"You've officially ruined her for any man who would have taken your place when you perish."

Xavier slowly looked up to meet Tristan's gaze. "Ruined her for other men...or you?"

Tristan said nothing in reply and stormed away.

Xavier once again looked down to Leawyn, staring at the still steaming mark of his forefathers.

A horse's head with its mane blowing in the wind, taking shape of a woman.

"Mine," Xavier whispered.

When Leawyn awoke, the first thing she registered was the pain. It was sharp and fiery, causing instant tears to gather in her eyes and spill down her cheeks. Moving was agony, and when she tried, she yelped at the sharp pain.

"Lady Chief," the soft voice was sweet and tearful.

Leawyn blinked her eyes open, vision hazy until it cleared and she met Namoriee's eyes. Seeing the anxiety and sadness in Namoriee's gaze, Leawyn burst into tears.

She felt herself being wrapped up carefully into Namoriee's tiny arms in a comforting embrace. Every heavy heave of her sobs caused the pain in her hip to flare up with a vengeance, but she couldn't stop even if she wanted to. Leawyn simply clung to her handmaiden's arms, and bawled.

It was how her husband found them when he walked into the hut. He paused, taking in the scene in silence. Leawyn watched him hesitate, then harden his gaze with his decision. "Namoriee."

Namoriee stiffened, glancing up fearfully at Xavier. The dead, emotionless face made her shiver, and Leawyn clung to her a little tighter.

"Leave," Xavier ordered. Namoriee paused, glancing down at Leawyn with uncertainty. Clearly her loyalties were conflicted.

"Now," Xavier said darkly, leveling her with a piercing look.

Namoriee closed her eyes in defeat, and slowly stood up, untangling from Leawyn when she gripped her tighter.

"I'm sorry," Namoriee whispered, finally managing to get out of her grasp. Leawyn noticed she didn't make eye contact as she passed her chief and silently closed the door.

Leawyn hugged herself, bowing her head so her hair shielded her face. She flinched away when Xavier went to tuck her hair behind her ear. He scowled down at her; she could see his anger quickly mounting.

"Get out," Leawyn whispered.

"No."

"Get out!" she screamed at him, slapping him across his face.

Xavier's nostrils flared, his gaze icy. "Do that again, and you'll regret it," he warned menacingly.

"Why?" Leawyn challenged, a slightly deranged look in her eye. "You'll hit me?" She slapped him again.

"You'll punish me? Mark me?"

"Leawyn," he growled threateningly, flinching when her hand connected with his cheek again.

"Leave bruises on my body?" she screeched shrilly. "Well, too late for that—you already did!" she shouted, slapping him again.

Hard; her anger fueling her.

Smack!

Xavier snapped.

With a savage snarl, he grasped her shoulders and threw her down.

"I hate you," Leawyn tossed her head back and laughed.

It was a hideous laugh—deep and dark and unhinged.

"I hate you," she gasped, still laughing. "I hate you."

"Stop," Xavier growled, his face red with his fury. Grasping her shoulders in a tight grip, he shook her hard enough that her head wobbling back and forth from the force. It only caused her to cackle louder.

"I hate you!" she screamed at the top of her lungs, getting in his face.

"You hate me?" Xavier seethed, lifting her up. "Huh?" He shook her again, his anger completely out of control.

"Do you?" he bellowed, the vein in his neck bulging.

"Yes!" Leawyn cried back, refusing to flinch away from him.

"I hate you! I've always hated you, and I always will." Her lips twisted up in scorn. "I should have killed you when I had the chance."

"But you didn't, and that was your mistake."

Their bodies heaved together, their breaths coming out in sharp, quick outbursts.

Like a whip, they both snapped.

Their lips crashed together in a kiss, their teeth clinking together as their tongues battled. Leawyn took Xavier's bottom lip, and sunk down until she could almost feel her teeth meeting together. He let out a shout, yanking his head back.

She met his gaze defiantly, her breaths coming out in gasps. He snarled, shoving his hands between her legs, until his fingers dove into her warm heat.

"You don't hate me when I do this, do you?" His thumb brushed against her nub before sliding his fingers into her warmth. Leawyn moaned, her body spasming against the pressure.

Xavier shifted so she lay on her back, his hand still buried inside her, pumping furiously. He pulled back, just enough to slide his finger out so he could add another, and shoved them both back into her roughly.

Leawyn yelped at both the intrusion and the pain as her hips bucked. Her burn mark stretching painfully, her legs spread wider as Xavier nestled between them. He leaned forward, his body flush against hers as he bit her neck, hard.

"I own you," Xavier growled. "Everything belongs to me." He slid his other hand beneath her, lifting her hips enough so his thumb brushed against her anal entrance. "You might hate me, but your body doesn't." He brushed the fingers of his other hand against her clit, while his thumb pressed in, filling her.

Leawyn screamed, her body convulsing against her orgasm.

Xavier pulled his hand away. Leaning back on his knees, he lifted her body up, then slammed her down on his length in one hard pull.

Not giving her body time to get used to the intrusion, he continued to thrust up against her, pulling out almost all the way, and then slamming into her again.

Her eyes rolled back into her head from the painful pleasure of it, her mouth opened in a silent scream as he plowed into her relentlessly. His big hands gripped the inside of her thighs as he sprawled her out, opening her wide for him. Her body jerked forward with each powerful thrust of his hips. The sound of his length pushing into her warm crevice mixed with their grunts and moans.

The intensity of it was almost too much for Leawyn. Their bodies grew slick with sweat, making it hard for them to stay together. She slid away from him with each jerking motion of his hips.

Xavier reached out and grabbed her throat, holding her down as he used one hand under her ass to lift her hips up, making him go deeper. His pelvic bone bumped her clitoris with each stroke.

"Give it to me," he grunted, continuing his brutal thrusts into her slick, tight body.

Leawyn moaned loudly, shaking her head. He bared his teeth as he gripped her neck tighter. "Give it to me."

"No!" she shouted defiantly, choking against his hold, and if anything, his thrusts grew more powerful, rocking her to her core.

He moved so his weight was resting on his arm; using his grip around her neck, he forced it back so her chest was arched up to him.

The stroke of his tongue against her nipple made her convulse around him. The nip of his teeth made her scream. And when his hand left her neck to pinch her nub—

She shattered.

The very moment Leawyn's scream ripped out of her throat, Xavier lost the battle and came in giant bursts inside of her. He slumped against her.

As they both tried to catch their breath, her body still shook with the aftershocks of her climax.

Xavier brushed his thumb against her burn, making her yelp and flinch away from him. He ignored her, and did it again, this time with more pressure.

"Xavier!" Leawyn yelped again, the pain stabbing. She pushed against his chest, trying to get him off of her.

"This mark...this pain," he said softly, staring down at the raised, angry flesh of her hip. Blood seeped through the skin that had scabbed over, reopened from the movement of their joining. "It belongs to me, just like you do," he whispered, looking up at her when he pushed against the burn again, making her cry out.

"You might hate me, Leawyn, and I don't blame you if you do." She sobbed, still fruitlessly trying to push him away.

"But this?" Xavier grabbed her hair and made her look down at his hand, pushing on the burn again, irritating it further. "I own you. You're mine."

She cried again in pain, and he bent his head and kissed the irritated, heated skin.

"I need you."

"Why?" Leawyn sobbed. Big, fat tears rolled down her cheeks as her anguished eyes met his own empty ones.

"Why, Xavier?" she gasped out, her body trembling violently. "Why me?"

"Because," he said, his voice almost inaudible and thick with emotion, making him sound less like the fierce warrior he was.

"You make me feel again."

With his admission, Leawyn stopped pushing against his shoulders, shocked. Xavier closed his eyes and rested his head on her flat stomach, snaking his arm around and under her, nuzzling into her.

Her tears still ran unchecked down her cheeks as she stared down at him. In that moment, Xavier looked like a child to her. He looked like a lost boy confined in a hardened man's body. Slowly, as if unsure of the movement, Leawyn brought her hand up so it rested upon his shoulders.

"This has to stop," she whispered, defeat heavy in the words.

Xavier slowly looked up at her, and she met his eyes. What she saw in them took her breath away.

Pain.

Regret.

Anger.

Hope.

Need.

Xavier's eyes were like her own; the only noticeable difference was the color. She knew they were both lost in a deep sea of the unknown, and the more they swam, the deeper they went. The more they fought and resisted the waves, the quicker they sank.

Unwilling as she was, she knew their lifeboat was acceptance and each other.

"Xavier." Leawyn lifted his chin with her slender fingers so he had to see her, to hear the gravity of what she had to say. It was the same thing he had done to her on multiple occasions.

"This has to stop." Her voice hitched. "You win; I have no one," Leawyn cried, the first tear spilling down her cheek.

"I'm alone."

Dropping her grip on his chin, she bowed her head, body shuddering as she sobbed. The sound was heavy and grief-filled as each sob tore from her throat.

She was startled when he gently cupped her cheeks, bringing his face close to hers. He studied her vividly, watching every tear that slid down her fair skin and taking her in.

"You're not alone," Xavier whispered thickly. "You are the most beautiful flower, Leawyn. Don't let people crush you. Even if it's me."

Then, he kissed her.

The sound of horses and loud voices of men woke her up.

Still in the firm grips of sleep, it took a moment for Leawyn to realize Xavier was no longer in bed with her. Leaning up on her right elbow, she looked over her shoulder to Xavier's side of the bed. The sheets were still rumpled. She placed a hand on the pallet and frowned.

It was still warm.

Leawyn squinted up at the small window inside her hut, the midday's sunlight bright in her eyes.

Xavier slept in?

For the sake of her own sanity, Leawyn decided she didn't want to think too much about it and flopped back on the bed. She winced at the flare of pain that shot from her hip at her sudden movement. She glanced down at the raised mark, studying it for the first time.

If it wasn't on her own body, and if she didn't feel the absolute pain of the symbol being branded into her skin, she would think the mark was quite beautiful. It was a woman's face, with long, flowing hair that morphed into the mane of a horse. It was Saviero and his love.

The mark of Xavier's forefathers. Of his ownership.

Leawyn's hands hovered above the raised skin as she thought about the night before.

After Xavier kissed her, he had laid her down as if she were a child being put to bed. He had touched her with a care and gentleness that she didn't know he was capable of. He had rubbed the cooling salve on her hip with gentle fingers until the entirety of it was covered. Once he was done, he gathered her up into his arms and went to sleep.

Before she could give any more thought to it, the wooden door opened and in walked Namoriee, her thin arms piled high with new clothes. Leawyn raised a brow as one by one, the village women, Tamanina and Thaarima, followed behind her.

Tamanina and her twin sister were carrying a large wooden tub, and their daughters, Tanessa and Talma, each carried large pails of water collected from the river.

Namoriee dumped the load of garments onto Leawyn's bed with a relieved sigh.

"Namoriee," Leawyn picked up the garment closest to her and raised it to eye level, "what are these?"

"Those, Lady Chief," Leawyn's brow arched higher when Namoriee snatched the garment out of her hands and tossed it back on the bed, "are your new dress clothes."

"Yes, I can see that," Leawyn said dryly. "But why do I have new clothes?" She peered to the side of Namoriee, watching Tanessa and Talma dump the water into the waiting bath as their mothers went about throwing in lavender. "And why are they preparing a bath?" She wrinkled her nose in her confusion. She watched the women leave the hut after the bath was prepared, then turned her attention back to Namoriee.

"Chief Xavier gave me the order to fetch you a bath and deliver these clothes this morning," Namoriee shrugged in answer. "And," she reached over and tugged the sheet Leawyn was using to cover herself, ignoring her squeak of surprise, "what Chief says, I do."

Namoriee scanned down Leawyn's body, taking in the fresh bruises on her throat and hips, as well as the scattering of the ones more faded with time. Her grin faded.

"Lady Chief..." Namoriee trailed off sadly, and Leawyn's heart constricted when she saw the young girl's eyes attempt to blink back tears.

"Oh, Namoriee," she soothed, wrapping the sixteen-year-old in her embrace when she fell into her crying. "Don't cry, I'm okay." She cupped Namoriee's cheeks as the girl pulled back to look at her.

"How could you be?" She sniffled. "When I heard Chief Xavier would marry, I was afraid for his bride, knowing how the chief is. I just didn't think it would be anything like this." Namoriee's eyes filled with tears anew. "I'm so ashamed, and I'm eternally sorry I left you last night when you needed me. I'm *so* sorry." She sobbed, throwing herself back into Leawyn's arms and clutching her tightly.

Leawyn sighed. "Look at me, Namoriee," she said, rubbing her back. "Namoriee, look at me," she said more firmly, leaning back to catch Namoriee's eyes as she guided her chin up. "You have nothing to be sorry for, you hear me?" She smoothed Namoriee's dark hair away from her face. "You did what you were ordered to do by your chief. If anything, it was wrong of me to cling to you so."

"Do you think you could ever forgive me?" Namoriee choked out, dejectedly.

Leawyn smiled gently, wiping a tear away with her thumb. "There's nothing to forgive. Okay?"

Namoriee smiled weakly and nodded. "Okay."

"Good," Leawyn said. She hugged the girl, rubbing her back twice before letting her go. "Now," she said cheerfully as Namoriee shyly stood, brushing the rest of her tears away from her face. "Why do you think Xavier ordered this?" She once again examined the various clothes scattered atop her bed.

Namoriee snaked an arm around Leawyn's back, supporting her as they made their way to the tub. Though it ached to walk, it wasn't nearly as painful as it was before. Whatever salve Xavier put on the burn had numbed it greatly.

"It might have something to do with all the tribesmen pouring into our village," Namoriee commented casually, helping Leawyn ease into the lukewarm water. Leawyn grew tense, her eyes flying up to meet Namoriee's startled gaze.

"Tribesmen? When?" Leawyn asked with urgency.

"They've been pouring in the last two nights. Men from all our tribes, and some from tribes I don't know." Namoriee picked up the soap-soaked cloth and lightly started to scrub Leawyn's shoulders. "The only tribe that's missing is the Rhoxolani. Though, I'm sure it's just taking them longer to arrive since they have a greater distance to travel."

Leawyn looked down at her hands, clenching them together. "No," she said. "I don't think they will come."

Namoriee paused, glancing down at Leawyn, slowly dipping the rag back into the water. "Why not, Lady Chief?" she asked hesitantly.

"Because," Leawyn replied, turning to look at Namoriee over her shoulder with a haunted look in her eyes.

"They're dead."

30

Xavier restrained himself from pinching his brow against the headache that was slowly but surely forming. His emotionless mask was in place. It hid his frustration from the tribe leaders of Siraces and Asori who stood in front of him.

"What makes you so sure this army means to attack us?"

Xavier heard Tyronian snort beside him.

"Besides the fact they demolished the Rhoxolani tribe, you mean?" Tristan asked coolly.

"Could have been a message to Boers. He always was an uncaring fool," Kisias, Chief of the Siraces, scoffed. "They were worthless anyways. If anything, it did us a favor."

Kisias and Yoro laughed at their joke, while Tyronian and Tristan each flexed their hands into tight fists. Xavier felt his blood boil.

"That is enough!" Xavier launched himself up and slammed his fist down on the table with a loud bang, making the various objects on top jump from the force of the blow. Yoro and Kisias quieted instantly. "How *dare* you," he hissed, fury and disgust coiling inside of him. "This is the Rhoxolani we're talking about." Xavier's heated gaze met both Kisias's and Yoro's. "They were a part of us!" His fist slammed the table again and caused Kisias and Yoro to jump.

"That tribe is where my wife was born," he said. His anger mounted with each word he spoke. "The Rhoxolani were her kin, and now she's the only one!" He picked up a goblet and threw it at the wall, shattering it to pieces. Kisias and Yoro jumped out of the way.

"Yet you laugh at the fact a whole century of our people, our *history*, are gone, never to be reborn!"

Yoro and Kisias glanced at each other wearily. Xavier's fury was almost tangible as it poured out of him. He marched up to them, and Tyronian and Tristan stepped forward when both Yoro and Kisias reached for the hilts of their swords. They did the same, ready to back up Xavier.

"Mark my words, this army will attack Siraces and Asori," Xavier said, crowding into their space until he was nose to nose with the two chiefs. "And when they do, and we hear the screams of your women and children being slaughtered, I will look upon the horizon and laugh as you are doing now." He smiled grimly, his eyes cold as he backed away from Kisias and Yoro and their fury.

"Don't expect the Izayges to fight your battles and save you." With that said, Xavier stormed out of the tent.

Tyronian, Tristan, Yoro, and Kisias all stared after Xavier, the tension still lingering between them. Slowly, Yoro and Kisias turned toward Tristan and Tyronian, loosening their grips on their swords as they did.

"Good to see Xavier still has his temper," Kisias said dryly.

"I can agree with Xavier over the fact it was wrong for us to laugh at the misfortune of Boers and the Rhoxolani, and for that I'm sorry," Yoro said.

Kisias nodded. "Yes. Me as well. It was wrong of us."

"Does this mean you will fight?" Tyronian asked.

Kisias and Yoro shared a glance. "No, we will not fight," Kisias said eventually. "I cannot risk my people's safety. We haven't been at war for many winters. I would rather not have to go to war in *this* one. Especially since this army does not seem a threat to us."

"I as well. I'm sorry," Yoro said, shaking his head.

"They ambushed my brother, and wiped out Rhoxolani." Tristan gritted his teeth, his leather wrist guards stretching was the only inclination at how tightly his fists were clenched. "How much proof do you need?"

"Yes, but both of those things have a direct connection to Izayges, not to our tribes," Yoro argued.

"And to Xavier," Kisias added. "With as many battles as he has fought, it would not surprise me if he were to make an enemy with a vendetta against him." He looked at Tyronian and Tristan, his face showing his sympathy. "It is not our fight."

Tyronian chuckled, shaking his head. Walking up to Kisias, he placed a hand on his shoulder. "I understand," he said reassuringly.

"What?" Tristan growled, taking a tense step toward his cousin. "Tyronian—"

"No, Tristan," Tyronian cut him off, glancing at him briefly before wrapping an arm around Kisias, clapping him on the shoulder and squeezing good naturedly.

"As Chief of the Siraces, Kisias has to do right by his tribe." Tyronian grinned at Kisias. "Right?"

"Right. I'm glad to hear you understand, Tyronian." Kisias grinned back.

Tyronian laughed heartily. "Oh, I understand." Quicker than Kisias could see, he slammed him face-first into the table.

"I understand you're a gutless fool," Tyronian hissed furiously.

Yoro shouted in alarm, moving to help Kisias, with his sword drawn. Before he could take a step, however, Tristan was ready.

Tristan kicked out, catching Yoro in the stomach. The chief doubled over, breathless. The young warrior bent down, his elbow catching Yoro in the nose while his hand gripped the man's wrist and jerked it forward. Yoro cried out in pain and dropped his sword. Tristan twirled on his knees, catching Yoro's sword and pulling out his own simultaneously as he stood and faced the chief.

Yoro's head was trapped in a scissor as Tristan glared down at him, holding the two swords to his neck.

"Now," Tyronian said, keeping Kisias's face flush against the wood as he struggled. "You forget my mother was the daughter of the chief before you. Do you know what that means?" Tyronian asked conversationally.

Kisias growled up at Tyronian, bracing his arms to push himself up. Tyronian jerked him against the table again, grinding his face deeper into the wood.

"Do you?" Tyronian yelled. He suddenly pulled Kisias up, spinning him around. He slammed his back onto the table, holding a dagger to his throat.

"It means, I can kill you right now," Tyronian said darkly, jerking Kisias up by his hair so the dagger nicked his flesh. "I can kill you now and become the Chief of Siraces, for it is my birthright," he said softly, his voice feral.

Tristan raised his two swords higher in warning when Yoro went to move forward.

"But you see, I don't really want to do that," Tyronian said conversationally. "It's too early for killing, and I'm feeling particularly nice, 'cause I'm usually a nice guy." He shrugged, his tone modest.

"You dare threaten me?" Kisias shouted in rage.

"Threaten you?" Tyronian said in surprise. "Tristan, you hear that? Kisias thinks I threatened him." He chuckled in amusement.

Tristan grinned. "I heard. It was very rude of him."

"I think I'm quite insulted." Tyronian pouted. "Let's get one thing clear, Kisias." He took the knife away and pulled his fist back. He struck out and connected to Kisias's face. It made a sickening crunch as his nose broke from the impact. Not stopping there, Tyronian pulled Kisias up again and slammed his fist into his face twice more in quick succession.

The force behind the last punch was so powerful, Kisias toppled over the table and brought it down with him.

"Stop!" Yoro yelled out, shooting forward again. He stumbled back when Tristan used the toe of his boot against his chest to shove him back.

"Shut up," Tristan growled in warning.

Tyronian calmly walked around the fallen table to stand in front of Kisias. Kisias moaned in pain and flopped over on his back, holding his nose. Reaching down to grip the front of Kisias's leather armor, Tyronian jerked him up.

Then he leaned down and got right into the chief's face. "I don't threaten— I make promises." Tyronian's grin was all teeth as he tilted his head. "Want to guess what the promise is?"

"I'll fight," Kisias moaned. "I'll fight with the Izayges."

"That's great!" Tyronian exclaimed happily. "You hear that, Tristan? Good ol' Kisias changed his mind." He glanced over his shoulder at Tristan.

"That's great news. Yoro here said the same." Tristan nudged Yoro's chin up with the tip of one of the blades. "Isn't that right, Yoro?"

"Yes," Yoro gulped, glancing down at the sword as sweat ran down his temples. "Asori will fight with you."

"This is great. I knew you two would make the right decision." Tyronian beamed, clasping Kisias's shoulders with both hands and tugging him up. "Now, I don't need to tell you what happens if you decide to change your mind, do I, Kisias?"

Kisias shook his head, blood running down the length of his face.

"Good," Tyronian grinned at him a moment before slamming his forehead into Kisias's with a *crack*. He dropped his hands and watched the chief slump to the floor. "Nice chat." Tyronian stepped over Kisias's body and out the door.

Tristan slowly backed away, holding the two swords steady, still pointing them at Yoro. When he was just outside the door, he dropped his hand and tossed Yoro's sword on the ground. He saluted them as he ducked down and exited the tent, leaving bloody and frightened chiefs inside.

31

Xavier dodged the busy bodies of his village and visiting warriors as they settled in. He was practically vibrating with fury. How *dare* they!

How can they laugh at the demise of the Rhoxolani? Xavier was not a sentimental man at the best of times, and he certainly wasn't known for his caring nature, but even he felt the loss of the Rhoxolani as if they were his own. They were his people, part of his history.

Xavier stopped and scrubbed his hands roughly down his face. Everything was a mess. His life of order, control, and power over himself and his village was falling apart. For years, he could look at everything objectively. He'd witnessed others become sloppy, so consumed by their emotions, it made them irrational and unable to see the bigger picture of the hard choices.

But Xavier always could think with his head and instincts.

Detached.

Calculating.

While others crumpled, he stood strong. He was reliable, and he was a fierce leader.

But in just a few short months, the years of training he was subjected to since he was seven years old were being destroyed.

"Xavier?"

He opened his eyes and dropped his hand from his temples, lifting his head to meet the eyes of the one who had spoken. His loss of control started when he first laid his eyes on her, and it hadn't stopped since.

~

Leawyn had to stop herself from fiddling with her dress when Xavier continued to just stare at her. "Is this okay?" she asked, growing more uncomfortable with the silence.

"You look beautiful."

Leawyn blushed. She looked down and smoothed the material. "It's the dress. It's very beautiful." She looked up at her husband, her smile shy. "Thank you."

And beautiful it was. It was colored a deep moss green, with long golden sleeves that flared out at the elbows. Golden beads and dried wild flowers covered the length of the gown. Two studded strips of heavily beaded material crossed over her breasts and held the dress together with a single clasp behind the neck.

Xavier nodded. He seemed to hesitate before he lightly traced the beaded embroidery on the neckline with one finger.

"It was my mother's," he said softly. He dropped his hand and took a small step back, meeting Leawyn's gaze.

At his admission, she glanced down at the dress, biting her bottom lip. "Well," she said finally, "she had good taste."

Xavier's lips tilted up in a barely-there smile. "Yes, she did." His eyes scanned her body appreciatively.

Leawyn flushed for the second time under his attention, not quite used to this side of her husband.

"There will be a feast tonight. I will need you to help the women prepare." Xavier watched avidly when his wife's eyes lit up in excitement. "Can you handle that? I don't want you in..." he trailed off, and an uncomfortable silence engulfed them. Leawyn knew that he was going to say *pain*. They both knew the reason she would be in pain was because of him.

"I can get Namoriee to help," she said, looking anywhere but his eyes.

"Good." Xavier cleared his throat.

He stepped forward and gripped Leawyn around the neck to tug her closer. He lifted her chin with his finger. Her breath whooshed out of her when he dipped his head, his lips hovering over hers, waiting. She hesitated, then tilted her chin. Xavier stared into her eyes when he brought his mouth down to hers in a kiss.

"I'll come collect you before the feast starts," he murmured against her lips. Then he pulled away.

"Okay," she whispered back. She closed her eyes when Xavier smoothed her hair away from her face.

He was already walking away from her when she opened her eyes.

"I think we're about ready, Lady Chief," Namoriee said proudly, placing the cylinder filled with animal fat and cloth on the table and lighting it.

It took the full efforts of all the village women—big and small— to prepare for the Izayges people and their guests for the night's festivities.

It would be the first feast they'd had since Leawyn and Xavier's wedding, which had been nearly nine months ago. Leawyn stood up from her crouched position, looking around as she wiped her hands on the rag that lay ready beside her. Namoriee was right; everything did seem to look ready.

Much to Leawyn's annoyance, most of the women would not let her see to more than simple tasks. Their reasoning was that it would not be appropriate for the lady chief to be seen handling such tasks.

"We wouldn't want you to ruin your dress," they said, but Leawyn knew it was because of her mark.

Instead, they respectfully listened to her direction and requests when needed, but for the most part Leawyn's sole duty was to set the surrounding tables with plates and silverware. It was both sweet and frustrating.

"This looks amazing. I can't believe we pulled everything off so quickly!" Leawyn laughed.

The feast was set to be in the middle of the entire tribe. The girls had to quickly gather as many tables, or things that could be used as tables, to fit all the tribespeople and guests. Two giant fire pits sat in the center of two separate squares of combined tables, while another separate fire had two wild hogs roasting over it. Namoriee wiped her hands on her dress and stood beside Leawyn, staring proudly at their work.

"All we need now is the men," Namoriee said wryly.

Leawyn laughed in agreement. "Indeed, we do."

She glanced at Namoriee, taking in her ragged and dirty clothes. "Namoriee, you should go change. I can take care of things here while you do." She looked around at their surroundings again before returning her gaze to Namoriee. "There's really not much left to do."

Namoriee shook her head in disagreement. "I can't. I won't even be attending the feast, really."

Leawyn frowned. "What are you talking about?" she asked in bewilderment. "Of course, you are!"

Namoriee wrung her hands together nervously. "Lady Chief..." she faltered. "I appreciate how well you treat me, but you m-m-must know I don't hold a very h-high stature."

Namoriee glanced up at Leawyn, still seeing her confused expression, she flushed anew. "My j-job is to be with the other serving wenches, serving food and ale." Leawyn could tell Namoriee grew frustrated with her stutter, but it had gotten better, only coming out when she was nervous.

"Namoriee," she grabbed her small shoulders, "you are *not* just a serving wench, or in low stature."

Namoriee opened her mouth to refute, but Leawyn cut her off with a stern "*no*" and continued.

"You are my handmaiden, and more importantly my *friend*," Leawyn stressed in sincerity. "You *will* be attending the feast, and you *will* be sitting with me."

Namoriee's eyes widened, shaking her head madly. "N-n-no, Lady Chief! My duties! I c-can't just—"

"Okay," Leawyn soothed. "I understand, Namoriee. You don't want to abandon your duties." She gave in to stop the young girl from having a panic attack. "You can serve with the rest of the women." The girl's shoulders sagged in relief. "But only for the first half, after that, you're done and you're going to enjoy yourself."

Namoriee's elation deflated. But she knew better than to argue. "Yes, Lady Chief," she mumbled compliantly.

Leawyn grinned in triumph. Using her grip on Namoriee's shoulders she spun her back around in the direction of her hut. "Now, go and pick out one of my dresses—not the ones Xavier gave me though." Now that she knew they belonged to his mother, she didn't want anyone to wear them but her. It said a lot that Xavier kept them in the first place, and that he gave them to her.

Namoriee's eyes widened again. "But—" Once again, Namoriee was caught off.

"Go!" Leawyn ordered sternly. She gave Namoriee an encouraging, but forceful, nudge to get her moving.

Namoriee stumbled forward, glancing back at Leawyn, who simply pointed at her hut as she would to a dog. She didn't pay attention to her surroundings, or the pair of blue eyes that followed her there.

32

The night was loud with laughter and roars of men as they drank deeply from their goblets of ale and wine.

Different members of the family tribes and the Izayges occupied the tables, men and women alike. Though the atmosphere was cheery and lighthearted, there was an air of pretense.

Word of the annihilation of the Rhoxolani quickly spread throughout the visiting soldiers, and the busted faces of the Siraces and Asori chiefs only added to the suspicion something dark was on the horizon.

Leawyn scanned the crowd with her eyes. She watched the interactions between all the men of the tribes gathered around with equal amounts of fascination and disgust. She overlooked the men who sat at their respective tables enjoying the meal of wild boar and mead, their arms wrapped casually around the women warming their laps. Occasionally, some of the men would grab one of the serving girls as they passed them by and haul them onto their lap with a squeal from the girl.

In the far corner stood a group of men who were engaged in a game of throwing knifes at the makeshift target carved out of tree bark. A short distance away, Leawyn could see men gathered around in a broken circle, cheering on the two opponents as they traded blows with each other with their fists.

After a particularly hard punch thrown by a fellow Izayges tribesman to the face of his Siraces opponent that made him instantly crash to the ground unconscious—which made the Izayges men roar—Leawyn grimaced and turned her attention elsewhere.

She had to do a double take, barely managing to keep her mouth from dropping open in surprise at what she saw.

A girl who couldn't have been much older than her, had her head thrown back, eyes closed in pleasure, as her bare breasts bounced from the force of two men thrusting into her. A group of men stood around them, watching.

It was like seeing a dead body for the first time. She knew she should look away, but couldn't because of the morbid fascination and curiosity of the ordeal.

When another man stepped forward—undoing his breeches as he did so— the man who was thrusting into the woman from underneath grabbed a fistful of her hair and yanked back until her neck was arched. Leawyn looked away.

Her eyes met her husband's, who was watching her. They stared at each other silently for a moment. Xavier looked over at the trio again, smirking at what he saw before he turned his attention back to Leawyn.

There was a challenge in his eye when he did so.

He dared her to look again. To watch.

Leawyn's eyes narrowed against his, causing his smirk to widen. He leaned forward, the scruff of his beard scratching against the top of her ear.

"Are you ashamed?"

Out of all the things Leawyn thought her husband would say— that was not one of them.

She tilted her head towards him, as he whispered in her ear again.

"Does it make you uncomfortable?" his lips brushed her ear, causing her to tense up as he said his next words. "Seeing the pleasure on their faces?"

Xavier looked at her calmly when Leawyn flinched away from him, glaring.

"All I see is the men's pleasure as they take that poor girl between them," she snapped. She resolutely kept her gaze down at her half-empty plate of food when her husband crowded into her space again.

"Look again," Xavier cupped her chin and turned her head toward the public display. "Look at them, Leawyn, closely, and tell me what you see," he encouraged against her ear softly.

Her body grew more tense, trying to yank her chin away from his grip, but she knew it was in vain.

He had her.

Leawyn had no choice but to watch.

There was a different man behind the woman now, his breeches around his ankles, ass flexing with each thrust his pelvis made against the woman's behind. The man underneath the woman had both of her breasts in his hands, tugging at them as they swayed in front of his face.

"I only see—"

"Look closely, Leawyn," Xavier interrupted, lowering his head so his bearded cheek meshed with her smooth one, keeping his hold on her jaw.

"Look at her face. Watch her."

Leawyn's lips pressed together, but she did as he bid and watched the woman who was being taken by the two men. Though her black hair was still being clutched in a tight fist by the man behind her, it didn't seem he was forcing her head back. Her dark features were flushed, her eyes closed, her mouth hanging open in...

Leawyn gasped.

"You see it now, don't you?" Xavier asked as he chuckled huskily, turning so his lips brushed her earlobe with each seductive word he spoke. "You see the pleasure on her face." He gave her chin a gentle shake, reminding her to keep watching. "You see the men's expressions, as they thrust into her tight, greedy body?"

Her breath grew ragged as she watched them, taking everything in. Both men wore grimaces on their faces, as if they were in pain, but Leawyn knew otherwise. If she sat closer, she was certain she would be able to hear their skin slapping together.

"See how they fill her up?" Xavier whispered in her ear. "How she cries out in passion as they do?" His voice was deep and hypnotic, and Leawyn felt that somehow, with him whispering words in her ear as they both watched the joining, he made it more erotic.

Made it more daring.

Arousing.

Both men kept a steady rhythm, when one thrust in, the other pulled back. Filling her with perfect unison. "They both want her, and she loves it."

The two men started to thrust faster into her, each holding some part of her body as they did. The woman reached back, wrapping her hand around the neck of the man behind her, while her other hand clawed at the chest of the man below her. It was moments later when the women screamed her release, shuddering against the two as she did.

"Sex can bring more than pain, Leawyn," Xavier dropped his hand away from her chin. She watched as the two men pulled out of the spent woman, the one below her holding her close to his chest as he stood up with her in his arms, uncaring of his nakedness. "It can bring pleasure too."

Leawyn tore her gaze away from the couple and looked into Xavier's eyes.

There was a message there in those dark orbs of his. For her.

A message she wasn't ready to accept.

Leawyn broke first, looking back down at her plate. She ignored Xavier's chuckle of amusement and instead focused on finishing her food.

She couldn't get the girl's expression out of her head though.

It can bring pleasure too.

Leawyn shook the thought out of her mind and ate.

"You seem to find something over there awfully interesting, Cousin," Tristan commented lightly.

Leawyn paused, the goblet in her hand poised at her lips as she shot a look at Tristan. Noticing Tyronian's scowl and Tristan's amused smirk, she looked to the area where they were both staring at. It didn't take long for her to find what they were focusing on so intently and what had Tyronian so riled.

Namoriee, as promised, was serving the first half of the feast. Leawyn noted she looked beautiful wearing her deep blue dress embroidered with light browns and golds that complimented the girl's caramel skin and hazel eyes. It also seemed Leawyn was not the only one to take notice of the young girl's beauty.

Which was the problem.

Namoriee currently was in polite conversation whilst pouring ale in the cup of a man Leawyn never saw around the village before, which made her assume he was a visiting warrior from the other tribes.

Judging by his dark hair, brown eyes, and the armor he wore, he was a Siraces.

"Who is that?" Leawyn asked, finally taking a sip of her drink.

"Cantos," Xavier said shortly, his eyes flashing up briefly to look before turning his attention back on the half-eaten leg of boar on his plate.

"What's she even doing serving food and drink anyways?" Tyronian grumbled with a scowl as he watched them with narrowed eyes.

"She insisted. Said it was her 'duty,'" Leawyn quoted, glancing at Tyronian from the corner of her eye when he scoffed around his mug of ale. "I finally managed to convince her she would only serve the first half of the feast." She shrugged, breaking a piece of her bread and popping it in her mouth.

Leawyn gave a Tyronian a weary look when his fists clenched. She looked back to Namoriee.

Cantos had his hand wrapped around Namoriee's wrist as he smiled flirtatiously up at her. He said something to her that made Namoriee shake her head in refusal, turning away from him. Cantos grinned, and with a quick tug, an unsuspecting Namoriee was spun around. She stumbled, sprawling across his lap.

Yes. Cantos was definitely Siraces, Leawyn mused.

She gave a startled jerk in her seat when Tyronian stood up abruptly from his chair.

Three pairs of eyes followed Tyronian as he marched over to where Cantos and Namoriee sat. He stopped in front of them, and reached down, and with one sharp tug, he yanked Namoriee off Cantos's lap, pushing her behind him in one smooth motion. Cantos shot to his feet.

Tyronian and Cantos exchanged heated words before Tyronian shoved Cantos back down into his seat. The two men glared at each other a moment more before Tyronian escorted Namoriee away with a hand on her lower back.

Cantos went to his feet again and said something to Tyronian's back.

Leawyn gasped, eyes shooting up in shock when Tyronian spun around and sent his fist sailing into Cantos's chin.

The men cheered when the force behind Tyronian's punch caused Cantos to stumble back into the table, holding his hand against his now bloody lip.

Without another glance at the fallen man, Tyronian spun about and made his way back to them at the table, his hand clasped around Namoriee's wrist as he hauled her resisting form with him.

The men cheered and whistled in their approval.

The table was quiet save for Tristan's amused chuckled when Tyronian righted his chair and plopped down into his seat, pulling Namoriee onto his own lap. He made a show of tucking her securely into his side, and calmly resumed his eating.

"Come with me," Xavier ordered, standing from the table and offering a hand down to Leawyn.

She glanced nervously around them. "What about our guests?" she asked, placing her hand in his and rising from her chair.

"They'll be fine," Xavier dismissed, impatiently tugging her with him.

He nodded to Tyronian, who simply grinned after them, his arm thrown casually but possessively around Namoriee's waist to keep her close to him. Leawyn frowned at Namoriee's wide-eyed and uncomfortable expression, shooting her disapproving glare at Tyronian.

She rolled her eyes when Tyronian simply winked at her in response.

Leawyn had to quicken her steps, practically jogging to keep up with Xavier's long and determined strides.

"Xavier, I can't walk as fast as you," she panted. She narrowly avoided colliding into his back when he stopped suddenly and twisted around to face her. She squawked when he dipped his shoulder until it met her stomach. He quickly scooped her up and stood, gripping her around her thighs, and continued his walk as if she were no more than a sack of potatoes.

"Xavier!" Leawyn yelped, resting her hands against his lower back and pushing herself up. "Put me down!" She hit his back, her face blushing furiously at all the catcalls and whistles being thrown their way.

"Everyone is looking at us!" Leawyn hissed at Xavier in embarrassment. She squealed when he slapped her bottom.

"Quiet," he ordered.

"Xavier—" Leawyn yelped again when his palm smacked against her backside once more. This time harder.

"Ow!" she complained. "Stop doing that!"

"Then be quiet," he said smugly. He chuckled when Leawyn just growled in annoyance at him in return.

Opening the door to their hut with one hand, Xavier ducked down and kicked the door closed. He flipped Leawyn over his shoulder and tossed her onto the bed in one smooth motion. His smile was dark with male intent as she scooted backwards, wide-eyed.

"Take off your clothes," Xavier ordered, already in the process of unbuckling the straps of his leather shoulder guards. His chest was bare when he reached for the ties of his breeches.

Leawyn's eyes followed the movement of his hands. The fabric around his waist fell to the ground in a heap. She stared when his erection sprang free and slapped lightly against his defined abdominals.

"Clothes, Leawyn," Xavier reminded, placing one knee down on the bed and boxing her in with his arms, surrounding her as he looked down to catch her blue eyes with his brown.

Leawyn let out a shaky breath as she slowly reached up with both hands and unclasped the dress behind her neck. Heat flowed through her, traveling up her chest and neck when Xavier's eyes stayed fixated on her as the dress opened and spilled her breasts free for his gaze to devour.

His head dipped, and she let out a startled gasp when his tongue flicked out against her pebbled nipple before he took it into his mouth. Her eyes fluttered closed at the sensation. His tongue continued giving attention to her nipples while his mouth continued to suckle her mounds with soft, sure, pulls.

She let out a little moan of disappointment when Xavier pulled away with a soft *pop*. He reached for her, one hand on her lower back and the other gripping her inner thigh. He jerked her forward so her legs draped over his broad shoulders.

"What are you...?"

Leawyn's eyes bulged and her mouth gaped open in a silent moan when Xavier immersed his head between her creamy thighs and spread her open, giving one long lick straight up to her clit.

"Oh, Gods!" Her hips bucked involuntarily against Xavier's mouth. His beard scratched her thighs and against her nether lips, which only amplified the pleasure.

"You taste so good," he murmured against her between lapping at her slick folds. "I've been wanting to taste you. You're so sweet against my tongue."

Leawyn whimpered.

Slowly, she leaned back until her body met the sheets, her legs falling open, creating more space for Xavier to bury his face in between her curls. Leawyn wasn't sure if this kind of talk was normal, but with each whispered word he said against her, heat flashed through her and made her more wet.

She liked this dirty talk.

"You're so wet for me," Xavier said, pulling his head back and Leawyn's arm shot out, reaching down into his long hair to try and keep his head right where it was. He chuckled huskily.

"Don't worry, I'm not going anywhere. I'm going to stay until your cream coats my tongue."

Xavier lowered his head again, and pulled Leawyn's bundle of nerves into his mouth once more, and sucked. Hard.

She gave a breathy moan in response, her legs shaking from the swift pleasure of it. He slid his hands underneath her thighs and jerked her up against him until her ass met his chest.

He kept her hips angled toward his mouth as they bucked involuntarily with every stroke of his tongue. He alternated between flicking her nub with his tongue and sucking on it until finally, he slipped his finger inside her soaked entrance and curled it upwards.

It was incredible. Leawyn couldn't hold back her cry even if she tried.

"Xavier!"

He hummed against her in encouragement, his fingers pumping in and out of her in a steady rhythm. He made his tongue flat, licking her cleft continuously and rapidly.

Between his fingers buried inside her and his continuous licks and nibbles against her nub, it didn't take long for Xavier to bring her to orgasm.

As she screamed her release, her hands tugged relentlessly on his hair as he lapped up her juices until there was none left.

Slowly, Leawyn broke through the fog of pleasure, blinking her eyes open to see Xavier now on his knees above her, one of his fists stroking his engorged cock with smooth, sure strokes.

"Open," he ordered gruffly, reaching his hand out and tangling it in her hair gently. He gave her locks a light tug, guiding her mouth until her lips almost brushed against the silky head. She noticed the small beads of fluid on the tip.

Leawyn looked apprehensively at his member, then up at him. Xavier's hooded eyes met her gaze, and she noticed his breathing was slightly ragged. He brushed his fingers through her hair, smoothing the errant strands away from her face. He trailed a finger down her cheek in an almost gentle caress once before fisting his hands back in her hair and holding her head steady.

"Open your mouth, Leawyn," Xavier growled. His arousal was prominent, the blood flowing through his member making it hard and thick. The veins woven on the underside of it like bulging vines on a tree.

Leawyn hesitated.

She'd never done anything like this before. She knew what her husband expected from her. He wanted her submissive and willing. If she wasn't submissive, it would be painful and rough. If she submitted, it would be gentle and almost pleasurable.

But this...was this normal?

Leawyn licked her bottom lip nervously. Her eyes shot up, startled when Xavier let out a small groan at the action.

"Leawyn..." he gasped. His breath coming out in quick and ragged breaths, his muscles taut and straining with need.

"Open your mouth. Now."

Otherwise, he'd do it for her.

Xavier gripped his cock, slowly brushing the head against her lips, swiping it back and forth against them, coaxing her. The precum made her lips sparkle from the moisture, and it drove him crazy with want. He pushed harder against her mouth, nudging her lips open bit by bit with his persistent thrusts until—finally—her lips pulled apart and the head was inside her mouth.

"Good girl," Xavier panted in relief, his hooded eyes watching her. "That's my good girl. Now, use your tongue," he ordered, and Leawyn, still looking unsure and nervous, tentatively swiped her tongue on the underside of him and around his sensitive head.

Xavier grunted, his thrusts faltering at the sensation. He gave her time to adjust; he could see she was nervous and scared. But he could also see she was aroused; it was clear in the glazed look in her eyes.

The knowledge that Leawyn was his—truly his—made him want to roar in triumph.

No one had seen her the way he had.

No one could touch her like him. No one could shove their cock so far down her mouth until she choked, lips stretching tight as he thrusted inside her slim, elegant, throat.

She was *his*.

Xavier gripped her hair tighter, making it so only he could control her movement. He thrust his hips toward her mouth, and at the same time he pulled her forward, he pushed his cock downward until he could feel it touch the back of her throat.

Leawyn gagged harshly, her eyes instantly watering and her hands flying to his hips to try and put some distance between them.

Xavier let out a guttural groan, and just when Leawyn was starting to panic, he pulled back. She gasped in relief, breathing deeply through her nose to try and catch her breath. He petted her head, swiping the loose tendrils away from her face and clenching them in his fist again in a loose ponytail.

"We're going to do that again, and this time, you're going to relax your jaw and suck."

Leawyn looked up at him with wide eyes. The slightly panicked glaze in her blue orbs made his cock twitch in anticipation. But he saw curiosity, too.

"You want to please me like I did you, Leawyn?" Xavier asked her. "You liked when my mouth was on you...licking you?" Her breath hitched, and the flash of heat in her eyes almost made him come right then.

"This is the same. Take me in your mouth, Leawyn," he panted, brushing himself against her lips again with his small thrusts. "Pull your pretty lips apart and take my cock. Let me watch you as you swallow it whole."

Leawyn shivered.

"Don't be scared; it will be good."

Slowly, she relaxed. She flicked her eyes up to Xavier, and he felt his jaw clench tight, his muscles taut with the strain of holding himself back. His wife looked down again, studying his thick arousal. He'd pulled the foreskin back, exposing its head with little clear beads of liquid seeping from the tip. It was long and thick for her, the veins interwoven as it arched upwards towards his stomach.

She finally looked back up at him. "Okay," she whispered, glancing down at his member again and then back up to him. "I'll do it."

Xavier sighed in relief, closing his eyes and swallowing against his suddenly dry throat. He would have had Leawyn suck him off anyways—with or without her consent; it was his right as her husband, after all.

But, some part of him wanted her to do this willingly.

He *wanted* her to want to do this for him, give him the pleasure of her mouth like he did with her. Xavier had pictured her lips wrapped around his cock since the first moment she'd spoken back to him all those months ago, standing tall with her blue eyes flashing defiance, blatantly daring him to disagree with her. He'd never seen anything more beautiful in his life.

It was in that moment he'd known he had to have her.

"Open wide, Leawyn—yes, just like that." Xavier sighed, his cock sliding in and out between her lips. His hand twitched in her hair, tightening and then releasing the long locks as he held her head steady. He groaned; the wet suckling noises she made as she took his cock made him want to push in deeper, and he did.

Leawyn gagged around him each time he pushed a little too deep, her hands flying up to his hips to try and ease him back.

"So good," Xavier groaned as he avidly watched his member slide in and out of her mouth. He used the grip he still had on her hair to arch her to him, neck bared.

"Keep your mouth open," Xavier ordered, barely giving her enough time to do as he said before he was thrusting into her mouth completely, his hips bumping her chin with each quick movement. Her eyes watered from the force, and her throat constricted around him each time he thrust deep, making her gag and cough, which only served to spur him on.

"I love that you gag around me. I can feel your throat constricting, and it's amazing. My wife is sucking me so good that I'm going to come, and you're going to be a good girl and swallow every bit of it," he ordered. He didn't give Leawyn time to comprehend his words before he was thrusting as deep down into her throat he could go. He let out a deep, drawn-out groan as he came spurting down her throat.

Leawyn swallowed his hot liquid down, choking at the suddenness of it. Some of it dribbled down the side of her lips, and to Xavier, it was a beautiful sight. Slowly, he withdrew from her mouth, his body still shaking from the aftermath of his climax.

He cupped her jaw, swiping his thumb under her lip as he tilted her head up to meet his sated eyes. "Good girl."

At the praise, Leawyn's cheeks—which were already rosy in color —grew brighter.

When no other words were spoken, she rolled off the pallet, clutching her dress to her chest as she made her way to her things.

She was just about to grasp her nightgown when Xavier pressed himself against her back, nuzzling his nose along her neck as he caged her in with his arms on either side of her. Her eyes fluttered closed when he inhaled deeply. He reached his hand up and swiped her hair to the side so his lips brushed her heated skin.

"We're not done," he whispered huskily against her ear before he swung her around to face him and hauled her back up into his arms.

She gasped, instinctively wrapping her legs around his waist. Using one hand to hold her up under her bum, Xavier reached with his other and tangled it into her hair as he kissed her.

His tongue brushed against her bottom lip before diving into the crevice of her mouth. Their tongues battled against each other as he carried her back to their bed. Bracing himself with one arm, he lowered her onto her back without breaking the kiss.

Leawyn moaned breathlessly against Xavier's mouth when he touched her breast, palming it. She tilted her head to the side as he rained kisses and nips from her lips down to her chin and neck.

"Xavier—ah!" she gasped when he nipped where her neck met her shoulder. "Please," she begged, clawing at his back.

"Please what, Leawyn?" he mumbled against her skin, flicking his tongue out against the mark he just left, causing her to shudder. "Tell me what you need."

She whimpered when he started to slowly thrust against her. He was already hard for her again, and he brushed his arousal against her most sensitive area. "Tell me." He pulled away from her neck, looking down into her blue eyes that were flushed with her arousal. Her mouth dropped open in a silent moan when he brushed against her main source of pleasure with a particularly hard thrust.

"What do you want?" Xavier whispered raggedly.

She grabbed the back of his neck, fingers twirling around his hair, and brought her face up so her lips brushed against his with each word she spoke. "You," Leawyn whispered, her eyes lifting to meet his. "I want you."

Xavier's gaze softened, his body relaxing against her as he pressed into her. His hips arched back and slid forward, slowly filling her, going as deep as he could go.

Their gaze stayed locked as he set a slow rhythm, his hips thrusting into her at a leisurely tempo.

They took pleasure in each other's bodies the rest of the night until they were spent, and both collapsed with exhaustion in the early morning light.

33

Weeks passed since the feast, and the Izayges people grew accustomed to having the extra bodies of the Asori and Siraces men in the village. But with the extra population came more mouths to feed and more chores.

Since the feast, Leawyn and Xavier hadn't had much time together during the day. They were too busy with their respective duties of running a village. Xavier was kept busy with council meetings. He wouldn't tell Leawyn what they were discussing, but it wasn't hard for her to figure out it had to do with her people being slaughtered.

Leawyn kept busy with the responsibilities as the lady chief, overlooking the day-to-day activities in their village. Most days, with Xavier gone, she took over the responsibility of holding court, hearing and settling disagreements within the tribe. On other days, she could be found helping out wherever she was needed, whether it be preparing the nightly meals, or doing laundry.

She found herself with her fellow tribe women down at the river bank washing clothes when Namoriee came to her early in the morning—hand clasped tight around the wrist of young girl about the age of twelve winters—explaining how she would be unable to help the other women with the laundry today because of a fever she had.

The girl was clearly scared of Leawyn's reaction and fruitlessly tried to deny what Namoriee said, insisting she was well enough to do her chores. Leawyn took one look at the girl and could clearly see she was indeed very sick. She insisted the girl spend the day resting, and offered to take her place. The look of shock that covered the girl's face was comical.

Hours later, Leawyn, Namoriee, and various other women of the tribe were all spread out up to their knees in the water as they scrubbed the dirty articles of clothing against the rocks.

Leawyn stood up, sighing tiredly. Swiping the back of her arm against the sweat on her brow, she glared against the sun. "Why must you be so bright?" she grumbled to herself.

It was a particularly hot day. The sun was bright and shining down on them all, and the few times they were lucky enough to feel a breeze, it was warm.

"It's not that bad. You're just not used to working in the sun without a nice ocean breeze," Namoriee teased, shaking out the shirt she was washing and placing it in the floating basket beside her.

"Well, that's true." Leawyn grinned back at her.

"Last summer was the worst, Lady Chief," Tana, a woman in her early fifties with hair streaked with white, commented on the other side of Leawyn.

"Really?"

"Oh yes." Tana nodded as she scrubbed a pair of breeches rather viciously against a rock on a particularly dirty spot around the knees. "It was a day like this, but with heat heavy in the air. Each breath you took was as if you were drinking steam. Quite a few women got sick."

"That sounds miserable," Leawyn frowned.

Tana nodded in agreement. "It was, Lady Chief."

"I hope it's not like that this summer. Otherwise you'll have to manage the laundry without me!" Leawyn teased. "I'm already hot as it is."

"Would you like to cool down, Lady Chief?" Garnette, who was there helping her mother, Micka, asked innocently in her sweet, child voice.

"I would to love cool down, Garnette," Leawyn smiled over at her.

"Okay." Garnette grinned mischievously, and—before her mother could stop her—she scooped up water with her hands and threw her arms forward, splashing Leawyn.

All the women stilled, holding their breath.

Leawyn looked down at her soaked front in shock, strands of her hair sticking to her face. Slowly, she looked up to Garnette, who seemed to have realized her playful action wasn't the best idea.

"Oh, you're going to get it now!"

It was the only warning Garnette received before Leawyn hauled her into her arms and tossed her away from her. Garnette let out a little squeal right before she sunk into the water.

Garnette reappeared with a gasp, blinking against the water in her eyes as she wiped her face. "Not fair!" she shouted, swimming her way back to them.

"Is too!" Leawyn laughed, matching the glare on Garnette's face mockingly.

"That was a mature response, Leawyn," Namoriee snickered. "Garnette, you still have clothes to wash."

Leawyn and Garnette looked at each other, before turning their attention back to Namoriee. The matching grins on their faces made Namoriee instantly nervous. "Don't you dare," Namoriee warned them.

It was too late.

Leawyn and Garnette charged Namoriee—Garnette letting out a mighty battle cry as she did—and tackled the handmaiden into the water.

It was a good many hours later before the all-out water war ended, and the women continued their work.

"You're sure?" Yoro asked. He looked to Xavier, who stood across from him.

Xavier met Yoro's eyes and nodded.

Xavier, Tristan, and Tyronian, along with Yoro and Kisias, had their most trusted men in their war councils gathered around a large wooden table. They were all looking down at a massive map sprawled out in front of them.

"It had to have been someone who knew the land," Xavier said, frowning gravely. "Likely a member from Rhoxolani, or someone who was familiar with that landscape."

"It's the only way that makes sense," Tristan agreed.

The room fell silent. Lost in their own thoughts.

It was a troubling thought indeed. To think the destruction of the Rhoxolani tribe was done from within.

"If what you say is true, and the Rhoxolani had a traitor in their midst, then we're all in danger." Kisias sighed. His expression was apologetic when he met Xavier's gaze. "These are troubling times. We were wrong to doubt you."

Yoro hummed in agreement, frowning in thought at the map below him. "When did you say was the last time you came across this army?"

Xavier shared a look with Tyronian and Tristan.

"Few months back. They captured a child from my tribe...and my wife."

Yoro and Kisias snapped their heads up to stare at Xavier. "They captured your wife and a child? Here?"

Xavier shook his head, holding back his smirk. "No. My wife followed them and managed to get the child to safety by sending her off on her horse before she was captured as well."

Kisias and Yoro both raised an eyebrow, which caused Tyronian to chuckle under his breath, and Tristan to grin.

"Your wife went after the girl?" Yoro said slowly, not quite believing it.

"She's very..." Xavier searched for the right the word to describe Leawyn. "Stubborn."

Tyronian snorted.

"Most women are," Kisias agreed.

"How would you know? You haven't had a woman in years."

Yoro dodged the punch Kisias aimed at him, the men around them snickering.

"I'm a Siraces. I have lots of women!" Kisias defended, spreading his arms out to his side proudly, grinning. "Look at me!"

"We are. That's why we don't believe you," Tyronian said dryly. The men around the table burst into more laughter.

Xavier held his hand up, and the room slowly quieted and gave him the attention he commanded.

"I know not when they will attack, or how many their numbers are," Xavier said seriously. "But I do know they're smart, and deadly. It's not a matter of 'if' they will attack again, but when." He met the eyes of the men around him, the severity of his tone registering with them all. "We *need* to be prepared."

Yoro and Kisias looked at each other again. "We are with you," Yoro told him, speaking for them both. "What will you have us do?"

Xavier hid the relief on his face and leaned forward so both his hands braced the edge of the table. "Keep a lookout. Scout your areas every day and night, focusing on these places." He pointed to the areas on the map. "Don't travel alone, try to keep everyone inside your village. Assign guards if they travel outside the borders."

Xavier stopped and looked around to make sure they understood what he was saying. Seeing he still had their attention, he continued. "At the end of each week, we will report to each other and compare our findings."

"How will we send word?" Tyronian asked.

"It's too dangerous using horseback." Xavier paused. "Use your birds to give the message."

Yoro and Kisias nodded in agreement.

"Then what?" Tristan asked, frowning at Xavier. "Even if we do all these things, that doesn't change the fact one of us will be attacked by them. How will we be any different than the Rhoxolani?"

Murmurs of agreement went around the room.

"We need to know where they're coming from. We can't do anything without knowing where they are, and having all the tribes in one place is too dangerous. They *want* that, but it might be the only way to draw them out."

"Then what?" Yorick, one of Kisias's men, spoke. "We wait

for them to attack us? Like sitting ducks?" The man scoffed in disbelief. "I say we strike now, and hard. Let them dread the day they tried to go against Samaria!" Yorick slammed his fist on the table with his point, the men from his tribe riling behind him.

Tristan narrowed his eyes at Yorick, while Tyronian stiffened. Xavier's facial expression however, remained smooth, not relaying his growing ire.

"Tell me, Yorick," Xavier leveled him with his stare. "How many battles have you fought?"

"He's always fighting!"

Yorick grinned at Kisias's joke.

"That's not what I asked," Xavier said lowly, silencing the room. "How many battles have you fought?"

Yorick paused, his body stiffening. Though Xavier's question seemed harmless, Yorick reacted to the tension that suddenly filled the air.

"Well?" Xavier asked sharply.

"None."

"None," Xavier's voice was soft but deadly. It carried a heaviness that was palpable, as if each vowel could strike out and draw blood at any given moment. The atmosphere in the room dropped in an instant by the presence that was Xavier. "Killed a man?"

Yorick's Adam's apple moved as he swallowed loudly. Gone was the cocky man he was before, and instead stood a man who sensed danger when it loomed before him. "No."

Xavier rose slowly, keeping Yorick ensnared with eyes, reflecting the great warrior he was.

"I have killed many men. Boys too, much like yourself."

Yorick tensed at Xavier's softly spoken threat. Sweat slowly beaded across his temple and slid down the side of his cheek.

"I could sever your head clean off your shoulders with a flick of my wrist before you even saw it coming," Xavier growled. "And while your head was too busy falling to the ground in a bloody heap, I would have already had three more deaths to my name."

Try as he might, Yorick couldn't hold back from flinching when Xavier suddenly moved so that they were nose to nose.

"I could do all this easily, and without remorse. Because I have killed my entire life."

Xavier stood suddenly, leveling his ferocious glare to every man in the room. "Izayges have protected you for years. We protected you against foes you didn't even realize you had. Our blood soaks the ground you all step on, all for the sole reason yours doesn't."

Xavier turned his attention to Yoro and Kisias, who were both stiff. "My men are the deadliest on this earth. I've been in more battles than I could count. Never have I been beaten, and never have I been caught unaware. Until now." He turned his heated gaze down to the map on the table spread out in front them.

"Until this army."

Xavier looked back up to his fellow leaders. "We need to be prepared. We need to *plan,* and when the time is right—we need to strike. Hard and fast. Because if we don't," Xavier paused, his brows furrowing together as he met the eyes of every man in the room. "There will be no more Samaria. Only echoes of our despair will remain as our bones turn to dust."

It was silent, each man processing the foreboding outcome Xavier envisioned to themselves.

It was Yoro who broke the heavy silence. "What's your plan, Chief Xavier?"

"Are you sure you're all right, Lady Chief?" Namoriee frowned down at Leawyn, who was in the same position she found her in—huddled up under a blanket on her bed pallet.

"You look sickly. I think I should get the healer." Namoriee worried her lip between her teeth, her eyes concerned.

Leawyn did feel sickly. Her normally lightly tanned skin was now a shallow pale white. Her slight frame was every so often wracked with shivers as if she were cold, but she was hot and sweaty.

Her symptoms pointed to fever. "I'm fine, Namoriee," Leawyn all but croaked out, which did not help to alleviate Namoriee's worry in the slightest. If anything, her handmaiden looked even more concerned. "I think the heat just got to me today."

Namoriee's frown deepened, unconvinced.

"Lady Chief— "

"Leawyn," she corrected in a halfhearted mumble, which caused Namoriee to roll her eyes in response.

"Fine, Leawyn," Namoriee amended wryly. "You need to see the healer."

Leawyn shook her head, pulling the blanket higher up on her shoulders and closing her eyes. "I just need to rest. I'll feel better then."

Namoriee's mouth opened to respond, but she was interrupted by Leawyn's hut door opening.

Namoriee tensed when Tyronian's tall, blond frame ducked through and closed the door behind him. He caught her eyes when he turned to face them, and his lips pulled up in a smirk.

"Ah, my two favorite beautiful ladies—just who I wanted to see!" Tyronian said jovially as he made his way to them. "I've come to escort you to the feast. Xavier is a bit indisposed at the moment."

Namoriee turned away, looking down so her mop of brown hair covered her face and shielded her from his view. Tyronian's smirk broadened at the action, but he otherwise let it go. He turned his attention to Leawyn instead, and his smile immediately disappeared into a frown.

"You look terrible. You should see the healer."

"Not you too, Tyronian," Leawyn groaned tiredly. "I just got done telling Namoriee I was fine and needed *rest*. Which is the same thing I'll tell you." She shut her eyes when they became too heavy to hold open. "I need rest," she mumbled into her pillow.

"But, Lady Chief—" Namoriee started to protest.

"Enough!" Leawyn snapped, eyes popping open again with her frustration. "I'm fine, I just want to sleep!"

Namoriee shut her mouth and looked down while Tyronian tensed, eyeing Leawyn.

"Please," Leawyn said less sharply. "Just let me rest a moment, and I'll meet you out there."

"Yes, Lady Chief," Namoriee mumbled softly, giving her one last worried look before she turned to make her way from the hut and to the feast.

Namoriee's body tensed again when a warm hand grasped around her arm and drew her to a sudden stop.

"I'll walk with you," Tyronian said lightly, as he drew up beside her. Leawyn noticed he didn't give her much of a choice when he forcibly tucked Namoriee's arm into the crook of his elbow and guided her with him to the door.

"Sleep well, Leawyn," Tyronian called over his shoulder as he opened the door and ushered Namoriee out with a hand resting on her lower back.

The distant sounds of loud laughter and chatter floated into Leawyn's hut for a briefly before the door closing instantly silenced it.

Leawyn sighed in relief as she burrowed deeper into the comforts of her bed.

A few moments later, she was sound asleep.

The farewell feast was already well underway when Xavier emerged from the meeting hut. His muscles ached from being in a slouched position as he went over the plan for hours. He wanted to make sure they didn't miss anything, and they were prepared to have a course of action if they did.

Hours and hours Xavier stood over the map. He thought over every angle and possibility, and something didn't sit right with him. The idea of asking Leawyn if she knew someone within her tribe who could have been a traitor crossed his mind multiple times. But each time it surfaced, he quickly pushed the thought away. But still...something felt wrong.

Xavier growled under his breath in frustration.

"Hungry, or angry?" Tyronian asked in amusement.

Xavier hesitated for a moment, the move barely distinguishable, before he sat down at the table, his mug instantly filled with ale by a serving girl.

Xavier glanced at Tyronian out of the corner of his eye. He hid his smirk around his cup as he took a deep pull of the pale liquid inside.

Namoriee was, once again, perched on Tyronian's lap, looking as uncomfortable as ever as Tyronian softly twirled a strand of her chocolate hair. His arm wrapped tight around her waist to anchor her there.

Xavier frowned, lowering his mug down on the table. Namoriee was there but...

"Where is my wife?"

Namoriee stiffened in Tyronian's lap at Xavier's growl. Tyronian's hands paused before he continued to stroke his fingers through her hair, as if to soothe her.

Xavier gritted his teeth when no one answered him.

He turned his full attention to Namoriee, who seemed to shrink into herself under his gaze. "Why isn't she here, and why aren't you with her?"

"I-I was b-but..."

Xavier's impatience with her halted answer was evident, which seemed to make Namoriee more frazzled.

"I stole Namoriee away from my dear cousin earlier when they were in your hut," Tyronian drawled, calmly turning his attention to Xavier. "She's probably still there."

Xavier's expression darkened. He stood from his chair and looked down at the sixteen-year-old. "Your job is to be with her. I can easily find someone else to replace."

"Yes, C-C-Chief Xavier," Namoriee whispered, quickly looking down so her hair hid her face. Tyronian's grip around Namoriee's waist tightened.

Xavier turned back to Tyronian. "The second your little obsession interferes again—she's gone."

"Perhaps you should look after your own little obsession better then, instead of bullying mine," Tyronian replied coldly, his heated stare steady with Xavier's.

Namoriee sucked in a quick breath in shock.

Xavier ground his teeth together but said nothing in reply before he stormed off. He took long, angry strides towards his hut, his anger mounting with each step. He was still seething with anger when he burst into his hut. "Leawyn!" he bellowed angrily.

"Leawyn, where are you—"

Xavier froze at the sight before him before he quickly moved into action. "Leawyn!"

34

Leawyn stared out at the dark ocean, watching the white foam fly high into the air as the dark green waves crashed against the cliffs, the force of the collision creating a deafening boom akin to the sound of thunder.

It was hypnotizing to watch...the dance of the ocean.

It was a constant game of catch and release. The ocean water formed into a great wave, recklessly charging up to the jagged cliffs, unafraid of the doom that awaited. Then, when the wave slammed home, its foamy white water flying in all directions, the calm current would gather the destruction in its watery, comforting arms. Over and over, the daring and heart-breaking cycle would repeat.

Catch and release. Catch and release.

It comforted Leawyn to sit and watch the playful but deadly dance. It was why she often found herself sitting in this exact spot, in this exact position, when her mind was troubled and her emotions too strong for her to hold.

Here, on the cliffs. Watching the waves with her knees pulled up to her chest, she hugged her legs with her arms as she rested her cheek against her knees. Her hair blew playfully behind her, the golden locks catching the light of the moon as it whipped and twirled in the wind.

The salty air stung her cheek as the single tear spilled over it before being swept away.

She felt so alone.

Leawyn's throat burned from the effort it took not to let the sob caught in her throat break free. She needed to be strong.

Her people needed her to be strong.

But...they were dead. How could she be strong for people who no longer existed? Whose only evidence was their blood staining the ground and bones turning to dust or being feasted upon by the wilderness?

"Why?" Leawyn whispered to herself, her question caught in the wind, floating soundlessly before it was carried off and drowned out by the symphony of the ocean.

"Leawyn?"

Leawyn swiped her fingers across her cheeks quickly to rid the evidence of the few tears that managed to escape before she looked over at Asten behind her.

He was frowning down at her, concern in his eyes. "Are you alright?"

On instinct, Leawyn started to nod, but then she really thought about the question. The image of her father's head on a spike, surrounded by the decaying bodies of her village flashed before her eyes, and her eyes instantly flooded with tears again. She shook her head.

"No," she answered softly, her voice clogged with emotion. "I don't think I'll ever be all right again, Asten."

Asten's face transformed with his compassion, and he instantly went to her, wrapping his strong arms around her shoulders and pulling her in close. His hand cupped Leawyn's cheek, and he held her against his chest as the sobs she tried so desperately to hold in broke free.

"They're gone," she gasped, her body shuddering with the force of her sorrow being released. "They're all gone. Brees...my father...I'll never see them again."

Asten held Leawyn tighter at her words, but offered no words of comfort. Instead, he let her discharge her grief in the way she needed as she clutched his tunic in a tight fist and her tears soaked it through.

"How could anyone do this? Why would anyone do this?" Leawyn pulled away slightly to look up at Asten.

His eyes darkened with an emotion she didn't quite understand, but before she could comment on it, it disappeared. She thought maybe she imagined it.

The pad of Asten's callused thumbs met her cheeks as they wiped away her tears. His thumbs went on to caress her cheekbone, before moving down her jaw and—Leawyn's breath hitched—her lips.

Lust flared in his gaze as he watched his thumb swipe back and forth on the bottom of her lip. The top of his nail briefly dipped into her mouth as he pressed down, testing the plumpness there.

"Leawyn..." Asten inhaled through his nose sharply, his eyes never leaving her lips as he continued to play with them. "I want to kiss you."

She sucked in a sharp breath, her mouth dropping open.

His eyes shot up to hers at the sound. His breathing was irregular as he said, "I know it's wrong. You're hurting, and you saw something you had no business seeing, but..."

Asten looked down to her lips again, and the heat Leawyn was still so unused to seeing in his eyes flared again.

"But even though what happened was horrible, I can't help but think about how it brought you back to me."

Asten brought his hand up to be buried in Leawyn's hair. Holding her steady, he moved closer, and his eyes bored into hers. She could feel the heat of his breath with each word he spoke. "I'm going to taste those lips again. I have to."

Then his lips crashed onto hers...

Leawyn woke with a startled jerk when a hand slammed onto her lips, muffling her scream as she was pulled up by her hair and spun around.

"None of tha' now," a baritone voice said in her ear when she struggled against her captor. She froze immediately when she felt the cool steel of a blade being pressed against her throat.

"Now, you an' I are jus gonna wait here quietly 'till yer husband comes home. Aren't we, lovie?"

Leawyn gave a short, jerky nod. "Atta girl," he murmured against her ear. "Won't be long now. You've been sleeping for a long time. Poor dearie missed the start of the feast."

She closed her eyes, her breathing erratic against his hand still pressed to her lips as he held her. Though it was impossible for her to be able to get a look at the man by the way he was holding her in front of him, she could guess, even though he had to bend down to her ear when he talked, he wasn't as tall as her husband. He had a hard chest, and since he wasn't in armor, it meant the firmness she felt was made of solid muscle.

Leawyn flicked her eyes downwards. His wrist guards were made up of some type of leather she wasn't familiar with. It was dark brown in color, with small, jagged slits that held spikes from his wrist down. They looked as if they were made from animal bones that were filed to razor sharp points. Almost like talons. They held no notable tribe markings, which meant he was from *them*. Part of the army bent on destroying them.

The army that destroyed her village.

Filled with fury, Leawyn renewed her struggles with more vigor.

"You were doin' so good, lovie, why you'd have to ruin it, eh?" She heard him tut in exasperation in her ear, seemingly not at all phased with her fight. Leawyn screamed in frustration against his hand, which came out muffled, and she jerked her body wildly. She even went as far as to drop all her weight, hoping to unbalance him.

It didn't work.

All she managed to do was make him chuckle huskily in amusement as he lifted her higher in his arms.

"Nice try, sweetens. But tha' not gonna work with me. I was warned about yer spirit." Leawyn tensed with fear at his words. He was *told* she had spirit?

"Lucky ferya, I like me girls with some fight in them."

"*Leawyn!*"

They both stilled at her husband's cry.

"Ah, finally." The hand against her mouth pressed more firmly around her as he adjusted the grip he had on the dagger. He pulled her in closer so her ear was adjacent to his lips just as the door to the hut door burst open, slamming against the wall with a loud bang.

"Leawyn where are you—"

She watched her husband freeze in shock as he assessed the

picture they presented. Anger quickly ignited his eyes as he saw the dagger pressed into her skin. Along with something else.

Worry.

"Leawyn!"

She couldn't help it; her eyes instantly watered with tears as she met Xavier's furious gaze. His features smoothed to an expressionless mask that told Leawyn his warrior training was taking over.

"Chief Xavier, how nice of ya to come. We've been waitin' for ya."

Xavier's dark eyes locked on the person behind her, his face a picture of terrifying fury. "Let her go. Now," he growled lowly. The threatening tone made Leawyn shiver in both fear and relief.

"Why would I wanna do tha'?" Leawyn felt him chuckle against her back. "Me and Beauty here were just getting to know each other. Weren't we, Beauty?"

She flinched away when her kidnapper brushed his lips against her temple, tears of fear spilling over her cheeks. Xavier's eyes zeroed in on her tears, and if possible, he looked even more furious.

"Let her go now, and I might still let you keep your head." Xavier's growl was almost inhuman, it was so deep and guttural.

He kept his gaze on Leawyn's kidnapper, his insides feeling as if they were going to explode with his rage. Every fiber of his being wanted to charge at the bastard who dared to kiss *his* wife. His Leawyn.

Xavier almost lost it when he saw the tear slide down her cheek. A red haze was slowly clouding his vision, making him irrational, which was something he couldn't let happen. He couldn't afford to let his emotions cloud his judgment. He needed to be the warrior he was known to be. *Leawyn* needed him to be the warrior he was known to be.

Cold.

Calculating.

Ruthless.

He needed to not be the man who was seized with an ungodly fear for his wife's safety.

Trouble was, Xavier needed this man alive. He needed answers.

"Who are you?" Xavier growled out, slowly starting to circle his prey. His eyes never wavered from the man who held Leawyn as he mimicked his movements, dragging her along with him each step of the way.

"Me names' nay important, but—for courtesy's sake—you can call me Hiinex." Hiinex grinned back at Xavier. Xavier studied him silently.

Hiinex couldn't have been much older than Tristan and Tyronian. He was lean with solid muscles. His hair was an interesting mix between copper brown and black, with a shadow of stubble along his angular jaw.

Though his face looked young, and had lines from laughter, Xavier saw the calculation in his multicolored eyes that was a glimpse of the warrior within. That look alone put Xavier's guard up. Hiinex was a seasoned warrior, and that meant he wasn't just some foot soldier sent for the suicide mission of testing the waters.

He held importance, and a mission.

"Why are you here?" Xavier barked out, his voice noticeably more demanding as he stopped his slow prowl, which in turn made Hiinex stop as well.

Xavier positioned them so Leawyn was closest to the hut's door while Hiinex and himself were parallel to each other and the fire pit that dominated the middle of the room. His hope was Hiinex would throw Leawyn aside, directly beside the door, before he attacked him.

In Xavier's mind, Hiinex hadn't hurt Leawyn thus far, which made him believe the man wouldn't condemn her to the pain of flames eating her flesh and would instead choose to throw her to the safer option: the door.

It would give Leawyn just enough time to escape and for Xavier to disarm Hiinex. Judging by the look in Hiinex's eyes and the slow grin tugging the corner of his lips, he knew exactly what Xavier had planned.

It also proved Xavier's hunch. Hiinex was a seasoned warrior.

"This is gon' be fun, I can tell." Hiinex chuckled, his knowing eyes bright with amusement.

"Last chance," Xavier said over Hiinex's humor. "Why are you here?"

"All in good time," Hiinex replied. Dipping his head, he whispered to Leawyn. "You really are a beauty, sweets. Excuse me poor form, but I canna resist any longer."

It was the only warning she got.

Hiinex dropped his hand an inch from her mouth, tilted her jaw to him, and smashed his lips onto hers—tongue and all—before Xavier's enraged roar shattered the moment.

Tearing his mouth from hers just in time, Hiinex gave Leawyn a hard push away from him as Xavier crashed into his body, lifting him clean off his feet and slamming him down on the ground.

"You dare kiss my wife!" Xavier bellowed in fury as he pinned him to the ground and immediately brought his enclosed fist down onto Hiinex's face with a quick, hard, jab.

Blood instantly burst from Hiinex's nose and covered Xavier's hand as he broke the bone. Xavier pushed aside the arm Hiinex threw up to block his punch effortlessly, and landed another hard blow into the soft flesh of Hiinex's cheek.

The assailant's head snapped to the side from the force, but he quickly recovered. Grabbing Xavier's shoulders, Hiinex yanked him down toward his face and slammed his forehead upwards in a hard head-butt.

The blow disoriented Xavier just enough for Hiinex to throw Xavier over his head with his leg. Once Xavier was thrown off, Hiinex catapulted his body up and onto his feet so he was once again standing upright.

Xavier pushed himself up quickly, bracing his body when Hiinex's shoulders slammed into his stomach, throwing him back against the table, which instantly broke under his weight. Xavier landed with a short grunt, his elbow flying up to block the right hook Hiinex sent his way.

"Xavier!" Leawyn screamed out in warning. Xavier snapped his head up, looking toward Leawyn at her scream. "Look out!" She pointed at the flash of metal in Hiinex's hand as he brought the dagger straight for Xavier's stomach.

"No!"

It happened in seconds.

Hiinex thrust the blade forward, but Xavier hollowed himself out, ducking his head as he did so, and blocked the knife using the back of both his arms. One hand hooked around Hiinex's elbow, and Xavier used his grip to pull Hiinex toward his chest. The attacker fell forward, his only free arm slamming on the ground to try and catch his balance. He let out a pained scream when Xavier stomped on his hand with a heavy boot. In quick succession, Xavier jerked his knee up into Hiinex's temple, knocking him out.

The knife clanged to the floor when Xavier dropped Hiinex and stepped back, wiping the blood out from under his nose with the back of his hand as he did. After kicking the knife away, Xavier looked up and caught his wife's eyes. Leawyn sobbed once.

It took three long strides.

The first step, he was in front of her. The second, he had his hands on her cheeks in a tight grip, keeping her captive.

By the third, he had her pushed against the wall, his lips slanted against her own in a searing kiss.

Leawyn whimpered into his mouth desperately, throwing her hands around his neck and clutching him closer to her as her tongue dueled with his. The kiss spoke volumes. Pouring everything they were feeling into the contact.

Fear.

Anger.

Relief.

Need.

The kiss said it all. It was the words they were unable to speak, both to themselves...and each other.

Leawyn gasped for breath when Xavier broke the kiss, pulling away from her slightly to look down at her. "Are you hurt?" he asked, his voice laced with quiet urgency.

Her nails bit into his shoulders as his hands tightened on her cheeks. He forced her head back and away from his lips as his eyes roamed over her form. "Answer me!" Xavier shook her chin, catching her eyes when they flew up to his.

"Did he hurt you?" Xavier gritted out beneath clenched teeth. His body was wound tight with anger and worry for her.

"No," Leawyn whispered huskily, her voice thick with tears and fear. "No, he didn't hurt me. I just...he had a knife," she said shakily. "Oh Gods," she gasped out, her eyes growing wide as the shock slowly wore off and realization hit. She looked from the knife on the floor, then back up to Xavier's face, as if noticing for the first time how swollen and bloody he was.

"He had a knife! He could have—" Her eyes filled with tears and she cried once, running her hands down Xavier's sides. Feeling for blood.

"I'm fine," he said shortly, soothing her in his gruff way. "But he could wake up any minute. I need you to listen to me, okay?" He ducked down, making sure he held her eyes and that they were clear and not dilated with shock.

Xavier nodded his head in approval when Leawyn's blue eyes locked onto his with her undivided attention.

"You're going to go outside, find Tyronian or Tristan—whoever you see first—and you bring them here. You *do not* tell them what happened in front of anyone else, and you *do not* go anywhere else. You find them, and you bring them straight here," Xavier ordered sternly. She gulped at the vehemence in his tone.

"Do you understand me, Leawyn?"

She gave a quick jerk of her head to show that she understood. Xavier gave another nod of approval to her and dropped his hands from her shoulders, stepping back so Leawyn could go.

She shot a nervous look down to where Hiinex was as she stepped around Xavier and toward the door.

"Leawyn." He snagged her wrist as she went to slide past him. He stared at her for a long moment. She looked up at him, eyes unblinking, plump lips set in a grim and determined line.

"Be careful," Xavier said gruffly.

Leawyn's shoulders dropped some of their tension as her face smoothed over, the hard lines of fear and worry softening. Without any hesitation, she took the two steps needed to get close to him. Reaching up and placing her hand on his cheek, she pulled his head down as she went up on her tiptoes and placed her lips on his in a soft, tender kiss.

"You too," she whispered.

Xavier gave a subtle nod and Leawyn smiled softly, her fingertips trailing down his chin once before she turned away and hurried out of their hut.

He watched her go until a low groan brought his attention back to the body on the floor. Hiinex was waking up. Good.

Using his toe, Xavier kicked Hiinex onto his back. He felt his lips pull back in a sinister grin.

He had some questions that needed answering.

eawyn tried not to show her urgency by running, but she
did not think she succeeded. The pace of her fast walk was
just a step away from a jog, as if she were a horse who
wanted to sprint, straining against the bit, but its master controlled
its pace.

In that moment, she vowed to herself the next time Deydrey
wanted to run, she wasn't going to hold her mare back.

Finally, she was amongst the crowd of her village and the visiting
warriors who were already well on their way to being inebriated.
Pushing her way through, she strained on her tiptoes to try and see
over the shoulders that blocked her, but between her short structure,
and the height Samaritan men seemed to be blessed with by the
Gods, it was a futile attempt.

At least it was until she caught a flash of blond hair from the
corner of her eye. Turning her head, she spotted Tyronian. He was
talking to Namoriee in what looked like an intimate discussion. His
arm was braced above her head against the wall of the hut Namoriee
was leaning against as she stared up at him. Tyronian's lips were
pulled down in a slight frown, and his brows were furrowed as he
dipped his head lower towards her eyes. She saw Namoriee's lips
move, and whatever she said caused Tyronian's face to harden, and
his jaw clenched as the muscle there jumped.

He looked like a wolf who was about to eat its prey, and poor
Namoriee was the meal.

"Tyronian!" Leawyn called out to him as she hurriedly pushed her way through the crowd.

Tyronian snapped his head around at the sound of Leawyn's call, his eyes scanning the crowd until they found hers. He frowned when he saw the distressed look on her face.

Tyronian met her halfway, placing his hands atop her shoulders as he looked down at her.

"Leawyn?" he asked, concerned. "Are you alright?"

She felt her eyes fill with tears before she stubbornly pushed them away. "Something happened. I... I'm not to tell you here," she said, glancing at the crowd around them nervously.

"Xavier needs you. I am to get you and Tristan and return with you both to our hut right away. You need to come *immediately*."

Tyronian's face twisted in worry, but he nodded to Leawyn, wrapping an arm around her shoulder and pulling her close in a one-armed hug.

"I will, don't worry. I'm not sure where Tristan went, but last I saw him he was over by his hut," Tyronian said, nodding his chin in that direction.

His eyes lifted to where he left Namoriee, and his expression grew stormy when he saw she wasn't there anymore. His lips pursed in anger and annoyance, but he returned his attention back to Leawyn.

"I'll walk you to Tristan's hut. We'll get him together and head over to Xavier."

Leawyn bit her lip, uncertainty filtering across her face. She thought about Xavier alone in the hut with Hiinex. About them fighting. Though she knew her husband was more than capable of handling himself, she worried about him being alone.

"No," Leawyn shook her head in disagreement. "You go to Xavier. He needs you, and I will go get Tristan."

He looked like he was going to argue with her, but she gave him a stern glare. "Go, Tyronian."

Tyronian blew out a frustrated breath from between his teeth, his hand running through his long blond hair and pulling at the ends. He groaned and looked back at Leawyn.

"Fine," he conceded. "But if Tristan's not there, you forget about him and go back to the hut."

Leawyn nodded. She tried to give him a small smile, but it came out more of a grimace. "Please, hurry," she whispered.

"I'm going now. Remember, if you can't find Tristan, come straight to me." At her nod, Tyronian gave her a chaste kiss on her head and quickly made his way in the direction of her hut.

She watched him go for a moment, then turned around and started to walk to Tristan's hut at a brisk walk. She dodged and weaved between the crowd, many of whom were drunk, fighting, and enjoying open displays of pleasure.

Finally, Leawyn reached her brother-in-law's hut, and without knocking, she pushed open the door and went inside.

"Tristan, Xavier needs you—"

Leawyn's words cut off immediately, and her mouth dropped open in shock.

The naked woman straddling a naked Tristan had her head thrown back and her eyes closed in pleasure as she bounced on top of him, moaning loudly.

Tristan had his hands on her wide hips, seeming to guide her up and down his shaft. His eyes cut to Leawyn's shocked ones, and she noticed surprise there for a moment before they cooled, and he gave her a smirk. He slid his hands down to the woman's bare bottom and gripped, spreading her cheeks.

When he pulled out and started to guide his erection into her ass, she quickly left the hut, slamming the door behind her.

Leawyn slumped against the door, trying to process what she just witnessed. Tristan just lay there and looked at her, almost as if he were daring her. Daring her to do *what* exactly, she didn't know. And when he started to guide himself into her...into *there*—

Leawyn shook her head to rid herself of the unwelcome thoughts and images that burned into her memory.

She needed to get back to her hut and check on Xavier.

Leawyn stilled.

Xavier said to get Tristan *or* Tyronian. Technically, Leawyn mused, she didn't have to get Tristan now, but.... she had come all this way. Sudden anger coursed through her. Xavier needed help, and as his brother and Xavier's second in command, he had responsibilities to this tribe.

Leawyn steeled her spine, cheeks flushing with anger, and turned right back around and barged back into Tristan's hut. They were still going at it, but this time Leawyn did not shy away. No. This time she marched right up the bed and stood before it.

"Get out," Leawyn said first to the woman. "Get dressed," she said next, looking at Tristan.

They both froze, the woman's eyes opening in shock to Leawyn's, her expression a bit startled. Leawyn didn't waste much time surveying the women, and only gave her a quick glance to see it was Kassia, the tribe's whore.

She turned her attention back to Tristan. "I need you to come with me. Right now."

He gave her a bland look and resumed giving his attention to Kassia, his hips thrusting up into her with a soft slap.

"Go away, Sister, I'm busy," Tristan dismissed.

Kassia looked from Tristan to Leawyn, and Leawyn could see the exact moment she decided to give her the same dismissal as her brother-in-law. Leawyn bristled.

"I'm not going to say this again—get up, and get *dressed.*"

They both froze at the tone of her voice—Leawyn herself was a bit surprised at the ferocity of it—and looked back up to her. At the look on her face, Kassia grew nervous, glancing back at Tristan as if to ask what to do.

Leawyn narrowed her eyes at her.

"I am Lady Chief of this tribe, and I'm in charge. You *do not* look to him for answers," Leawyn hissed angrily. "You do exactly what I tell you, *when* I tell you, and I'm telling you to *Get. Out!*"

The last sentence was said in a yell, and they both blinked at Leawyn with shock. Kassia seemed to snap out of it and quickly got off Tristan. Leawyn stepped out of the way so Kassia could gather her clothes. Throwing them on quickly, Kassia hurried to the door.

When the soft thud of the door closed behind her, Leawyn looked to Tristan, who was glaring up at her.

"Get dressed, Tristan," she growled angrily at him. She turned her back to avoid looking at something she had no desire to see again when he stood up.

"This better be good," he growled out in annoyance. "What's this about?"

Leawyn gritted her teeth, listening to the sounds of Tristan getting dressed. "I was held against my will in my hut, and Xavier was attacked—"

She was spun around, and suddenly she was looking up at Tristan, who held her tight. "What do you mean you were held against your will in your hut?" he yelled.

Leawyn shrugged herself out of Tristan's hold on her arm and glared up at him.

"Exactly what I just said. Xavier defeated him, of course, and now he's holding him captive. He told me to come get you and Tyronian and then come straight back."

Tristan yelled out a curse in their native tongue suddenly, and Leawyn jumped. "Who else knows about this?" Tristan asked, his voice vibrating with anger.

"No one. Xavier told me not to speak to anyone and just come get you and Tyronian. I think..." Leawyn hesitated, her voice trailing off as she looked down. Tristan gripped her shoulders again and looked down to her.

"Tell me, Leawyn," Tristan asked softly, "what do you think?"

Leawyn bit her lip uncertainly, her eyes sad and vulnerable when she looked up at him. "I think there's a traitor in our tribe...and I think Xavier thinks so too," Leawyn finally whispered.

Tristan scowled darkly, but didn't disagree with her, which made Leawyn even more fearful. He grabbed her arm, urging them to the door of his hut. He paused and jerked open the door.

"Let's go," he said shortly and dragged her through. They set a brisk pace back to Leawyn's hut.

Leawyn couldn't resist. "So, is this important enough for you?"

Tristan's grunt assured her he was not at all amused with her sass.

"Anything?" Xavier asked as he entered the hut they reserved for prisoners and stopped beside his brother, staring at the spectacle in front of them.

Tristan's lips were pursed in a thin, angry line as he glared out in front of him. The room echoed with the wet smacking sounds made from flesh meeting flesh, pain-filled grunts, and air pushed harshly out of abused lungs.

Xavier narrowed his eyes, his fists clenching. He watched impassively as his cousin continued to rain blows on their prisoner. The cracking sound that assured a broken rib after a particularly hard jab caused a low, painful moan to leave the split and bloody lips of the man who was currently suspended with his arms high above his head.

"I'll ask again," Tyronian said lowly as he made a circle around his hostage. "Who sent you?"

Hiinex spit blood out of his mouth and coughed out a short laugh. "I don' hafta tell ye somethin' you already know," he wheezed. He lifted his head to meet Tyronian's hard glare.

Hiinex's left eye was swollen shut, the right eye looked to be following close behind, and his face was decorated with a collage of dark bruises. He had to blink against the blood the cut above his eyebrow gushed out in a steady stream.

"Who me am isn't important," Hiinex gasped, giving Tyronian a blood-filled grin. "What matters is your interrogation skills. 'Cause if this is all ye got...I'ma hafta wonder how you're going to protect your wee lass I saw you with earlier tonight."

Xavier and Tristan tensed along with Tyronian. He'd been watching them.

"A bit too ripe for me, but she is a beauty, so I'm sure she'll be sweet enough. Tell me, is she as pure as she looks? Or can I just dive in and taste her crea—"

Hiinex never got to finish his sentence. With a rage-filled yell, Tyronian charged him once again. In rapid succession, Tyronian's tightly closed fists met Hiinex's stomach and sides. The force behind the blows caused his body to sway against the ropes binding him.

"You don't talk about her, you bastard!"

When another *crack* sounded, Xavier stepped forward.

"Enough."

Tyronian paused with his fist raised. His broad shoulders heaved as he panted against his anger. With much difficulty, Tyronian stepped away when Xavier stepped forward to take his place. His murderous glare never left Hiinex.

Xavier looked at Hiinex with a cold expression. "Why are you here?"

Hiinex closed his eyes, breathing harshly. The slight wheezing sound he made when he took a breath assured that multiple ribs were broken and it was a struggle to breathe.

"Answer me!" Xavier barked out, kicking Hiinex with his foot. He gasped in pain.

"You have...something...we want," Hiinex gasped. His words choked out of him as he coughed until blood pooled inside his mouth. Tyronian and Tristan stepped forward, sharing a glance with each other. This was the most informative thing they'd gotten out of Hiinex yet. Xavier's eyes narrowed, his jaw clenching as he took another step toward him. He reached up and stilled Hiinex's swinging body by his neck.

"What do we have?"

Hiinex shook his head weakly, refusing to say more. Xavier growled low in his throat.

"WHAT. DO. WE. HAVE?" Xavier roared, shaking Hiinex in his impatience. When he continued to say nothing, he sneered in disgust and pushed Hiinex away from him.

"Kill him," Xavier ordered as he turned away to leave. "He knows nothing."

"Why don't you ask your wife?"

Xavier drew to a sudden halt; everything about him was tense when he slowly turned around to face Hiinex.

"What did you say?" Xavier breathed, his voice dark with a deadly combination of warning, disbelief, and fury.

Hiinex let out a humorless chuckle, which cut off into a coughing fit. He winced at the pain the action caused his broken ribs.

"I said, ask your wife," Hiinex finally managed to wheeze out, watching as Xavier slowly started his way back to him.

"What would Leawyn have to do with any of this? With you?" Xavier growled down at Hiinex when he was standing right in front of him again. Hiinex shook his head, his smug grin taunting that he knew something important Xavier didn't. Which he did—and that pissed Xavier off more.

"You're blind," Hiinex said. "You all are," he added, shooting a look over Xavier's shoulder at Tyronian and Tristan, who stood there with faces the picture of anger at Hiinex's accusation.

"That's why you're going to fail." He sneered up at Xavier.

"You're going to lose, and I'm going to enjoy watching you all die. *Especially* you," he glared at Xavier.

The air grew unbearably tense. Xavier bent forward, their face inches apart.

"You are nothing but a calf pretending to be a bull," he said, his voice dangerously low.

"You need to reevaluate your situation. You're bound, helpless, and the chances of you living through what I'm about to do to you are very, very, slim," Xavier promised darkly, his eyes filling with malice.

"But I can save you a slow and painful death, if you answer my three questions, and tell my cousin and brother here," he nudged his head behind him in the direction of where Tristan and Tyronian stood, "anything else they would like to know. Otherwise, I promise you, I'll strip you of your skin piece by piece. Now," Xavier held out his hand behind him, and Tristan stepped forward, pulling his dagger out from its hip holster as he did and placing it in his brother's outstretched hand.

"First question," Xavier said as he turned back to Hiinex and placed the dagger under his armpit. "Where is the army hiding?"

Hiinex met Xavier's eyes bravely, his face twisting up in a hateful sneer. "Fig're it out yerself."

"Wrong answer," Xavier growled, and without further warning, he smashed the dagger into the soft flesh and twisted. Hiinex jerked against the chains holding him up, but otherwise didn't make a sound except a long groan of pain.

Xavier yanked the dagger out swiftly, blood rushing to the surface and spilling down Hiinex's side.

"I'll ask again, where is the army hiding?" Xavier growled out. Hiinex stayed silent, shaking his head as sweat gathered heavily on his brow and lips. Xavier smirked and stabbed the blade back into Hiinex's body and dragged the dagger downward, cutting the flesh in a smooth line as blood splayed out of him and stained Xavier's shirt.

"Where?" Xavier asked calmly over Hiinex's muffled shout. But still, he didn't answer.

Xavier's eyes flashed, and the hand not holding the dagger into Hiinex's flesh reached up to where his skin protruded from the broken rib bone. Xavier quickly pushed against it, forcing the bone back in roughly.

Hiinex let out a terrifying pain-filled scream, jerking against the chains in his agony as his feet kicked out.

"Where is the army hiding?" Xavier yelled at Hiinex over his screams. "Tell me!" He jerked the dagger down and out, and with a quick flick of his wrist, a clean strip of Hiinex's flesh landed on the ground in a bloody mess.

Xavier stepped back from Hiinex as he slumped against the ropes, his body shuddering with agony and shock as blood continuously oozed from his wounds. As promised, the skin was completely flayed from underneath Hiinex's armpit all the way down to his ribs.

Xavier stared coolly at Hiinex, not at all fazed by his heaving breaths or the prisoner's blood that had gushed all over him.

"Where?" Xavier asked calmly.

Hiinex weakly lifted his head to meet Xavier's cold eyes.

"Just kill me," Hiinex said in a whisper, his breaths ragged and uneven as he spoke. "Because I'll never tell you."

Xavier looked upon Hiinex with grudging respect for his tenacity. But that didn't change anything. He needed answers.

Xavier tossed the dagger from hand to hand as he circled Hiinex. He would get the answers he needed, one way or the other. He was a man of his word, after all.

He raised his bloody knife again, and Hiinex's screams filled the air as Xavier tortured him.

For hours, Xavier did as promised and stripped Hiinex's skin off his body piece by piece.

The door slammed open with an almighty crash. Leawyn let out a short, startled scream and shot to her feet from the bed. Her mouth dropped open in shock at the sight of Xavier, who was covered with blood from head to toe, as he charged toward her with a murderous expression.

"Xavier, what—"

Leawyn choked on her words when he grabbed her around her throat with one hand and lifted her clear off her feet until her back slammed hard into the wall behind her. Her shocked cry of pain was short-lived when he squeezed her throat tight.

"What do you know?" He growled down at her, his eyes icy. "What did you do?!" he yelled, slamming her against the wall again and holding her up higher.

Leawyn's eyes bulged in shock and fear, her hands flying up to clasp Xavier's hand around her throat. "I don't know what—"

Xavier let out what could only be described as an animalistic growl as he pushed his weight into Leawyn.

"Don't you dare lie to me!"

Her eyes filled with tears of fear; she choked when his hand flexed around her slim throat. "Please!" She gasped.

"What did you do, Leawyn?" Xavier roared, enraged.

"I don't know what you're talking about!" Leawyn cried fearfully, clawing at his hands. "Xavier...please!" she begged, her tears streaking down her cheeks.

He stared coldly at her a moment, lowering himself so his face was close to hers. Even though Leawyn was suspended high by his hand, her toes barely made contact with the floor, Xavier still towered over her.

"What are you hiding?" She could feel the rage from his grip, and she was quickly losing her air supply if the dots in her vision were any indication.

"Please," Leawyn whispered, squeezing her eyes closed. "I... don't...know what you're talking...about."

Just when she thought she would pass out, Xavier released his grip around her neck with a sneer and stepped back. She dropped to the floor, coughing roughly as oxygen quickly rushed back into her lungs.

She didn't get much respite; Xavier gripped her by her upper arm and jerked her into a standing position. She slammed against the wall again and she couldn't control her flinch when he raised his hand to slam his palms on the wall on either side of her, caging her in.

"I swear, Leawyn, if you're lying to me..." he warned dangerously. "I'll—"

"You'll kill me?" she interrupted. "What else is new?" she spat hatefully.

"Why don't you just do it, then? I'm so sick of you threatening me, you bastard!" Enraged, Leawyn pushed against his chest roughly.

He didn't budge, except to narrow his gaze.

She quickly reached down between them and pulled Xavier's dagger free, brandishing it in front of them. Xavier narrowly avoided Leawyn slicing his chest.

"Do it!" she growled, thrusting her hand forward and offering him the knife.

"I have *nothing* left! Kill me and get it over with! You sure threaten me enough, so do it!"

Xavier gritted his teeth, staring her down silently. His chest heaving just as much as Leawyn's with the emotions swarming within him.

"DO IT!" She shoved the blade toward him. Taunting him.

Challenging him.

Pleading with him.

Xavier snapped.

With a savage snarl, he effortlessly swatted the knife away so that it clattered to the floor. They silently stared at each other, their eyes spitting with rage.

Groaning low in his throat, Xavier dipped his head and captured Leawyn's lips in a soul-shattering kiss. Their breaths rushed out of them when their lips meshed together, and their tongues battled to express everything they were feeling.

Leawyn lost herself in the kiss for a second before she wrenched herself away from him with a cry.

The sharp echo of her slap penetrated the air when her hand met Xavier's cheek, the force behind it causing his head to tilt to the side.

The room was silent sans their harsh breathing.

"I wish I never was given to you," she whispered hatefully. "I wish I didn't have you as a husband, and I wish—" She stopped, her breath hitching as her bottom lip trembled.

"What do you wish?" Xavier gritted out, his eyes boring into her fiery gaze.

"I wish my body didn't want you the way it does," she whispered brokenly, her tears making a silent trail down her cheeks.

"My heart will never alight with happiness. I'm *stuck*. Captured and caged by you. Like a bird with broken wings denied the freedom to soar." Leawyn hiccuped, blinking against her tears, her face compressed in torment and loss.

Xavier turned his back to her as she spoke.

"I will never know the touch of a lover who *loves me*," she said, a sob escaping her. "You have *ruined* that for me, Xavier. You're ruining *me*."

"You're ruining me!" Xavier bellowed, whipping around to look at her, neck muscles bulging. A tortured sound ripped out of his throat.

"I can't get you out of my head! You're all I think about. I can't concentrate! I can't be the leader I need to be because all I can think about is *you!*"

Leawyn flinched at the volume of Xavier's voice. In seconds, he was in front of her, towering over her. He glared daggers at her, his eyes like liquid fire.

He lowered his head until they were eye-level, his palms smacking the wall above her head again.

"You. Are. Ruining. Me," he said through tightly clenched teeth.

Leawyn was silent, her eyes spilling over with more tears as she looked at him. This broken, hardened man who didn't know what it was to love, or be loved. The warrior who conquered everything he set his eyes on—including her.

They were both trapped in each other. The harder they fought, the more explosive they would be. They expressed hate and pain in their touch to hide the fear of themselves. They couldn't accept they were both broken. How could they grow if they constantly suffocated each other?

It was in that moment Leawyn made a choice. She reached up and grabbed Xavier around the back of his neck, bringing his face down to hers.

"No," she said, her voice a touch above a whisper. One of her tears caught on his lips when she pulled him closer. "I'm saving you."

Xavier's face crumbled and his eyes closed as Leawyn trailed a finger down the long scar that ran from his eyebrow to his cheek.

Then, she crushed his lips to hers.

"Where are we going?" Xavier grunted, trying to ignore his instinctive reaction and jerk his hand from Leawyn's as she dragged him behind their hut and toward the mass cluster of trees that surrounded their village.

He scanned the trees warily. They shouldn't be here. He shouldn't be letting her drag him here. It wasn't safe. Though, he mused to himself, nowhere is safe if his instinct was right, and it always was. It's what kept him alive for this long.

"You'll never be able to wash all that blood off in our small basin," Leawyn said, looking over her shoulder at him. Her face pinched in both disgust and fear before she quickly masked it and turned away. "You need to wash in the lake."

Xavier studied his small wife, taking advantage of the moment, she couldn't see him. In such a short time, she'd grown; physically and mentally.

Gone was the shy, timid girl who knew nothing about life, from the weakest tribe in Samaria. Tiny and petite, Leawyn no longer dressed in the soft, flowing material of the Rhoxolani, and instead took on the garb of the Izayges women. Dark brown tops that often showcased her stomach, while the dark brown skirt made from deer hide hugged her hips and thighs, the twin slits in the material at mid-thigh offering a peek at the creamy skin of her legs with each stride she made. Seeing Leawyn in the clothing of his people made the possessive beast part of him roar in triumph and desire, but Xavier was surprised at the distant pang in his chest he felt about her

251

forgoing her Rhoxolani dresses. Absentmindedly, he made a note to give her more of his mother's dresses.

Her hair, though still as bright as the sun's rays, was longer. The curls draped over her shoulders and back in long, lush waves, which curled a little below her bottom.

And what a nice bottom it is, Xavier thought to himself with a smirk.

Leawyn was undoubtedly the most beautiful girl Samaria was ever blessed with. Between her bright blue eyes, curly hair, and the soft curves that stopped men in their tracks, she was the closest thing to a Goddess that mortals could gaze upon.

It wasn't her beauty which captivated Xavier, though. It was the look in her eyes.

The moment her sky-blue eyes met his, he could see there was more to this slip of a girl than met the eye. The defiance reflecting in them both irritated and captivated him. Until that point, no one dared to challenge Xavier. They were too afraid of him. They naturally bowed down to him. But with Leawyn...he saw it.

He saw the hidden strength there, deep inside. Nothing about her was weak. It was what captivated him in the first place. But it was the all-consuming love Xavier saw that touched his dark soul. Leawyn loved. She loved selflessly and unconditionally. She was pure good. She was the light of the moon and the stars, guiding him home, and the sun that lit his everlasting darkness.

It was why he was so consumed with her. Why he had to have her, and why he hated her all at once.

He needed her.

"Strip."

Xavier snapped out of his musing at Leawyn's voice, and the sound of rushing water penetrated his ears. The fact they were now standing at the foot of a small waterfall both startled and annoyed him. He lost awareness of his surroundings, and that was unacceptable.

"Strip," she repeated, giving him a pointed look.

Xavier arched his eyebrow at her command. He gave the commands, not her.

Leawyn rolled her eyes, an action that shouldn't have amused Xavier but did.

"You can't expect to get clean if you stay in your bloody clothes," she huffed, annoyed. "You need to bathe; you're filthy, and you stink."

This time, both his brows rose at the comment, an amused smirk tugging at the corner of his lips.

"I stink, do I?" Xavier said wryly, enjoying the flush that appeared on Leawyn's cheeks. "If you want me naked so badly, take off my clothes yourself."

Leawyn narrowed her eyes at Xavier, seizing him up.

Was he serious?

Yes, she decided when he merely held her gaze in a challenging sort of manner.

He was very serious.

"Fine," Leawyn growled, reaching for the hem of his tunic. She saw the brief flash of surprise in his eyes right before she tugged the ruined garment up and over his head, throwing it down uncaringly onto the ground. She unbuckled his belt with deft fingers and, with a swift jerk, pulled it free to meet the same fate as the pants.

She was just reaching for the ties of his breeches when Xavier seized her wrist. Leawyn met his eyes, and seeing the heated look in them, she swallowed.

Oh, Goddess help her.

"You have exactly three seconds to take off your clothes," Xavier said, his voice thick with arousal.

"Why would I want to do that?"

Leawyn was ashamed to admit her voice was just as breathy and husky as his. Judging by how his eyes heated more, he could tell the effect he was having on her.

"Time is about to be up," Xavier warned, and her heart skipped a beat when he fisted the ties to her top around her neck with both hands.

She closed her eyes when he bent, his lips trailing small soft kisses starting from her brow and down her cheek until his lips hovered above hers.

"Decide," Xavier whispered, and Leawyn tilted her head away from him and lifted her eyes.

When he reached out to grab hold of her, she stepped away from him. He paused, his hand hovering in the air. He seemed to hesitate for a moment before, slowly, his hand fell back to his sides. His eyes never left Leawyn's retreating form as she walked backwards towards the lake. She paused when her feet were just about to touch the water. She kicked off her shoes first, and then her skirt quickly followed. She could see that his breath hitched when she looked him straight in the eye and took off her shirt.

Leawyn tilted her head back to look up at Xavier when he was suddenly standing in front of her. His arm wrapped around her waist and he tugged her to him, his naked arousal pressing against her stomach.

"I'm not doing anything with you until you get yourself clean. You really are disgusting," she said, eyeing the crusted blood that covered his arms and shoulders. The only clean part of him was where his clothes had covered him. Even then, his wide chest had streaks of red from where the blood seeped through the material.

Xavier's lips quirked, and his eyes showed his amusement as he looked down at her.

Her nose was scrunched up with disgust, and her hands hovered above his shoulders as if she was unsure if she wanted to rest her palms there.

"If you insist," Xavier murmured, and before Leawyn could utter a single word, he hefted her up by her waist and tossed her into the lake.

She let out a startled shriek before she submerged into the water with a splash. A few seconds later, she surfaced, sputtering and coughing water out of her mouth. "Xavier!" She cried in irritation, smoothing her wet hair out of her face. "I can't believe you did that!"

He stared at her for a moment, saying nothing. Then, for the first time since she'd known him, Xavier laughed aloud.

Leawyn stilled, her eyes widening in astonishment at the sound. It wasn't his usual low, dark I'm-Xavier-and-I'm-scary chuckle. No, this was a full belly laugh that had his shoulders shaking as if the earth were moving.

It was husky, as if his vocal cords weren't used to the strain, and deep, just as his regular voice was, but the sound was almost lighter...more carefree.

It was so unexpected and mesmerizing.

"What...?" Leawyn asked, bewildered. Seeing the look on her face, Xavier only laughed harder. She rolled her eyes at him, but she couldn't help the grin that spread across her lips and the small giggle that escaped them.

His laughter abruptly stopped when he suddenly found himself soaked with water. He looked back up at Leawyn, who wore a grin that was far from innocent. She shrugged one dainty shoulder. "Oops."

"Three seconds."

Leawyn frowned.

"What?"

Her eyes widened, and she covered her face against the splash of water Xavier's dive caused.

When Leawyn turned back around, he still hadn't surfaced, and the only thing that remained of his presence was the lingering ripples in the water.

"Xavier...?" Nervously, Leawyn looked around her. Each passing moment Xavier did not surface, the more anxious she got. He was planning something, she could just feel it, and whatever Xavier plans, usually it did not bode well for her.

Hands grasped her hips, and Leawyn shrieked in surprise when Xavier popped up behind her and tossed her over his shoulder.

"Don't—!"

Leawyn's scream was cut off when Xavier threw himself backwards, dunking them both. She gasped when he pulled her up with him, glaring up at his grinning face. "That was not funny!" she growled, shoving his shoulder angrily. His grin widened, and she had to try extremely hard not to stare at the sight in awe.

Xavier was good-looking, but Leawyn found that when he smiled, he was beautiful. Perhaps it was because she'd never seen him look so carefree, or perhaps it was because something had changed between them the night before. Or maybe it was because for once she wasn't feeling as sick as she'd been the past few weeks.

Either way, Xavier needed to smile more, because the sight was something to behold.

"It was a little funny," he chuckled. Leawyn rolled her eyes at him again.

"At least your swan dive made you a bit cleaner," Leawyn said, looking at the small swirl of red around them. "Still, you need to go over there and wash it off," she ordered, pointing to the three-tier waterfall off to the side of them.

Xavier didn't reply. Leawyn took that as his acceptance, and started to swim towards the waterfall. The sound of his arms cutting through the water assured her he was following.

The waterfall was in the deepest part of the lake. The foundation of rocks that surrounded it was in the formation of steps that could be walked up. The rock stairs led to the platform of a small cliff that overlooked the lake and formed a smaller waterfall. Leawyn looked over her shoulder, waiting for Xavier to swim up beside her before she braced her hands on the bottom layer of rocks and hauled herself up. He quickly followed, and together they climbed up until they were standing a breath away from the trailing water.

"There should be some wash oils here..." Leawyn muttered, and she walked into the water, to the small cove behind it. When she found what she was looking for, she came back to him. Xavier raised an eyebrow when she held up the small vial of light purple liquid in her hand, grinning.

"Found it!" she chirped proudly, pulling the small cork off the top and bringing the via of soap to her nose, smelling it.

"Why are you laughing?" Xavier asked, staring at Leawyn

strangely when she started to giggle. She bit her lip, trying to still her giggles but failed.

"No, don't," she protested when he snatched the bottle from her hand and brought it to his own nose to smell. His face scrunched up, and glared at his wife accusingly.

"You're not washing me with lavender."

Leawyn snorted, but gave Xavier a stern glare. "I never said I would wash you, and you are too using that. It's the only one left."

He snatched her hand and tugged her to him, staring down at her. "The only way I'll use this is if you're the one to put it on me."

Leawyn searched his eyes when his hand came up to gently tuck in a wisp of her wet hair back into place. Xavier stepped back a bit, holding the vial of oil out to her. Sighing, she took it from him and poured some of it into her hand. She lathered a generous amount between her hands before she slowly brought them to Xavier's chest, rubbing it all over.

It was quiet between them; the only sound was the trickling of water falling. Leawyn nervously looked up from her task to Xavier multiple times before he stopped her with a hand on her chin, making her keep eye contact with him.

"Ask me."

Leawyn nibbled on her lip, a nervous gesture that had Xavier's full attention.

"Did you kill him?" Leawyn asked softly. Hesitantly.

He was quiet for a moment. He seemed to struggle with what to say before he answered her. "No," he finally said, his voice gruff. "I didn't kill him." Leawyn paused in her washing, staring at her hand and the blood she was washing away.

"This is a lot of blood," she whispered.

"He will not live to see the morrow," Xavier confirmed her unspoken question. Leawyn shuddered, swallowing around the bile that suddenly appeared.

"Today...in the hut, you..."

Her exhale came out jerky when he placed his finger on her lips, silencing her. "Enough, Leawyn."

She frowned around his finger. "But—"

He grabbed the back of her hair and tilted her head back right before he slammed his lips onto hers, his tongue pushing inside to play with her own, effectively silencing anything else Leawyn was going to say.

After a moment, he pulled back, staring down into her glazed eyes.

"I am the Chief of the Izayges, and I will protect every member of my tribe with my dying breath," Xavier told Leawyn, his voice fierce. "Even against someone I love." Her eyes widened, and she opened her mouth to speak, but he beat her to it.

"But I am also your husband, and I will protect you with my life," he said vehemently, his eyes boring into hers. "You don't trust me, and I get it, you shouldn't." Leawyn's mouth snapped closed, staring at him in shock. "The only person you should trust is yourself. Trust this." He placed his hand on her chest, right over her heart. "It's the only thing that will never fail you. You are the most beautiful thing I have ever seen," he said roughly, and the thickness in his voice brought tears to her eyes.

"I may have hurt you, Leawyn, and I can't take that back or make up for anything I've done, but I will *kill anyone else* who hurts you, who makes you cry. Because I am your husband, and it's my job to protect you. To protect what's mine. And you are mine, Leawyn. In every way." Xavier caressed her cheek, taking in all her features before meeting her eyes again, staring straight into her soul. "You're the only thing I can't stand to lose."

Tears spilled over from her eyes, and she shook in Xavier's arms when he pulled her forward gently, cradling her against him.

They stood like that for a long while, as another broken piece of their hearts settled into where it belonged.

Each other's.

They were quiet as they trekked back up to their village. When they were done bathing, Xavier found there were two sets of clean clothes waiting for them hanging on a tree. When he looked over at Leawyn in question, she just smiled and threw on the dress that was set out for her.

She came prepared.

It did not escape his notice that most of the villagers did not meet his gaze as they walked past. The few who were brave enough smiled at Leawyn, and gave him a jerky nod before hurrying away. It didn't surprise him. They were bound to have heard Hiinex's screams as he tortured him. It didn't seem to bother Leawyn in the slightest as she continued to smile and call out pleasantries in return to those who did so with her.

When they finally reached their hut, Xavier was relieved. He wasn't sure how much longer he was going to last. He waited until Leawyn shut the door before he turned on her.

She gasped when he spun her around, her hands slamming onto the wall to balance herself. She moaned and arched her back when Xavier flipped her dress over so her bottom half was bare. Her breath seemed to be coming out in short pants. He was sure that she could hear him undoing his belt, the soft sounds of metal clinking together. He knew the moment she felt his silky-smooth head brushing against her entrance, because her muscles coiled in anticipation. It made him want to tease her more. He wanted her to beg for it. More than that, he wanted her to tell him she wanted him.

Xavier paused, leaning over Leawyn and brushing her hair away from her neck with one hand so his lips were at her ear.

"Tell me you want it," he said huskily, thrusting against her in slow, deliberate movements so she felt his length sliding against her, getting covered in her slickness. Leawyn moaned softly, shaking her head in refusal. He felt her shiver as his low chuckle raised the hairs on the back of her neck.

"Tell me," Xavier persisted, and Leawyn growled in impatience, thrusting back against him. He chuckled again and moved back, his hand grasping her hips to still her.

"Tell me, Leawyn, and I'll give you what you want," he said softly, his voice like smooth silk. Xavier gripped himself, slowly rubbing himself against her. Every so often, he would push the engorged head in, gathering her juices, but every time Leawyn pushed back against him to impale herself, he would pull away.

"Xavier..." she whimpered in need when he slipped a hand between them and played with the nub that brought her pleasure. "Please..." she gasped against the sensation.

Xavier's fingers were slick with her juices, making it easier for him to rub his fingers against her in slow circles. He used just enough pressure to build her up until she was gasping and moaning, but not enough to let her climax.

"Bastard," Leawyn gritted out when, once again, he pulled his fingers away right when she was a breath away from orgasm.

"Tell me, Leawyn, and I'll give you exactly what you want and more," Xavier growled, pulling her hips against his so she could feel exactly how hard he was.

"Just say the words, Leawyn. I'll take you so hard until I'm balls deep, and you'll be screaming my name until your throat is raw. You'll be begging me to stop, to let you rest, but I won't. I'll keep ravishing what's mine until your knees are weak, your body is shaking, and you're too damn tired to stand up. All you have to do is say. The. Words."

Each word spoken was followed by a thrust of his hips.

"Tell me to take you, Leawyn," Xavier growled into her ear, reaching out and grabbing a fistful of her hair, holding her steady as his lips locked around her neck, suckling and biting the skin there as his fingers started their steady rhythm on her most sensitive place of pleasure. Pressing down, then rubbing, then pressing down again, all in quick succession.

It was too much.

"Xavier," Leawyn gasped out, her body shaking as the slow swirl of need pooled at her gut. "Please...take me. I need you inside me."

She barely finished her sentence before Xavier slammed into her, doing exactly what he promised and filling her to the brim the exact moment he pressed his fingers fully against her. With a cry, Leawyn shattered, and he groaned as she clamped around him, her inner muscles spasming with her climax.

Still, he didn't stop. He never faltered at his teeth-chattering pace. The sounds of their joining filled the room, and Leawyn's moans and cries of pleasure got progressively louder.

"You like that?" Xavier panted, digging his fingers into her hips. He was sure to leave bruises, but she didn't care. As long as he didn't stop.

"Tell me!"

A sharp slap on her ass made Leawyn gasp in surprise and arch her back against him. He leaned over her so his harsh breaths were right in her ear. "I think you like that too, don't you?"

Another slap landed on her ass, the sound reverberating around them. Leawyn whimpered, arching her back at the sting. "You do like it; I can feel it. How wet you get around me," Xavier grinned carnally as she grew even slicker with her arousal.

"You might not want to admit it, but that's fine because your moans and whimpers are about to turn into screams. Loud enough for the whole village to hear you. Want to know why?"

Xavier slapped her ass again, hard enough to cause Leawyn to cry out and throw her head back.

"Because you're mine, Leawyn," he growled, and with that, he stopped holding back.

Grabbing her shoulder, he pushed her down so she was completely bent over for him, her ass high in the air as he thrust into her with an almost brutal intensity. His palm smacked her globes rhythmically, each one slightly harder than the last. She knew they blushed a rosy red.

Leawyn couldn't describe the sensations that were taking her over. Each soul-shattering thrust Xavier made inside her brought her higher and higher, the inferno inside unkempt. She lost count of how many times she'd climaxed, and she was delirious from the pleasure.

She didn't want to admit it, but he was right. Each slap against her bottom brought a sharp sting of pain that quickly morphed into pleasure. Her body was a traitor. The sticky wetness sliding down her legs was evidence enough.

She felt Xavier bend over her form, his hands grasping her breasts and pulling her back, forcing her to cling to his legs with the back of hers as he controlled their movements, tossing her up and down so she slid over his length continuously. The sharp stab of uncontrollable pleasure this new position caused as Xavier hit something deep inside her gave him what he wanted so desperately.

Leawyn screamed, her body spasming wildly as if she were possessed when she lost the battle and was overcome with her near-orgasm.

"Who do you belong to?" Xavier whispered sensually into her ear, lifting her higher up his body. When she didn't respond, he stopped his movements and spun her around in his arms, bending so her back met the wall.

She cried out in indignation, her climax that was in reach slowly dissipating. Her eyes flew open to stare at Xavier with anger, and she scowled.

"You bastard!" she cried out, jerking against his hips to urge him so she could find the release she was craving.

Xavier smirked smugly at her, thrusting into her leisurely, keeping her on the brink. "Who do you belong to?" he asked again, his smirk growing when she hissed at him like a wet kitten.

"Xavier, if you don't shut up and finish what you started..." Leawyn trailed off, her eyes flashing with heat and arousal.

"I don't think you're in any position to make threats, Wife," Xavier told her, and Leawyn whimpered when he pulled her down and impaled himself deep within her. He clasped her hips tight to keep her still when she went to raise herself up. "Who do you belong to?" His voice was husky with his arousal, and she felt satisfaction that he was just as affected as she was.

Her arousal and annoyance with him not giving her what she wanted was the only explanation she had for what she said next.

"Well, if you made me scream your name like you said you would, you wouldn't have to ask me that question, now would you?"

It was silent as Xavier stared at her blankly, as if he didn't fully comprehend what she said. Leawyn felt a shot of victory. She bent forward, grabbing a fistful of his hair and jerking him closer to her so they were a breath away from their lips touching.

"I'm not screaming, so what are you going to do about it?" she taunted in a sexy whisper. His expression grew stormy; his eyes flashing as his strong arms lifted her up effortlessly and slammed her home. Her pelvis dug into his, as over and over, he lifted her and slammed her down onto his length until she was sure he was hitting her cervix. The only thing Leawyn could do was grip his shoulders, her nails digging into the skin as she clung to him weakly. Xavier took complete control of her body and their movements.

For hours, Xavier didn't stop, and before long, he got exactly what he wanted. Repeatedly, Leawyn screamed out his name until her voice was raw, and she was too tired to move.

She opened her eyes weakly, her vision hazy with the exhaustion that came from a woman being satisfied, when she felt her back meet the soft animal furs of her bed.

Meticulously, Xavier undressed her. Unbuttoning the front of her dress and lifting her arms up one by one to pull it off her. Leawyn tiredly watched him as he then started to untie her underskirt. He brought his arm underneath her to lift her hips up as his other hand slid her skirt down her legs. He stood long enough to take off his own clothes, before he climbed back into bed and pulled her back against his chest.

Leawyn sighed contentedly, the heavy weight of Xavier's arm lulling her into a deep sleep.

She thought she heard him whisper something to her, but she was out before she could ask him what he said.

It was dark and silent as the weakened and bloody form hung from the ceiling with his head hanging down. The air shifted, and slowly, painfully, Hiinex lifted his head to meet the eyes of the man standing before him.

"I was wondering when you'd come," Hiinex gasped out, his voice garbled by the blood filling his mouth. Each word he spoke brought him pain as the leftover flesh of his face stretched with the movement his jaw made. Hiinex's body was indistinguishable by the blood that covered his entire form and the few patches of skin he had left hanging by a thin membrane.

"I did what you asked," Hiinex gasped, coughing. "I won't survive the night. Please...just put me out of my misery," he whispered at his silent leader.

"You did good," the voice spoke, the twinge of pain in the words hinting at the sense of loss he felt. If Hiinex could have managed a smile, he would have given it to him.

"Say goodbye to her for me, and tell her I did not suffer," Hiinex whispered, his voice thick with loss as his eyes softened with love.

When the man nodded, Hiinex sighed in relief and closed his eyes. He held onto the image of the little brown-haired girl with curls as she smiled up at him with childish delight.

The soft whistle of a knife being thrown sounded right before it embedded itself between Hiinex's eyes.

The door shut silently as Hiinex's body went slack and hung limply with death.

Once again, the air was still.

"How long has he been like this?" Xavier asked, glaring at the sight in front of him with barely concealed fury.

"The kid, Hassef, found him this morning," Tristan answered.

Hiinex hung there, his dead weight suspended by the ropes that cut into his wrists. A massive puddle of blood was at his feet, the blade square between his eyes now only trickling a small amount of blood from the wound.

"Why am I just now being notified?" Xavier demanded, whirling around to face Tristan. His scowl deepened when Tristan smirked at him with ridicule.

"We didn't want to interrupt yours and Leawyn's uh, *late night activities.*" Xavier's hands bunched into fists, not appreciating the challenging look in Tristan's eyes. "The whole village heard her screaming. My, my how she's changed."

Tristan looked up unflinchingly when Xavier took the step needed to stand toe to toe with his shorter and less muscular brother.

"It's good the village heard my wife screaming her pleasure; it means I did exactly what she *wanted* me to do." Tristan's smug smirk quickly fell, his eyes spitting fire. Xavier grinned condescendingly at him. "Does that bother you, brother?" he asked. His voice was light, but the unmistakable threat lingered in the tone. "That Leawyn begged me for *my* cock?" Xavier stepped even closer to Tristan, who was steadily becoming angrier.

"Because she did. She begged me to put my cock into her, to make her scream. For me to take her over, and over again, until she couldn't take it anymore. Because she knows she is *mine*."

Tristan grunted when Xavier, quick as a cobra striking, gripped the back of his younger brother's neck so his thumb pressed firmly behind his earlobe. "And if you *ever* pull what you did to her again, I'll kill you myself. Do you understand me?" When Tristan started to slump against Xavier, a sure sign he was close to fainting, Xavier continued to press against the pressure point behind his ear. Just before he passed out, Xavier let go and pushed Tristan away from him so he sprawled on his back in the dirt.

"Clean this up. And send Hassef to me," Xavier ordered, disgusted. He made a point to step over Tristan on his way out of the hut, and slammed the door closed.

The birds were singing when Leawyn woke, and the first thing she noticed was how unbelievably tired she was.

Her bones felt heavy, as if a great weight were inside them and holding her down. Her head felt as if she were underwater, and it was difficult opening her eyes.

She was also sore in the most intimate of places.

Even half awake, Leawyn flushed at the memory of the night before. Of how many ways Xavier took her. Of him bringing her multiple releases...the way he spoke to her. Of how he spanked her...how she liked it.

Leawyn shifted, the memory causing the wetness Xavier was so fascinated with to gather between her thighs.

The sound of the door opening quietly snapped her out of her musing as she turned her attention to see who came in.

She saw Namoriee's long brown hair as she closed the door gently. When she turned around and saw Leawyn looking at her, the girl gasped in surprise, but quickly looked down to her feet.

"I'm sorry, I didn't know you were awake," Namoriee said quietly, walking past Leawyn toward the trunk of clothes. Leawyn frowned, confused at the girl's behavior. Though Namoriee was, at times, still shy and timid around Leawyn (and everyone else), she was usually a bit more relaxed, and Leawyn thought they had built a solid enough friendship that made Namoriee comfortable around her.

Today showed differently.

"Namoriee? Are you alright?" Leawyn asked softly, pushing herself into a sitting position, keeping the animal skins pressed against her naked chest.

It was a bit silly, seeing how Namoriee had seen her fully naked, but it was the principle of it all.

Namoriee's shoulders tensed for a brief second before they relaxed. "Y-y-yes, Lady C-C-Chief. I'm f-fine."

Leawyn's eyes narrowed further. Namoriee's stutter was another thing that had relaxed. The stutter only became worse when she was nervous or...lying.

"I-I have some other w-w-work to do today, Lady C-C-Chief. I will come b-b-back with your lunch. Here is your d-dress," Namoriee managed to stutter out quickly, setting the dress down on top of the trunk and hurrying her way back to the door.

Leawyn halted her escape before she could open it.

"Namoriee, come here," Leawyn said sternly, her voice booking no room for argument.

Namoriee's shoulders tensed again, but didn't make a move toward her. "P-please, Lady Chief," she whispered, her voice trembling.

"Now," she ordered.

Namoriee's shoulders slumped in resignation, slowly turning around and making her way to Leawyn with her head down until she stood before her at the foot of the bed. Leawyn studied Namoriee, taking in her posture and the fact she had yet to look up to meet her eyes. "Look at me, Namoriee, please."

Namoriee sighed, hesitating for the briefest of moments before she bravely lifted her head and met her lady chief's blue eyes.

She gasped in horror, reaching out and grabbing Namoriee's arms and pulling her close to her, taking hold of her chin and pulling it to the side. "Namoriee, what happened to you?" she asked in alarm.

Namoriee's left side was completely swollen and bruised a ghastly black and blue. The bruising expanded from her cheekbone all the way up to her temple. Her eye in particular was extremely bruised, with a ring of dark red underneath.

Namoriee jerked her chin out of Leawyn's hand, looking down self-consciously.

"It's nothing, Lady C-Chief," she mumbled, going to stand from the bed. But Leawyn's tight grasp of her arms forced her back down.

"This is not *nothing*, Namoriee," Leawyn growled out angrily, her eyes stern when she nudged the girl's chin up to meet her eyes again.

"Who did this to you? Did—" She hesitated uncertainly. "Did Tyronian do this to you?"

"No!" Namoriee glared at Leawyn, jerking her face away and pushing herself off the bed and away from her. "Of course not! Tyronian would never hurt me! How can you even ask me that?"

Leawyn hid her surprise at how quickly Namoriee admitted that and placed her hands out in front of her in a soothing motion, seeing how upset she was. Another surprise. "Of course not, Namoriee. I just wanted to—"

"You wanted to make sure Tyronian isn't like your husband? Well he's *not*. He would never hit me, even if I were to deserve it. Unlike Chief Xavier, Tyronian is *good*."

Her mouth closed with an audible snap. Namoriee, seeming to realize how insulting she sounded, covered her mouth in shock.

"Lady Chief, I-I'm sorry, I-I didn't mean to..." she trailed off, shame compressing her face when Leawyn waved her off, looking down.

"It's okay, Namoriee," she said softly, her voice tinged with hurt.

"Leawyn..." Namoriee stopped, at a loss for words. Leawyn took a moment to gather herself before looking up at Namoriee and giving her a small smile, motioning her to sit back down on the bed with her, which she did, her face still sullen with her guilt.

"A long time ago," she began, "someone told me not to be so quick to judge my husband. That there were many things I didn't know about him."

Leawyn swiped a loose tendril away from Namoriee's face and tucked it gently behind her ear.

"What they said was true. There are many things I don't know, or like, about my husband. Then again, there are flashes of the man deep inside I know I'm lucky to get a glimpse of. Of the man, I think even he fears, because of how good he can be."

Leawyn looked away from Namoriee, her gaze wistful as she gazed out the window.

"Those flashes give me hope that perhaps...we can learn to treat each other kindly. That maybe one day...I will not look to the morrow with a deep, painful longing of a different life."

She stared out the window for a moment more. "Tyronian said that to me." She smiled at Namoriee gently.

"You're right, he is good. You'll be lucky to have him, as I have no doubt that soon you will be my cousin as well."

Namoriee shook her head, looking down at her hands she wrung together nervously. "I will not. I don't deserve him," she whispered, her voice a mixture of sadness, pain, and resignation.

Leawyn frowned, her brows knitting together in confusion. "Why would you say such a thing? I've seen the way he looks at you, my friend. It's the same way Xavier looks at me. He's but a wolf dying to devour his prey," she teased Namoriee, who immediately looked even more uncomfortable.

"He does not. Even if what you say is true, I will not be married to him. I don't *want* to be married."

Leawyn pressed her lips together, not wanting to upset the girl even further, as she was fully aware that if Tyronian decided to make Namoriee his, he would see it so whether she wanted it or not. But Leawyn didn't tell her this, and instead chose to let Namoriee live in her naiveté a bit longer and get back to the task at hand. Which was to find out who raised a hand to her sweet handmaiden?

"Who hit you, Namoriee? You must tell me." When she looked to protest, Leawyn straightened her spine and stared at the girl with steel in her eyes.

"As your lady chief, I command it."

Namoriee sucked in a sharp breath, staring at Leawyn in shock. This was the first time Leawyn had ever used her title against her, to command her as the slave she was.

Leawyn fought desperately with herself to stay strong. She didn't like the look Namoriee was giving her, but she reminded herself she was doing this for her own good, as it was the only way she would get the answers she sought.

"It was—"

The hut door flew open, banging against the wall with great force. Both Leawyn and Namoriee jumped, startled. Namoriee paled as she watched Tyronian march up to her, a murderous expression on his face. She jumped up from Leawyn's bed and hastily backed up, lifting a shaky hand, trying to halt Tyronian's advances. Her back met the wall at the same moment his chest met her palm.

Tyronian moved fast as lightning, lifting Namoriee up in his arms effortlessly and bringing her close to his face even as she struggled.

"You will show me who did this to you, and you will do it now," Tyronian growled down furiously in Namoriee's face. Leawyn, sensing this situation was rapidly becoming dangerous, grabbed her robe and hastily threw it on.

"Tyronian..." Leawyn warned, now standing to the side of him and looking between him and Namoriee nervously.

"This does not concern you, Cousin," Tyronian snapped, not sparing Leawyn a glance and keeping his cold blue eyes on Namoriee's.

Namoriee looked over Tyronian's shoulder to meet her stare before a shake brought her eyes quickly back to his.

"Show me, and after, we'll have a talk about why I had to hear about your attack from a fellow warrior and was not notified by you personally."

Namoriee glared up at him mutinously. "What happens to me is not your concern," she snapped, and Leawyn had to hold in her groan at the words.

That was, probably, *not* the best thing to say to him. Judging by the sudden feral stillness that surrounded Tyronian, Leawyn was right.

"You are *mine*, Namoriee," Tyronian said, his voice soft with menace. "*Everything* that happens to you is my concern."

Namoriee's eyes matched Leawyn's wide-eyed ones, but before they both could really say anything, Tyronian swung Namoriee around in his arms and stalked back to the door. Leawyn followed them with her eyes, turning her body as Tyronian passed her. He was not even remotely fazed by her struggles to free herself.

"Where are you taking her?" she sputtered, wide-eyed. Tyronian paused only long enough to switch the girl's weight so he could pull open the hut door.

"Namoriee has someone to show me, and then she's going back with me to my hut. Don't expect her again today," he said curtly, ducking under the hut's door and stepping outside.

Namoriee's petulant shout of "No!" was cut off by the door slamming.

It wasn't until after they left that Leawyn realized a very important detail.

"She never did tell me who it was."

271

Months later.

Leawyn groaned when another heave constricted her body, only for nothing to come out of her stomach. She had been feeling sick for an hour now, and it was with the *worst* possible timing.

Ever since Hiinex's assassination, Xavier had been busy with meetings with the elder council members and other warriors of the three main tribes. In fact, the only time she really saw Xavier for long periods of time was late at night when he woke her body up with pleasure.

Today was also the day half the village was to pack up and get ready to travel to the sacred grounds for the warrior games.

The warrior games were an event where tribes gathered together and fought each other for sport. They were designed for the leaders to pick which child would officially start his training as a warrior. Each tribe hand-selected and volunteered warriors who would compete against each other, and in the final round, fight. Whatever boy was left undefeated from their tribe was to be the warrior who began training.

The games were also for the seasoned warriors to compete against each other and show off their skill. All in all, it was a friendly activity for the tribes to unite, and ensure there would be no revolts.

This tradition only happened once every five winters, and it was the most treasured tradition of their people. Leawyn *could not* afford to be ill, as it was necessary for her to be present with Xavier as the wife of the Chief.

The hut door opening forced Leawyn to push to her feet and straighten out her appearance behind the safety of her screen divider.

"Lady Chief, are you ready? We are to head out now," Namoriee's voice called out to her. Despite Leawyn's best efforts, Namoriee remained tight-lipped about what happened between her and Tyronian. She never gave any details away, and after awhile Leawyn stopped pressing her.

But whatever *did* happen between them changed Namoriee. There was a seriousness in her brown eyes that had not been there before. Some promise or understanding had happened, and Leawyn wasn't quite sure it was shared mutually.

"Yes, go ahead and take my bag to the cart. I'll be out in a moment," Leawyn called out.

"You will be riding Tasselfell today. The chief will be riding up ahead with the others." Since Deydrey was pregnant, Leawyn was unable to ride her. Usually, she would be stuck riding with her husband atop Killix.

"Thank you, Namoriee, I'll be out there in a moment."

She listened to the sound of Namoriee gathering her pack before the silence assured her she had left.

Leawyn sighed in relief, pressing a shaky hand to her forehead. She just hoped she would be able to handle the six-day ride well enough to stay on her horse.

It was day two in their journey when Leawyn started to admit something was seriously wrong. It felt like a herd of horses were running on her skull, and her body felt like a dead weight. The newest development: her vision was spinning.

Leawyn gasped, pulling Tasselfell up short with a startled jerk of his reins, which he *did not* like, and he showed it as he snorted angrily and kicked out his hind legs.

But Leawyn didn't care because *her vision was spinning.*

Quickly, and without any finesse, Leawyn slid off Tasselfell's back so her feet met the ground. She stumbled forward, knocking into a Siraces villager.

"Sorry," she mumbled, disoriented, stumbling away from the woman she bumped into. She caught a glimpse of the angered expression on the woman's face before it morphed into a more alarmed one.

"Lady Leawyn?"

Whispers and words of alarm spread like wildfire around Leawyn, when more and more of the villagers who were walking alongside and in front of her became aware of her strange behavior.

Leawyn squeezed her eyes shut, shaking her head a bit to get rid of the black dots quickly overcoming her line of sight.

She was going to faint, she realized too late. *Xavier is going to be upset.*

And with that last thought, Leawyn collapsed in a heap on the ground, the various cries of alarm going unheard as she slipped into unconsciousness.

There were hushed voices whispering all around, the tones both urgent and calm, that floated into Leawyn's consciousness.

"It's been more than a day..."

"Why hasn't she awoken?"

"We need to move. We're already behind the other tribes..."

"I am not leaving until I know what is wrong. Why isn't she waking up? You're the healer; you're supposed to fix her!"

"Xavier, calm your—"

"Don't tell me to be calm! Why hasn't she wakened?"

"Chief Xavier, I assure you—"

"You assure me nothing! Do your job, or I'll find someone else who can!"

Heavy footsteps faded away, then a crashing sound followed as if something had fallen or been knocked over, before the room was silent once more for a few moments. The whispering continued.

"Why *hasn't* she woken up yet?"

"Why are we whispering? Don't we *want* her to wake up?"

A soft smacking sounded and a yelp of "Hey!" quickly followed. She heard a grumbling that sounded like, "It's a valid question."

"As I've told the chief, with Leawyn unconscious, it is hard for me to determine anything substantial. But it is my belief Lady Leawyn needs rest, and her body made it so."

"So, basically, she's been having too much sex?"

There was a feminine gasp before a soft *thump* could be heard with a muffled *"ompf,"* followed by a drawn-out groan.

"Be that as it may, we must leave the lady to her rest. I will linger until nightfall and until my chief retires, should she awaken before then."

There were murmured agreements before the sounds of shuffling feet as they walked away. The sound of a chair being dragged on the floor met Leawyn's ears, before a soft, withered hand rested on her forehead and whispered softly to her. "Rest, Lady Leawyn. You shall get respite for another day."

Sighing, Leawyn slipped back into peaceful unconsciousness.

Xavier sat across the room, his elbows resting on his knees and hands clasped in front of him. His eyes were fixed on his wife sleeping on the pallet of furs. When word reached him that Leawyn had fallen off her horse and was swept with a dark spirit, he immediately left the council of chiefs and rushed off to see to his wife.

A healer was already seeing to Leawyn when he arrived at the tent that had been hastily put together for them. Unfortunately, as Leawyn was still unconscious, the healer couldn't inform him of much.

That was midday, and the sun had long past set. Yet Leawyn still did not wake.

His brows furrowed, the only significant sign of his worry. He already lingered too long. The other tribes had a two-day head start, and they were due to participate in the warrior games in a day's time.

Xavier couldn't afford for the Izayges to stay any longer.

Sighing, he pushed himself to his feet, walked over to the small table positioned off to the side, and went about removing his armor until he stood in only his breeches. His sword and daggers made soft thuds onto the wood as he placed them onto the tabletop. He made sure almost everything was off his person before he made his way to the bed his wife slept in.

He never took his eyes off her as he bent, placing the unsheathed dagger on the floor beside him before he slowly sat down, as to not jostle Leawyn.

He lay on his side, gathering Leawyn to cradle her against his chest with one arm while he lifted the fur pallets to cover them both with the other. Once settled, Xavier reached over to the side of the bed and grabbed the dagger once again to place it under his pillow.

He fell asleep like that, wrapped around his wife protectively as he gripped the hilt of the deadly dagger under his pillow with his fist.

Protective.

Dangerous.

Ready.

~

"Are you certain this will work?"

Xavier looked over at Yoro, his eyes shooting around to the other men who surrounded him. The men consisted of the Asori and Siraces tribe leaders and their high-ranked and best warriors. Xavier had his tribe had somehow managed to arrive at the sacred grounds before the *warrior choosing* which is set to take place tomorrow.

At first, Xavier had been worried about traveling the way they did to ensure that they would make it on time, but Leawyn had assured him that the healer said she was fine, and that her fainting spell was only due to the heat.

He wasn't sure he believed that.

The fact that she didn't quite meet his eye, or that she seemed flustered when he first asked her what the healer said was wrong, made him suspicious and believe that she wasn't telling him every-thing. But, because he knew that they couldn't afford any more delay, he let it go.

Tyronian and Tristan stood to the side of him with Xavier's own high-ranking warriors standing behind them. They were all looking at him with tense expressions. Their eyes were hard and focused, their attention completely on him.

"Yes," Xavier said confidently. "If not tonight, then soon."

"What makes you so sure, Chief Xavier?"

Xavier turned his attention to the Siraces warrior who spoke, stepping forward a bit with his question.

"This is the perfect time," Xavier explained.

"We're all converged into one space. All the tribe's best warriors are here, leaving the unseasoned warriors to guard our villages. Not to mention all the women, children, and elderly. But more than that, it's our *sons* who are the prime target," he said, meeting the eyes of every man.

"Our future generation of warriors, of all tribes, all here in one spot. Tell me, what were to happen if they were killed?" He paused, seeing the comprehension dawn on the hardened faces around him.

"We would be the only warriors left," Yoro said gravely, his tone matching his expression.

Xavier nodded slowly. "It's the perfect plan, and the perfect time to strike. It's what I would do," he admitted, and all around him murmurs broke out.

"But if you know this, then why did we come? We gave them exactly what they wanted!"

Murmurs of agreement sounded around Xavier, and he felt the air around his warriors' tense and shift closer to him, their loyalty clear. They did not appreciate their leader being questioned.

"Because," Xavier spoke, instantly quieting the murmurs, "we have the advantage."

"And what advantage is that?" Kisias asked, and Xavier turned his attention to him. The sinister expression and the smirk that quirked Xavier's lips made all the men pause, shifting restlessly.

"They think we're unaware of what their plan is, but they're wrong," Xavier growled, his eyes flashing with the bloodlust and anger that had been simmering in him for the last six months.

This army had been the dark clouds of a looming storm, dark, angry rain clouds that consumed the sky as lighting struck in an ominous warning of the destruction to come. The attack at the lake, the head delivered to Xavier, Leawyn's attack—it was all just the beginning. A warm up. It was the monsoon that came just before the hurricane that destroyed everything it touched.

"We'll be waiting, and we'll be ready. We will wipe the victorious smiles—victory they do not have a right to—off their faces. Our swords will be stained with their blood as we smile down at their severed heads," Xavier growled in fury, turning around to meet the gazes of all the warriors around him. He saw the same bloodlust in their eyes he felt as he called to the warrior within them. They all had the urge to spill blood—the blood of anyone who dared to question the ferocity of the Samaritan men. Who dared to challenge them and try to destroy their home?

"They want to destroy us, take what is ours," Xavier's voice grew louder as the air around them crackled with energy, each word he spoke bringing a spark to flame. "They will kill our daughters, our sons, our *people*. They want a day where Samaritans will no longer lay claim to this land. They want to take what is ours. Do we let them?" Xavier shouted at the men.

"No!" they cried back.

"They want to destroy us. Do we let them?"

"No!" the men cried back louder, fists raising in the air with their passion. Every face clouded with determination of victory, victory against the men who dared to challenge them and threaten their way of life and land.

"They think they can beat us, that they can kill us. We are Samaritans; we do not bow down to anyone!" Xavier slammed his fist against his chest, and all around him the warriors did the same. Creating a cadence, their fists represented an audible pulse of their hearts.

"This is our land, our fathers' blood in the soil who died protecting this land. This is *my* home, and I will give my very last breath to protect it," Xavier said vehemently, eyes blazing. "Will you?"

"Yes!" they roared back in answer.

"I say let them come," Xavier bellowed above the roars of the men. "The last thing they see will be our swords soaked in their blood!" The cheer was deafening as each warrior echoed Xavier's bellow.

He met Tristan's eyes as the warriors around them continued their challenging cries.

What Xavier failed to mention, what he purposely left out, was that the army wasn't just trying to take over Samaria, though that would be a bonus.

This army wasn't just starting a war for control.

Xavier's eyes reflected the same icy coldness which resided in Tristan's, locked in a silent battle only between them. Their eyes expressed the things they didn't dare voice out loud.

The army wasn't just starting a battle for glory and land.

Tristan broke first, turning around and walking down the hill. Xavier watched him go, following him with eyes that never lost their hardness.

These attacks...they were personal.

The sun was shining bright on the day of the warrior choosing. Leawyn sat next to Xavier on a wooden throne, built from strips of oak that were fused together. The other tribe leaders and their wives sat alongside them on the flat rock platform that overlooked the designated fighting arena.

The arena was once a grassy plain but had been worn down due to the many years of fighting, causing it to be reduced to nothing more than loose soil. Small boulders on the ground created the circumference of the four large circles that interlinked together. Each tribe had their own circle where the young hopeful warriors would fight against each other until only the strongest few remained. They were tested first on their archery, which had taken place earlier that day. Now it was time to test their swordsmanship.

Leawyn stared at a circle which was noticeably empty, and her eyes misted as her heart clenched in sadness. This would be the first warrior choosing the Rhoxolani would not be a part of. She jerked, startled. She looked down to the hand that had embraced hers. Her eyes shot up and met Xavier's, who was also looking over at the empty circle where the Rhoxolani should be. Leawyn closed her eyes, taking strength in the small act of comfort. She returned the comforting squeeze he gave her before letting go of his hand.

Both the Siraces and Asori had a fair amount of young hopeful warriors in their rings, to which her eyes scanned over quickly before moving over to the Izayges' circle. The hopeful warriors wore stoic expressions as they held their weapons in their hands. Each of them looked ready to face real battle, instead of just their fellow tribesmen. Leawyn supposed that going against each other *was* like going to real battle with the amount of time they trained for this moment. When her eyes landed on a familiar face, Leawyn choked on her surprise. She smacked Xavier's arm, making him still. She glared when he slowly looked down to his arm and back to her face, eyebrow raised.

"Why didn't you tell me Castic was part of the warrior choosing?" she hissed angrily, pointing. Xavier glanced to the ring briefly before meeting her eyes again.

"Why would I need to tell you?"

"Why would you..." Leawyn sputtered incredulously, looking at Xavier like he had two heads. "Why wouldn't you!"

"You seem upset."

"Of course, I'm upset—it's Castic!"

At Xavier's blank look, Leawyn huffed and looked back to the ring, a frown wrinkling her smooth features.

Great. Now she was going to be *really* nervous watching the battles.

Xavier stood to address the young faces that were lined up in their respective rings and the tribes people surrounding them.

"A challenge has been made," he said loudly, his voice strong and clear as it echoed out to the crowd. "Come forth, Cantos of the Siraces, and meet your challenger."

Leawyn sat higher in her seat, watching as Cantos stepped forward. The crowd parted for him as he made his way to the Izayges ring and met with...Tyronian.

She gasped in shock, her eyes flying over to Namoriee, whose eyes were riveted on the two men, stoic. Leawyn looked to the ring again. Tyronian and Cantos's chests were bare of armor; the only thing they were equipped with were their weapons and hateful stares.

"It is a fight to the death, of which only one shall be victor." The words were spoken solemnly, and irrevocably. Xavier sat back down on his throne, and she couldn't understand how he could be so undaunted.

"Xavier..." Leawyn whispered shakily, her eyes glued to Tyronian's form as he and Cantos started to circle each other, sizing each other up.

"You know our laws, Leawyn."

"But Xavier, it's—"

"Quiet," he said, looking over to her. "It is his choice, Leawyn."

Her mouth snapped shut, having nothing to say to that. Xavier was right. She did know their laws, and she knew that challenging a fellow warrior was a rare and grave request that wasn't made lightly.

There was nothing she could do. Not caring how it may look, Leawyn reached over and gripped Xavier's hand, holding it tightly as she prepared to watch her friend and kin fight for what could possibly be the last time.

Cantos attacked first. With a loud cry, he swung his sword up in a high arc, causing Tyronian to bend his arm to parry and shove Cantos away from him.

And thus, the battle began. The clang of steel meeting steel echoed as Leawyn watched with bated breath the two solid warriors fight against each other. The men of the two tribes were yelling, cheering their tribesman on as they fought. Tyronian and Cantos seemed evenly matched. With each jab, swing, and strike Cantos made against Tyronian, Tyronian would match with his own in equal fervor. It seemed like ages that they battled, and Leawyn grew more and more fearful.

"He's done," Xavier said suddenly, his voice smug with humor. Leawyn glanced at him from the corner of her eye, too concerned to take her eyes off the battling men.

"What?"

"Cantos," Xavier explained. "Tyronian is done playing with him. He's going to end it."

Leawyn looked to Xavier, perplexed.

"What are you talking about—" A loud cheer cut her off, and her eyes instantly whipped back to the battle. It was then she understood what Xavier had meant.

For it seemed that Cantos was no longer evenly matched. Leawyn sat up higher in her seat, watching in amazement as Tyronian seemed to come to life with his attacks. They were swift, powerful, and unrelenting. Cantos was barely able to block the blows in time.

She watched as Tyronian shot his arm forward, his blade whistling as he whipped around to face Cantos.

Cantos only had a moment to watch his sword flying out of his grasp before his body jolted, pain etched on his face. He looked up at Tyronian, his expression glazed with stunned disbelief at the sword that was now protruding from his chest. Tyronian's grip on his sword's hilt twisted. The awful sound of flesh tearing and blood squishing together permeated the air.

Tyronian's shadow fell upon his opponent, and Cantos looked up at him, dazed.

The cheering stopped. The battle was over and thus no longer exciting. The only thing left was to claim victory.

Leawyn flinched, turning away. The sure *thump* of Cantos's decapitated head split the silence. The head bounced once when it met the soil, rolling before it settled.

Tyronian bent at the waist, snatching the head up by the hair and raising it high. His scream of triumph was drowned out by the audience's.

Leawyn sagged in relief, sitting back in her chair. Xavier met her gaze, and she smiled back at him when he grinned at her.

Xavier stood when Tyronian came to him, head still firmly gripped in his hand. He slapped Tyronian's arm in a job well done before allowing him to pass so he could present his prize to Kisias, who somberly accepted it.

Xavier waited until the crowd settled before he addressed them again. "Tyronian of the Izayges has defeated his foe, and in such, claims victory!"

The Izayges side roared with their approval, and Leawyn could admit she found their good spirit contagious. "If there are others who wish to challenge, speak now," Xavier commanded. It was silent, no one really expecting anyone to challenge.

"Let us start—"

"I challenge Xavier to the right of chief."

Leawyn gasped, her hands flying to her mouth. She stood slowly, her steps unsteady. She watched as the form of Xavier's brother pushed through the parting crowd and made his way to the center of the Izayges ring. Shocked murmurs broke out. Never in Samaritan history had there been a challenge for chief, much less between brothers.

"I challenge Xavier, Chief of the Izayges, for the right of chief of the tribe," Tristan called out again, his voice matching his stoic demeanor.

Leawyn appeared at Xavier's side, watching as Tyronian marched up to Tristan and spoke to him quickly and quietly. Tyronian grabbed Tristan's arm, his voice rising. Tristan shrugged out of his hold. "You can't stop me," Tristan said before pushing past him and staring up at Xavier

"I challenge Xavier, Chief of Izayges," Tristan repeated, speaking directly to his brother.

"Why are you doing this?" Leawyn whispered numbly, her eyes filling with tears. Tristan cut his gaze to her, causing her to inhale sharply as he did. His eyes were clear and remorseless. He turned his attention back to Xavier.

"Do you accept?"

Xavier's eyes met Tristan's, an unspoken war raging between them. Xavier broke first, turning to look at Leawyn, whose tears instantly spilled over. Xavier didn't have to say it. She knew what his answer would be.

"No," Leawyn whispered through trembling lips, shaking her head. Xavier held her eyes as he said the words that would change everything.

"I accept."

"Xavier, you can't do this." Leawyn gripped his arm, trying to hold him to her. He turned to face her fully. Her eyes were distraught, tear tracks already showing on her cheeks. She was looking at him with

such desperation and grief that it made his own heart clench in the unfamiliar way only Leawyn seemed to make him feel.

"You know our laws, Leawyn," Xavier said gently, knowing she didn't truly need another reminder. She gripped his arm tighter, her clutch desperate. She moved closer to him, her head tilting back to meet his eyes.

"Please don't do this." Her knuckles turned white with her grip. "You don't know what you're doing, what you're opening yourself up to." Leawyn searched his eyes, pleading.

"He's your brother, Xavier. Please, I don't..." She paused, looking down and swallowing against the emotion choking her. Xavier tipped her chin up with his finger, forcing her to meet his eyes.

"You don't, what?" he prompted.

"I don't—" Leawyn exhaled shakily. "I don't want to lose you. Not now. Not when I feel like I'm finally starting to find you."

Xavier reached up, wiping the tear that fell away from her cheek. "You won't," he promised softly.

He gripped her cheeks with both hands, her hands flying up to grip his wrists. Xavier could feel her hand shaking as he turned her head, urging her to reach up to meet his kiss. She opened her mouth, and he could taste the salt of her tears as his tongue lightly brushed against her own.

The kiss was tender, but searing. Xavier could taste her fear and desperation. Finally, he pulled back, staring into her watery gaze for a moment before he turned and tugged out of Leawyn's grasp.

Xavier met Tristan in the middle of the ring, facing him calmly.

"Last chance to back out of this, little brother."

Tristan smirked, his answer clear when all he did was unsheathe his sword. Xavier's gaze narrowed, but he followed suit and unsheathed his as well.

There was no buildup, no need to prolong the fight, testing to find out their strengths and weaknesses. They knew exactly what kind of warriors they were, and they had no weaknesses.

Like two bears, they charged each other, sparks flying when their blades met.

Leawyn felt sick, her stomach revolting at what she was watching. Xavier and Tristan's movements were so fast, it was hard to keep up. Unlike Cantos and Tyronian's fight, Xavier and Tristan's battle was almost graceful. It was a dangerous dance between two predators, both equally skilled in the art of killing and swordplay.

It was a battle that would be told for centuries, the day the greatest warrior in their history fought against his own brother.

Tristan attacked first, swinging his sword wide. Xavier jerked back, ducking against another attack. Xavier pressed forward, making a sweep for Tristan's stomach. Tristan jumped away, just as quickly pushing forward and swinging his sword overhead and down towards his brother's neck. Xavier spun, his sword already up to block Tristan's next blow.

Their movements were fast, with no hesitation in their attacks. They met each other with speed, force, and precision. Tristan attacked again, his wrist flicking out his sword and coming at Xavier in a blur. Xavier blocked, pushing Tristan back, but Tristan was quick in his retaliation. He swung around, slashing at Xavier's neck. Xavier deflected, but Tristan pushed forward, putting on more pressure. Their swords shook and wavered, each gaining and losing ground. Tristan swung, his fist colliding with Xavier's jaw and knocking him sideways.

"Oh, Gods," Leawyn breathed in horror, watching as Tristan slashed at Xavier's exposed back. Xavier narrowly avoided the strike, whirling around and bringing his sword up.

Xavier pushed Tristan back with enough force to make him stumble. Xavier advanced, and gripping his sword with both hands, he swung wide and low. The blade caught Tristan's feet, and with a yell, Xavier swung up, sweeping Tristan off his feet and landing him on his back.

Leawyn shot up from her seat as Xavier advanced, his sword held lightly at his side. Xavier lashed out, slashing at Tristan and cutting across his forearm, drawing first blood. Tristan hissed, yanking his arm back.

Leawyn didn't see an end. They were too skilled, too practiced. The clangs of steel were so consistent it blended into one sound. But then, things changed; it happened so quickly.

Tristan struck downward. Xavier deflected, elbow pointing out with his down-strike. Xavier used interlocking blades to his advantage, moving them in a circle, wrist flicking. Tristan's sword went flying. Xavier brought his blade up, slashing Tristan across the face.

Leawyn stumbled forward, everything seeming to move in slow motion.

Tristan looked up as his brother approached. Blood streamed down and hindered his vision in his left eye. The ragged column from Tristan's left temple down to mid-cheek was filled with blood, the skin no longer there. He was defeated.

"You never should have challenged me, baby brother," Xavier told him, glaring down at him. "Now, I have to kill the only relative I have left. Why?" he asked. "Why did you challenge?"

Tristan raised his chin, sneering. "Because you're weak. You lost your way. Blinded by your obsession." He spat blood at Xavier's feet. He looked up at him, his smile bloody and scornful. "She'll always hate you. You're chasing a dream, Xavier."

Xavier's knuckles turned white around his sword hilt. He slowly moved it so it hovered at the side of Tristan's neck.

"Farewell, Brother."

Xavier raised his sword high, about to deliver the killing blow.

"*No!*"

Xavier stumbled forward, barely catching himself in time so he didn't slice Leawyn in half. She had caught his wrist with both hands.

"Leawyn, what—"

"You can't kill him!" Leawyn cried, pushing Xavier's hand down. He tore himself out of her grasp, rounding on her with anger.

"You care for him? You would risk your life for him? Answer me!" Xavier growled, his voice dripping with jealousy.

"No!" Leawyn cried, shoving him back hard enough so she stood between him and Tristan. "I care for you!"

"Then get out of my way," Xavier growled, reaching to shove her aside.

Leawyn resisted, pushing him back again. "If you kill him, you'll never forgive yourself. His death will haunt you, and you'll never come back. I can't let you kill him."

Xavier stared at Leawyn in shock. Her eyes were vivid blue, made brighter with the glistening tears in her eyes. Her expression was intense, compressed with pain and some other emotion he couldn't pinpoint. He shook his head, hefting his sword higher in his hand.

"You know our laws. I have to do it."

"You don't," Leawyn beseeched, eyes full of tears. "Change the rules. Banish him. Let him live a life of exile. You don't have to kill him, Xavier."

Xavier held her gaze for a long time, searching for answers in her blue eyes. He glanced down at Tristan, who was staring at Leawyn like he couldn't quite believe she was there. Xavier looked around him, at all the eyes staring at him. They were waiting for him to uphold tradition.

Xavier looked to Leawyn again. She gazed at him as if she saw something in him. A lightness. She looked at him as if he wasn't a monster. She had faith he would make the right decision. She was protecting him. Trying to save his soul from the torment of killing someone he loved.

He didn't want to let her down.

Leawyn recoiled at the scream of frustration and anger Xavier let out, slamming his sword in the ground. She sobbed in relief, willingly moving out of the way as he stormed over to her.

"You can never come back," Xavier growled down at Tristan, wrenching his sword up and sheathing it.

"Tristan of the Izayges is exiled. Any who try to stop his escape will answer to me," Xavier yelled, turning in a circle so everyone met eyes with him. Xavier grabbed Leawyn around the wrist, tugging her along with him.

"Tyronian, take my place," he ordered darkly as he passed him.

Xavier didn't look back to see if Tyronian followed his orders. He never once turned around when Tristan was hauled to his feet and escorted away.

Xavier didn't look back.

Not once.

I t was strange to be walking through the camp and not seeing a single person. Not that it was surprising; they were all witnessing the *Choosing*. Leawyn glanced at her husband, trying to get a read on his mood.

He was still dragging her behind him, his steps quick—almost urgent. His guard was up, his emotionless mask in place. She couldn't get a read on how mad he was, which made her nervous. It never boded well for Leawyn when he was mad at her.

She stumbled, her outstretched arm jolting as she started to fall while Xavier kept walking. He turned, simultaneously catching her, and hauling her up into his arms and over his shoulder, growing impatient with her.

Leawyn wisely kept her mouth shut as she rolled her eyes behind the safety of Xavier's back. It wasn't *her* fault he walked too fast for her to keep up.

A few tense moments later, he reached their tent, pulling aside the curtain and storming in. He swung her around so she was facing him, holding her by the globes of her ass. Her legs wrapped around his waist.

Xavier walked forward, his eyes staring into Leawyn's with a strange intensity that had her heart pounding in both fear and excitement.

"Xavier..." she bit her lip uncertainly, watching his eyes zero in on the action. Her back met the modest bed pallet that was provided in their tent, and Xavier followed her down so he hovered over her.

Goosebumps broke out on Leawyn's skin when she felt the long, hard length resting against her thigh through his breeches.

"What you did today..." Xavier's voice trailed off, teeth grinding together as his fists clenched. Her heart pounded, fear gripping her throat.

"Xavier, I'm sorry. Please, I didn't—"

Leawyn quieted when he put a finger to her soft lips. Her breathing accelerated as he stood, his hands going to his belt and undoing it. His swords clattered to the ground, followed by his pants. He gripped the collar of his shirt and pulled it over his head, tossing it aside. Xavier stared down at her, fully naked. His erection touched his stomach, hard and ready.

"Xavier..." Leawyn said nervously, sitting up so she could scoot backwards. He reached for her as his knee touched the bed, pulling her forward and effectively stopping her escape. His rough hands trailed down her body, and before she knew what was happening, her dress was ripped over her head and landed with the rest of the clothes.

Xavier gripped her cheeks with both hands, tilting her head up, positioning her right where he wanted. They both exhaled hard when he slammed his lips onto hers in a searing kiss. He wrenched his mouth away, and Leawyn stared at him dumbly, a bit dazed.

"What you did today," Xavier said, his voice a husky growl, "no one has ever done anything like that for me before." He lowered her to the bed again, his hand burying between her legs. Leawyn gasped, back arching as he brushed his thumb against her nub, slowly rubbing.

"Why did you do it? Why did you stop me?" Leawyn whimpered when Xavier lowered his fingers, dipping to gather the wetness there before continuing his ministrations until he had her gasping and writhing beneath him in need.

"Why, Leawyn?" he asked again, bending down to capture a nipple with his mouth. She groaned when he sucked hard, tongue swirling around the puckered bud. Her body started to shake, her climax building rapidly.

"Xavier," she whimpered in need, her eyes squeezing shut.

"Tell me," he said against her skin. His hand dipped to slowly thrust a finger in and out of her, curling it inside her as his thumb brushed against her clitoris with each stroke.

"Because," Leawyn gasped out, her whole body jerking when he added another finger inside of her, pumping faster.

"He's your brother. I couldn't let you," She cut off with a moan, eyes closing when he added a third finger, curling it upwards. "I didn't want—"

"You didn't want to lose me," Xavier interrupted, ignoring her frustrated cry of "no!" when he stopped moving his fingers. "Answer me," he demanded, his other hand gripping her chin and making her look at him. Leawyn's eyes were hazy with lust when she met his own.

"You said you didn't want to lose me," Xavier said seriously, eyes blazing with emotion. "Did you mean it?"

"I didn't want you to do anything you would regret. I couldn't watch you destroy yourself, and if you killed Tristan, it would haunt you for the rest of your life. I couldn't do it." Leawyn's eyes watered. "I couldn't watch you kill someone you love. So, whatever you plan on doing to punish me, do it. Because I'm not sorry...not about that."

Leawyn blinked as Xavier leaned forward. He watched in near fascination at the tear she felt trailing down her cheek. For once, this tear wasn't *because* of him, but *for* him. She had never cried for him before.

Xavier wiped said tear away and lifted his eyes back to hers.

"I'm going to make you love me," he whispered roughly, his eyes fierce.

"You can't make someone love you, Xavier," Leawyn whispered back. "It has to be their choice."

"Then I'll make you choose me."

"Why?" She breathed, closing her eyes as he started to slowly rock against her, mere inches away from entering her.

"Because I want you to...I need you to," Xavier said, kissing along her ear and trailing down to her neck.

"I didn't think you needed anything, or anyone."

"I didn't," Xavier replied, pulling away from her neck to ensnare her eyes with his. "Until I met you."

Leawyn was silent, searching his eyes. He was a fierce warrior—she saw proof of that today. His body was riddled with scars, the canvas for his art of war. But, for the first time, she saw past the hardness in his eyes. She saw past the cold depths of merciless feelings shielded by the absolute loneliness within. In that moment, he was a lost boy to her, trapped inside a man's body he couldn't escape due to expectations and responsibilities.

Having no words to offer, Leawyn simply lifted her head, claiming his lips with her own in a soft, sensual kiss. She wrapped her arms around him and pulled him down so he was flush against her while her legs snaked around his waist.

Xavier gripped her thighs, his nails digging into the soft flesh as he brought his lips to her ear.

"Choose me, Leawyn," Xavier whispered, and then he shifted, pushing into her slowly, inch by inch. He didn't stop until he filled completely, and she didn't know if she could survive the pleasure of it all.

His hips rocked into her with soft, unhurried movements. The pleasure was a slow build, bringing them higher and higher with each thrust. Their heavy breaths mingled together, bodies slick with sweat, and as each minute passed, they grew more desperate for each other. They used each other to chase away the pain inside of their hearts they didn't know they possessed until fate brought them together.

"Xavier..." Leawyn whimpered, fingers digging into his shoulders at her peak. He reached up and cupped the back of her head, fingers fisting in her hair as he brought her up to meet his mouth, swallowing her cry of release. Xavier wrapped both his arms around her, lifting her by her ass. She had no choice but to dig her fingernails into his back and hold on as he pounded into her, no longer being able to be gentle as he chased his own release.

"Xavier! I can't..." Leawyn moaned, the familiar heat rising within as she felt another orgasm coming.

"You can, and you will."

Xavier reached between them, pinching her *there* as he continued to pound into her.

"I'm going to own your heart, Leawyn. I'm going to make you want me. Make you crave me. You're mine. I claimed you the moment I saw you, and now I'm going to make you need me. Because this?" Xavier drew back until he was almost all the way out of her hot, needy warmth. He watched in rapt desire as he gripped his length and rubbed it up and down her slit.

"This wants me. This needs me, and sooner or later, you will too. I'll make sure of it." Xavier continued his assault, rubbing himself until he was covered in her juices. He caught Leawyn's hands and held them above her head.

"Look at me," he ordered huskily, staring into her pleasure-filled eyes when they fluttered open. He thrust back into her, burying himself to the hilt and causing Leawyn to cry out, gripping his hands tightly. His hips slammed into hers in rapid succession, his hand squeezing her hands tightly as he came closer and closer to his own climax. It only took a few minutes of his pace inside her for her to orgasm again, her mouth open in a silent scream.

It didn't take much longer for Xavier to follow. As Leawyn felt her pussy muscles squeezing his cock tightly, she watched as his eyes rolled back in his head. His thrusts were disjointed, growing more urgent the closer he came to climax.

He squeezed Leawyn's hands tightly as he stilled, going rigid as he pulled out, watching his cum shoot onto her stomach. Marking her.

"Do you still hate me?" Xavier panted down at her, smoothing back her sweaty hair from her face.

"Yes!" Leawyn groaned, low in her throat. Her body was still thrumming with the after effects of her orgasm.

His grin was absolutely carnal.

"No, you don't." Then he flipped her over onto her stomach. She shrieked when his palm swatted her ass, hard.

"Xavier!" Leawyn yelped when he swatted her again, trying to wiggle away from him.

"Don't ever come between me and my sword again when I'm in battle," Xavier growled, swatting her other cheek. She could feel the heat of his slaps, no doubt leaving red handprints on her skin.

"Stop!"

"By rights I should take my belt to you, like any other husband would," he said. "Do you have any idea what could have happened to you if I didn't stop myself? I could have killed you!"

"I'm sorry!" Leawyn gasped, jerking when he slapped her ass again in quick succession. Her eyes stung with tears, and she couldn't help but try to shy away from the fiery pain his spanking caused her backside. He hold held her down, forcing her to take his punishment, until she was begging him to stop around her tears.

He brought his palm down one more time before he flipped her back over, gripping the back of her neck.

"I mean it. That cannot happen again. No matter what the reasons are. I don't want to risk hurting you," Xavier told her gravely.

"I understand," she sniffled. He sighed, using his grip to bring her head down to his chest as he lay down, pulling the covers over them both to ward off the chill.

"I definitely still hate you," Leawyn mumbled petulantly against his chest.

Xavier let out a low chuckle in response. "No, you don't."

A few moments passed in silence, both lost in their thoughts. Even though it was still early, Leawyn was too emotionally exhausted to stay awake.

"Xavier?"

"Hmm?" he hummed, his fingers pausing in her hair, tilting his head down to look at her as she propped herself up on her elbow.

"I'm sorry about Tristan," she said softly.

Leawyn lay back down when Xavier didn't reply. She was moments away from sleep when she heard his whisper.

"Me too."

~

"Some might not be as accepting of me breaking tradition by sparing Tristan's life," Xavier told her, lifting his head to look at her as he finished cinching the straps of his belt that held his swords. He made his way over to her, stopping in front of her and tying the rest of the strings that held her dress.

"You'll have to be careful," Xavier told her seriously, dropping his hands when he finished.

Leawyn's brows furrowed. "You think someone will try to hurt me?"

"You did stop me," Xavier pointed out. "It could put a target on your back."

"Because I stopped you from killing your brother?" Leawyn frowned.

"Because I listened."

She swallowed at the look in his eyes she couldn't quite place. She didn't think that by stopping Xavier she could potentially endanger them both. That was the problem, wasn't it? She didn't think.

"Well...what about you? Wouldn't you be in danger too?"

Xavier smirked. "You don't need to worry about me. I can handle myself."

"Yeah, but I'm still going to. I can handle myself too, you know."

"You haven't been trained like I have," Xavier pointed out. Leawyn watched in interest as he went to where he kept all his weapons. He plucked up a short bow and its quiver of arrows. He held them out to her, and she tentatively grabbed them. Looking up at him, she saw he was smirking at her confused expression.

"I want you to start carrying that with you, as well as a small dagger you can hide in your dress."

Leawyn raised a slim brow. "You trust me with a bow?"

"I've seen what you can do with a bow," Xavier replied wryly. "I think you can handle it." He watched as she swung the bow and quiver onto her back, settling it in place.

"Carry it everywhere; I mean it. It's not just the tribes people you have to worry about," he said gravely. "It's only a matter of time until they attack, and it won't be to test our strength. This attack will be for annihilation."

"I understand," Leawyn whispered with just the slightest tremble. "How do you know this?"

"Because my gut is telling me so, and it's never wrong. Something is coming, soon, and it won't be good."

Well, that certainly is comforting, Leawyn thought, but nodded in understanding.

The Izayges won the competition, which wasn't surprising.

They always won.

All the tribes were set to celebrate before they made the journey back to their homes. Everyone was in good spirits, the huge feast well on its way.

Yet...Leawyn could feel the stares many gave her as she walked past. Whispering about her behind her back, some merely curious and praising her for her bravery—she stopped two brothers from killing each other, after all. But it was the other looks and whispers that bothered her and made her hand itchy for her bow.

Leawyn knew what they were saying about her. How she ruined tradition, their laws. But what really bothered her was what they said about her husband. How can a man be chief if he was swayed by a woman? Xavier wasn't powerful; he was weak in their eyes now.

Because of her.

The whispers were like a disease, spreading through her mind and consuming her heart until she felt like she was going mad. She had to escape, which was how she found herself on top of a modest hill that overlooked the camp and the celebrating bodies below. The sounds of laughter and music floated up to her as they ate and danced around the multiple fires.

She would have to return soon. Xavier wouldn't be happy to know she wandered off.

"It's a funny thing, isn't it?"

Leawyn jerked in surprise at the sudden husky voice behind her.

She turned around and was met by the stare of a woman she had never seen before.

Her skin was dark, darker than Leawyn had ever seen. It was the color of wet soil. She had long, thick, straight black hair that fell over her shoulders and down to the middle of her back. One side of her hair was shaved, revealing a spiraling tattoo on the side of her head.

She was exotic, but the most shocking thing about her was her eyes. They were multicolored: the right eye a vivid green that was the exact color of grass, while the other one was such a light gray it looked almost white. It was the color of the sky right before it rained. She would have been beautiful if it weren't for the hideous jagged scar that ran from the top of her brow straight down to her chin, as if her attacker tried to cut her face in half.

"What is?" Leawyn asked finally, hesitant. Her eyes followed the strange woman as she walked towards her. Her steps were light and silent, the dirt underneath her bare feet not once making a sound. Leawyn shifted a step away from the woman as she came to a stop beside her, looking down to the bodies below.

"War," the woman said in her rough voice that sounded like two rocks grinding together.

"Life is such a fickle thing," the woman mused. "It can be created by both love and hate, and then destroyed for the very same reason which made it possible in the first place. It's an ugly truth that is beautiful in a tragic way. Don't you agree, Lady Leawyn?"

"Who are you?" Leawyn whispered, her voice thick with unease. "How do you know my name?"

"I've come to warn you," the woman said in lieu of answering Leawyn's question, her gaze still locked on the people below.

"Warn me of what?" Leawyn asked shakily, a chill going down her spine.

The woman met Leawyn's eyes, and she gasped at what she saw reflected in her strange-colored gaze, stumbling back away from her. The look was pure ice; cold and lifeless. It instantly brought goosebumps to Leawyn's skin.

"Death."

It was at that very moment a shrill scream shattered the silence, the pain within it echoing to the depths of Leawyn's soul.

~

"I can't believe he betrayed us," Tyronian said, nursing his cup of ale as he glared broodingly at the liquid. "That traitor," he growled, launching his cup angrily. It shattered when it hit the ground.

"He made his choice; there's no use lingering on the subject," Xavier said, taking a long pull of his ale.

"How can you be so calm?" Tyronian asked incredulously. "He's your brother!"

Xavier's eyes narrowed at Tyronian. "He was my brother," he said darkly. "He's not my brother anymore."

Tyronian was silent, his heart heavy with pain and betrayal. Xavier took another big gulp of his drink, slamming it down on the table hard enough for the whole table to shake when he was done. He scanned the crowd, looking for Leawyn.

There were too many people; he'd have to go look for her. Xavier stood, looking down to his cousin as he did.

"He made his choice, Cousin," Xavier said again, the only form of comfort he could offer.

Tyronian sighed. "I know, I just—"

A scream broke out. Tyronian shot to his feet at the sound.

"What was that?"

"I don't know but—"

There was a whistling sound, a moment of stillness before Tyronian's pain-filled grunt shattered the silence.

An arrow lodged into his arm.

Everything turned to chaos around them.

"Ambush!" Xavier bellowed, his shout cutting through the air a sparse moment before arrows fell from the sky like raindrops. The air lit up with terrified screams of the women and children as hundreds of men swarmed around them with battle cries.

Tyronian broke the shaft in half, grunting once in pain before throwing it down on the ground in disgust as Xavier pulled his bow over his shoulder, aimed, and let the arrow fly, hitting its mark dead-on.

"Whoever shot me is going to pay," Tyronian growled in annoyance, ripping his sword free from its scabbard with his other hand.

"Get the women and children to safety!" Xavier yelled out to the warriors around him, most of whom were already in the throes of battle. Xavier was rapidly shooting his arrows, one after the other, aiming for the archers on the other side.

"I need to find Leawyn," Xavier yelled to Tyronian as he reached for another arrow, swinging it back over his shoulder and yanking out his sword when he had none left.

Three men rushed them, each with swords raised high above their heads. They were wearing the same armor as the men who attacked Xavier the first time. He and Tyronian wasted no time in dispatching them.

"I need to find Namoriee," Tyronian yelled back, dodging sideways as another man swung his sword at him. Not a second later, the attacker found himself dead on the floor.

"Go! I'll find you when this is over."

Xavier nodded before running and submerging himself in the heart of the battle, clinging desperately to the hope Leawyn was safe.

Leawyn had never been more scared in her life as she ran, dodging bodies everywhere. All around her was pandemonium. Men fighting against each other, the symphony of swords slamming against others, the yells of victory, pain, and the terrified screams of women would haunt Leawyn for the rest of her life.

She had to find Namoriee.

She had to get the children out of here.

More importantly, she *needed* to find Xavier.

A familiar scream had her head whipping to the right, her heart stuttering to a stop in horror.

Well, she found Namoriee.

Before Leawyn even registered what she was doing, her arrow was soaring through the air.

Leawyn ran to her friend, helping her push the corpse who had an arrow lodged in the nape of his neck off her. As soon as Namoriee was free, she scrambled back on her hands, staring at the dead body in shock.

"Get up, Namoriee!" she ordered, hauling her handmaiden to her feet. "We have to get out of here!"

Namoriee nodded quickly, and together they ran, trying desperately to maneuver past the fighting warriors.

They didn't get very far.

43

Xavier was in his element.

His blades were a flurry of movement, striking down his enemies as effortlessly as breathing and leaving a trail of bodies with each step he took.

It was exhilarating, exciting, and he loved every single second of it.

At least, he did...until he just happened to flicker his eyes upwards and to the left.

"What is she doing?" Xavier growled to himself, ducking from the spear aimed at his head distractedly. His eyes never left the scene a few feet away from him as he thrust his sword into the stomach of his attacker, discarding him to the side as if he were nothing more than trash.

There was Leawyn—and Namoriee, he noticed—pointing the bow he gave her earlier that morning at a man who was twice her size.

As if she had a chance.

Xavier growled, attacking with a vengeance as he hurried his way to her. He hoped he'd get to her in time before she got herself killed.

～

Things did not go as planned.

Namoriee and Leawyn were running to what they hoped was

safety, and then somehow, she found herself a having a stare-off with a man who looked as if he'd never had a bath in his life.

It was comical, really, considering he had a hooked sword and all she had was her bow that was dangerously low on arrows.

"What you plannin' on doing with that?" the man chuckled, grinning maliciously, his rotten teeth on full display.

Good question, Leawyn thought.

"You care to find out?" she challenged instead.

Their attacker blinked at her dumbly a moment before he let out a howl of laughter.

"I might just have to keep you," he chuckled, eyeing Leawyn in consideration. "You and your friend sure are pretty. Too bad I have strict orders to take you to my leader."

It was Leawyn's turn to blink at him dumbly, faltering.

"What's that supposed to mean?"

The man's grin grew, and she felt more nervous than she did before.

"I think you know the answer to that."

Leawyn's expression grew grim. They'd been watching the Izayges. Of course, they knew who she was.

Without any kind of warning, the man charged at Leawyn, his grubby hands reaching for her. Namoriee screamed as he tackled Leawyn to the ground, her arrow flying off course as she crashed with a grunt.

They grappled for a few seconds, Leawyn desperately trying to get away from him with no success.

"No!"

Namoriee came flying at the man, attacking him with all her strength. He grunted when she landed a fist to the side of his ear.

"Get her," the man growled, annoyed, pushing Namoriee away from him and into the arms of another one of his men who came up to them. He stood and threw Leawyn's struggling body over his shoulder.

"Namoriee!" Leawyn cried out when her captor struck her across the face, effectively knocking her out and ceasing her struggles.

"Let's go," Leawyn's captor ordered. "We have what we came for."

Leawyn's heart seized in terror.

Something told her if she got taken now, Xavier wouldn't be able to find her this time, and she'd never see him again. She struggled harder as they began to move swiftly away and back towards the trees they came out of.

"Leawyn!"

Her head snapped up, her eyes landing on Xavier, who was frantically trying to fight his way over to her.

"Xavier!"

"Damn," Leawyn's kidnapper muttered when he turned to look over his shoulder and saw that Xavier was getting closer to them. "Take him out!"

Leawyn watched as more men rushed Xavier, causing him to stop his advance as he took them all on at the same time.

Leawyn was getting farther and farther away.

"Xavier!" she screamed, her voice ringing with panic and despair as she was thrown onto a horse sideways, her captor quickly hopping on behind her before she had the chance to throw herself off.

"Leawyn! No!" Xavier roared, viciously stabbing the men attacking him and shoving them away, his desperation to save her evident.

"*XAVIER!*"

But he was too late.

"*No!*"

All she could do was watch helplessly as more distance grew between her and Xavier while her attacker rode off, taking her with him.

It seemed like days since Leawyn had been taken. The last time she saw Xavier kept replaying in her mind. The way he fought so desperately and ruthlessly to get to her. The look in his eyes when he realized he wouldn't be able to do the one thing he promised he would always do...save her.

Leawyn's eyes burned with tears. Her throat felt raw from her sobs, and she knew her eyes were swollen from the countless tears she shed. She tried to be strong, but the overwhelming pain and feeling of despair in her heart made it difficult for her to draw breath.

She wanted to go home.

She wanted to see Xavier again.

But the sinking feeling made it impossible to hope. How could Xavier find her when the army had managed to evade him all this time?

It was then Leawyn thought back to the moment Xavier first saved her. She could hear his voice as clearly as if he were right beside her.

"I knew that you'd come for me. I knew you'd save me."

"Always."

Leawyn snapped out of her daze as the horse below her skidded to a stop.

They had arrived. Leawyn was about to meet the leader, but it didn't matter because it was at that moment she made a vow to herself.

This time, she was going to save herself. This time...she was coming for Xavier.

And she was going lead him right to this base, right to this leader, and she was going to enjoy the moment when he destroyed them all.

"Let's go," her captor said, jerking her off the horse and holding her arm tightly, his grip bruising as he shoved her in front of him and caused her to stumble. Leawyn looked around, struggling against his grip, as she tried to remember every aspect of where she was at.

It was hard to see anything because of how dark it was. But it looked like they were in between two mountains. Or at least deep underground. It was covered and secluded, and Leawyn remembered they traveled across water to get there. It would explain why Xavier had such a hard time finding them.

Leawyn gasped in pain when she was suddenly tossed forward, falling hard onto her knees. Without her hands to catch herself, which had been tied after they made leeway in their escape, she fell face forward.

"Now, that's no way to treat our guest. Especially a beautiful lady."

It felt like a blow to her stomach. She knew that voice.

Leawyn's head snapped up, her face contorting in astonishment before rage took over.

"You!"

"Y**ou're** the traitor?"

"Nice to see you too," Tristan said, grabbing Leawyn's arm and hauling her back up to her feet.

"Don't touch me!"

"I'll take her," Tristan said to the man who had brought Leawyn, who was eyeing her with clear lust in his eyes. Leawyn shifted uncomfortably, moving closer to Tristan out of habit.

"What about her friend?" Leawyn stiffened. Her captor had looked at Namoriee with the same lust in his eyes he had now. Leawyn didn't want Namoriee to be at the mercy of this vile man before her.

"Bind her in the tent set for them," Tristan ordered. His voice grew stern and his eyes narrowed when he said, "If she is touched, you'll be answering to me."

The man straightened, and Leawyn could tell he didn't appreciate taking orders, but nonetheless he nodded stiffly before walking away. Even with Tristan's threat, Leawyn was worried about her friend.

"C'mon," Tristan muttered, yanking Leawyn around.

"Don't touch me!" she snapped, pulling at her arm as he manhandled her. "The Rhoxolani were innocent! You murdered them! Why? How can you betray your own tribe? How can you betray Xavier?"

"Easily," Tristan replied, ignoring her struggles.

"You're despicable," Leawyn snarled. "I should have let Xavier kill you."

"Yes, you should have," he agreed, smirking.

They stopped in front of a dark gray tent that was significantly bigger than the others before Tristan turned and jerked her forward. He held her bound wrists long enough to cut the bonds before grabbing her arm again and shoving her inside the tent. The interior was simple; a desk situated in the back-right corner, two closed trunks sitting across from the desk, and a large bed pallet covered with wool blankets.

"I said don't touch me," Leawyn said sharply, jerking her arm away from Tristan when he went to grab her.

"There was a time when you wished for my touch," he chuckled lowly. "I guess my brother broke you in just fine after all."

"You *bastard*," Leawyn hissed, incensed. "You don't get to say his name! He's not your brother anymore—you don't deserve that title!"

"You know, I can't help but think that if the other Rhoxolani's had as much fight as you do, they might still be alive."

Leawyn saw red.

Tristan easily caught her wrists when she went to attack him, holding her at bay. She could tell he enjoyed her thrashing as she tried to lash out at him, then he grew bored.

"I was hoping we could be pleasant, but I see now that was a dream, so you'll have to forgive me."

"What—" Leawyn started to say, but it was cut off when Tristan suddenly spun her around so her back met his front. Her scream was muffled when he placed his hand over her mouth and nose, pressing in tight, cutting off her air supply.

"Shh," Tristan soothed, holding her tight against her struggles. "Don't fight it."

Slowly, Leawyn's thrashing weakened, and it wasn't a moment later she felt herself slump against him, losing consciousness.

The battle created by the ambush was over. Bodies that were just moments before celebrating tradition were now lying on the ground and lifeless. Xavier surveyed his surroundings. The only small blessing of the Gods was that there seemed to be more of the enemy's bodies littering the ground than his tribesmen. He knelt, studying the corpse below him. He had never seen this man before. His skin was fair, and his eyes—frozen wide with death—were a dark brown color. Xavier reached over, turning the corpse's neck to the side, revealing a strange mark carved into his skin: three separate loops swirled close together to make one continuous swirl.

"What is that?"

"Symbols," Xavier answered, grim. He stood up straight when Tyronian moved to stand beside him.

"Have you seen it before?" Tyronian asked, looking down at the fallen warrior.

"No," Xavier frowned, "but they seem familiar."

"I don't get it," Tyronian glowered, kicking the corpse once in his frustration. "Their numbers were too little. We outnumbered them, so why attack now? It doesn't make sense. What do they want?"

Xavier swallowed, his chest aching as he thought about Leawyn. Of her reaching out to him, her eyes shining with terror and desperation to save her. He would never forget the look in her eyes when she realized he wouldn't be able to. He could only watch as the most important thing in the world to him was taken away.

"They have what they came for."

Tyronian looked over to Xavier, and at his tone, his eyes narrowed. "Where's Leawyn?" Xavier looked away and didn't answer his cousin. "Xavier, where is Namoriee?"

At his continued silence, Tyronian jerked him forward. "Where is she?" Tyronian yelled.

"She's gone. They took her."

"What do you mean they took her? Why?"

"We'll get them back, Tyronian." Xavier stumbled backward when Tyronian suddenly released him. His cousin turned away, a shaking hand coming to run through his blond locks.

"How?" Tyronian turned back to Xavier, wearing the same lost expression on his face that reflected Xavier's own. "How can we find them when we can't even find their base?"

311

"I can't tell you—"

Tyronian scoffed, turning away again.

"But trust that we will. I have a plan," Xavier finished, as if Tyronian never interrupted him. "Tyronian."

Tyronian stopped his aggravated pacing, and his shoulders slumped in defeat. "Do you love her? Your wife?"

"I'm incapable of love." Xavier looked away, his teeth grinding together.

"She seems to think otherwise."

"She's wrong. I don't love; I own," Xavier said.

"Sometimes knowing the fall is over is harder to accept than the pain of impact once you reach the ground. The question is...will you forgive the person who pushed you?"

"I don't have time for your riddles," Xavier growled in annoyance.

"She should have left you a long time ago, and she didn't. You tried to break her, yet she stands strong. You don't deserve her, yet she stays."

"She stays because I won't let her leave."

"She stays because she believes in you. If it were her wish to leave, she knows I would see it so."

"You speak of treason," Xavier accused, irrationally angry. "You'd betray your own chief and kin?"

"I'd do it for her," Tyronian said unflinchingly. "Stop fighting with her, and start fighting *for* her."

"Do you?" Xavier challenged, his only way of attack as he felt himself being backed into a corner and forced to confront the feelings he didn't understand.

"Namoriee will never agree to be yours. Not willingly."

"Namoriee is the *only* thing I fight for. I knew she owned me the moment she was brought to us. So, I'll ask you again." Tyronian took a step closer to Xavier, his face hardening as he jabbed a finger at him.

"Will you forgive her? Because if you can't, then just let her go. Let her find someone who deserves her love."

At Xavier's silence, Tyronian exhaled roughly, frustrated.

"Call me when your so-called plan is ready," Tyronian muttered angrily as he brushed past him.

He was right; Xavier should let Leawyn go. As heartless as Xavier could be, he knew Leawyn deserved better. Her heart was pure, filled with innocence he often tried to destroy. He tried to let her go in the only way he knew how. He recalled the night he was poisoned from the arrow. He was awake when she held the knife to his throat.

He was weak, barely hanging onto consciousness, but he could have stopped her. And he didn't. He was giving her a way out. No one would blame her.

Xavier was going to let her kill him...but she didn't.

"I tried to let her go," Xavier called out. Tyronian froze. "In my own way," he told him when Tyronian slowly turned to face him.

"How?"

Maybe it was wrong of him. Xavier knew Leawyn was pure, and good—too good to kill.

So, he gave her another chance. It was the night before he gave her his mark—when Tristan offered to help her escape him.

What Leawyn didn't know was that Tristan didn't offer out of the kindness of his heart.

"I had sent Tristan to set Leawyn free. He gave her a chance to run away before I branded her," Xavier admitted. Tyronian took a step toward him.

"Maybe it was guilt, or—" he grimaced, looking away from him. "Maybe it was the last bit of humanity I had left that made me offer to do the very thing that brings me into a rage just thinking about... letting her go."

Xavier clenched his fist, taking a moment to calm said rage. "I don't know why I did it; all I know is that she didn't run." He looked up, meeting his cousin's stare head-on.

"You're right," Xavier said, taking in the flash of surprise in Tyronian's eyes at that admission.

"She deserves better, but I gave her a chance and she didn't take it. That will never happen again. She made her choice." And it was him.

Whether Leawyn admitted it or not, she was his. Xavier just hoped he'd someday hear it from her lips.

Tyronian was silent. He was studying Xavier in a way that made him uncomfortable. Finally, he spoke.

"You love her."

Xavier stiffened.

"You might not think you're capable of love, Xavier, but I know you're wrong." With nothing else left to say, Tyronian turned and started to walk away again.

"Call me when your plan is ready."

Xavier watched him go, dizzy with the conflicting emotions Tyronian's statement caused. Did he love Leawyn? How was he able to feel love, when he didn't even know what the emotion felt like? Love was never a possibility in Xavier's life.

It wasn't something he deserved.

He looked down at the corpse, pushing the thought of love to the back of his mind. He had more important matters to deal with. He crouched, forearms resting on his knees as he studied the symbol. He was missing something.

It came to him like a flash of lighting.

Xavier surged to his feet. The symbols! He *had* seen them before. They were on Hiinex, the same exact symbols.

It was a tribe brand.

This was how they'd identify the traitor. Xavier immediately started to walk back to camp.

I'm coming for you, Leawyn, Xavier thought. *I promise.*

Leawyn slowly came to, the sound of hushed voices arguing with each other nearby.

She groaned, and the voices instantly silenced. She felt, more than saw, someone kneel by the bed.

"Leawyn?"

Leawyn sat up slowly, blinking into focus.

"Easy. Don't overdo it."

"Asten?" she said, shocked when she opened her eyes.

Asten frowned at the hoarseness of her voice and surged to his feet.

"I told you not to hurt her!" Asten yelled at Tristan, his face red with his anger.

"I didn't," Tristan replied coolly. "She's breathing. I think the important question is how you two seem to know each other."

Tristan's eyes were narrow and guarded when he looked between Leawyn and Asten.

"We're old friends," Asten said, his expression softening when he looked back at Leawyn. She blushed when he trailed the back of his fingers down her cheek. Tristan's eyes zeroed in on the intimate gesture.

"Just friends?" Tristan asked, his tone more suspicious than before.

Asten tensed, and Leawyn shifted uncomfortably at the sudden strain electrifying the air around them.

"What does it matter to you?" he asked, his tone just as suspicious as Tristan's when he turned around to face him.

"Just curious is all," Tristan shrugged noncommittally. "Leawyn never mentioned you, and I don't remember seeing you when she wed my brother."

Something about the way Tristan said that sentence tickled something in Leawyn; an unmasked emotion she couldn't quite place. It sounded almost...accusing.

"That's because I wasn't there." His eyes bore into Leawyn's. "I couldn't watch the woman I love marry another man."

Leawyn felt more than saw Tristan's glare at that proclamation. She was just as shocked. Up until that moment at the cliffs, Asten never showed signs of caring about her as more than just a childhood friend.

"So, attacking the Izayges wasn't just about power." Tristan shot a look at Leawyn. "It was about her."

"I made a promise to save her."

"How dare you," Leawyn said with quiet fury that surprised both men. She shot to her feet. "You attacked the Izayges long before you made that promise to me. Do not use me as an excuse to hide behind your ulterior motives. You slaughtered my tribe!"

Asten straightened, his expression sliding into an emotional mask. His eyes were cold when they met Leawyn's. Tristan turned away and—distantly—she thought it was strange he looked guilty.

"You murdered my entire family! They were innocent. You *know* they aren't fighters like the Izayges. You didn't have to do that—you *chose* to!" Angry and bitter tears filled Leawyn's eyes as she looked at Asten, who still didn't seem at all remorseful. "How *dare* you stand there and say you did all this for me. You didn't do this for me—you did this for *you*."

"You want to go back to him," Asten accused, and Leawyn was boggled that was all he had to say. "To Xavier, the man you hate."

Just hearing his name made her heart ache with such intensity, it was crippling. She could only imagine what he was going through. How worried he must be. Leawyn needed to remember her promise.

She needed to get back to him.

"I want to go home," Leawyn lied. "I want the fighting to stop."

Asten's eyes darkened. "They were never your home, Lea."

Her eyes narrowed. She was *really* tired of men telling trying to control her, and her opinions.

"Besides," Asten continued, "it's too late. Half my men are already stationed for attack, waiting for me."

"Where?" Tristan spoke up suddenly, which startled Leawyn. She forgot he was still in the room. Asten looked over at him, taking in the eager gleam in his eyes.

"We leave at dawn. Come nightfall..." The malicious smile that lit up Asten's face made her stumble back in shock. "I'll enjoy hearing the dying screams as I wipe out the disease that is the Izayges and the Samaritan people."

Leawyn paled and swayed unsteadily on her feet. One day. She only had one day to form a plan of escape and warn Xavier.

. . .

"I'll get what I was promised?"

"Yes, yes." Asten waved his hand dismissively at Tristan. "You'll get your own precious tribe."

Leawyn couldn't believe what she was hearing. How could her eldest friend who had always been so loving and kind to her— someone she often thought would never be as cold-hearted as Xavier —talk about killing hundreds of innocent people so callously?

"What happened to you?" Leawyn breathed out. "Why are you doing this?"

"What happened to *you*?" Asten yelled, incensed. He yanked her to his side and glared down at her. "What sorcery did he bewitch you with?"

"He didn't!"

"Then why are you fighting this?" Asten asked condemningly. He looked at her the same way she looked at him—like he couldn't believe what she was saying.

"Because I don't want there to *be* any fighting!" Leawyn said in exasperation. "Especially now that I know who we're fighting against."

"What *we're* fighting against?" Asten repeated. He chuckled humorlessly, shaking his head. "See, *that* right there is what I have a problem with."

. . .

His expression softened slightly. "It's okay, Lea. I know it's not your fault."

Leawyn's confusion didn't lessen in the slightest, even as he gathered her into his arms for a hug. He kissed the side of her head, keeping his lips there as he murmured, "I'm going to save you, Leawyn. You *and* your mind."

Understanding dawned on Leawyn, but before she could do anything, Asten shoved her away and into Tristan who caught her, gripping her arm tightly.

"Put her with her friend," Asten ordered. "Same treatment."

Tristan nodded and proceeded to drag Leawyn away.

"No!" she cried, Tristan easily containing her struggles. "You don't have to do this!"

"I'm sorry, Lea," Asten said sorrowfully. "But now more than ever, I see that I need to kill him. It's the only way to free your mind."

"Don't do this!" Leawyn pled desperately, straining against Tristan's hold. "Please!"

His expression was full of pain as he watched Tristan drag her away. "When I get back, you'll be better. You'll be *my* Lea again."

Leawyn looked over and panicked when she realized how close

they were to the exit. "Please!" Tears of frustration and terror clouded her eyes.

Tristan held the tent flap open. One more step, and they would be outside.

"Asten!"

The last thing Leawyn saw before the tent flap closed was Asten's back as he turned away from her and her pleas.

Leawyn was still reeling from shock as Tristan dragged her away from Asten's tent. In a detached way, she could almost see the irony. She begged Asten to run away with her to escape Xavier, and now, she wanted to run to Xavier to escape Asten.

"How long?" Tristan barked out, setting the pace at a brisk walk that had Leawyn struggling to keep up.

"How long have you been letting him between your legs behind my brother's back?"

"What?" Leawyn sputtered.

"How long have you been lying to him, huh?" Tristan laughed humorlessly. "You talked of me being a traitor, when you have been betraying Xavier all along!"

Leawyn stopped short, completely mystified by the judgment in his tone and expression, as though he was concerned for Xavier and her loyalty to him.

Why would it matter to him if she were unfaithful? She wasn't, of course. Tristan's reaction didn't make sense.

"Why do you even care? You *left!* You tried to kill him, remember? You—"

Tristan stopped abruptly, whirled Leawyn around and pushed into her space. He leaned in, his eyes icy.

"I should just kill you," he said with soft menace. "Save everyone the trouble."

Leawyn's eyes widened, her expression a picture of disbelief before it quickly morphed to outrage.

"I could do it right now," Tristan's hand crept to her throat like a snake, squeezing it with just the right amount of pressure to ensure Leawyn he could hurt her. "No witnesses."

It was then Leawyn realized how isolated they were. It was dark, no torches or fires to guide them, and it was dead silent. The hand around her throat tightened, bringing her attention back to Tristan, who stared down at her with cold eyes.

"Scared?" he taunted.

Leawyn's eyes narrowed and her spine straightened. "You don't scare me. You're a coward," she hissed heatedly.

"You don't compare to your brother,"— she saw his eyes narrowed into slits—"in any way. As a warrior, as a man, or as someone to fear. You're *nothing*."

"Shut up," Tristan growled, vibrating with anger.

Leawyn pushed forward, making his hand press hard into her throat. "You. Don't. Scare. Me."

She yelped when he released her suddenly. She watched as he paced like a captured animal until he suddenly stopped, staring out into the darkness.

"So many people love you, Leawyn," he mused. The abrupt change of topic made her dizzy.

"What do they see in you?" he asked, spearing her with such great intensity in his eyes that it stole her breath. There was an almost longing look in his orbs. "What is it that's so special about you?"

"What—"

"You destroyed him."

Leawyn's breath hitched, silencing whatever she was going to say. Tristan studied her, taking in her face and the emotions that caused it to change.

"You have so much power over him. He revolves around you. One look at him with those blue eyes of yours and you bring him to his knees." He frowned. "Why?"

Leawyn's lip trembled. He didn't need to elaborate; she knew he was referring to Xavier.

"You're beautiful, there's no denying that." Tristan smiled, fingering a golden lock of her hair. "You were the girl the Gods were sad to lose. They say the sky cried when you were born; did you know that?"

Leawyn's face cracked, and he watched as a tear slid down her cheek.

"They all love you," Tristan said quietly. "You touch the heart of every person you meet...even mine."

He swiped his thumb underneath her eye, smearing the tear onto her cheek. He looked up at her, and for a moment, he let her see the real Tristan. Then he stepped back, and it was gone.

"It's your eyes," he decided, straightening. "It's what's behind them." He gripped her arm again.

"They reflect the purity of your heart and the damage in your soul. That's why you scare me, Leawyn, and that's why I hate you. You made him wish he was worthy of you."

They didn't speak to each other the rest of the way. By the time they reached their destination, the only evidence of Leawyn falling apart was the tear tracks on her cheeks.

"What are you doing?" Namoriee eyed Leawyn curiously.

Leawyn had sat compliantly and didn't resist when Tristan brought her in and bound her. She was filled with relief at seeing Namoriee unharmed as he tied her feet first, then her hands behind her back and around the pole in the middle of the tent.

That was quite some time ago, and until now, Leawyn hadn't so much as moved a muscle. Now she was flailing her legs about.

"Hey!" Namoriee snapped, moving her legs out of the way when Leawyn almost slammed her heel onto the girl's foot.

"We gotta get out of here," Leawyn said, still flopping around like a lunatic. "Asten is planning an attack. Only this time it's to completely annihilate the tribes. We have to warn Xavier before that happens."

"Why?"

"What?" Leawyn huffed, slumping against the pole. She blew an errant strand away from her face, frustrated.

"Why *do* you want to go back?" Namoriee hesitated, avoiding Leawyn's eyes when she looked over at her. "I thought this would be what you wanted? To escape Chief Xavier?"

Leawyn stilled, the question throwing her off guard. Why did she want to go back?

By all accounts she shouldn't want to. Why would she want to go back to a man who was more acquainted with her tears than he was her smiles?

She bit her bottom lip thoughtfully, thinking about her time spent with Xavier and the conflicting feelings that arose. For the longest time, she couldn't understand why he was so horrible to her. He gave her every reason to fear him. To hate him.

It wasn't easy, being married to Xavier. Every day was a battle to stay strong, to survive. But when Leawyn thought back at all the times he was being horrible, and *really* examined the way she felt... she realized she was never as strong as she was when she was with him.

Each terrible thing he did to her, Leawyn could have used as an excuse to end her life—to be a coward. But she chose to live. He pushed her, but she pushed back just as hard. She learned to be strong when she was at her weakest. None of that would have been possible without Xavier. He made her find her strength.

She wouldn't abandon him.

"Because he needs me," Leawyn answered with a soft smile. "And I need him."

Namoriee looked up at her, clearly shocked.

"I can't pinpoint when it happened, but somewhere along the way, I stopped seeing Xavier as a monster. He's just a man who's never had love, and it's up to me to show him love isn't a weakness...it's powerful."

Leawyn raised an eyebrow when all Namoriee did was stare at her with her mouth agape.

"Any more questions? Or are you ready to help me save our men?"

"Tyronian is *not*—"

"Yeah, yeah. Save it," Leawyn cut off her protests impatiently. "Can you reach that?"

Namoriee was startled to see a small dagger was now laying on the floor a few inches away from her feet.

"When did that...?" Namoriee trailed off, confused.

"Xavier gave me that. It's been in my boot this whole time. Bad breath guy didn't even think to search me. Idiot," Leawyn mumbled. "So, can you get it?"

"I believe so." Namoriee stretched out her leg trying to nudge the dagger closer.

"Try taking off your shoes," Leawyn suggested helpfully. "You can grip the hilt better with your toes. Just be careful you don't cut them off."

"Not helping," Namoriee mumbled but kicked off her boots nonetheless.

It took some maneuvering, but it wasn't long before it was close enough for them to reach. Leawyn awkwardly sawed at the ropes binding her wrists. She broke free and quickly reached forward to untie her feet.

"What now?" Namoriee asked, rubbing her sore wrists when Leawyn was done freeing her.

"Now we have to try and escape." Namoriee rolled her eyes at Leawyn's stating the obvious.

They walked up to the opening of the tent; loud male voices could be heard from the other side. Leawyn pulled back the flap enough for them to duck their heads and peek outside; they pulled back immediately.

"Well, that's not good," Leawyn deadpanned. Namoriee nodded her agreement, eyes wide.

"What are we going to do?"

The tent was guarded, which didn't particularly surprise Leawyn. What *did* surprise her was the number of guards stationed. Two guards stood at the ready directly outside of the tent, with a huddled group sitting around the fire in the center of the quad. The other guards stationed on the outskirts solidified the fact they were surrounded.

Leawyn looked around their sparse tent thoughtfully. "As far as we can tell, they only had one guard in the back, so if we can take him out, we'll sneak away."

"How are we gonna do that?"

"We'll cut a slit in the tent," Leawyn pointed over to the corner and the silhouette of the sole standing guard.

"And after?"

Leawyn shrugged helplessly, giving her handmaiden an exasperated look. "I don't know, Namoriee! I'm doing this as we go."

"We have to get out of this camp—unnoticed—and then there's the fact of somehow getting *back*," Namoriee pointed out obviously. Dubiously. "We'll never make it."

"We have to try." Leawyn said firmly. "If we don't, hundreds of people will die. Gather your courage, Namoriee," she ordered grimly, "because we're *going* to get out of here."

Namoriee inhaled shakily, but she pushed back her shoulders in determination. It made Leawyn grin. Namoriee was stronger than she thought she was.

They tiptoed to the back of the tent, careful to avoid direct firelight so as to not create their shadows.

When Leawyn was stationed directly behind the guard's silhouette, she looked over to Namoriee, who nodded at her, her face bleak but determined. Leawyn gripped the dagger tighter, pointing the tip so it was level with his skull.

It was just when Leawyn finally found the strength to plunge the dagger into his skull that he jerked, reaching up toward his neck, before slumping to the ground.

The women looked at each other in alarm. They jumped when the flap to the tent was wrenched opened.

"You!" Leawyn said in surprise, lowering the dagger from in front of her. "What are you doing here?" she asked in bewilderment.

The strange woman with the colorful eyes threw a bow to Leawyn, who snatched it out of the air on instinct. Leawyn looked down, seeing that it was her bow. She looked up.

"We don't have much time. Come."

The dark-skinned beauty turned on her heel, disappearing as quickly as she appeared.

"Who was *that*?" Namoriee asked, wide-eyed.

"I have no idea." Leawyn shrugged. "But for right now, she's on our side. Let's go."

Namoriee groaned and followed Leawyn outside where the strange woman was waiting for them impatiently.

"What did you do to them?"

Bodies were everywhere Leawyn looked.

"Fast-acting dart. Quick and silent." The woman pointed at the thin sticks lodged into the necks of the men.

Leawyn prodded one of the bodies with the tip of her toe. "Are they dead?"

"Yes," the woman answered simply. Namoriee and Leawyn shared a stunned look.

"But I did not kill all of them. Just the ones who would hinder your escape. We must hurry; it won't be long before someone finds one of the bodies."

Leawyn didn't ask any more questions. She was right; they didn't have time to ask questions. They ran a different way than she was brought in, and when the woman stopped in front of the rocks that made up the base of the cliff with a long, thick rope hanging down from it, she stopped and turned to face the younger women.

"We must climb up."

Leawyn's brows shot up to her hairline. Was she serious? She tilted her head back. It was too dark to gauge how far up it was, but if it was anything like what she saw earlier...it was high.

"She's not serious, is she?" Namoriee's horrified whisper sounded behind Leawyn.

The woman's face remained impassive as ever, but she could have sworn she seemed a bit impatient. Wordlessly, Leawyn held out her hand for the rope, wiggling her fingers in a "give it here" way.

Leawyn gave the rope a couple of pulls, testing the strength. It seemed sturdy enough.

"It will hold," the woman said in her strange voice. "Now hurry, time is running out."

Leawyn nodded. She looked over her shoulder at Namoriee, who looked at back at her anxiously. Leawyn could see her trembling.

"Courage, Namoriee," Leawyn reminded her. "Once I've climbed a body-length distance, start to climb up after me. Okay?"

"I'm scared of heights," Namoriee whimpered.

"Courage," Leawyn ordered firmly and waited until Namoriee gave her a jerky nod before she started to climb up the rope.

It was a lot harder than she thought it would be.

The rope wobbled. Leawyn clung to it fearfully. For a moment, she pictured the rope snapping and her falling to her death.

"Keep moving, Leawyn."

Leawyn looked down when the rough voice floated up to her. She sighed in relief. No falling to her death for her. She resumed climbing.

It was daunting. Her arms felt weak; it was getting harder and harder to pull herself up. She was covered in sweat and out of breath. When she finally reached the top, she collapsed on the ground in relief, panting. A few moments later, Namoriee's leg appeared over the edge. Leawyn helped pull her up when she struggled to do it herself. Namoriee collapsed much like Leawyn did, sucking air into her lungs.

"I'm...never...doing...that...again," Namoriee gasped out, wiping the sweat on her forehead with a trembling hand. Leawyn agreed with her wholeheartedly.

They both looked over when the woman pulled herself up, not looking the least bit disturbed. Leawyn narrowed her eyes in envy.

"We must hurry," the woman urged. "That took too long." She

turned and pulled a dagger out, cutting the rope so it fell to the ground.

As if to prove her point, shouts rang out, the sound carrying up the mountain.

"Hurry!" the woman said sharply, taking off into the trees.

Leawyn stood quickly, hauling Namoriee up with her, and they followed. They ran until they burst into a small clearing where three horses stood waiting. The woman made a beeline for them, quickly untying the buckskin and tossing Leawyn the reins.

"This one is the fastest," she told Leawyn. "And he'll run until his heart stops if you ask it of him."

Leawyn climbed up smoothly, turning the stallion in a tight circle when he sidestepped impatiently.

"You must ride hard, Leawyn. Do not stop. When you get to the river, head east. It will be a straight shot from there."

Namoriee pulled up beside Leawyn, riding a dapple-gray mare.

Leawyn looked down at the woman. "You're not coming with us, are you?" she asked, already knowing the answer.

"No, I am not."

"Why did you help me twice? You must have been watching me for a while. Who are you?"

"Let's just say we have a common enemy," the woman replied mystically.

"That answer is unacceptable," Leawyn told her, scowling.

"It's the only answer you're going to get."

"At least tell me your name!" Leawyn called out desperately as the woman started riding away.

"Don't worry!" she called over her shoulder, riding farther and farther away. "We will meet again. Ride hard!" Leawyn could only watch helplessly as the woman rode away, quickly disappearing into the night.

Leawyn looked over at Namoriee, putting the mystery woman in the back of her mind. She had more important things to think about.

"Don't worry," Namoriee said before Leawyn could open her mouth. "I'll keep up, no matter what."

Leawyn nodded. They both knew it couldn't be any other way. Without saying anymore, she dug her heels into her horse's side and took off, Namoriee quickly following.

They rode hard and fast at neck-breaking speed, desperate to reach their men in time.

~

"You were right," Tyronian said quietly. Xavier looked over at him when he sidled alongside him. "You did have a plan." His eyes were regretful. "I should have trusted you, I'm sorry."

"You were scared." Xavier looked away, staring out into the distance. "I know all too well how it feels to have your woman kidnapped."

The air was a symphony of noise as the gathered tribes made and sharpened their weapons of choice. The sounds of the warriors blended together with the clatter of carts being loaded as the woman and elderly raced to pack up and leave, the prelude associated with an upcoming battle.

"She's not my woman," Tyronian glowered, which was the expression he wore often whenever they talked of Namoriee, Xavier noticed. "Yet," he pointed out as an afterthought, "still, that's no excuse." He sighed. "I won't doubt you again."

"Did you kill him?" Xavier said, changing the subject. He didn't handle apologies well.

"Hassef is no more," Tyronian confirmed, his expression murky. "I still can't believe he was the traitor. I never would have guessed."

Xavier thought of the young warrior who had betrayed them all.

He was young, only nineteen winters, and had still clung to his innocence and humor, that had not yet been jaded by life. Xavier always figured his age was why he wasn't the best fighter; he was young, still had things to learn. Now that he thought about it, that was why it made sense for him to be the perfect spy.

"I suppose that was the point," Xavier said, letting Tyronian in on his musing.

"He was easy to bypass. Were you able to get any information out of him?"

"No," Tyronian spat hatefully. "Little bastard cut out his own tongue. He must have known it was over for him, but knew he wouldn't have been able to escape."

Xavier's brows rose, impressed. "Guess he had guts after all."

Tyronian laughed bitterly. "I guess so. What do we do now? We're no closer to knowing where their camp is now than we were before."

Xavier went to reply, but a loud shout rang out, interrupting him.

"Riders approaching fast!"

Xavier and Tyronian shared a look and took off running down the small incline.

Swords were already unsheathed and archers placed at the ready to shoot when they reached the camp.

"How many?" Xavier barked out to the scout who shouted out the warning.

"Two, but—" The scout gasped in shock.

Tyronian and Xavier looked up sharply at him.

"They're women!"

Xavier grew rigid. Hope helplessly consumed him. *It couldn't be...*

The riders drew closer, their speed recklessly fast. When they approached close enough for him to glimpse their faces, Xavier almost collapsed in shocked relief.

It was Leawyn and Namoriee!

"I can't believe it," Tyronian breathed in astonishment, eyes wide. "How can this be?"

Xavier couldn't answer. His shock quickly morphed into alarm when he realized they weren't slowing down.

"They won't be able to stop in time!" Tyronian yelled out, horrified.

"Get out of the way!" Xavier yelled out to his men in panic.

They narrowly avoided getting slammed into as they all quickly dived out of the way, just moments before Leawyn and Namoriee zoomed past them. Xavier was running towards his wife even before he was aware of getting up. Tyronian was right alongside him.

"Leawyn!" Xavier watched in horror as both the horses' legs buckled when they skidded to a stop, sending two bodies flying and to the ground.

Xavier's feet slid beneath him as he fell beside Leawyn and scooped her up in his arms before he even hit the ground.

"Are you okay?" he asked frantically, looking her body over as she sat up, dazed.

"Fine," she winced. "I'm not that—"

"What were you thinking?" Xavier screamed, shaking her roughly. "You could have been killed riding that fast!"

"I had to get to you! I had to warn you. Xavier, I know where the ca—"

A horrible screeching sound ripped through the air, and they all looked at the horses who were thrashing on the ground.

"What's happening to them?" Namoriee cried, horrified and near tears as the horses continued to let out pain-filled neighs.

"They're dying," Xavier said grimly.

"Please, put them out of their misery!" Namoriee wailed, clutching Tyronian's arms as they all watched the horses struggling to breathe.

Xavier stood and unsheathed his sword as he strode toward them to do just that. Just when he raised his sword to end the first horse's suffering, an arrow zoomed past him and lodged into the creature's head, killing it instantly.

He looked up to see Leawyn load another arrow into her bow, tears dripping down her cheeks and face pinched in despair and guilt. She released the second arrow and lowered her bow. It was silent around them once again.

Leawyn looked into Xavier's eyes as he came and stood, looking down at her. He cupped both her cheeks, his thumb catching the salty liquid that dripped from her beautiful eyes.

"They served their purpose," Xavier told her softly.

Leawyn's lip still had a tremble even when she pursed them together in false acceptance. "I know." She clutched his wrists tight with urgency.

"I have a lot to tell you." He watched as fear and an emotion he couldn't place flashed in her eyes. "I know where they're hiding. They're coming, Xavier."

His breath shuddered out of him. "When?"

Xavier only had eyes on Leawyn even as Tyronian and the other men surrounded them. They all heard her response.

"They're already here...and they're going to attack tonight."

Leawyn wrung her hands together, her body strung tight with nervousness as she watched Xavier pace like a captured wild animal inside their tent.

She had just confessed everything to him. She told him about the camp, the enigmatic woman who had helped her and Namoriee escape, Tristan's involvement...Asten.

Leawyn's heart wouldn't stop pounding as she told Xavier she'd kept Asten a secret since the first time she was captured, when he was there to save her. She had cried when she told him the true reason why she ran back to her native tribe; she hoped Asten would be there.

Through it all, his expression grew stormier and stormier with each word that tumbled out of her mouth, but he had stayed silent.

When she got to the part of how she kissed Asten back when he confessed his love for her, Xavier had shown the first sign of how furious he was when he surged to his feet.

Leawyn had covered her mouth to quiet her sobs when he picked up the table and threw it across the room. He had smashed anything that he came across: chairs, cups, chests—nothing was safe from his wrath. He didn't stop until nearly everything inside their tent was destroyed, and then he just stood there with his back to her in the aftermath, his shoulders heaving. Then, he started to pace, not once looking up at her.

That was where they were at now.

Xavier stopped suddenly, still not looking at her. The air was electric with his emotions.

Rage. Betrayal. Fear...*jealousy.*

"Is there anything else you need to tell me?" His tone was vibrating with anger.

"Yes," Leawyn whispered, voice thick with angst.

"What is it?" Xavier bit out through gnashed teeth.

Leawyn started to tremble and tried to speak around the fear that clogged her throat, as she choked out her biggest secret of all.

"I am with child."

The air grew deathly still.

"What," Xavier's tone was indistinguishable, "did you just say?"

"I am with—"

Her husband's enraged scream echoed around them. It tore Leawyn's heart apart. He whirled around, his eyes pure fire as he marched toward her.

She screamed when he gripped her arms tight enough to make his knuckles white and bruise her skin.

"Is it even mine?" Xavier screamed down at her. "Is. It. Mine?"

When Leawyn only cried harder, he released her as if she'd burned him. He stumbled back away from her as she slowly crumbled to the floor, her shaking hand covering her mouth.

She saw the look on his face. For the first time, she was certain he wanted to kill her.

It was silent between them for a long time, with Leawyn falling apart on the floor, and Xavier watching her in shocked silence. Suddenly, he moved towards her.

His hand tangled into her hair. He wasn't gentle, but he wasn't overly forceful when he tugged her head back until her red-rimmed eyes looked into his.

"Is it mine?" his voice cracked. He blinked rapidly against the liquid she saw pooling in his eyes.

"Yes," Leawyn wailed. She reached up to cup his face, but Xavier kept her from touching him by strengthening his grip on her hair. It would have been less painful if he'd slapped her. He gave no notice to her pained expression and forged ahead.

"How do you know?" Xavier asked, unconvinced.

"I didn't sleep with him—no, wait!" she cried, her nails digging into his skin to keep him with her when he tried to pull away. "Please. I know you don't believe me—"

"Why should I?" he snapped.

"I didn't give him my body, Xavier, I swear. I was having symptoms before I ever saw him, but I didn't tell you because I was scared. Please," Leawyn whispered.

Her hand shook against Xavier's skin when she reached up and cupped the back of his neck. He stayed stiff, refusing to bend down to her, but she tugged until he relented. Her eyes closed when his forehead rested against hers.

"I'm horrible to you," Xavier said suddenly, his deep voice almost garbled from his emotion. "I don't deserve you. I never did. *Nothing* I do in the future can ever forgive what I've done to you."

Her eyes squeezed shut; his words like a physical blow to her heart. He was saying exactly what Tristan had said.

"I don't want you to forgive me." Leawyn looked up at that. "I hurt you, I know that. It seems to be the only thing I'm good at. But for the first time—" Xavier swallowed against the hurt she had put on his face. "For the first time, we're even."

Leawyn's breath shuddered out of her. It was difficult for her to breathe. "I'm sorry." She threw herself at him, her arms wrapping around his shoulders and hugging him tightly, crying into his neck.

Xavier closed his eyes. Clutching her close to him, he buried his nose in the crook of her neck and inhaled deeply. "I'm no good for you, Leawyn." Her arms squeezed his neck tighter. He pressed his lips to her skin. He didn't move as he uttered the words she suddenly realized she feared the most.

"I was already planning on sending you away. I didn't want you here when they attacked. I want you to go, and I don't want you to come back. "

Leawyn jerked back. "What?"

"I'm letting you go."

"What are you saying?" she whispered through numb lips, suddenly terrified.

"I have nothing to offer you, Leawyn. Do you understand me?" Xavier jolted her. "I can't change. Not even for you. All I do is hurt you. I won't hurt my child too."

"Don't do this," Leawyn begged. Xavier growled low in his throat, swooping down and stealing her lips in a hard kiss. She opened her mouth, eagerly twining her tongue with his. He cupped the back of her head. His grip was painful, but she didn't care. She was desperate for him. She clutched him so tightly, she had trouble breathing. She whimpered with need against his mouth as her hands explored his body.

The kiss ended just as quickly as it started.

Leawyn tried to follow Xavier's lips when he tore his away from hers, but he held her back as he stood, tearing his arm away when she grabbed it.

"No!"

"Killix is saddled and waiting for you. Everything you'll need is with him. He'll keep you safe." Xavier exhaled shakily. "He'll keep you both safe."

"Xavier..." Panic flared in Leawyn's heart when two of Xavier's men came in behind him. They wore grim faces as they came towards her. Her eyes flew back up to Xavier. He wore his expressionless mask. He'd turned the man into the warrior again.

"No!" Leawyn called out, her back bowed as the men each gripped her around the arms. "Xavier, *please* don't do this!"

He did nothing to stop his men when they carried her out of the tent and outside towards the setting sun.

"Leawyn!"

She looked over to see Tyronian watching with desperate eyes, but he was being held back by his tribesmen.

"What are you doing?" Tyronian shouted at Xavier when he came out of the tent. Xavier ignored him.

Leawyn found herself put on top of Killix, and before she could attempt to climb off, Xavier was suddenly there, face fierce. He forcibly put her hands on the horn of the saddle before he slapped Killix hard on the rump. Killix took off and immediately gained speed, leaving Leawyn no choice but to hang on or risk falling off. She called out to Xavier with every hoof fall.

~

Xavier turned around, looking around at his men. Tyronian looked like he was in shock.

"Do you have any idea what you've just done?" Tyronian asked him, wrenching Xavier around by his arm when he tried to walk away from him. "You let her go off alone!" he yelled, pointing to the space where Killix and Leawyn had been. "Who's going to protect her?"

Xavier pulled his arm away. The blank glare was more terrifying than any other look he'd ever given Tyronian.

"I took your advice. I let her go," Xavier said, his voice monotone. He looked out to the distance, his mask wavering for a split second before he brought it back up. "Get ready. It will be dark soon."

With nothing else left to say, Xavier walked away to get ready to face the army that had eluded him.

He had a score to settle.

~

How had Leawyn's life gotten so messed up so fast?

She couldn't believe what just happened. How could Xavier send her away?

I want you to go, and I don't want you to come back.

She hasn't been able to stop crying, or Killix—no matter how many times she tried.

It was like he knew he was supposed to carry her as far away as he could.

The sun had set a long time ago, and Leawyn was sick with worry and "what ifs.'"

Had Asten attacked?

If he did, were the Samaritans winning or losing?

Was Xavier *alive*? Was Tyronian?

Leawyn couldn't take it anymore. She pulled Killix's reins so hard, it snapped his head back. The horse showed his displeasure by skidding to a stop and rearing up on his hind legs. He landed on his feet hard, stomping in place and throwing his head in anger. She climbed down from him while she had the chance. Killix snorted behind her and she heard him come up behind her.

"It doesn't make sense," she told Killix angrily as she paced back and forth in front of him.

Leawyn knew how pointless it was to be talking to a horse since they don't talk back to you, but she didn't care. Thanks to her husband (Or was it ex-husband now?) she had no one else to talk to. Her anger fought with her sadness when she thought of Xavier.

"That bastard!" she hissed. She had risked her life to get back to him. She had told him she was carrying his child and he sent her *away?*

"How can he do that?!" Leawyn shouted, stomping abruptly and spinning around to face Killix, whose ears flicked forward at her raised voice.

"He took everything from me! Do you know how many times I wanted to run away from him? I wanted to leave, and he made me stay!" she ranted. Her shoulders sagged, and she flopped down on the ground, emotionally drained.

"I thought things were getting better between us," Leawyn lamented.

Killix bent his head down, nudging Leawyn's shoulder with his wet nose. He sensed her sadness. She reached up and held his face to her chest, hugging him close. She scratched behind his ears. She didn't move from her spot, and after awhile he got bored of her and started to graze. While Killix chomped on the grass, everything Xavier had ever said to her replayed in her mind.

You will become my wife, Leawyn.

You'll never escape me, Leawyn. Wherever you are, I'll find you.

Every single distinct moment between them came to her like a flood. The memories came to her one after another—the good, and the bad, until it was a continuous stream.

You are the most beautiful flower, Leawyn. Don't let anyone crush you...even me.

You're the only thing I can't stand to lose.

I'm going to make you love me.

I don't deserve you. I never did.

Leawyn shot to her feet, heart pounding. All this time, she thought he had the power, that he controlled her—but she was wrong.

She had the power over *him*. Xavier didn't get to drive her away.

She was going back.

Killix must have sensed her resolution because he came up beside her, rippling with energy and ready to head into what would undoubtedly be a dangerous journey.

Whoever was reborn into Killix was an amazing warrior in his lifetime.

"Run hard, Killix," Leawyn whispered into his ear when she climbed up his back. She barely had to tap his sides before he shot off, clumps of dirt and grass soaring behind him as his hooves flew over the ground, going the opposite direction as before.

47

Xavier had a moment of déjà vu.

The camp was up in flames, and all around him people were fighting for their lives. He grudgingly admitted that Asten was smart with his battle planning—but so was Xavier.

Just as Leawyn promised, their enemy attacked at nightfall. Fittingly, the moon was kidnapped by a thick fog that had come so swiftly, he felt it was the great Goddess Ianna, preparing herself to watch the battle and judge who was to be reborn into her precious warhorses.

Xavier had no plan of dying today, and as such, he would not be joining the fate of his forefather Saviero.

Asten's army had been the one to attack first, and as much as Xavier hated to admit it, he did it creatively. Huge balls of kindling had been set alight with flames and rolled down the incline. It was a tactic meant to catch them off guard and eliminate most of their men. It would have worked, too, if Xavier had not prepared his own surprise tactic.

While there were casualties with Asten's attack, it wasn't the amount he was sure Asten had hoped for.

The tents had been empty.

Xavier had waited until the army had charged down the hill before he revealed himself with a volley of arrows tipped with fire.

The sound of their warriors colliding with each other was akin to the crash of thunder.

The Izayges, Asori, and Siraces warriors were strong—but so were

Asten's. He had no idea where Leawyn's friend had managed to get this many men. Xavier could admit they were outnumbered. Where did they come from?

It seemed, for the first time in a long while, the Samaritans had a worthy challenger. But the foot soldiers weren't the ones Xavier wanted to challenge. He wanted the leader.

Just the thought of Asten brought his bloodlust to the surface. He hacked off the arm of a man who tried to slice his side; his sword was a blur when he swung. He was moving on to his next victim before the body even hit the ground.

His sword effortlessly fell into a pattern of strikes, both the offensive and defensive. Xavier didn't know who was winning, nor did he care. The night reverberated with men dying, swords clashing, and sounds of victory. His sole focus was on the man who was decapitating Xavier's tribesmen as easily as Xavier himself, which could only mean one thing—he was the leader.

Just then, the man in question looked up, hazel eyes colliding with Xavier's. The hate that flashed in their depths and contorted his face was all the confirmation he needed.

He had found Asten.

They cut a path towards each other with a vengeance, bodies dropping with each step they took until they stood in front of each other, not but a foot apart, and stared each other down as they prepared to partake in what was sure to be the fiercest battle of the night.

"I've been waiting a long time for this," Asten called out to Xavier loudly so his voice wasn't drowned out by the sounds around them.

"What do you want?" Xavier said in reply, skipping to the point.

"I want you to die." Asten's expression filled with menace. "I want what's rightfully mine."

Anger made Xavier's hands grip his sword tighter.

"You mean my wife?" He kept his face emotionless, but felt satisfaction when Asten's face turned red with his anger at the taunt.

"She won't be yours for long," Asten replied self-assuredly. "You'll be dead, and she'll be in my bed tonight, and every night after."

Xavier's face hardened.

"That will never happen."

Then he lunged.

Leawyn was pleasantly surprised to find she wouldn't be the only one charging head-long into battle on horseback. She should have known the Samaritan warriors would fight with their war horses—they were known for their incredible horsemanship, after all.

Few have noticed her yet presence, and she supposed that was understandable considering how much chaos there was. It was an advantage she gladly took, and she didn't take it for granted. Leawyn reached back, yanked an arrow, and had it sailing in the air before she fully registered she'd raised her bow.

If the fighting warriors didn't notice her before, they did now.

Steel met steel in a flurry of parries and thrusts. Nothing was held back as Xavier and Asten fought. There was no toying with each other; they didn't test each other's skills. It was a dance between two predators who had everything to lose. Their movements were practiced, precise, and quick.

Asten lurched forward, making a daring jab for Xavier's throat. Xavier brought his sword up on reflex, neck straining back from the tip of glistening steel. Asten pushed forward, their swords shaking as they both wrestled to keep from being cut.

"I thought you were supposed to be the greatest warrior?" Asten taunted. "I'm almost disappointed."

Xavier growled. That was the second time Asten had gotten the leg up on him and Asten knew it.

"At least you've heard of me."

Xavier knocked Asten's sword away from him and swung a right hook straight into Asten's cheek. Asten stumbled back, blood trickling out of his nose.

Xavier didn't let him recover, and this time, Asten was the one who brought his sword up to narrowly avoid getting his neck sliced in half. Xavier pushed forward, his speed leaving Asten no choice but to try and deflect every shot aimed at him.

Their deadly dance continued.

As far as fighting went, Leawyn felt she was doing a pretty good job at not getting killed.

She had lost Killix some time ago. It became too difficult for her to shoot her bow with Killix constantly bowling through any warrior he could reach. Being it was her first battle and all, she wasn't aware of just *why* they were called warhorses. She certainly understood now.

The horse was nuts.

When her fellow Samaritans realized she was amongst their numbers, they had tried their best to protect her. But it became apparent there were just too many enemies, and they couldn't afford to lose their focus. Leawyn tried to stick to the outskirts as best she could, keeping her eye out for her husband and Tyronian in between arrows.

No sign of them yet.

Leawyn lost herself in the motions; notch, pull, release.

She didn't notice the man behind her and the arrow he pulled from his quiver until it was too late. She turned at the sound to see his arrow aimed and ready. Her fear made her immobile, her feet refused to move. Her attacker sneered, joy lighting up his eyes at the fact he would be the one to kill her. He raised his bow and pulled the string back. Leawyn's eyes squeezed shut. This was it. She was going to be responsible for killing herself and the life inside her.

A whinny rang out, and the ground thundered. Leawyn's eyes

snapped open, and she watched, horrified as Killix charged at her attacker—who had turned at the distraction— full force.

Killix slammed into her attacker's body at the same time he released the arrow.

"KILLIX!"

It was too late.

Her attacker went sailing through the air, and his body making a sickening crunch when it landed dead on impact.

"No, no, no," Leawyn chanted, falling to her knees beside Killix's massive body. "Please no," she sobbed, her hand hovering over his beautiful, muscled form. "Killix!"

The arrow meant for her was now lodged into his chest, and he wasn't breathing.

He had saved her life at the cost of his own.

Leawyn screamed, her grief echoing in the sound. Not caring that she was in the middle of a battlefield, Leawyn threw herself on top of Killix's body and sobbed.

eawyn didn't know how long she laid over Killix and cried. She knew it was dangerous—she was in the middle of a battlefield, but she didn't care.

He was still warm. His shiny black coat was wet with sweat. It was almost like she could pretend Killix was sleeping.

But he wasn't, and that fact broke her heart.

It was the blood that finally made Leawyn move away from Killix's body. She stood up, refusing to look down and into his dead eyes. That's when she took in her surroundings. She gasped, hope blossoming in her chest. It seemed that the Izayges were no longer outnumbered, and were now driving their opponents back.

They were winning.

A flash of movement from the corner of her eye got her attention. She turned her head in the opposite direction and looked up at the hill.

Leawyn froze, her heart leaping in her chest. She snatched her bow up from the ground and ran.

Asten's sword slammed into the dirt where Xavier's head would have been if he hadn't rolled away at the last second. But roll he did, and his boot connected with Asten's chest and kicked him away, giving himself time to pop up onto his feet.

They had been fighting for what felt like hours. Xavier's arm had gone numb quite some time ago, and he dripped with sweat and blood as he panted with exertion, physically exhausted. Asten was just as bad.

There was an underlying respect for each other as fighters in their eyes, but it didn't overshadow their hate.

"Give up," Xavier panted at Asten. "You have nothing to gain now. Your men are retreating."

Xavier watched as awareness flashed in Asten's eyes when he took in his surroundings for the first time and realized Xavier was right. Asten turned and glared at Xavier. He had a desperate look in his eyes now that made Xavier's body coil with tension. Desperate men were dangerous.

"I found her, you know, when we were kids. She was beautiful, even then."

Xavier eyes narrowed, not sure where this was going.

"She was clueless. I think that's why I fell in love with her. She was innocent. It made my mission harder."

"What are you talking about?"

"We were always destined to meet, Xavier, way before your marriage to Leawyn. I knew about you my whole life," Asten explained. "She assumed I was a part of one of the nomad merchants who frequented there."

"Get to the point!" Xavier barked.

"It was my father's tribe who attacked your village and killed your parents."

Xavier's blood ran cold, stumbling back in shock.

"The Rhoxolani were going to betray you. It wasn't hard for me to convince Leawyn's fool of a father to do it, either. But then you had to ruin everything and agree to a marriage," Asten snarled. "Leawyn was supposed to be mine. She was *my* reward. But you took her away from me, just like you took everything else away from me! You killed my father!"

"Your father deserved to die," Xavier bellowed. "If I could do it again, I would—but this time I would make sure he suffered more than an arrow to his throat!"

Asten let out a battle cry and slammed into Xavier. He gripped him around his legs, lifting him off his feet as he continued to run forward, before slamming him on the ground.

Xavier landed hard on his back, the breath knocked out of him. Asten took his moment of weakness to pound his fists into his face. Xavier grunted in pain, but blocked Asten's next blow, then landed one of his own. They grappled each other for a while, giving in to a much more primal way of fighting. They rolled, both trying to get the upper hand.

Xavier brought his leg between them and wrapped it around Asten's neck, giving his torso a sharp twist that sent him tumbling sideways. He choked as Xavier squeezed tight, cutting off his air supply.

"How's it feel to know you're going to die by the same man who killed your father?" Xavier snarled hatefully. "Oh wait," he said sarcastically, dark humor lighting his eyes. "I wasn't a man yet when I killed him."

Asten was furious. Xavier realized he shouldn't have gotten cocky. Asten reached behind him, pulling out the dagger from a holster hidden inside his pant leg and ramming it down into Xavier's leg.

The pain made his grip on Asten's neck loosen enough for him to take advantage of that weakness and pull away, yanking the dagger out of Xavier's leg as he did. Xavier stumbled to his feet, blood seeping through his fingers as he limped away from Asten. He breathed through his pain.

They realized at the same time they were without their swords, having been too enraged with each other to keep them in their grips. Xavier eyed the ground; their swords had landed right next to each other. He looked up, exchanging a glare with Asten.

There was a split second of hesitation before they both dove.

Xavier knew the moment his feet left the ground, arm stretched out ahead of him, he wasn't going to be the one to reach a sword first. It all boiled down to luck. Asten was closer.

Asten fell to the ground. His hand gripped the hilt, and he turned. Xavier couldn't stop him.

His body heaved as Asten's sword pierced through his flesh as easily as lightning sliced through rain clouds.

Asten's eyes flashed with victory when Xavier slowly looked up, dazed. For the first time since he was seven years old, he had been bested. Asten's eyes slanted, and with great zeal he wrenched the blade free.

Xavier jerked, pain compressing his face. Asten stood and looked down at Xavier when he toppled over sideways.

Asten pointed his blood-tipped sword down at Xavier, his expression filled with sadistic pleasure.

"How's it feel to know you're going to die by the son of the man who killed your parents?" Asten questioned, throwing Xavier's words back at him.

Xavier didn't give him the satisfaction of replying. Asten's face twisted into a snarl. He raised his sword above him to deliver the finishing blow.

"Stop!"

Asten froze, his sword still held high above his head as he stared in front of him, shocked.

For there, in front of them, stood Leawyn. With an arrow notched in her bow, she pointed it straight at Asten.

"Don't make me do it," Leawyn pleaded with Asten, her voice desperate.

Asten studied her. Taking in her white-knuckled grip around her bow, the notched arrow had the slightest quake as her hands trembled.

"Drop your sword, Asten."

When Asten didn't move, Leawyn pulled the bow string back tighter, the sound of the string going taut seeming to echo around them. "Do it!"

Slowly, Asten lowered his sword. "You won't shoot me, Lea," he told her, his tone confident.

"I can't let you kill him." Leawyn's bottom lip quivered with her tears as she spoke.

"Everything will be okay, Lea. I'm going to take care of you," Asten reassured her, his face softening when he looked upon her glassy eyes.

"But this?" He looked down to Xavier, who, despite being mortally wounded, met Asten's eyes fearlessly. The nerve of that action caused his eyes to harden.

"This *thing* needs to die. He needs to pay. Don't you see, Leawyn?" Asten glanced back to her, and she couldn't fight the sob that escaped her lips at the maniacal glint in his eyes. "This is the only way."

"What about you, Asten?" Leawyn challenged. "What about what you've done?"

Asten frowned. "I haven't done anything wrong, Lea."

"You annihilated my tribe! Women and children!" Leawyn cried. "You killed innocent people!"

"The Rhoxolani were weak. They didn't belong."

Leawyn recoiled, shocked. She couldn't believe these hateful words were coming from her childhood friend. From Asten, the boy who made her smile even when she felt her world was falling apart. Who once looked upon her with love. Her best friend. She thought she knew everything there was about him. But looking at him now... she realized she never really knew him at all.

"What about me?" Leawyn said softly, her voice barely carrying over the sounds of battle around them. "I was Rhoxolani. Do I not belong?"

"Of course, you belong, Lea." Asten said, his hard expression softening. And for a moment, she saw the boy she grew up with in that look as he took a step towards her.

"You belong with me. Which is why I had to kill them. Which is why I'll enjoy killing him. They took you away from me."

The moment was broken, and Leawyn's heart broke all over again.

"I said I'd save you. We'll finally be together," Asten continued fervently as he took another step towards her. "It will be a fresh start, with the rightful people. I'll not harm your friend, Namree?"

"Namoriee," Leawyn's whispered, sorrow overcoming her as she watched him step closer.

"Yes, her. I'll spare her because she's important to you. We'll rule our people together."

Leawyn shook her head slowly, one solitary tear escaping her eyelashes to trail down her cheek.

"These are not my people."

Asten stopped, his face dawning with understanding, then rage.

Leawyn's tear dropped from her chin.

He swung his sword up, fire reflecting off the blade as he turned towards Xavier.

Leawyn closed her eyes.

The world went silent.

Her fingers released the fletching the second she opened her eyes.

The arrow whistled through the air.

Mere moments.

Mere moments were all it took for Leawyn to kill her best friend.

The arrow that pierced his chest mirrored the pain in hers.

"Xavier!" Leawyn's bow tumbled out of her hand as she ran over towards her husband's prone body. She fell to her knees beside him, hands shaking as she pulled his head onto her lap.

"Xavier..." she whimpered. She let out a relieved sob when his tired brown eyes met hers.

"Leawyn..." Xavier breathed, his relief evident. "Asten—"

"He's dead," Leawyn said bluntly, giving him a weak smile. "I took care of him."

"I told you not to come back."

Leawyn choked out a laugh. "Since when did I ever listen to you?" She sniffled.

"Never," Xavier's lip twitched with a start of a smile before his face scrunched up in pain, clutching his side. They both tried not to pay attention to the blood that was seeping through his fingers.

"Why?" Xavier whispered hoarsely. Leawyn tenderly smoothed back his hair from his face, trying to ignore how shallow his breathing was. "Why did you kill him for me?"

"You shouldn't talk," she whispered, worry creasing her brow.

Xavier lifted his other hand, and Leawyn immediately grabbed it and pressed it against her cheek, squeezing gently.

"I need to know." He coughed, and she clutched his hand tighter with worry at how much blood he seemed to lose. His once bronzed skin was starting to pale. His eyes, which had looked at her with such intensity, were now becoming glossy and far away.

It terrified her.

"I couldn't let him kill you. If anyone is going to kill you, it's me." Xavier's lip quirked in humor at that.

Leawyn's worry grew when a wave of pain compressed his face. He was getting weaker. Each breath he took became more ragged than the next.

"You...should...go. Hide until it's...over."

Leawyn frowned. "I'm not leaving you," she said resolutely. How could he even ask her to do that?

Xavier made a sound of frustration.

"I'm not asking you, Leawyn. I'm telling you. The battle—"

"I'm not leaving you again!" Leawyn snapped down at him. She softened her expression and her tone when she whispered, "I'm sorry." She wasn't apologizing for snapping at him.

Xavier's thumb caught one of her tears as it brushed her cheekbone.

"It wasn't your fault, Leawyn," he told her quietly.

"It is all my fault," she said tearfully. "You asked me what I was hiding so many times. If only I'd told you sooner. I'm the reason this happened. This is *all* my fault. All the lives I've cost tonight...it's my fault."

"We all make mistakes. My biggest mistake is that I ever let you go."

Leawyn sucked in a sharp breath at that admission, squeezing his hand tighter.

"You just deserved...so much better. I wanted the chance to do the right thing," Xavier rasped out before he coughed, and her fear continued to mount at how weak he was getting.

"Do you still hate me?"

"No, I don't hate you," Leawyn cried. "I love you. I was just too scared to admit it."

The relief and happiness reflecting on Xavier's face should have made her happy, but it was the other look he had that made fear and anxiety grip her. He looked like he had everything he needed—before he gave up.

"Don't you dare leave me," Leawyn said fiercely. "Don't you dare give up. We need you. *I* need you. I refuse to raise our child without you. You don't get the luxury of dying."

His hand lifted, shaking as it traced her cheek and the tears running down her face in rivulets. His dark eyes traced her features, memorizing her face. "Our child," Xavier repeated softly, a contentment entering his eyes at the knowledge.

"Xavier..." Leawyn jolted, panic splayed across her face. "Xavier!" she said urgently as his gaze grew dim.

His hand slowly dropped from her face, and his eyes closed.

"*Xavier!*"

They didn't open again.

49

"So, you never betrayed Xavier? It was planned all along?" Leawyn asked, confused.

"Everything was planned." Tristan met her eyes, and she could see the truth in them. "Xavier was never going to kill me the day I challenged him. The plan was for him to exile me, to give them an opening to make contact with me. We didn't expect you to stop him." He smiled wryly. "Though, I'm sure that was a bonus for him."

Leawyn blushed.

"Why didn't you tell me?"

"I'm sorry, Leawyn, but I couldn't," Tristan said, looking at her earnestly. "He made me promise. Xavier was the one who came up with the idea. He knew the only way to find out where they were hiding, and who the traitor was, was to use their plan against them."

"Did Tyronian know?"

Tristan shook his head, a look of pain and regret clouding his face. "No," Tristan said. "Xavier didn't want me to tell him. He knew we were close, and that Tyronian wouldn't have the right reaction when I challenged Xavier to that duel. It wouldn't have made sense for him to just accept it and not try to stop me. His reaction had to be genuine."

Leawyn's heart hurt for Tristan. She knew they were close. It had to be hard for him to keep something like this from him.

"So, you pretended to betray Xavier," she said, understanding dawning. "You knew they would ask you to join them."

Tristan nodded. "Once I was inside the ranks, I was able to find out who the traitor was so Xavier could take him out. But as you know, he had already figured it out before I even had a chance to tell him." Tristan's lips quirked in amusement. "Then you escaped before I could warn Xavier of their plans to attack."

"Why you?"

"Xavier knew it had to be someone important, otherwise they wouldn't bother. It would make sense for it to be me, since things were already tense between us because...." Tristan trailed off, and Leawyn knew the answer by his look.

"Because of me," she said despondently. "Things were tense because of me."

Tristan hesitated, which was telling enough. A humorless laugh escaped Leawyn. "What didn't I cause? Your rift with Xavier. Asten's attack. What else? What other suffering shall I bring the Izayges?"

"Leawyn—"

"I have to know," she said suddenly, cutting him off. "Do you have feelings for me?"

"Leawyn..."

"I need to know, Tristan," she said more firmly. "I won't make the same mistake I did with Asten."

Tristan's brow furrowed, looking at Leawyn with sympathy. "Asten wasn't your fault. You said yourself you didn't know he was behind everything."

"That's where you're wrong," Leawyn said, shaking her head as her eyes clouded over with tears of regret. "I knew about Asten long before the battles. When I was kidnapped, Asten was the one who saved me. He was there before Xavier. And after I found out my tribe was killed..." She trailed off, eyes pained.

"Go on," Tristan urged her gently.

"When I ran back, he was there. I confronted him about something before I was given to Xavier. He..." Leawyn exhaled shakily, swallowing against the sudden lump in her throat. "He admitted he loved me. He...kissed me. And I kissed him back."

Leawyn looked up to Tristan, her gaze watery with regret. "Don't you see? I *encouraged* him. Even when I knew in my heart I didn't *truly* want him. I was scared...because I wanted Xavier. I think I knew I was falling in love with him, but I couldn't understand why. I didn't *want* to feel that way. He terrified me. He abused me, yet..." Her fists clenched, her neck flushing with anger.

"Xavier didn't deserve my love, yet my body craved him and my heart called out for him."

"Leawyn," Tristan whispered, stepping forward and wrapping her in his arms, even when she tried to resist. "You can't blame yourself for that. You don't have to explain your heart to anyone except to the person it beats for. We don't get to choose that. Our heart chooses for us."

"I saw the way everyone looked at me. Even you," Leawyn looked up at Tristan when he wiped a tear away with his thumb. "I saw the pity in their eyes. They looked at me as if I were broken."

"You were afraid they would look at you differently when they knew how you started to feel," Tristan stated gently.

"Sometimes, I wished to die," Leawyn said in a wistful tone. "It would've been so much easier to just cease existing. My life was full of pain, despair, and heartbreak. There were times when it got too hard to keep going...to keep fighting. To live."

Leawyn pulled away, and Tristan watched her as she turned away from him. She turned and faced him again. He swallowed, his throat dry at the emotion in her crying eyes.

"I wished to die, but then I would think of him. Of the way he looked at me when he thought I didn't notice. He looked at me like an orphaned boy. Strong, yet yearning for the thing forbidden to him— love. That was the moment I knew...I had to keep fighting for *us*. Xavier couldn't love, so I had to do it for the both of us."

"I don't love you," Tristan said suddenly. "I care for you, but I don't love you. You must understand, it was just me and Xavier for the longest time. We were *orphans*. But then you came along, and it's like he just...woke up." He gave Leawyn a small smile, and her heart broke a little at the pain hidden there. "I was jealous, I think. Of him. Of you... Do you understand what I'm telling you?"

Leawyn nodded. She did understand. The rift between Xavier

and Tristan was to do with her, in part, but it wasn't because of Tristan's hidden romantic feelings for her. He had realized he was just as lost as Xavier was before he married her. Now, Tristan was just as lost, and even more alone.

"I understand why Xavier didn't want you to tell me. I would have given you away." Leawyn sighed, turning away from him once again. "Even so...I need time. I don't think I can be around you."

"What are you saying?"

Leawyn's shoulders slumped, and Tristan had to stop himself from rubbing his chest from the pain that suddenly appeared there at the look she gave him.

"I want you to leave. "

"How—" Tristan cleared his throat, emotional. "How long?"

She didn't answer right away, studying him. "I think you'll know when you're ready to come back."

Tristan kept eye contact with Leawyn, and she could see her unspoken message was heavy in his heart. Though she needed time away from him, she was also giving him an out. Tristan needed time away from them both; he didn't know how to be anything other than the Xavier and Tristan duo.

He had lost himself.

Xavier found his home in Leawyn, and now Tristan needed time to learn how to be his own person.

"Thank you." His voice was barely audible.

"Of course," Leawyn said softly, her look gentle. "I'll make sure Tyronian knows what you did, that you didn't really betray us. I'll make sure *everyone* knows."

Tristan brushed a tendril behind her ear, cupping her cheek and smiling at her softly. "You truly are the most beautiful girl in the land, Leawyn. Inside and out." He kissed her cheek, pulled back and started to walk away. She watched him go for a moment. She stood up straight, a thought appearing to her.

"Tristan!"

He looked back, expectant.

"There was a girl. Woman, really. She had a scar on her face, and she was...different. She warned me of the attack, and she helped me escape when..." Leawyn shrugged. "I never got to thank her."

"What's her name?"

"I don't know it." Leawyn grinned and Tristan barked out a laugh.

"I'll ask her myself, then." He waved at her, and she watched as his form disappeared into the distance.

Come back to us soon, Tristan. Leawyn thought sadly. She heaved a heavy sigh and turned away to get back to work.

There was a lot to do in the aftermaths of war, after all.

EPILOGUE

The morning air was cool, the sky a soft gray with tinges of pink in the morning light as Leawyn quietly made her way past the slowly waking village. The tribes' grazing horses paid her no attention as she walked past them and up to the small incline in the field.

Leawyn stopped, her hands raised up to her brow to shield her eyes from the sun that was glowing steadily brighter. Her eyes scanned the field and hillside.

"C'mon," she muttered under her breath. "Where are you?"

The sun was becoming a beautiful blend of colors now as it peaked. Soft pinks, blues, and tangerines created the beautiful chaos of morning light.

More moments passed, and she was just about to head back up to the village when she heard it.

A soft whinny echoing from below the hill.

Leawyn stilled, watching the hilltop with bated breath.

Deydrey's silver mane appeared first, slowly walking up the hill until her chest was visible. She stopped, her neck turning to look behind her, waiting.

Leawyn's hand flew to cover her mouth, blinking back tears.

The pure black colt burst over the hill, his longs legs still uncertain and wobbly as he hurried over to his mom's side and stayed close.

"He looks just like him."

Leawyn jumped in surprise, looking over her shoulder to see Xavier staring at the foal ahead of her.

"He's beautiful," she said with emotion thick in her voice, turning back around. Xavier's arm rested around her shoulders, pulling her close to his side.

They watched the colt run around, testing out his legs and speed. The colt kicked out his legs, and they both laughed when he wobbled precariously as his feet landed back on the ground, the momentum throwing him off balance.

A soft cry caught drew their attention behind them.

Xavier and Leawyn both turned, watching Namoriee walk towards them, her arms cradling a blond-haired baby close to her chest.

Xavier stepped forward and met her halfway, Namoriee gladly handing their son over so he could take him in his own arms and hold him close. The girl turned to leave as soon as she did so.

Leawyn smiled softly at the sound of her son's happy gurgling as his dad tickled his stomach. Xavier walked back over to her, and she sighed in contentment, leaning back against him when he wrapped his arm around her waist from behind.

"I love you," he whispered into her ear, meeting her eyes when she tilted her head back to look up at him.

Leawyn and Xavier didn't choose their beginning, it was chosen for them. They were forced on each other for the sake of their tribes. For a long time, Leawyn's life had felt hopeless. She was stuck with a man she hated, with no chance to escape, and she had often wished-for death.

Xavier and Leawyn tore each other apart with their words, and then put the pieces back together with their actions. They wanted each other to suffer, because they were scared. Of themselves, of each other...of love.

Hate brought them together; fear tore them apart.

They hurt each other to try and hide their own pain. They were lost in the sea of loneliness, yet, somewhere along the way, they found each other, and instead of drowning, they swam.

It took Leawyn awhile, but she finally figured it out.

Xavier was a warrior first, and a man second. That was a fact that would never change.

Their love wasn't easy, and it wasn't conventional. But it was theirs. Their love was painful. It was hard. It was heartbreaking. But most of all...It was everlasting.

They fought the battle, and won.

Leawyn smiled, fingers caressing his cheek. She went up on her toes and Xavier bent his massive form down to meet her halfway. Before their lips touched, she told him the truth.

"I love you, too."

The End.

Turn the page for an exclusive bonus scene in Tristan's point of view!

BONUS CHAPTER

"Tell me, Tristan...what would you do if you lost your freedom?" Leawyn asked him.

"To be forced to spend the rest of your life as nothing more than an object; tied to a man who cares so little about you, he would feel no remorse for killing everything inside of you."

The wedding party continued to dance around them and even though they kept tempo, it was like time had slowed and everyone faded away until it was only them and this moment. An air of melancholy surrounded her, and when she met his eyes... it took everything he had to not react to what he saw reflecting in her ocean blue eyes.

"Would you accept your fate?"

It was a simple question, one that she couldn't possibly know how much it would affect him. The hollowness that he saw in her depths was the same kind of emptiness that reflected in his own.

Because like her, he wasn't free. He was trapped in the prison of his creation.

Unexplained anger coursed through him to which he unfairly directed at her. But just as quickly as his anger, came wariness.

Leawyn might seem like an innocent and defeated girl now, but she was far from it.

She was dangerous—she just didn't know it yet.

From over her shoulder, he saw his brother get up from his and Leawyn's shared table and make his way towards them.

Their time together was coming to an end.

She was still waiting for his answer; the fact that he was about to crush the glimmer of hope he saw in her gaze weighed heavy on him.

Because instead of admitting the truth, he did what he always did. Lie.

"No," he said softly, watching avidly as the light in her eyes dulled. "But you will, Leawyn."

He released her and stepped back, hiding his shaking hands by dropping hers. He watched Xavier escort Leawyn to his horse, Killix. Her expression was more akin to a woman being led by her executioner instead of her husband.

If Tristan truly believed that he was capable of feeling anything, he would imagine the tight feeling in his chest would be sympathy.

You're a liar.

The whisper in his mind made him clench his fists.

Filthy, dirty liar. You don't feel sympathy for her. You want what he has. As always.

The toxic thought was one that he refused to acknowledge. Turning away, he pushed through the crowd that was still celebrating the union of the Izayges and Rhoxolani.

From foe to friend.

He snorted at the thought. He knew for a fact that the only reason Xavier agreed to the marriage was because he wanted the Rhoxolani's land so that he could turn it into another Izayges settlement. His brother was a great warrior and masterful liar. He was cunning, ruthless, and cared only for the Izayges people. No matter the cost.

Unlike you.

He grabbed a mug of ale as he passed by the serving wench, ignoring the suggestive look she sent his way. Usually, it was easy for him to play his part of the carefree brother of the Izayges chief, but not now.

His mask was slipping and Leawyn was to blame.

The Tristan people saw didn't care that his brother was regarded as the best warrior of Samaritan history. Or that he was passed over to be the one to bride the beautiful daughter of the Rhoxolani.

If only they knew the true nature of what he was.

He was so lost in his thoughts, that once he stopped walking, he was surprised to find himself at the cliffs behind the village. He downed his drink and in a bout of bitterness, he threw launched his mug. He watched as it arched and then crashed into the ocean below.

He heaved a sigh.

"Tired of the wedding?"

He whirled around at the voice, his dominant hand going for the hilt of his sword on instinct.

No one was there. He scanned the darkness with his eyes.

"Who's there? Show yourself," he demanded.

Everything remained still and quiet. He narrowed his eyes; his sword made a quiet slinking sound when he started to pull it free.

"There's no need for that," the voice spoke again, sounding amused. If he wasn't on such high alert, he would ponder the uniqueness of that voice. It was raspy, but decidedly feminine and had a strange accent.

"I will not ask again," he warned.

"And what will you do?"

He whirled to the right, where the voice was now coming from.

"Come and find out."

Laughter floated out to him, this time to his left. He jerked his attention that way. How was she moving so silently?

Witch, his mind hissed. He tensed, unease coating him.

"Relax, brother of Xavier. I mean you no harm."

At the mention of his brother, he pulled his sword completely free despite her assurance. "How do you know who I am? Enough games. Show yourself!"

"Very well."

It was quiet, then like a forest sprite, she stepped out of the darkness and robbed him of breath.

He realized why she had been able to blend with the night. Her skin was darker than what he had seen before. Her midnight hair framed her face and was ramrod straight. The length of it covered breasts that he was sure were bare. Smooth, unblemished skin glowed in the moonlight, despite her color. But what was most remarkable about her was her eyes.

They were two different colors.

She was the most exotic thing he had ever seen, and she was beautiful.

"Who are you?" he breathed, entranced.

She tilted her head curiously. "What difference would my name be to you?"

"Are you a witch?"

"To some," she replied cryptically. "To others, I am many different names."

She was close enough to him now that he could smell the woodsy scent of her.

"Are you the Goddess Ianna?"

She laughed quietly under her breath. "I am no Goddess."

His breathing became slightly uneven when she reached up, smoothing her hands up his chest.

"What are you doing?" he asked huskily.

Her lips tilted. "Isn't it obvious?"

His lids grew heavy while he watched her untie the strings holding his shirt together; starting from the base of his throat, downward. She might claim not to be the Goddess Ianna, but her actions screamed otherwise.

After all, Ianna was known for her trickery over warriors who fell for her sexual prowess.

"What do you want from me?" He should be asking more pressing questions and demanding answers, but it was like she had cast a spell on him. He couldn't move—could hardly breath from the arousal she awakened within him.

"I want nothing from you right now besides this," she whispered, cupping the firm bulge hidden beneath his trousers. "Will you deny me?"

He didn't answer her right away, his eyes flying across her face.

He shouldn't do this.

Something about her wasn't right, and he now, more than ever, was certain that she was a witch. But instead of voicing his thoughts and pushing her away like he should have, he bent his head and captured her lips in a kiss.

He groaned softly when her tongue met his eagerly, her arms wrapping tight around his neck and pulling him closer. He snaked his arms around her, his hands traveling until they gripped her ass. He hauled her up, making her moan against his lips. She wrapped her legs around him as he carried her away from the cliffs before lowering her to the ground.

He trailed his mouth from her lips to her jaw while her frantic hands unbuckled his belt. His body lurched slightly from the force of her pulling it free from the loops and pushing the fabric of his pants down his hips.

"Gods," he grated against her neck when her hands gripped him firmly. She stroked his length, using the exact amount of pressure that he liked, but usually had to teach the women he slept with how to do.

"I am not a lover," he growled against the delicate skin of her neck. "I will not treat you like some flower." He gripped her throat, urging her head back forcibly to better look her in the eyes.

"I don't care about you. I only care about the pleasure I can find inside of your tight cunt, you got that witch?"

"Do I look like I want a lover? Why do you think I chose you?" Her multicolored eyes darkened with arousal.

"You're good for only one thing, Tristan," —she reached down and squeezed her fist around him almost to the point of pain— "and that's this."

He snarled at her, pulling back enough so that he could use both of his hands to tear her skirt in half— uncaring that it left her without one once they were finished.

His hand back at her neck, he used his other to hoist her leg around his hip at the same moment he filled her entirely with his girth with on hard thrust.

There was no buildup. No foreplay.

He did exactly what he promised and used her with the same

gentleness of a man using a whore. His thrusts were brutal and punishing. Forceful. If it wasn't for his hand against her throat holding her down, her body would be sliding away from his after each impact.

"Tristan!" she cried, her nails raking down his back, leaving crescent moon indents that beaded with blood.

"You don't get to use my name," he rasped. "Not when you withhold yours."

She whimpered in response, her bare breast bouncing as her inner muscles clasped him. She wasn't the tightest, but her cunt gripped him with encouragement while he battered into the delicate tissue. Arousal spun through him like a storm. Each time he pulled out of her greedy body and slammed back in, it was like a spike of pure euphoria to his engorged member.

He consumed her. Abused her. The sounds ripping out of his throat were animalistic, her mews and whimpers fueling his primal hunger.

He wanted to tear her apart with his cock, and he felt no shame for it.

Sweat dripped down his brow and chest, his lungs puffed for air as he owned her. He was always a rough lover, something the women in the village knew and willingly endured when they sought out his bed.

But this was different. He was completely unbidden.

Maybe it was the fact that he didn't know this woman. Or maybe it was because some part of him was angry with her for being able to entice him so much and make him lose control.

Whatever it was, it liberated him.

She gasped in protest when he pulled out of her, reaching out to him desperately. He ignored her and flipped her over. With a sharp slap on her bottom, he tugged her up by her waist so that she was on her hands and knees.

She shrieked when he hammered back into her roughly. The force caused her to fall forward, but he simply followed her down, his hips pistoling inside of her.

"You're so wet," he rasped. "You like the feel of my cock inside of you, don't you witch?"

She gasped in shock when his palm smacked against the skin of her ass again.

"I asked you a question."

"Yes!" she wailed, jerking when he spanked her again. Painfully.

"Yes what?" he taunted, spanking her again— this time on her other cheek. "Tell me what I want to hear."

"I like your cock inside of me," she moaned. "I want to come."

"You'll come when I say you can."

His fingers curled over her hips hard enough to bruise. When she went to look back at him, he tangled his fingers in her hair and held her head forward to prevent her from doing so.

The waves drowned out the sound of their bodies slapping together in a frantic tempo. He kept her captive, not letting her control any aspect of their joining. Eventually, she stopped trying and just submitted herself to the fact that her body was his to control, and there was nothing she could do about it.

Time seemed endless. He lost himself within her body, until finally he felt close to combustion. His balls drew up tight, his spine tingled and he knew he was close to coming apart, but he held back.

He didn't want it to end until she screamed his name whilst she fell apart.

It only infuriated him more that he cared enough to make sure she got her release before he did.

His hand left her hip to come between her spread legs where the meat of his cock was spreading her folds apart. She jolted when he touched her swollen nub, rubbing it in harsh circles.

"What are you—ah!" she choked, his hand squeezing around her throat preventing her from finishing.

"Shut up and come, witch," he hissed cruelly into her ear, taking the lobe between his teeth.

He pressed down against her nub simultaneously his hand left her throat and pushed his thumb inside of her puckered hole.

She screamed as she spasmed around him with her release. A moment later, he followed with a groan.

Their heavy panting broke the otherwise silent night. Still buried inside of her, Tristan squeezed her hips once before pulling out of her warmth and got to his feet unsteadily. As he dressed, the mysterious woman rolled onto her back, not at all ashamed of her nudity. He finished and stood straighter, his gaze roaming her naked body lazily.

The sweat that misted her skin made her body shimmer in the moonlight. Her long hair was wild from his hands being buried inside of the tresses. She looked sated, and extrinsic and it made his blood heat with the knowledge that he was the one to make her look that way. A sudden, fierce desire hit him, confusing him.

"Who are you?" he asked again, mystified by her mere presence. "You're not from here."

The husky laugh that poured out of her lips went straight to his dick.

"What was your first guess?" she teased, rising to her feet with movements that seemed almost too graceful to be human. He watched as she came to him until her chest brushed his.

"Do not worry, Tristan," she said softly. "We'll meet again." He caught her wrist, preventing her from leaving when she turned away. She glanced down at his grip, then back to him.

"Let go."

"Not until you tell me who you are," he countered.

She faced him again, and before he knew it, her lips were on his. He immediately deepened the kiss, forcing his tongue into her mouth. She broke away much too soon for his liking.

"Who are you?" he whispered, desperation coating his tone. He couldn't understand what he was feeling. He only knew that she lit him up from the inside out, and his heart was pounding a frantic tempo. His body responded to her presence like nothing he had experienced before.

"Do not fear," she caressed his bearded cheek. "What you feel will fade, and with it this night in your memory."

"What does that mean?" He held her to him tighter, but she still somehow managed to detangle herself from his arms and step back.

"What does that mean?" he yelled, stumbling after her. The onslaught of sluggishness that hit him was sudden, and startling. He fell to his knees, his lids growing heavier and his lips tingled.

"What...did you do?" he slurred, watching as she continued to step back from him, the darkness seeming to embrace her with each step.

"I never kiss and tell."

"You..." he fell forward, his cheek meeting the hard ground with a thump, "witch," he whispered. It was becoming harder to keep his eyes open, his vision swimming.

"You...poisoned...me."

"It will wear off by morning. Goodbye, Tristan. Until we meet again."

He blinked sluggishly, trying to keep his eyes open, but it was futile.

The last thing he saw was the witch being swallowed up by the night and disappearing from his sight.

***

The sun woke him up.

He groaned softly, the bright rays were blinding when he blinked his eyes open. Gripping his head, he slowly pushed himself up to his elbows. It felt like he took an axe to the skull.

He squinted against the sun, taking in his surroundings.

How did I get here?

He rolled to his side. It was purely his sheer will that prevented him from losing the contents of his stomach when he pushed himself up. He stumbled to his feet, swaying when his surroundings spun together.

What *happened* last night? Did he get that drunk? He thought back to last night, trying to piece the night together. The last thing he remembered was walking here after his brother left with his new *wife*. The word left a bitter taste in his mouth.

He must have drunk more than he thought, because try as he might, he couldn't remember anything else.

He guessed it was midday by the height of the sun. His men were probably looking for him. He and Xavier's men are supposed to stay another night and leave in the morning, but he hadn't count on his reaction to his brother's marriage. The farther away he could get from the Rhoxolani, the better. Besides, it would take about half a days' journey to meet Xavier at the rendezvous point.

Might as well get a head start by leaving today.

He started to walk away, but paused. The back of his neck prickled with awareness, making him go on alert. He jerked his gaze behind him, scanning his surroundings.

Nothing.

He hesitated before forcing himself to turn back around.

His tension didn't ease though, because even as he started his trek back to the Rhoxolani village...the feeling of being watched lingered.

But that wasn't what made him so on edge. What disturbed him the most was that the gaze felt familiar and even though he couldn't explain it, he had a nagging feeling that something important happened last night.

***

"It's done." She said upon arriving. The man who had been casually leaning against his horse stood to his full height at her arrival.

"Don't sound so upset," he told her, amused. "At least the Rhoxolani had one night of celebration before their demise."

But Dkésea was upset, though she made sure to keep her expression emotionless.

There were innocent women and children in that village.

She looked to the man she had quickly learned to despise.

"And my sister?"

"Ah, yes," he grinned. "Your precious sister. That was the deal, wasn't it?"

She didn't give him the satisfaction of answering him. He knew perfectly well what the deal was. It was the only reason that she would have sold her soul to him.

370

Her sister was the only thing she cared about.

"Your sister was traded, and is now on a ship."

"Where?" she demanded, her heart jumping in her throat when her fears were confirmed. She knew in her heart that that was the only explanation for why her sister was missing from the compound she was being held in prior after Dkésea went back for her.

Just like she knew it was her fault that her sister was sent away in the first place.

"Ah, ah, ah," he waggled a finger mockingly. "We're not done yet."

"But you said—"

She cut off with a choke when his hands were suddenly wrapped around her throat. He leaned in, his eyes glistening with malice.

"What I *said* was that should you destroy the Rhoxolani village and everyone in it, I'd tell you where your sister is. Now, did I not just do that?"

He didn't give her a chance to answer, just continued to squeeze around her windpipe as he talked.

"But what I *didn't* tell you to do was to grow a damn conscious." Her breath—if she had any—would have caught at the pure evilness that clouded his eyes. "When I tell you to kill everyone—I mean everyone! How is it that the Izayges managed to escape, hmm?"

Even as her head felt like it was about to pop, she refused to grip his wrists. Not for the lack of her will to live, but because he would enjoy her fight. He always did.

He watched her and just when she realized that he planned to choke her until she passed out, he let her go.

She fell to her knees instantly, her throat burning while she coughed; her deprived lungs filled with precious air once again.

"You didn't follow orders, Dkésea. And because of that, consider our contract renewed. You fail me again....I'll make sure you'll never see your sister again."

She bowed her head, the only thing she could do to hide the tears that glistened in her eyes. Her sister was the only thing she cared about, and he knew it. It's why he had so much control over her. She had been *so close*. She risked everything, and for what?

371

All she had to do was poison Tristan so that the Izayges would be forced to stay. But instead of killing him, she saved him. The worst part? She didn't even know why. All she knew was that when she saw the pain behind his eyes, the same pain that reflected in her own... she couldn't do it.

Then she followed him.

He claimed that she put a spell on him, but in that moment, it was he who had cast a spell on her.

"Now," he said, bringing her attention back to him. She waited until the threat of tears were gone before she looked up. Her blood chilled at the intent she saw. His hands went down to his belt, unbuckling it.

"How about we not draw this out? You know as well as I do that failure doesn't go unpunished from my pathetic pet."

She did nothing but clench her jaw at the name. She learned long ago to not trust him, and to hide her emotions from him. After all, that's how she got into this mess. He had tricked her by saving her from execution, and promised to save her sister, too. But it was all a lie.

The only reason he saved her was to exploit her for his own personal gain.

She went down on her hands and knees, presenting her back. He pressed up behind her, and when she felt his flesh brush against her netherlips before he forced himself inside the cleft between her legs, she made a vow.

Somehow, someway, she would see to Asten's demise.

He began a punishing pace that she escaped by closing her eyes. And like so many times before, the same vision flashed behind her closed lids.

A little boy with russet skin running into the arms of his mother while his father trailed behind him. He rests his hand on her shoulder, bending to kiss her cheek... her long black hair blowing softly in the breeze. His expression content and beautiful, even with the nasty scar running diagonally down his face.

Just as quickly as it came, the vision faded away and like always, it left her wondering:

Was the woman with Tristan her...or her twin sister?

**Tristan's story
is coming...eventually.**

OTHER BOOKS

ABOUT NICOLE

Nicole René is a San Diego native living with her grumpy kitty, Sebastian and her crazy cute Boxer, Walter.

When she's not busy creating sexy alpha males, you can most likely find her with her nose stuck in a book reading OTHER sexy alpha males, kicking back with her friends and family, at the movies, or further fueling her "The Little Mermaid" and "The Lord of the Rings" obsession.

She is a certified klutz, often tripping over invisible objects, dropping things like they were hot, and playing ping-pong with the walls. She has lots of tattoos, loves to eat sushi—but hates eating cooked fish, hates going to the beach (even though she's surrounded by them), and is still waiting for her Hogwarts letter to come in the mail.

Want to be in the loop and know what's next? Sign up for my newsletter and never miss and update!

Or join my Facebook group!

I like to procrastinate using social media. You can add me by click on the links below.

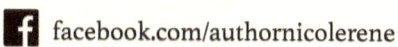 facebook.com/authornicolerene

ACKNOWLEDMENTS

To my readers both, present and future—Thank you for taking a chance with your hard earned money and buying this book. I hope that you enjoyed reading it as much as I enjoyed writing it, and I look forward to (virtually) getting to know you all!

My family— Thank you for all your continued support, and love. Dad, thank you for all your help with making this possible. I know there was quite a few (a lot) times that you caught me writing instead of doing my office work like I was suppose to be doing, yet you continued to support my dream. Mom, thank you for always picking me up when I fell with self-doubt and fear. You were always ready to listen to me read and blab about my book ideas. You were quick to offer me words of encouragement and gave me strength to work through my fears. I love you. To my brother, you're my best friend and one of my favorite people. I love you lots! To my sister, even though we tend to fight like cats and dogs, I hope you know how much I love you. Because I do. Thank you for supporting me!

To my friends— Even though I was a bit tight lipped about what exactly I was writing, you still supported me through it all and were always ready to support me in any way I needed. I truly have the best group of friends, and I'm so thankful to have found true friendship in you all.

To Joanne—You're the best employee ever! You're always quick to encourage me, and your excitement and willingness to listen to me read whatever I write means so much! I hope you enjoyed this book as much as you thought you would!

To Lauren Funtootie (told you I would, ha ha!)— one of my best, and closest friend who was lucky enough to meet Mike, her closeted-romance-book-reader boyfriend who inspired some of my personal favorite quotes in this book. You rock Mike!

To my beta readers — You all took a chance on a first time author by beta-reading this book and I cannot thank you enough. All your insight, enthusiasm, encouragement, and feedback helped me and this book so much. Thank you!

Krista— For rising to the challenge of editing this book when I decided to revamp it. Thank you so much!

To Carian Cole— I don't think I can truly express how thankful I am for you. I adore you. You have been so incredibly helpfully, and supportive. You took the time to listen to your fan, and completely blew expectations away by the helping hand you offered so freely. Thank you for being so patient with me, and for answering my endless (and sometimes annoying) questions about this crazy self publishing world, and all the encouraging words and advice you have given me. There are no words to truly express how thankful I am of you. You're truly one of a kind! I hope that we can one day meet so that I can hang out with my girl-crush face to face!

To Book Enthusiast Promotions and Bloggers— Thank you so much for all your shares, reviews, comments, and likes and making my first book release a massive success! Us authors would be completely lost without you.

To Kari Ayasha—Thank you for my beautiful cover! It's every-thing I ever could have imagined and more! I couldn't help but stare at it for hours in complete awe. I love it! You're the best!

To Joel Hicks, and Tillie—Thank you both so much for making my first book cover/photoshoot so amazing. Joel, you were so patient with me and you made this experience that much more amazing with your excitement and willingness to work with me. Your creative eye is amazing! You both brought my beloved characters to life, and made them that much more beautiful— I can't thank you enough!

To Murphy Ray and Indie Solutions—Murphy, you have made

the editing experience so amazing. You were such a joy to work with, and I cannot wait to continue to be working with you!

To my editors Holly, and Meghan— Holly, I absolutely loved working with you! Your notes were so spot on and such a joy to read. Your time, dedication, and love for my characters inspired me, motivated me, and made me want to make this book the best it could be! I hope to be working with you for many years to come! Meghan, thank you for fine-tuning my story and making it even better. Between you and Holly, I know my book is the best it could be! Thank you so much!

To Wattpad— I don't think "thank you" is enough of a word for what you have done for me. I took a chance posting a chapter of HOW THE WARRIOR FELL, and was prepared to discontinue the story 'because I thought there was no way that anyone would want to read a story like this one. I was wrong. You took a chance with me, and this book would not be possible without all of your encouragement and support. You were the reason that I decided to publish this book, and to follow my dream. I especially want to thank my "warrior tribe" of original readers who have been with me since the very first chapter. Thank you for sticking with me through everything!

HOW THE WARRIOR CLAIMED:

HOW THEY FELL:

www.ingramcontent.com/pod-product-compliance
Lightning Source LLC
Chambersburg PA
CBHW030630020726
47493CB00006B/1640